## "Dinah Halstead?"

"I'm Charlotte. I'm Dinah's identical twin sister," she said. "But those criminals think I'm Dinah. I don't know what's going on."

He heard the voice of the unknown assailant; it was clear he was angry. And it sounded like he was headed their direction.

"My truck's parked near the alley where I first saw you. Come on, let's get out of here." He held out his hand, praying she would reach for it and let him take her to safety. After a moment's hesitation, Charlotte grasped it. They took off running. Wade slowed his pace as they approached his truck.

"What?" she asked in alarm.

"I just want to make sure everything's okay." If he were one of the bad guys, he'd be waiting here for the bounty hunter to return.

Overhead the clouds were moving, and in the subtle glow of moonlight he saw a large puddle behind his truck, the standing water's surface perfectly smooth.

But then it rippled. For no discernible reason.

"Back up!" Wade ordered.

"But why? I thought—"

*Bang!*

**Jenna Night** comes from a family of Southern-born natural storytellers. Her parents were avid readers and the house was always filled with books. No wonder she grew up wanting to tell her own stories. She's lived on both coasts but currently resides in the Inland Northwest, where she's astonished by the occasional glimpse of a moose, a herd of elk or a soaring eagle.

### Books by Jenna Night

### Love Inspired Suspense

### *Range River Bounty Hunters*

*Abduction in the Dark*
*Fugitive Ambush*
*Mistaken Twin Target*

### *Rock Solid Bounty Hunters*

*Fugitive Chase*
*Hostage Pursuit*
*Cold Case Manhunt*

*Last Stand Ranch*
*High Desert Hideaway*
*Killer Country Reunion*
*Justice at Morgan Mesa*
*Lost Rodeo Memories*
*Colorado Manhunt*
"Twin Pursuit"

Visit the Author Profile page at LoveInspired.com.

# MISTAKEN TWIN TARGET

## JENNA NIGHT

**LOVE INSPIRED** SUSPENSE
INSPIRATIONAL ROMANCE

# LOVE INSPIRED® SUSPENSE
### INSPIRATIONAL ROMANCE

ISBN-13: 978-1-335-58826-5

Mistaken Twin Target

Copyright © 2023 by Virginia Niten

Recycling programs for this product may not exist in your area.

For questions and comments about the quality of this book, please contact us at CustomerService@Harlequin.com.

Love Inspired
22 Adelaide St. West, 41st Floor
Toronto, Ontario M5H 4E3, Canada
www.LoveInspired.com

Printed in U.S.A.

Let not mercy and truth forsake thee: bind them
about thy neck; write them upon the table of thine heart.
—*Proverbs* 3:3

To my mom, Esther.

# ONE

Charlotte Halstead hurried down the dark street, anxious to reach her SUV and get out of the wind and rain rolling through Range River, Idaho.

Her dinner meeting at a steak house with a literacy advocacy group had run late and she was the only member at the gathering who'd parked in the municipal lot a couple of blocks away. The street was nearly empty, and as she passed by a jewelry store and then a real-estate office, both shuttered up for the night, a nervous itch crawled up her spine.

She slowed down and threw a quick glance over her shoulder. Of course no one was following her. "Get a grip," she muttered to herself as she resumed her quick pace. "You're in Range River, not Seattle." She'd been back in her hometown for six weeks, focused on work and defying her mother's push to pursue a romantic life because pouring her heart into a cold, businesslike relationship like her parents had and calling it a *marriage* was the last thing she wanted. She took a breath to calm her squirmy nerves. Apparently it was going to take her a little longer to readjust to safer, small-town living.

A band of heavier rain swept up the street toward her; she could see it coming in the amber glow from the streetlights, and she pulled the hood of her jacket farther down over her face.

Finally, she reached the parking lot. She approached her SUV, hit the key fob to unlock it and then quickly slid into the driver's seat, pulling the door shut beside her.

Safe and sound. Nothing to worry about. She tossed her tote onto the seat beside her, pulled back her hood and turned to the rearview mirror to fix what she was certain would be an unruly head of hair.

A stranger sat behind her.

Inside her SUV.

Charlotte's body startled at the shock of it.

Her lungs locked up and she couldn't scream, couldn't even take a breath. Fear washed over her like a giant wave, leaving her light-headed and numb. She fumbled for the door handle, desperate to obey the internal voice screaming, *Get out now!*

The intruder catapulted himself forward from the very back of the SUV to the second row. In an instant he was just inches behind her. He scooted even closer and slung an arm and shoulder over her seat back so he could press a gun to her temple.

She was finally able to scream, but it did her no good.

Too late, she realized that the phone alert from her car alarm an hour ago had not been the random, nuisance triggering she had assumed it to be when she'd hit reset and continued with her meeting. Because of that mistake, her life now hung by a thread.

*Oh, Lord. Help!*

A surge of adrenaline and fear sent her body shaking.

"Don't make a move unless I tell you to." The intruder's voice was low and gravelly and she caught a whiff of stale cigarette smoke on his breath. "You try to get away, try to make noise to get people's attention, and I'll kill you. Believe me. I don't care whether you live or die."

The oddly emotionless tone of his voice made him all the more believable.

"What do you want?" Charlotte's words came out breathy and puffy now that her lungs had loosened and she was gulping in air. Her heart galloped in her chest and a matching pulse pounded in her ears.

"My bag is right there." She started to gesture toward her tote, but caught herself at the last moment when she realized that any movement might give him an excuse to pull the trigger. "It's in the seat next to me," she finally added. "Go ahead, take my wallet. Take whatever you want. I'll get out and you can have the SUV."

"I'll take what I want later."

*Later? Why not now?*

Charlotte turned her gaze to the rearview mirror. The intruder was staring back at her reflection. "Don't look at me," he barked. "Face straight ahead."

Charlotte forced her gaze back to the redbrick exterior of the building in front of her.

"Start the engine." The thug moved so that he sat directly behind Charlotte, and he tilted his gun so the barrel tip pressed against the back of her head. "I'll be watching everything you do. If you flash your headlights at an oncoming car to get the driver's attention, or blow through a stop sign, or drive too fast hoping a cop will pull you over, I will shoot you. I'm getting paid to deliver you to a specific location. Nobody said you had to be alive when you got there."

Somebody was paying him to kidnap her? Who would do that? Why?

Charlotte started the engine. "Where are we going?" She was still terrified, in some ways more so, but the light-headedness had eased and her mind was starting to clear. She needed to focus her thoughts and watch for any opportunity to save herself.

"Never mind where we're going. You just do what I tell you. Start by driving out of the parking lot and turning left."

Charlotte's knees shook as she alternately tapped the brakes and the gas pedal to back out of the parking slot and get to the street. She hesitated at the edge of the driveway when it came time to make the left turn. A right turn would take her toward the police department, although it was several miles and many more turns away. If she tried to go in that direction, the kidnapper would kill her.

It was eight o'clock on a Wednesday night in early March, so there wasn't much traffic. No one drove by for her to signal in hopes of getting help. The winter tourists were gone and the summer tourists hadn't arrived yet. Cold, rainy early spring wasn't much of a draw for the North Idaho mountain town.

The abductor shoved his gun harder against her head. "Get out of this parking lot and onto the street, *now*!"

Charlotte hit the gas and made the turn onto the street. She fought to take a deep breath as a rising surge of panic threatened to choke her. Range River was a moderate-size town surrounded by forest. If the thug made her drive past the edge of town, into the forest, what then? Nothing good, obviously. Beyond that, she didn't want to imagine.

Driving as slowly as she dared, Charlotte desperately tried to think of a way to escape without getting herself shot. But with that gun pointed at her, anything she did could get her killed in an instant.

A few moments passed and then she heard the criminal make a phone call while still managing to keep his gun pressed against Charlotte's head.

She could just barely hear the call go through and someone answer at the other end.

"I got Dinah," the abductor said. "We're on our way now."

*Dinah?*

"You've got the wrong person!" Charlotte called out. He'd let her go now, wouldn't he? "I'm not Dinah," she continued. "I'm Charlotte."

The person on the other end of the call must have heard her, because the man in the car said, "She's lying. She's Dinah Halstead. I've got the picture of Dinah you sent right here on my phone. This is her." A moment later he added, "Right." And then the call ended.

"No, seriously, you've made a mistake. Dinah is my sister. My identical twin sister." Charlotte felt a stab of guilt as the words poured out of her. But she wasn't shoving her sister under the bus, putting her in danger. She just wanted the creep to let her go. Then she could get to the police, report what had happened, and they would make sure Dinah was protected while the cops got this bizarre situation figured out.

"Identical twin sister? Give me a break." The gunman made a scoffing sound.

"No, wait," Charlotte said, fanning a spark of hope in the midst of the horrible situation. "If you would just search on your phone—"

*"Shut up!"* This time he shoved the gun hard to make her head snap forward.

"Okay, *okay.*" She gripped the steering

wheel tighter, fighting against her frustration. If she could stay calm, maybe she could get him to listen to her.

"Turn left," he barked as they approached the next intersection.

"Why do you want Dinah?" she asked while making the turn.

Several moments passed, but he didn't respond.

*"I'm not Dinah!"* Charlotte finally shouted.

So much for trying to appear calm. But the situation was absurd. "*Look* in my purse, *look* at my driver's license. You'll see my true identity."

"You just want to distract me so you can try to get away."

Charlotte huffed out a breath, a tight feeling of anger starting to overtake the grip of fear. "Why won't you just take a look?"

"Shut up." He didn't bother yelling this time. He just let the words ooze out, filled with contempt.

What would he and his accomplice do when they discovered he'd grabbed the wrong woman? Kill her so she couldn't turn them in to the cops? She wanted to believe they'd let her go, but it didn't seem likely.

But she wouldn't give up. She *couldn't.*

Charlotte leaned toward the passenger seat to grab her tote. "Look, let me just grab my wallet and you can see—"

*"Enough!"* The man grabbed a handful of her hair, twisted it and yanked her head back until it smacked into the headrest. "I don't *care.*"

"Okay," Charlotte said quickly.

He ordered her to make several more turns until they were in an industrial part of town.

"Slow down. Turn into the alley."

Fear turned into dread. A dark, heavy sensation sank into her chest. The kidnapper still pressed his gun to her head, still held on to a fistful of her hair. She made the turn into the alley. She had no choice.

She drove a short distance into the shadowy passage until he told her to stop.

She had to *do* something. She just needed a chance.

Charlotte hit the brakes and her SUV came to a stop. Her body tensed. Maybe he was going to shoot her right here.

*Dear Lord, protect me.*

He let go of her hair and took the tip of his gun away from her head. He moved to open the car door.

Charlotte yanked on her own door handle

and was out of the SUV in an instant, pure terror fueling her as she ran down the dark alley in the cold, heavy rain.

*Just to the end of the alley*, she told herself. *And then to the cross street where there might be somebody driving by and you can get help.* A few of the businesses were still staffed and functioning even at this late hour. Maybe she could flag down a worker and get them to call the police.

She was closing in on her goal when headlights swept around the corner of a warehouse and headed up the alley straight for her. The approaching vehicle slammed to a halt, the door flung open and the driver stepped out.

Charlotte could barely see his outline in the darkness, but she kept running. She couldn't turn around and run back toward the kidnapper. She dared to hope this new arrival would offer her help.

That hope was quickly dashed when her abductor—hot on her heels—shouted, *"Get her!"*

The driver stepped into the illumination cast by the car's headlights and pointed a gun at Charlotte. She came to a halt. Disappointment and hopelessness smacked her with a force that nearly knocked her to her knees. So much for her attempt at escape. She'd just run from one dangerous criminal to another.

\* \* \*

Bounty hunter Wade Fast Horse hit the brakes, pulled over to the side of the narrow road and brought his pickup truck to a stop. Ahead, red taillights reflected on rain-slicked asphalt at the end of an alley.

He was following bail jumper Brett Gamble, a fugitive who'd recently been arrested for residential burglary. The guy only had a couple of assault charges on his record, none of them involving weapons, so Wade figured he could capture him on his own rather than having someone from his team accompany him.

A warrant had been issued for Gamble after he'd skipped his court appearance earlier in the day. Range River Bail Bonds had bonded Gamble out of jail, so it was now Wade's job to find the bail violator and haul him back to county lockup. Wade had spotted Gamble a short time ago inside a Thai restaurant where the fugitive's girlfriend worked, but he hadn't arrested him on the spot because there were families with children around. Following the fugitive home and arresting him there seemed like a better choice.

But Gamble had not headed home after finishing his dinner. Instead, he'd driven to a section of town with warehouses and a few small factories where he'd just now turned down an alley and then stopped.

Had his fugitive figured out he was being followed? Was he trying to hide in the alley or was something else going on? It was possible that Gamble was more of a threat than his criminal record indicated. People committed crimes they were never charged for all the time. Maybe he'd done something dangerous that Wade didn't know about.

Wade grabbed his baseball cap from the seat beside him, hoping it would keep some of the rain out of his eyes, and then got out of the truck to see what his bail jumper was up to. The guy had been arrested for burglary, so maybe he was here to sell stolen items to someone.

Wade jogged over to a warehouse, pressed against a wall to stay hidden and then peered around the corner into the alley. What he saw wasn't anything he'd anticipated.

A woman stood in front of Gamble's car, frozen in place, while Gamble and a second man Wade had never seen before pointed guns at her.

Clearly the situation had the potential for explosive violence. Wade needed to call the cops. Bounty hunters were not law enforcement officers and there were strict limits on what they could do. At the same time, like any Good Samaritan, he was within his rights to help a person in harm's way.

Keeping his gaze locked on the trio in front of him, Wade reached for his phone. Just as his fingers touched it, Gamble suddenly moved toward the woman in an agitated fashion, gun pointed at her, saying something that Wade couldn't clearly hear. It looked like he was about to shoot.

"Freeze!" Wade stepped around the corner of the warehouse, going for his gun instead of his phone. "Drop your weapons!"

The fugitive spun around. Wade had the advantage of being in darkness. He hoped the bad guys would assume he was a cop. That they'd think they were surrounded and put down their guns.

Instead, the unidentified man fired several shots in Wade's direction, forcing the bounty hunter to retreat and go back to peering around the corner of the warehouse. Gamble ducked out of the way. The woman took off running up the alley and then darted into a passage between two buildings.

Gamble sprang up and ran after her.

Wade was determined to get to her first.

Instead of running down the alley behind them, he raced along the narrow, intersecting road, hoping to get ahead of them and reach the woman before Gamble caught up with her.

He raced past alleys and narrow service roads, looking down each one as he went by, hoping to see either his fugitive or the woman. He didn't see either one. Somehow, they'd gotten ahead of him. Or they'd turned down a connecting passage and gone off in an unknown direction where he'd never find them in time.

The smartest thing for him to do was to stop and *listen* for some indication of which way they'd gone. He stepped into one of the alleys, where sound bounced off the walls and carried a little better, hoping to hear footfalls or voices or trash cans being knocked over. Something, *anything*, that would give him an idea of their location.

For several seconds, the only thing he heard was rain splattering on the asphalt around him. And then, *footsteps*. Fast slapping and splashing sounds moved through a passage toward him.

The bounty hunter pressed against the side of a building, doing his best to make himself invisible in the darkness. Seconds later, the unidentified man ran into view. He had a phone in his hand, set to speaker. He stopped and spoke into it, coordinating with Gamble to locate the woman they were chasing. Looking up and down the alley, cursing, the man raked the fingers of his free hand through his hair.

Wade didn't move. Much as he wanted to tackle and handcuff the guy, it wouldn't keep the woman from danger since Gamble was still searching for her. But if he followed the thug, the assailant might lead Wade right to her.

The unidentified man started moving again, jogging up the alley before disappearing into another passage between buildings.

Wade started up the alley behind him, but after taking several steps he caught a flash of movement from the corner of his eye.

He slowed and turned for a closer look.

The woman sprang up from behind a stack of pallets and smacked Wade on the side of the head with a chunk of asphalt she must have grabbed from the crumbling edge of the alley.

Wincing in pain, he grabbed her wrists before she could do any further damage. "Shh!" he whispered as she opened her mouth to scream. "They'll hear you and find you."

By the faint illumination cast by a lone security light farther down the alley, he saw the cornered-animal look of sheer terror in her eyes. She dropped the chunk of asphalt. And then she kicked him, the pointy toe of her boot connecting hard with his shin. Again, he winced. But he didn't loosen his grip. "I'm trying to help you!" he said through gritted teeth, shaking her wrists, hoping to break the grip of panic that was understandably overwhelming her. "I'm a bounty hunter. I'm tracking Brett Gamble and I saw what happened. I saw him pointing a gun at you."

She stared at him as if he made no sense.

In that moment, he realized she looked familiar. "Dinah Halstead?" What was the daughter of the owners of the luxury Wolf Lake Resort doing in an alley at night with a couple of criminals?

She was probably just one more spoiled, rich young woman foolishly looking for excitement in the wrong place. Wade crossed paths with her type every now and then while in pursuit of a fugitive. There was no way he would put up with anyone like that in his personal life.

"I'm *Charlotte*. I am *not* Dinah," the woman snapped. Wade was pretty sure those were tears of frustration and not raindrops building up in the corners of her eyes.

"I'm Dinah's identical twin sister," she continued. "But those men think I'm Dinah." She tried to pull her wrists free and Wade released his grip. She rubbed her eyes. "I don't know what's going on."

The rain had slackened and then stopped, and in the relative quiet he heard the voice of the unknown assailant. He couldn't discern the man's words, but it was clear he was angry. And it sounded like he was headed back in their direction.

"My truck's parked near the alley where I first saw you. Come on—let's get out of here." He held out his hand, praying that she would reach for it and let him take her to safety.

He did have a gun. And if he had to, he could use it to defend the both of them. But he wanted to avoid a shoot-out if at all possible. Once people started firing, and bullets ricocheted off buildings and asphalt, there was no controlling where the rounds would go. Innocent people could get hurt.

After a moment's hesitation, Charlotte grasped his hand.

They took off running, to the end of the alley and then down the intersecting street toward Wade's truck. Gamble's vehicle had vanished but Charlotte's SUV was still there.

Wade slowed his pace as they approached

his truck. He stepped in front of Charlotte and stopped.

"What?" she asked in alarm.

"I just want to make sure everything's okay." There weren't any other passenger vehicles parked nearby, so it would have been obvious to the bad guys that this truck belonged to Wade. If he were one of the bad guys, he'd be waiting here for the bounty hunter to return.

Overhead the clouds were moving, and in the subtle glow of moonlight he saw a large puddle behind his truck, the standing water's surface perfectly smooth.

But then it rippled. For no discernible reason.

Maybe someone was crouched back there.

"Back up!" Wade ordered.

"But why? I thought—"

Wade stepped back, grabbed Charlotte's hand, and they ran toward the nearest building. It was some type of factory, closed for the night, with trucks and large storage containers parked in the lot that surrounded it.

*Bang!*

A shot blasted toward them from the direction of Wade's truck.

*Bang! Bang!*

Wade tightened his grip on Charlotte's hand

and he pulled her in front of him. A few steps later he gave her a slight shove, sending her between two semis with large shipping containers that were backed up and parked at a loading dock. He gave her a boost when they reached the concrete dock and then jumped up alongside her. They scooted over until they were hidden between the end of a shipping container and the loading dock roll-up door.

"Call the police," Wade whispered as he reached for his gun. If the assailants came upon them, he'd do what he had to do.

"I don't have my phone."

Wade handed her his.

She tapped the screen, and moments later she whispered into it, giving their location and explaining what had happened.

At the same time, Wade heard Gamble and the other assailant talking to one another as they converged near the truck where Wade and Charlotte were hiding.

"The cops have already gotten reports of shots fired out here and they're on their way," Charlotte whispered to Wade.

*Thank You, Lord.*

She had the volume turned down and the phone to her ear, but Wade could still hear the emergency operator talking to her.

The bad guys were getting closer and Wade was concerned that the sounds from the phone would carry and give away their location.

"We need to silence my phone," he whispered, taking it from her and tapping the appropriate side buttons.

The assailants' voices grew louder as they moved closer. Charlotte pressed against Wade's side. He felt her shiver in the cold, damp darkness.

A rectangle of light illuminated the area near where they were hiding. A second, similar type of light joined it.

"They're using the flashlights from their phones to search for us," Charlotte whispered into his ear.

Wade took a steadying breath, watching the lights move closer.

The men didn't bother to move quietly. But after a few moments, Wade heard something different.

*Sirens.* In the distance and rapidly drawing closer.

Charlotte squeezed his arm. "Police." She whispered the word barely louder than a breath.

Both searchlights suddenly went out. The bad guys must have heard the sirens, too. "You owe me, Dinah!" Gamble yelled. "And you're not going to get out of paying! I'll make sure of it." The threat was followed by the fading sound of rapid footsteps as the assailants fled.

Moments later, blue police lights flashed across the storage containers and the loading dock.

Charlotte scrambled to her feet. "I need to tell them my sister's in danger."

Wade helped her climb down from the dock and watched her run to the first arriving patrol car. He had no idea what the bigger story was here. Clearly, Dinah Halstead was the person the goons were after. But he couldn't help thinking that Charlotte might still be in danger, too.

# TWO

An hour later, Charlotte was at the police station. Officers had retrieved her SUV and checked it for potential prints left by the kidnapper. Her tote and phone had just been returned to her and she finally had the opportunity to call her sister to tell her what had happened and warn her that she was in danger.

Dinah had reacted with shock and disbelief.

"I don't owe anybody anything," Dinah responded emphatically after Charlotte told her about the assailant's threat. "The creep who says I do is delusional. Or he's the latest opportunist trying to get some of our family money."

"Well, he believes what he said, so you need to be careful. Don't go anywhere alone. Not until these men are caught. Where are you right now?"

"I'm at the resort. I was in the Garnet Banquet Room, but I stepped into the lobby to take your call. The Bellinghem Property Managers Association awards ceremony is still going on. Ethan is here, as well. He wanted us to stand by in case there are any problems. You know how he is."

Ethan Frey, Dinah's boyfriend, had started his career at Wolf Lake Resort working as a parking lot attendant when he was a teenager. He worked his way up over the years, leaving town to earn a couple of degrees, and then returning to eventually become the resort's chief operations officer. He was older than Dinah, steadier, and had a stronger work ethic. The two of them had started dating a year ago.

"Enough worrying about me," Dinah continued. "How are *you*? Shouldn't you go to the hospital to get checked for injuries?"

"I'm fine." Charlotte glanced around the police station conference room where she'd been sent to wait. She'd been given a blanket to wrap around her rain-soaked shoulders when she'd first arrived, along with a cup of strong, hot coffee. The bounty hunter who'd helped her escape the kidnappers—she'd learned his name was Wade Fast Horse—also sat in the conference room. Unlike her, he'd declined the offer of a blanket and he didn't appear particularly put out by having to sit at the oval conference table in soaking wet clothes. Maybe as a *bounty hunter* he spent a lot of time tracking people in the rain. Who knew what bounty hunters did?

"*Charlotte!*"

Charlotte moved the phone slightly away from her ear. "What? Why are you yelling?"

"I just asked if you wanted Ethan and I to come get you and you didn't answer."

"Oh." Charlotte shook her head and tried to redirect her thoughts. Now that things had calmed down, and she knew Dinah was safe, her body had started trembling again and her mind wouldn't stay focused. She recognized what was happening as an adrenaline crash and drew in a deep, fortifying breath, intent on holding herself together. "Thanks, but I'll ask an officer to drive me home." After all she'd been through, driving herself didn't seem like such a good idea right now. "I can retrieve my SUV later," she added.

"Have you spoken to Mom and Dad about this?" Dinah asked.

"Not yet. And don't you tell them, either. I want to wait until they can see me in person and know I'm okay."

"You don't sound okay," Dinah muttered.

Truth was Charlotte didn't feel okay. Not emotionally, anyway. She'd nearly gotten killed tonight, and the reality of that was hitting her hard, making her exhausted and jittery at the same time. "I should go. The detective will be here any minute. I guess she'll ask me a few more questions and then I can go home."

"I'm so sorry this happened to you." Dinah went from sounding like Charlotte's bold, confident younger sister—by sixteen minutes—to sounding fearful and worried, which was *not* like Dinah. And then it sounded like she'd started crying. "I'll see you when you get here."

They disconnected and Charlotte tossed her phone into her tote. She pulled the blanket tighter around her shoulders. Her gaze settled on the bounty hunter. "Thank you for saving my life." After the cops arrived at the crime scene, she hadn't had an opportunity to talk to the man who'd come to her rescue. Until now, the police had been intent on interviewing them separately.

He'd been politely averting his gaze since she initiated her call to Dinah. Now he turned to her. His deep brown eyes appeared hardened and determined, his expression angry. But then he blinked, offered her a faint smile, and his gaze brimmed with warmth and compassion. "Glad I could help."

Charlotte was taken aback by the sudden change.

She'd heard about bounty hunters, seen them in movies and on TV shows, and had the impression that they were rough, tough and hardheaded. She'd experienced what it was like to have this particular bounty hunter by her side in real life amid some terrifying moments. He'd been relatively calm and decisive. And while he hadn't exactly seemed *comfortable* with danger, he appeared to be used to it.

Now that they were in the conference room together, she was getting her first good look at him in decent lighting. Black hair, aquiline features, nearly black eyes, reddish-brown skin. A few seconds ago he'd looked fierce, but now the smile he offered bordered on shy.

Charlotte cleared her throat, remembering how she'd pressed against him for reassurance as they sat on the loading dock listening to the thugs closing in on them.

Turning to someone for emotional reassurance like that was unusual for her. Her childhood had been spent with distracted parents and resort employees who only pretended to

care about her because that was their job. She'd
learned early that depending on someone to
shore her up emotionally only led to heartbreak
and bitter disappointment.

Hence her determination to focus on work
rather than looking for a husband, despite her
mother's ambitions for her. Charlotte would
rather be single than be married and risk feeling the hollow pain of living with another person nearby yet still feeling alone. Yes, she felt
a little lonesome sometimes, but she was not
interested in building a life together with anyone. The truth was she could only safely rely
on herself.

Even so, the admittedly handsome bounty
hunter *had* shown up at just the right time to
keep her from getting killed, and she appreciated it. She searched for something else to
say to keep the conversation going, because
despite her intention to remain aloof, she was
curious about him. They'd crossed paths at a
profoundly significant moment in her life and
she wanted to know something more about him
beyond just his profession and his name.

But before she could say anything, the door
to the conference room opened and Detective Romanov, the auburn-haired investigator
Charlotte had spoken with briefly before being

ushered into the conference room, walked in. Wade got to his feet and waited until the detective was seated before he sat down again.

Charlotte couldn't help being impressed by his good manners.

Romanov looked at an electronic tablet for a few moments and then set it aside. She glanced at Wade and then Charlotte before settling her focus back on Wade. "Tell me how you and Ms. Halstead know each other."

"What?" Charlotte piped up before the bounty hunter could answer. "We don't know each other at all."

Romanov lifted an eyebrow, still gazing at Wade. "So you decided to jump in and risk your life for a complete stranger? She's not a client? Or connected to one of your clients?"

He offered a slight shrug. "Like I said in my initial statement, I was hunting Brett Gamble after his bond had been revoked when I came across him and another man I'd never seen before holding Ms. Halstead at gunpoint. It looked to me like Gamble was about to take a shot at her. I had to do something."

Romanov turned to Charlotte. "So, how are you, Mr. Gamble and our currently unidentified assailant connected? I need to know the truth no matter how ugly it might be."

"I honestly have never seen either of the men before in my life."

"In your statement you mentioned Gamble claiming that your sister owed him money for some reason. What do you think that was about?"

Charlotte shook her head. "I have no idea."

"Gamble was recently arrested for residential burglary. None of the stolen items, including several pieces of high-dollar jewelry, have been recovered. Might your sister have agreed to purchase something from him at a suspiciously reduced price? And then perhaps she didn't pay him?"

"Why would she do that?" Charlotte was starting to feel defensive.

The detective kept her cool gaze fixed on Charlotte but didn't respond to her question.

"No," Charlotte finally said. "I don't think she bought stolen goods."

"Gamble also has a history of violence," the detective continued. "Could your sister have hired him to threaten somebody? Maybe she needed him to frighten someone into ending some kind of dispute and she didn't pay him for his services?"

Charlotte stared wordlessly at her. What a bizarre string of accusations. "Dinah's n-not like that," she finally stammered. "She works at the resort, just like I do. I work in Marketing. Our parents assigned her the coffee shop on the plaza to manage and she's been doing a good job." Despite the fervor of her words, a shadowy uncertainty flickered through Charlotte's mind. She would know if things weren't going well for her sister, wouldn't she?

Charlotte and Dinah had gone their separate ways after high school, with Dinah attending their mother's alma mater on the East Coast while Charlotte headed for Seattle. A couple of internships plus some added courses had kept Charlotte away for an extra year. The sisters, women of very different temperaments, hadn't been emotionally close to one another for the last five years, despite being twins.

Charlotte had only been back in Range River for six weeks. Even so, if something odd had been going on with Dinah, wouldn't she have noticed?

Charlotte tried to shake off the feeling of uncertainty about her sister, but it stubbornly stayed in her mind. Detective Romanov had to entertain every plausible idea that crossed her mind in order to solve this crime. That didn't mean any of her far-fetched theories were true. She drew in a breath and lifted her chin. "Detective, I want to do everything I can to help you. I want the criminals who tried to kill me—*us*—" she quickly glanced at Wade "—to be captured and locked up. But I will *not* drag my sister's reputation through the mud. She is in *danger*, and I think your line of questioning borders on blaming the victim in this situation."

Romanov gave a slight nod. "A lot of people make bad decisions that get them into serious trouble," the detective said mildly. "Then they ask the police for help, as they should, but they withhold important details and that puts them in greater danger. I want to make sure that doesn't happen here."

While she understood the detective's point of view, Charlotte still couldn't help feeling insulted on behalf of her sister. She crossed her arms over her chest. "Why aren't you out looking for Brett Gamble and his low-life partner?"

"Officers are searching for Gamble at his home and elsewhere as we speak. I'll have a lineup of mug shots for you to look at tomorrow and hopefully we'll get a name for the unidentified assailant. As soon as businesses reopen in the morning, we'll collect all available security video near the location where you were initially abducted and also in the industrial district where you met Mr. Fast Horse. This investigation has not ground to a halt just because I'm sitting here talking with you."

That sounded reasonable. Charlotte nodded. "Thank you."

"You'll need to come back and have a look at the mug shots, too," Romanov said to Wade.

"Just let me know what time."

Romanov picked up her tablet and got to her feet. "All right, Charlotte. Let's get you home. I understand you live on the resort property?"

"That's right." Charlotte rose, took the blanket from her shoulders, folded it and set it on a chair.

"Does Dinah live on the resort property, as well?" the detective asked.

"Yes."

"Good. I want to talk to her. Tonight."

Wade stood. "I'd like to come along."

"Why?" Charlotte turned to him, uncertain how a bounty hunter could figure into a kidnapping and attempted murder investigation.

"Brett Gamble is still a bail jumper and I'm still going after him," Wade answered, shifting his gaze between Charlotte and the detective. "Your sister might have useful information about him without realizing it. Maybe when she sees his mug shot she'll realize she's seen him somewhere or that she knows him by another name. That information could help me find him."

Romanov gave a nod that seemed to indicate her approval of his request before walking out of the conference room.

Charlotte followed the detective, realizing as she did so that her knees had gotten wobbly again. She'd survived tonight's attack, but the memories of having a gun pressed to her head and running for her life down a dark alley rattled her to her core. Even more unnerving was the fact that the assailants were still at large. They were free to launch another attack on Charlotte—or her twin sister—at any time.

Detective Romanov, accompanied by a uniformed police officer, drove Charlotte to the Wolf Lake Resort. Wade followed in his truck. When they stepped into the marble-floored lobby, Charlotte's twin hurried forward to embrace her.

Dinah Halstead wore her blond hair tightly pulled back, twisted and pinned up. Her makeup was perfectly applied to dramatic effect. She wore black trousers and a gold sweater with a little bit of sparkle. She was a beautiful woman, no doubt, but Wade's gaze was drawn back to Charlotte. He found her casual appearance—jeans, flannel shirt and jacket—and the warm, open expression in her eyes more appealing.

Not that anybody asked him.

Dinah's boyfriend, Ethan, had come to the lobby alongside her. He sported a suit and tie and appeared to be a decade older than the Halstead twins.

The sisters held each other in a tight embrace for several moments. Charlotte managed to keep her composure, but Dinah burst into tears. After they let go of each other, introductions were made.

"A bounty hunter?" Dinah said to Wade when his turn came. "What do we need a bounty hunter for?"

"One of the attackers was a bail jumper," Wade answered easily. "It's my job to find him."

"I'd like to speak with you for a few minutes," Detective Romanov said to Dinah, redirecting the topic back to her investigation. "One of the assailants mentioned you by name."

"Yes, of course." Dinah wiped at her eyes. "Charlotte told me about that."

"Why don't we head up to your parents' apartment," Ethan suggested to Dinah after glancing toward several resort employees at the check-in desk who were casting curious looks in their direction.

The small group walked around a corner and through a door leading to a private elevator. Romanov and the officer followed close behind Dinah and Ethan. Wade brought up the rear. He was surprised when Charlotte dropped back to walk with him. "Our parents have an apartment on the top floor as well as a house on the edge of the resort property near the lake," she said.

"I know."

"You do?" Charlotte sounded surprised.

"My mother worked here when I was a little kid."

"Oh really?" She offered him a slight smile. "Which department?"

"Housekeeping," he answered as everyone stepped into the elevator. "She cleaned up after rich people who were on vacation." The sharpness in his tone took Wade by surprise. A cluster of memories and emotions were stirred up as the elevator took them to the top floor. There was nothing wrong with the work his mom did back in the days after his dad left them. And Maribel Fast Horse never complained about it. But she came home from work every night bone-tired. At some point Wade had started to feel like she was unappreciated, and that had bothered him.

Later, she'd joined forces with friend and neighbor Connor Ryan when he opened Range River Bail Bonds. Life had gotten much better for Wade and his mom after that. Connor and the other members of the Ryan family made it obvious that they were grateful for his mom's work as an investigator, a researcher and an administrator. He'd half forgotten how rough things had been in the early days. Until now.

Charlotte was admittedly an attractive and intriguing woman, but she represented a wide gap between people born into an easy life and those, like his mom and his friends, who had to work hard for everything they had. The thought brought with it a sting of recognition that the attraction he felt toward Charlotte was a betrayal to everyone he cared about. He needed to put a stop to it.

The elevator doors opened onto a short hallway with a single door to the right and another to the left. The door on the right opened and a woman who appeared to be in her early fifties, shorter and rounder than the Halstead twins but with the same blond, blue-eyed coloring, stepped out and made a beeline toward Charlotte, grabbing her in a tight hug. A man hovered close behind her. His features somewhat favored the twins, and he was tall, which must have given them their height.

Charlotte's mother finally let go of her daughter only to hold her at arm's length and scan her up and down. "Are you *sure* you're all right?"

"I'm okay, Mom. Really."

On the way into the apartment, Charlotte's father hugged her.

Introductions were made as the visitors were seated on chairs and one of the thickly padded leather sofas. Floor-to-ceiling windows covered one side of the room, with points of light from houses and businesses down below visible in the darkness.

"Perhaps we need our attorney present," Arthur Halstead commented as Detective Romanov pulled her tablet out of its case and prepared to question Dinah.

Dinah shook her head. "I don't need a lawyer."

Beside her, Ethan reached for her hand.

"It might be better if we speak privately," the detective suggested.

Dinah squared her shoulders. "I have nothing to hide."

"Our daughter had some problems with drugs and alcohol while she was in college," Kandace Halstead said calmly. "We know about it, and it's all behind her. We love her and there's nothing she needs to keep secret from us."

Wade watched as Charlotte's brows lifted and her eyes widened. Was she surprised to hear about Dinah's problems in college, or was she surprised that her parents knew about them? And more importantly—as far as Wade was concerned—were these past problems related to what had happened tonight?

"Could the kidnapping and threat be connected to drugs?" Romanov asked, despite the claims that Dinah had left that issue in her past. "Do you owe a drug dealer money?"

"No." Dinah shook her head. "Absolutely not."

"Are you involved in anything else that puts you in contact with criminals in town?"

"No."

Wade wasn't completely convinced by Dinah's protestations. It was fairly apparent that Romanov wasn't, either. Most likely she would find a way, on another day, to ask Dinah those same questions again in private.

"Why do you think someone would attempt

to kidnap you and then claim you owed them money?"

"I don't know." Dinah sighed heavily. "I create a lot of content for my social media accounts, trying to influence people to come visit Range River and stay at the resort. We've had a few celebrities stay with us recently, which I've posted about, and that has led to me having a good number of followers. I sometimes get disturbing messages from people who apparently feel we have a personal relationship because they follow my accounts." She grimaced and an expression of disgust crossed her face. "Maybe the attempt to kidnap me tonight is related to that." She shrugged. "That's just a guess."

"How do you know Brett Gamble?" Wade interjected.

Dinah turned to him. "I don't know anyone by that name."

"Someone remind me why we have a bounty hunter in our home," Kandace said in a frosty voice as she stared at Wade.

"Mom, he saved my life," Charlotte said. Her arms were crossed over her stomach and she looked anxious and exhausted.

Romanov tapped her device and handed it to Dinah. "This is Brett Gamble's booking photo. Does he look familiar?"

Dinah gazed at the picture. "I've never seen this man before."

Ethan leaned closer to her and peered down at the photo. "I don't recognize him, either."

After looking at the image, the Halstead parents gave a similar response.

"It's getting late and my daughters are tired," Arthur said to the detective after returning Romanov's tablet to her. "I think we should wrap this up for the time being so they can get some rest and continue your questioning tomorrow, if necessary."

"Actually, that's all I have to ask for now." Romanov and the officer got to their feet.

As the Halstead parents were seeing everyone to the door, Wade overheard Kandace ask Charlotte, "Do you want to stay here with Dad and I tonight? Or across the hall with Dinah?"

"Thanks, but I want to sleep in my own bed." Fatigue weighted Charlotte's response. "I feel like pulling the blankets over my head and hiding there for a week."

"I'll stay with you at your place." Dinah's tone made it less an offer and more a statement of fact. "So you don't have to be alone."

Their mother nodded her approval. "I'll tell Randall to have the security team keep a close eye on your condo tonight."

"Condo?" Wade asked Charlotte after she and her sister had hugged their parents good-night and the visitors were heading for the elevator. "You don't live here in the main building?"

It wasn't his business where she lived, and she was going to have resort security keeping an eye on her, anyway, but he still couldn't help worrying. Even if the creeps who'd kidnapped her had finally figured out she wasn't Dinah, they might still come after her. As long as the motivation for the kidnapping remained unclear, anything seemed possible.

"We have a few condos on the resort property that we rent out, and I live in one of them," Charlotte explained. "They're away from the main buildings, closer to the lake."

"I'm familiar with them," he said.

The head of the security team met them in the lobby. While Ethan and Dinah spoke with him, Romanov and the officer headed for the exit. Wade had turned to follow the cops when Charlotte placed her hand on his arm and stopped him.

"While you're tracking Brett Gamble, if you learn anything about Dinah that I should know, will you tell me?" she asked quietly.

"What do you suspect?"

"I don't know." She smiled sadly. "I'm just wondering what might be going on that I'm unaware of." Her eyes, already red from exhaustion, became shiny with unshed tears. "Dinah and I were so close when we were little, but over the years—the last four or five, especially—we grew apart. It took what happened tonight for me to realize I hardly know her."

Wade wanted to help her, but the request made him uneasy. "I'm a bounty hunter. I look at the details of a case only to the extent that it helps me do my job so I can recover a fugitive." He shook his head. "I won't spy on your sister. You need to hire a private investigator for that."

She kept her hand on his arm. "Do you have any brothers or sisters?"

Wade thought of the Ryan clan: Connor, Danny and Hayley. He and the two younger Ryans—Danny and Hayley—had gone to school together. They'd helped each other through tough times and now they worked together at Range River Bail Bonds. Technically, Wade did not have any siblings. Not related by blood. But the Ryans truly were his family. "Yes," he answered. "I have two brothers and a sister."

"If one of them were in trouble, involved in

something bad, wouldn't you want to know so
you could help them? I don't mean help them
escape the law. I mean help them to be safe, to
get their life back together, to hang on to some
bit of dignity."

*Yes.* If any of the Ryans was in trouble, he
would want someone to tell him.

Wade drew in a breath and blew it out. "If
I learn anything about Dinah that you should
know, I'll tell you about it. But only on the condition that you promise to stay vigilant until
the criminals we're looking for are caught.
And you need to make sure your sister is careful, too."

"Agreed." Charlotte offered him a tired but
grateful smile.

Wade found himself drawn into that smile
and it was a challenge to look away.

"Come on—let's go," Dinah called out to
Charlotte.

Ethan was no longer by Dinah's side. Presumably, he'd gone home for the night. But
the security manager was there to provide the
sisters an escort.

"Thank you," Charlotte said softly to Wade,
before turning and walking toward Dinah.

The bounty hunter let his gaze linger on her
for a moment. Even with the resort security

team keeping an eye on her, he couldn't help feeling she wasn't completely safe. There were always moments when a person was vulnerable.

He headed for his truck, determined to do everything he could to find the kidnappers and get them off the streets. Only then would he be convinced that Charlotte was truly safe.

# THREE

"That's him." Wade pointed at the image on Romanov's electronic tablet. "That's Brett Gamble's accomplice."

It was early in the morning the day after the attack. Shortly after awakening, Wade had received a text from the detective asking him to come to the police station to look at mug shots. He'd grabbed a couple of coffee drinks and huckleberry muffins on his way to the meeting.

Upon receipt of her gifted coffee and muffin, the detective had given him a suspicious frown.

"Not trying to butter you up," he'd said while taking a chair across from her desk. "I needed some breakfast and my mom didn't raise me to be rude."

That actually got him a slight chuckle in response, something he'd never seen the serious-minded detective do before. She'd taken a sip of her brew. "Mocha. Good call. Thanks."

She was sipping her coffee again as she looked at the mug shot that Wade had indicated. "Trey Murphy. Out on parole for armed robbery after serving six years in prison. Looks like he'll be going right back in." She picked up a desk phone, punched in some numbers and then requested officers to go to Murphy's last known address and arrest him.

"Do you really think he'll be there?" Wade asked between sips of coffee.

She shrugged. "A bold criminal is not necessarily a smart one."

A police scanner was audible in her office at low volume. Wade heard a couple of transmissions, one of an officer making a traffic stop and another of an officer reporting that she was back in service after a meal break. He knew that he likely wouldn't hear the dispatch of officers to check on Murphy. A call like that would go out via cell phone messaging on the patrol car's computer so eavesdroppers couldn't hear.

"I went by Gamble's house after I left our meeting at the resort last night," Wade said after taking a bite of his muffin. "A couple of your officers were there, watching the place, but they wouldn't let me in."

Romanov nodded. "Good. I'm glad to hear it."

The detective and her husband had moved to Range River from California a little over a year ago. The first attempts by the bounty hunters from Wade's office to work with her had not gone well. She'd been wary that they would disrupt her investigations and she had at first refused to assist them when they worked pursuits that intersected with her cases. Slowly, over the last few months, the bounty hunters had proved their professionalism and she'd warmed up to them. Somewhat.

"I know you won't tell me what your officers found inside Gamble's home." Wade tapped the lid on his paper coffee cup. "But would you at least let me know if it looks like he cleared the place out? I need to know if he planned ahead and could be anywhere, or if he's in the middle of a panic run and likely has to stay nearby because he's low on resources."

The detective leaned back in her chair. "Before I answer that, let me remind you that your job is to capture bail jumpers, not to run your own police investigation."

"Yes, ma'am." His job was simply to capture fugitives. But sometimes in the course of doing that job, he got caught up in broader criminal situations.

"If I find out that you intentionally withheld information from this police department and delayed the capture of Brett Gamble—or Trey Murphy—so that you could be the one to make the arrest and earn your bounty hunting fee, you and I are going to have a serious problem."

Wade had heard various versions of this speech from her before. But this time she sounded a little less concerned about that happening.

"Understood," he said. If the police captured a bail jumper, the bounty hunter didn't earn any money. Which meant bounty hunters could be motivated to put their own financial gain ahead of public safety. Range River bounty hunters didn't do that. But other bounty hunters sometimes did.

"I really want Gamble locked up before he can endanger anyone else," Wade said. Collecting the recovery fee would be a second-level priority. Whether he was the one to put cuffs on the guy, or the police were the ones to do it, didn't really matter. Not in this case.

"All right, I'll tell you what we found." Romanov tossed her empty coffee cup into the trash can beside her desk. "The front door at Gamble's house was unlocked when officers got there. They observed muddy footprints leading from the entrance to the master bedroom, where the closet door was left open and a safe was also left open. It was empty, of course."

"So he likely grabbed whatever valuables he had—probably cash and guns—from the safe and got out of there in a hurry," Wade said, thinking out loud. "His plans for whatever he meant to do to Charlotte, under the mistaken impression that she was Dinah, went sideways and now he's in a panic. That might make him a little easier to find."

"Let's hope that's true."

"Now that we've got Trey Murphy identified as the accomplice, will you show his mug shot to Dinah to see if she recognizes him?" Wade asked. "And then will you tell me what she said?"

Romanov arched an auburn eyebrow. "Are you starting to think I work for you?"

"No, ma'am."

Wade got to his feet, ready to take his leave, when an officer stepped into Romanov's office. "Detective, a call just came into the 9-1-1 center from Charlotte Halstead. She says her sister, Dinah, is missing."

Wade's heart clenched.

Romanov was on her feet in an instant. "Let's go!" she called out to the squad room as she headed for the door.

Wade grabbed his phone and tapped the screen. Charlotte had given him her number last night.

She picked up immediately. "Wade! Dinah is gone. Something has happened to her." Her words were oddly spaced, as if she were gasping for air.

"Take a breath," he said, managing to sound calmer than he felt. "Did someone break into your condo?" He imagined the two assailants from last night's attack reappearing in her life and terrifying her again. "Did they hurt you? Are you okay?"

"I'm all right." She started crying and Wade gripped his phone tighter.

"Can you come over here?" she asked after getting hold of her emotions enough to speak clearly. *"Please?"*

He was already out the door and striding toward his truck. "On my way."

Even without the details, Wade knew Charlotte was much too close to danger. He would do whatever he had to, to make certain she wasn't caught up in violence again.

The resort condos were built in Craftsman style and positioned to have dramatic views of Wolf Lake. Wade easily picked out Charlotte's residence. There were cops in front of it and a police forensic team just now walking inside. Romanov had arrived ahead of Wade, and he assumed she was inside with the Halstead family.

Torn between the desire to barge in and see for himself that Charlotte was okay, and the awareness that Romanov might ice him out of her investigation completely if he actually did that, Wade finally sent Charlotte a text letting her know that he was waiting outside.

She immediately replied, telling him to come in. Permission enough. Wade would show the text to the detective if she got mad at him for entering her crime scene.

As expected, the officer on the front step stopped him. But Charlotte, her eyes swollen and red, saw Wade through the open door and waved him in.

Romanov was in the midst of interviewing the Halstead parents and Ethan as they all stood in the living room. The detective shot the bounty hunter a disapproving look, but otherwise continued her questioning without missing a beat.

Kandace Halstead, however, was distracted by Wade's arrival. "What is the bounty hunter doing here?" she asked weakly. Her features were slack and Wade noted the stunned and confused expression in her eyes.

"He can help, Mom," Charlotte said. "He has connections in the criminal world."

When she put it that way, Wade couldn't blame Mrs. Halstead for being wary of him.

"It will speed things up to have the police *and* a bounty hunter searching for Dinah," Charlotte continued. "Having his help could get Dinah home faster."

Mrs. Halstead gave her daughter a curt nod of agreement. Beside her, Mr. Halstead rubbed at his eyes with a handkerchief and then blew his nose. Ethan, red-faced and shiny-eyed, had his arms wrapped tightly across his chest as if trying to hold himself together.

"When and how did you discover that your sister was missing?" Romanov asked Charlotte, refusing to have her interview derailed.

"After I woke up and went downstairs to start a pot of coffee, I knocked on the door of the ground-floor bedroom to see if Dinah wanted some, and she wasn't there." The last few words came out breathy, with Charlotte struggling to speak. She took a moment to compose herself and continued. "Her purse was on the nightstand. And her phone." Charlotte's voice cracked and she cleared her throat.

"At that moment I *knew* something was wrong. Even if she'd left to get some breakfast in one of the resort dining facilities or gone back to her apartment, she wouldn't have left her phone behind." Charlotte took a deep breath. "I looked around on the property for her, hoping that I was overreacting and she was somewhere on the grounds. But I couldn't find her anywhere." Tears began to roll down her cheeks.

The sight triggered a twisting sensation in Wade's gut, strengthening his determination to find Gamble. Someone must have broken into Charlotte's home at some point while she was asleep and vulnerable. The thought of that was beyond unacceptable.

"Did you hear anything last night?" Romanov asked.

Charlotte shook her head. "I was so upset about being kidnapped and chased that I was afraid I wouldn't be able to fall asleep. But I did. Quickly. I slept straight through until this morning."

"We went through all the video security feeds for the property and couldn't see her anywhere," Ethan added, his voice sounding tight.

"You live on the resort property, as well?" Romanov asked him.

Ethan shook his head. "No. I live a few blocks away. I came here as soon as I learned Dinah was missing."

A crime scene tech stepped into the living room from the bedroom where Dinah had been staying. "No sign of forced entry," he said to Romanov. "There's a slider door that opens to a patio. We found it unlocked and closed, but the screen door had been left pushed open. We're lifting prints right now. Also, a small table on the patio was knocked over. Looks like there was a potted plant on it that's lying beside it now, broken."

"The door could have been inadvertently left unlocked," Romanov mused. "Or someone could have had a key."

"What happened to the security employee who was supposed to be watching this place?" Wade meant to ask Charlotte the question quietly, but apparently Romanov overheard.

"Yes, wasn't someone from the security

team supposed to keep an eye on you and your sister last night?" she asked Charlotte.

"I already talked to the guy," Ethan interjected. "He admitted that he pulled up a chair and sat out front, looking toward the lake. He claims he got up and walked around the building every hour, but I'm not sure I believe him."

"How is it that there would be no security video of the rear exterior of this building?" Romanov pressed.

"We've got cameras scattered across the property, but there are blind spots, nevertheless," Arthur Halstead answered. "I now know that the backside of this condo is not visible to the cameras. I didn't realize that before." He wiped his eyes with the handkerchief again and cleared his throat before saying, "You are welcome to view as much security video as you want. Beyond that, I'll give you access to every inch of the resort buildings and the grounds. I'll arrange for you to interview my employees. Anything you need, just tell me."

Romanov nodded. "I'll start with having a couple of officers talk to your security employees and we'll go from there."

The detective left and Wade walked out behind her, figuring Charlotte and her family would want their privacy. He considered how to best start searching for Gamble and hopefully find Dinah. Or, alternately, he could set his sights on finding Dinah and hope that also led him to Gamble. Same goal, but the methods would be a little different.

"I need to speak with you." Charlotte caught up with Wade, stopping him on the footpath in front of her home.

Arthur and Kandace passed by on their way to the main building, both of them talking on their phones. Ethan stopped long enough to give Charlotte a side-hug before continuing on to the main building, as well.

"Let me work with you," Charlotte said to Wade when everyone else was out of earshot.

The bounty hunter stared at her and grasped for a polite way to tell her, *No. Absolutely not.* She was frantic and scared and had no idea what she was asking him.

"I already know the police won't let me work with them," Charlotte added, correctly reading his hesitation. "And the resort security team is here to keep guests safe. They aren't going to go searching for my sister."

Wade thought of a few choice things he had to say about the resort's security team, but decided to keep them to himself.

"Charlotte, *you* could be a target. An intentional one, this time." Wade was determined not to get pulled in by the pleading expression in her eyes. "Between what happened last night and now your sister going missing, nobody knows what's going on or what the motivations are behind it. The best thing would be for you to stay with your parents until Dinah is back home."

The expression in Charlotte's eyes shifted from pleading into something stronger. "You told me that you work differently from the police. And that your success at least in part comes from gathering information from people who won't talk to the cops."

Wade nodded. "That's true."

"Well, it's not just criminals who don't want to talk to cops. I know plenty of people in this town who care more about maintaining their reputations than helping anyone else. They'd give minimum information to the police, if they'd talk to them at all. They normally wouldn't even consider talking to a bounty hunter. But, because they know me or my family, they might give you the time of day if I were with you."

Her argument made sense. Wade found that alarming. He couldn't take Charlotte Halstead with him while he was working a case, could he?

"You'll get faster results with me along." Charlotte apparently sensed that her argument had found a foothold. "I can give you ideas on where Dinah spends her time and who her friends are. Together, we can find my sister. And your fugitive," she added.

Wade gazed down into her stubborn blue eyes and decided it wouldn't be an easy thing to talk her out of this idea, or anything else she set her mind to.

"I can't let you do it," he said. "It's not safe."

"It's not like I'm going to try to act like a bounty hunter or do anything dangerous or foolish. I just want to help you talk to people so that you can find my sister and the criminals who kidnapped me."

She might search for information about Dinah whether she was working alongside him or not. Wade would definitely rather keep an eye on her than have her out looking for Dinah alone and making herself an easy target.

He could only hope that after a few hours of bounty hunter–style grunt work—involving people with hostile attitudes, time wasted pursuing dead-end leads and having to untangle the flat-out lies they would be told—she'd get tired of it and want to go home.

"All right," he finally said, not feeling entirely comfortable with his decision. "Let's get started."

"It's only 10:00 a.m. I'm not sure we can get a whole lot accomplished this early in the day. Most of my informants are still asleep," Wade said.

Charlotte watched him complete and send a text before setting his phone on his truck's center console. They were parked in the resort garage, making plans to start searching for Dinah. Charlotte fought to ignore the coffee headache tightening the nerves at the base of her skull. Once she'd realized her sister was missing, she'd forgotten all about getting her morning caffeine. But her head was reminding her about it right now.

"I managed to get hold of a few contacts last night to ask if any of them knew Brett Gamble," he continued. "None of them did, but they said they'd ask around. It might take a little while to hear back from them, but at least that ball is already rolling."

"These informants are mostly criminals, I suppose," Charlotte asked.

Wade nodded. "In this case, all of them."

"I assume they help you for the money. How

do you know they aren't lying to you? Feeding you false information so they'll get paid?"

Wade shrugged. "It happens sometimes. But over time those people are easy to weed out. Now, what kind of leads can *you* give me to help us find your sister?"

Charlotte opened her mouth, but before she could speak he held up a hand to stop her. "I should tell you that the cops will go through the phone company to try and get a look at your sister's contact list and recent activity. We don't want to waste time duplicating their efforts. I'm not interested in the names of her friends that everyone knows about. I'm looking for something different."

"Like what?"

"I don't know yet. You tell me. Has she made any new friends recently? Maybe a man she hasn't told her boyfriend about?"

"No." Charlotte shook her head. And then found herself adding, "At least, not that I know of." Given the circumstances, the reminder that she and her twin weren't close carried an especially sharp sting. She shook her head, angry with herself. When they went their separate ways after high school, they'd let go of each other. Why had she let that happen?

"I couldn't miss hearing about Dinah's problems with drugs and alcohol in college. What can you tell me about that?"

"Nothing. I only learned about it when you did."

He didn't believe her. She could tell by his lifted brows and the slight tilt of his head. She could hardly blame him. What kind of parents would keep a secret like that from the rest of their family? From their other child? She knew the answer almost immediately. Parents whose foremost concern was their reputation and public persona. No wonder Dinah had turned out to be so much that way. Overly concerned about what everyone thought of her. Compelled to always look perfect. To be perfect.

Charlotte could only wonder what other secrets her family was keeping from her.

"Dinah said she quit college because she was bored, and I believed her."

As a tremor of worry and fear passed through her, Charlotte turned to gaze out of her side window, taking the opportunity to wipe away the tears forming in her eyes. She'd convinced Wade that she would be of help to him if he let her tag along as he searched for Dinah and Gamble. She refused to spend her time with him crying.

She shifted her thoughts toward her sister's recent activities. At least, the ones she knew about. She dug through her purse for her phone and tapped open a social media app. "Dinah likes to post pictures of herself all over town, not just at the resort," Charlotte told Wade. "Here she is at Club Sapphire over on Indigo Street. She's spent a lot of time there lately."

Wade glanced at the photo, a selfie of Dinah with a wall of deep blue glass behind her. "Okay, good. Let's head over there." He slid on a pair of dark sunglasses and started the engine.

"It'll be closed right now," Charlotte said.

"Somebody will be there getting things ready to open up tonight. Your sister's a local celebrity. I'm sure at least some of the employees have paid attention when she's been in there. Maybe somebody noticed something helpful."

He pulled out of the parking garage and drove northward, toward the river that gave the town its name, and the historic street that ran alongside the north bank and was home to handcraft shops, trendy clothing stores, nightclubs and restaurants.

As Wade drove, Charlotte scrolled through a couple of different social media accounts, searching for Dinah's posts.

"While you're looking at those, pay attention to the people around her," Wade said with a glance in Charlotte's direction. "So if we run across any of them later, you'll recognize them."

Charlotte studied the photos, doing her best to commit what she saw to memory.

They arrived at Indigo Street a short time later. The old cobblestone road was now a pedestrian-only thoroughfare, so they parked in a municipal lot at the end of the street and headed toward the main hub of activities.

As expected, Club Sapphire was closed. Wade led the way around the nightclub to the delivery entrance in the back.

He rang the bell and added a couple of loud knocks on the door. A few moments later, a man in jeans and a T-shirt and wearing a heavy cleaning apron threw open the door. "Can I help you?" His gaze strayed to Charlotte and stayed there. He squinted slightly, looking confused.

Uncertain how to respond, she nervously reached up to smooth her hair.

"We'd like to talk to you about a missing woman," Wade said. "Her name is Dinah Halstead. Do you know her?"

The man broke his gaze away from Charlotte and then laughed self-consciously. "Of course." He smiled at Charlotte. "I heard Dinah had an identical twin sister and that would obviously be you. Kind of threw me off at first."

Charlotte had experienced similar reactions before. Especially when they were younger, people regularly mistook one Halstead sister for the other. And thanks to her family's ownership of the Wolf Lake Resort, she was used to complete strangers knowing who she was. "I'm Charlotte," she said, figuring this was her opportunity to step up and show Wade that she could get someone to talk to them. "This is Wade Fast Horse. And we could really use your help."

The man opened the door a little wider and ushered them inside. "Stuart Dees. Officially, I'm the night manager. In reality, I'm the guy who does a little bit of everything." He gestured toward his apron. "The day manager called in sick this morning, so I was asked to come help out and make sure things were under control. Normally, I'd be home sleeping right now."

The main expanse of the club was in shadows. Stuart led the way to a section of the bar where circles of light shone down from low-hanging fixtures. Through an open door behind the bar, Charlotte saw into a kitchen where three or four people were bustling around cleaning and doing food prep work.

"So, you said Dinah's missing?" Stuart pulled out a couple of barstools for them to sit down on while he walked around to stand behind the bar. He picked up a mug and took a couple of sips from it. "I'm sorry to hear that. She's a nice lady. What happened?"

Charlotte started to speak, but was surprised to find herself getting choked up. Her emotions were still close to the surface and she quickly realized she wouldn't be able to describe finding her sister missing without starting to cry again. Her feelings of fear and sorrow were made even stronger in this place where her sister had been enjoying herself only a couple of nights ago.

Wade stepped in and gave a brief summary of the morning's events, leaving out the attack on Charlotte last night.

Stuart shook his head. "That's horrible. How can I help you?"

"Tell us who she hangs out with when she's in here," Wade said.

Stuart's expression shifted subtly and he chewed his lower lip for a moment. "Sorry, but I can't say that I've paid attention to that.

When I'm here, I'm busy working. Know what I mean?"

Charlotte knew what he meant. But she didn't believe him. She figured he observed a lot more than he was admitting to.

"We have good reason to believe Dinah's in grave danger," she said. "Maybe you could just give us a single name that would send us in the right direction."

He shrugged. "Sorry, can't help you."

The surge of frustration Charlotte felt was maddening. She wanted to reach out and shake some sense into the guy, but realized that probably wasn't a good idea.

Wade calmly got to his feet. Charlotte did, too. And then Wade handed over his business card.

"'Bounty hunter'?" Stuart read off the card, looking up with a surprised expression.

Wade nodded. "And like Charlotte said, we believe her sister is in serious danger."

Stuart pursed his lips together as if considering something, and for a moment it looked like he might help them. But then his expression shuttered again. He came around from behind the bar and walked them back to the delivery door. "I hope you find her."

"He's noticed who she hangs out with when

she's here. He just won't tell us," Charlotte fumed as they stepped outside and the door closed behind them.

Wade nodded at her and then reached for his phone. "Happens all the time."

"Doesn't it bother you?" Her head was starting to throb again.

"It doesn't help for me to get upset," Wade said while looking down at his phone's screen. "He might think it over and decide to call me later. That sometimes happens. Don't get discouraged. We're just getting started." He glanced up at her. "Looks like I've got an informant checking in. Let's see what he's got to say."

While he took the call, Charlotte walked around aimlessly behind the nightclub, hoping to burn off some of her aggravation and impatiently waiting for him to end the call and tell her what he'd learned.

She walked one direction and then the other, before noticing the back of a diner with the words *fresh hot coffee served all day* painted across the brick wall. She hadn't gotten any coffee this morning, and while it seemed like a petty concern in the light of things, she nevertheless thought caffeine might help her headache and ease her aggravation.

Wade was still engaged in his call. Rather than interrupt him and ask what he wanted to drink, she decided to bring him back a standard coffee with sugar and cream and hope he liked it. Figuring she should send him a text so he'd know where she'd gone, she reached into her purse for her phone. As she rounded the corner of the building where the coffee shop was located, she heard a noise behind her. Assuming it was Wade catching up with her, she started to turn. She felt a sudden, sharp pain on the back of her head, and then, darkness.

# FOUR

*Where is she going?*

Wade kept his gaze fixed on the corner of the building where he'd seen Charlotte disappear just a moment ago. He was still on the phone call with his informant, who had so far only offered general information about Brett Gamble, none of which was news to Wade.

While staying on the call, the bounty hunter began to follow his temporary working partner.

As soon as he spotted the word *coffee* painted on the bricks above an image of a steaming cup on the backside of the building in front of him, he knew exactly where Charlotte was going and why. He breathed in the rich aroma as he moved closer, figuring he could do with a caffeine reload, as well.

The sound of scuffling footsteps beside the building, just ahead of him and out of sight, caught his attention. A heavy feeling of unease quickly dropped over him.

"I'll call you back," he said into the phone, cutting off his informant midsentence. He shoved the device into the holder on his belt, just as he heard the soft echo of a sound that sounded like a woman's gasp.

He hoped he was mistaken. It could be some ordinary sound from the next street over carrying down the passageway and into the alley. But Wade had learned a long time ago to anticipate the worst and save hoping for the best for some other time. When exactly that time would come, he had no idea. Wade didn't think of himself as a pessimist. He was a realist.

The thought of Charlotte in danger already had his heart pumping and his legs moving faster.

His main worry for her had been that she might be caught in the cross fire when the bad guys came after Dinah again. Maybe he was wrong. Maybe this time they'd intentionally come after *her*.

"Charlotte!" He shouted her name as he cleared the corner of the building and his heart fell at the sight in front of him. At the far end of the narrow drive, where it met the intersecting street, last night's attackers, bail jumper

Brett Gamble and the accomplice now identified as Trey Murphy, had Charlotte. Even
more alarming, it looked as if Charlotte was
unconscious.

Gamble held her by the arms, Murphy had
her legs, and they were about to swing her into
the back seat of an idling sedan.

"Stop!" Wade yelled, summoning every bit
of strength he had to race toward them.

The kidnappers moved faster, with Gamble shoving the upper half of Charlotte's body
inside the vehicle and then letting go to race
around the back of the car and head for the
driver's seat.

Wade's blood ran cold. They were going to
get away. With Charlotte!

But then her body twisted, as though she'd
been startled awake. She twisted again, harder,
deliberately, aiming kicks at Murphy's head as
he kept his grip on her legs and tried to force
the lower half of her body into the back seat
of the vehicle.

*Good job, Charlotte!* Wade thought, proud
of her for putting up such a strong fight. *Hold
on!* He was almost to her.

Murphy let go and stopped trying to man-
handle her the rest of the way into the car. Instead, he turned his body so that he was facing

Wade. Using the weight of his own body, the thug backed into Charlotte, sitting on her to hold her in place. Then he reached for a gun and fired at Wade.

The bounty hunter had just reached the front of the diner and he dived behind a waist-high hedge in front of a plate-glass window. Bullets flew around him, chipping the brick building, punching holes in the steel rain gutters, and finally striking the large window and sending down a rainfall of shattered glass.

Wade was vaguely aware of the small shards scraping and scratching the back of his neck as he crouched behind the hedge, but he kept his attention focused on Charlotte and the assailants.

Behind him, from inside the diner, he heard screams and shouts and the scraping sounds of hastily moved chairs and heavy thud of tables tipping over. The patrons and employees were likely trying to get away from the window or take cover. Good. He figured at least one of them was already calling 9-1-1.

But he couldn't wait for the police. Any second now, Murphy would turn his attention from Wade back to Charlotte. With his gun pointed at her, she'd have no choice but to comply and pull her legs into the car so they could make their getaway.

The criminals had likely hoped to grab her in as low-key a manner as possible—at least, as low-key as it was possible to carry out something like that in broad daylight. Knock her unconscious in an alleyway, hustle her to a waiting vehicle, and figure that anyone casually glancing in their direction might not recognize that they were witnessing an abduction.

But now there was no longer any reason for the kidnappers to be cautious.

And for all Wade knew, they had no particular reason to keep Charlotte alive for very long. Maybe she was just a pawn in some kind of attempt to get money owed them by Dinah. Maybe Charlotte was valuable to them alive for only a short time. And after a short time, they'd do whatever they had to so they could get rid of her quickly.

He didn't dare shoot back at Murphy. The creep was still so close to Charlotte that he was leaning back onto her. A bullet sent in that direction could get her killed. But maybe Wade could take out the tires. At least one of them. Something that would slow them down, make them realize that they couldn't flee fast enough to escape law enforcement if they kept fighting to kidnap Charlotte. Just like Wade, they must be anticipating the cops' arrival at any moment now.

Wade scanned the area, hoping for a clear shot with no innocents in the way. It looked good. He aimed for the front passenger side tire, flicked off the safety, was just about to pull the trigger when he heard an approaching engine and a car drove past.

Wade held his fire, and to his horror, Murphy turned to Charlotte and started lifting his gun to point it at her. But before the perp could take aim, she landed a kick in the center of his gut. Clearly caught off guard, the kidnapper crumpled in pain. Charlotte grabbed her chance, shoved him aside as he was doubled over and pressed past him as she climbed out of the car and sprinted for cover.

Wade sprang to his feet and shoved through the hedge, angling toward Charlotte, who was looking around frantically as if uncertain which way to go.

Bracing himself for a shot that could come from the criminals at any moment, the bounty hunter cleared the expanse between himself and Charlotte and then leaped at her while twisting his body so that when they landed he would take the brunt of the impact. Holding her tightly, he continued the roll until they were behind a cement planter surrounding a tree in front of the dry cleaner next to the diner.

*Bang! Bang!*

Bullets struck the edge of the planter, sending chunks and smaller fragments of cement flying.

Wade got to his hands and knees, shielding Charlotte's body with his own as he inched forward to take a look. He assumed it was Murphy shooting at them, and if the kidnapper was advancing on them, Wade had to do something to get Charlotte to safety. "Get ready to run back toward the alley," he said without turning to look at her. "Head for my truck as fast as you can." He reached into his pocket for his key fob. Keeping his gaze focused toward the danger, he tossed it back in her direction.

"What about you?" she asked in a shaky voice.

"Don't worry about me." Wade could look after himself. It was a skill he'd picked up at an early age. After his dad vanished and his mom worked all hours of the day.

Still crouched, he pushed himself up onto his toes, readying to spring forward toward the shooter, figuring this was a case where the best defense was an offensive move and hoping to gain the upper hand by surprising Murphy.

*Bang! Bang!*

One more quick look around the planter before he made his move had gotten two more gunshots fired in his direction. But in that instant, he'd also been able to see that the kidnapper had shut the rear passenger door and moved toward the front of the car. A small ember of hope flared to life within him. *They're giving up!* It looked like they weren't going to keep trying to take Charlotte. At least, not right now.

Murphy yelled something. Wade couldn't make out the words over the rumble of the car's engine and he didn't much care what the jerk had to say anyway. The kidnapper's shouting was followed by the slamming of a car door and the growl of an engine after its accelerator had been punched. Tires squealed. Wade raised his head to get a clearer view.

The assailant's car was speeding away. "They're going," Wade said, watching the car for as long as possible while reaching for his phone to call Detective Romanov directly. But before he could tap the screen to make the connection, he heard a sound behind him that caught his attention.

He turned as Charlotte, who'd held herself together despite her obvious terror, began working her throat as she fought to hold back sobs. Finally, she burst into tears.

Wade was only too familiar with the feeling the moment after a terrifying ordeal when you realized you were safe and all the emotions you'd choked down while you fought to survive clawed their way to the surface. Thugs like Murphy and Gamble didn't just commit physical crimes. They did things that left behind emotional scars, some that lasted a lifetime. Knowing people like them existed was the motivation behind Wade doing what he did for a living. Taking criminals off the streets. Protecting innocent people who simply wanted to go about their daily lives.

"Everything's okay." Wade worked to settle his own intense emotions so that his voice would be calm and steady. "They're gone and you're all right."

She fought her way through a couple of ragged breaths, staring down at the ground where they were both still sitting. "They called me by name." Her words sounded scratchy and squeezed by emotion. "This time they knew it was me and not Dinah."

Her words confirmed his new fear. Now the

kidnappers were after Charlotte, specifically. Wade had heard the threat Gamble directed to Dinah when he and Charlotte were hiding on the loading dock. Clearly, Gamble had mistaken Charlotte for her identical twin. But now things had changed and he and his partner had targeted Charlotte. Why? What had changed? And what was the bigger story here?

"I don't understand any of this." Charlotte shook her head and then lifted her face, settling a searching gaze on Wade. Tear tracks marked the sides of her cheeks. Her shoulder-length blond hair, normally neatly parted on the side and tucked behind her ears, now fell across her face in twists and tangles. Before he knew what he was doing, Wade reached out to brush some of the errant strands aside.

His fingertips brushed the soft skin of her forehead and temples and he told himself he was just trying to make it easier for her to see, even as he felt the unexpected catch in his breath at the flush in her cheeks.

Awareness of what was going on hit him like a snap and he drew back his hand. This was not happening. He wouldn't let it. They were temporary working partners. She was a woman who needed the help and protection he could offer. That was all.

Although, she'd just now done a pretty magnificent job of protecting herself.

The thought brought a return of that catch in his breath.

Determined to get his thoughts—and the accompanying feelings—under control, Wade leaned back and got to his feet, all the while schooling the expression on his face to something appropriately serious. He didn't want to think about what might have been written plainly on his face moments ago. Something ridiculous, no doubt.

"Let me help you up." He extended his hand. When Charlotte grasped it, when she touched him, that feeling was there again. A gentle warmth that was something beyond simply the temperature of her skin. But this time Wade was ready for it and he immediately cut off the unwelcome feeling of connection, turning his attention from Charlotte to their surroundings.

Unfortunately, it took another few moments for him to realize he still needed to let go of her hand.

Sirens wailed at the end of the street, accompanied by the flashing red and blue lights of police cars speeding in their direction. People slowly emerged from the diner and the dry cleaner and several other businesses on the street after apparently taking cover inside.

"We need to have a paramedic check you over as soon as an ambulance gets here."

Charlotte blew out a deep breath. "I'm fine. I have a headache, but I had a headache before they hit me on the back of the head. And I never got my coffee."

Wade gritted his teeth. The thought of someone striking her like that soured his stomach. And it sharpened his determination to get the kidnappers off the streets. "Well, you still need to get checked out. Maybe go to the hospital for X-rays."

"I will if that seems necessary. Otherwise, I don't want to waste time on it." She crossed her arms over her chest and gave him a steadfast look that took him by surprise as the cop cars rolled up to them. "We need to keep looking for my sister."

Despite his best intentions to keep his emotions in check, Wade still felt the flutter of something warm and not altogether unpleasant in the center of his chest. Maybe Charlotte Halstead wasn't the soft, spoiled daughter of wealth that he'd thought she was. There was no denying that the woman had backbone. Hopefully, it would continue to help keep her alive.

\* \* \*

"We were able to get the plate numbers off the perps' car thanks to a couple nearby security cameras," Detective Romanov said. "It was stolen, of course, but patrol will be on the lookout for it. And I've got a unit canvassing the neighborhood where it was stolen searching for potential witnesses and seeing if anybody there has outdoor security video."

Charlotte nodded her understanding. Other than that, she had no idea what to say. Tracking criminals was not a normal part of her life.

She and Wade were in the detective's office a couple of hours after the attack outside the coffee shop. The detective had arrived on the scene shortly after the initial responding officers, where she'd conducted quick interviews with Charlotte and Wade.

Now, while two other police detectives along with patrol officers interviewed diner patrons and followed up on related leads, Romanov was ready to talk to Charlotte and Wade again.

"What exactly did Gamble and Murphy say to you?" Romanov asked.

It took Charlotte a moment to rouse herself to answer. Despite Wade getting her a very large and very strong espresso drink with lots of chocolate in it, she was exhausted and her mind was unfocused. It had to be the surge of adrenaline and subsequent drop that had her feeling an edgy combination of sleepy and jittery. But at least she had no symptoms of concussion and her headache had finally gone away. The coffee drink and a couple of ibuprofen had eased the throbbing pain. At the moment, she just had to make sure she didn't lean the tender knot on the back of her head against the chair or she'd quickly be reminded that not too long ago she'd been hit hard enough to lose consciousness.

That was a creepy thing to think about and she didn't want to dwell on it.

"As I've mentioned before, one minute I was walking to the diner and turning around because I thought I heard Wade walking up behind me, and the next thing I knew, I was being carried by my hands and feet. I recognized Gamble first because he was closest to my face." Charlotte stopped for a moment, as the stark terror she'd felt in that instant became immediate and real to her even though she was safe inside the police department. For a few seconds, she couldn't breathe.

"Take your time," Wade said gently.

She glanced at him, taking comfort in the

determined yet compassionate expression on his face.

"Breathe," he added.

Filling her lungs and blowing out the air a couple of times did seem to help.

"When I recognized Gamble, I tried to break free of his grip and I shouted, 'I'm not Dinah!'" Charlotte resumed. "He said, 'I know, Charlotte. This time it's *you* we want.'"

Romanov leaned forward, resting her elbows on her desk. "What else did he say? Or the other one, Murphy, did he say anything?"

Charlotte shook her head, carefully, just to make sure it didn't start hurting again. "Everything else was just them threatening to kill me if I didn't cooperate with them and them ordering me to get into the car." She swallowed thickly. "I was pretty sure they planned to kill me eventually anyway, so I fought back. I escaped. Murphy yelled something before they drove away, but I couldn't hear clearly enough to understand it."

The detective turned to Wade.

"Same," he said. "I could tell the guy was yelling, but that old car had a bad muffler. It drowned out his words."

"Why do you think they didn't just shoot

you in the passage beside the coffee shop and be done with it?" Romanov asked.

It was a harsh question. But not one Charlotte hadn't already asked herself. "Murphy could have killed me when he snuck into my SUV thinking I was Dinah. He didn't. But at the same time, both men seemed willing to use lethal force to make sure I didn't get away." She sighed. "Gamble said Dinah owed him. He had to mean she owed him money as opposed to, say, owing him a favor. Maybe he meant to grab me to get money, too."

"You mean he wants to hold one or both of you for ransom?" Wade asked.

"I don't know what I mean. I'm confused and I'm just doing my best to think of things that could help us figure this out."

"Do you think the Invaders could have a part in this?" Wade asked the detective. "Attempts at making quick money and use of violence are right up their alley."

"*Invaders?*" Charlotte asked, thinking maybe she'd misheard him. "What does that mean?"

"They're a criminal motorcycle gang that operates in and around Range River. They're involved in everything from illicit drug sales to auto theft to strong-arm robbery and crimes beyond that. More than one member has faced murder charges."

A sound that was a combination of a cough and a laugh came out of Charlotte's mouth. Because she could hardly believe what he was saying. "You're telling me that Range River has an outlaw biker gang running around?" She shook her head. "I've never heard anything about it."

"How closely do you follow crime?" Wade asked.

It was a fair question. "Until now, not too closely. I'd catch news headlines, but that's about it."

"They're not above kidnapping for ransom, extortion, blackmail. Whatever could be the motivation for these attacks, I could see them being involved in it." He turned to the detective. "Maybe we should take a look in that direction. See if Dinah's being held at the gang house out on Tributary Road."

"*The police* will deal with the Invaders. Not you." Romanov focused a hard stare toward Wade. "Don't try to talk to any of the gang members. I am explicitly telling you to stay away from them."

"You've got an ongoing investigation into them, don't you?" Wade said.

The detective didn't respond.

"Okay." Wade nodded. "I understand. If you've got an undercover officer or officers working with them, I don't want to get in the way."

Romanov responded with a sharp nod. "See that you don't."

"Meanwhile, we need to strengthen security for you." Wade shifted his attention to Charlotte.

His gaze, determined and protective, calmed some of the edginess that had her nerves so aggravatingly unbalanced. For a moment she let herself revel in the feeling—the dream, really—of having someone focused on caring for her and looking out for her. Someone she could rely on. Someone who would be there when she needed him to help her feel strong.

But then the moment passed, and she let the dream—because it really was just a dream—go. Charlotte had grown up seeing warm, close families. Some were friends; some were visitors she observed vacationing at the family resort. Their casual connectedness was visible in their body language, in the way they talked to one another, in the inevitable family spats that appeared to be quickly resolved. It was obvious that the various family members really, truly had each other's back.

Charlotte's family was good at keeping up appearances. Over the years there had been countless photos taken of the Halstead family with their blonde twin daughters, everyone looking cozy gathered around fireplaces in the winter or seated on boats on Wolf Lake in the summer. Charlotte would never claim that her parents hadn't taken care of her. They bought everything their daughters could possibly need, and then some. But Arthur and Kandace Halstead were very focused on their resort, on expanding it and increasing bookings not only for individuals but also for large conference events.

That took a lot of energy and a lot of hours in the day, so they needed to be focused and efficient. An extra hug, a few minutes away from the phone or meetings or their laptops to listen to an adolescent girl's worries or fears, was a waste of their precious time.

Charlotte often wondered if the emotional support she'd thought she'd seen in other families was real, or were they faking it, too? She couldn't be sure. But she had discovered a foundation of strength and comfort when she'd come to faith while away at college. And she'd met people through her church and prayer groups who were very supportive.

But even with that experience, she still couldn't bring herself to completely emotionally rely on another person in any situation that truly mattered. Maybe it had always been unreasonable for her to expect anyone else to care about her that much. All she knew was that she'd learned long ago not to get her hopes up. The crash that came when she'd leaned on someone and they'd chosen not to shoulder the burden and instead leave her on her own was just too painful.

She would rely on her faith, and herself, and that was it.

She would rely on the bounty hunter to protect her physically, because he'd proved he could do that. But there was no way she would give in to the pull that tempted her to trust him to be steadfast when she needed someone to lean on.

"We have a security team at the resort who can help keep an eye on me," Charlotte finally said in response to Wade's comment about her needing better protection.

He tilted his head slightly. "They didn't do much for your sister."

"True." What else could she say? At the end of the day, you couldn't pay people to care.

Perhaps the security employee who was

supposed to protect the twins had intentionally let Dinah get kidnapped. Maybe he'd been paid off. The thought sent a chill racing across Charlotte's skin and she shivered.

"Until we have a better handle on what's going on, I think you should stay at a secure location." Wade exchanged glances with the detective before turning back to Charlotte. "Connor Ryan, owner of Range River Bail Bonds and my adopted brother, inherited the old Riverside Inn five years ago. The grounds were overgrown and the building dilapidated, but he did some rebuilding and repairs and made it a private residence. He's got state-of-the-art security. We've had people who were in danger stay there before. My mother manages the property, and when necessary, she or Danny or Hayley Ryan move in temporarily to add extra security."

"You're asking me to stay with your brother?"

He offered her the slight boyish smile that completely eased his normally serious expression. It also made Charlotte's stomach do silly little flip-flops for some dumb reason. "I'll be there, too, along with my mom," he said. "It's quite large. Plenty of room. And I hope you like cats and dogs, because Connor's got several of both. He likes to pretend that they aren't actually his, and that some other mysterious person can't resist adopting abandoned animals."

Charlotte knew the building he was talking about. It was a beautiful structure surrounded by tall pines on the southern bank of the Range River. She was vaguely aware that the property had been given a substantial face-lift not too long ago, but she hadn't known the details.

It was a gorgeous location. And after today's attack, Charlotte did feel especially vulnerable. But she'd never laid eyes on Wade Fast Horse until last night, and now he was suggesting she move in with him and a group of strangers? *Bounty hunters*, at that?

"It's not a bad idea," Detective Romanov said. "I've worked with Connor Ryan and his crew for a year now. They're ethical people. I know of at least one woman who, like yourself, was in danger and needed a safe place to stay. She moved to the Riverside Inn until the men who were threatening her life were brought to justice. She told me after the fact that she was very glad she'd made the decision to do that."

Charlotte blew out a sigh. It was time to let go of her hopes that Dinah would be found quickly and things would go back to normal in a day or so. After all that had happened, that didn't seem likely.

Charlotte and Dinah had not been close for a long time. And now that Charlotte knew of her twin's drug and alcohol problems—which had been kept secret, with the possible result of making the situation worse—she was especially frustrated with Dinah and their parents. Why not let a problem like that see the light of day and try to heal it? Was the secretiveness something Dinah had requested, or was it a case of their parents wanting to put on a good face for the public?

And were these recent terrifying attacks and Dinah's disappearance somehow related to that addiction problem?

In spite of everything, Charlotte loved her sister. Even when she was annoyed by her. She wanted to help Dinah, to rescue her. She wanted to do what she needed to keep herself safe and alive, too. Despite having a paid security team at the resort, it looked like the Range River Bail Bonds crew would be her best choice.

"All right, thank you. I'll stay at the inn," she finally said.

What choice did she have? Her life was in danger, the Wolf Lake Resort was not as secure as she'd thought it was, and she had nowhere else to go.

# FIVE

"It looks like a fortress." Charlotte's gaze swept over the stone-and-heavy-timber building in front of her.

"Connor wanted to keep the feel of the original Riverside Inn," Wade responded. "It was designed to withstand harsh weather along with the occasional bandit attack when it was originally built back in the 1880s. The town of Range River afforded the only river crossing for miles around and a lot of tradesmen and merchants with gold or silver on hand stayed at the inn. That made it a tempting target."

Just beyond the building, the Range River flowed by with late-afternoon sunlight glinting on its splashy, riotous surface. Spring had announced its presence with rain and snow-melt resulting from warmer days. The runoff from the surrounding mountains made its way to the river, where it flowed westward toward the Pacific Ocean.

"Well, it's a gorgeous setting."

The resort had a beautiful view of the Wolf Lake and the surrounding mountains, but this particular spot felt cozier and homier to Charlotte. Maybe it was because of the surrounding trees, meandering blackberry vines and the neat redbrick path leading to the oversize front door.

Unlike the lodge, it didn't have an attached parking garage, a large staff and numerous guests wandering around.

In any event, here she was, with a suitcase full of clothes that she'd grabbed on a quick trip to her condo. She'd tried calling her mom and ended up leaving a voice mail with a vague explanation that she didn't feel safe in her condo, so she would be staying with "friends" instead. Any further explanation would have led to her parents questioning her decision. And telling them about the attack would upset them for no reason.

"I messaged my mom, so she's already here and planning to make dinner tonight," Wade said, carrying Charlotte's suitcase as they walked up to the front door.

"She doesn't normally stay here?"

Wade shook his head. "All of us have our own homes. But we've got rooms here for when we need them. Range River Bail Bonds has a storefront office in town—so no bail bond clients ever come out here—but we sometimes meet to discuss strategy here. If we've got an intense case, or a dangerous situation going on, we tend to all move in here and stay until the case or situation is resolved. Connor's generous about letting people visit for a while when they need a safe place to stay. When that happens, some or all of us usually move in to help out."

Wade punched a number into a keypad beside the front door and pushed it open.

They were immediately greeted with the sounds of barking dogs and canine toenails tapping on a wooden floor.

"They don't sound like guard dogs," Charlotte mused.

"Yeah, you'd think a home owned by a bounty hunter would have vicious attack dogs, but no."

The words were barely out of his mouth when they were greeted by several bundles of fur of various colors and sizes. A small white dog with an underbite and hair nearly covering its eyes seemed to be the boldest, and it stepped up to Charlotte, nose quivering, and delightedly sniffed her hand, which Charlotte held out in greeting.

Not wanting the other pups to feel left out, she made certain to hold her hand out to each of them, too, as she brushed by them while walking into the foyer. They were boisterous and happy dogs, but also well-mannered and refrained from jumping up on her.

"Hey, you hooligans! Back up and give the lady some room." A dark-haired woman with russet-brown skin who looked to be in her fifties and whose features favored Wade walked into the short hallway and gestured at the dogs.

"They're fine," Charlotte said, reaching down to the graying terrier mix that was nearest to her. "I love dogs."

"This is my mom, Maribel," Wade said to Charlotte as she straightened.

"Charlotte Halstead." She reached out to offer her hand to the woman, who grasped it and gave it a light squeeze.

"I haven't seen you since you were a tiny little thing. You and your sister."

That was right—Wade had mentioned that his mom had worked at the resort years ago. "I hope we weren't obnoxious brats," Charlotte said with a tentative smile. Was Maribel treated well when she was employed by the Halsteads? Charlotte certainly hoped so.

There had been a time, when she first went away to college, that Charlotte was certain she wanted nothing to do with the family business and she had figured on going her own way. Then the passage of time plus basic life experience made her realize that she not only had a wonderful career opportunity right in front of her with the family business, but by being employed at the resort, she could also do some good beyond her own self-interest. She could do things for the community, like working with the literacy group she'd met with before Trey Murphy kidnapped her in her SUV. Maybe she could do things to provide for a better quality of life for resort employees, too.

"You and Dinah were sweet kids. I remember you were crazy about a collection of little toy ponies you had with a plastic corral and stables."

Charlotte hadn't thought about those little ponies in years. The memory made her smile as it brought with it thoughts of times when she and Dinah were best friends and played together all day long. *What happened? Why did things have to change?* It wasn't like they fought all the time now. They didn't really have direct conflicts. They just had such a shallow, surface relationship.

And now it was possible that she might not ever see Dinah again. They might not ever have the chance to resolve whatever it was that had pushed them apart.

"Wade and I and the rest of the Range River team are going to do everything we can to help find Dinah," Maribel said, rightly discerning the direction Charlotte's thoughts had taken at the mention of her sister's name.

Charlotte nodded. "Thank you."

"Meanwhile, welcome to the Riverside Inn." Maribel gestured toward the end of the foyer and led the way into a great room with a high ceiling sporting exposed wooden beams and a second-floor gallery with what appeared to be doors leading to bedrooms. There was a large river-stone fireplace with windows on either side that offered a view of an outside deck, the river and the mountains in the distance.

Looking around, she could see hallways, part of a kitchen and dining room, and a slight bit of what appeared to be an office or a den.

"It's beautiful," she said.

"Not as luxurious as what you're used to," Wade said beside her, "but we like it."

Charlotte cut a glance at him because there

was no missing the edge to his comment. He was assuming that she'd make some kind of comparison, even if she didn't voice it, and find the inn somehow wanting. He assumed she was spoiled and critical.

Her glance lingered and he held her gaze, a hint of challenge in his eyes and a slight lift to his brows, as if throwing down a challenge and awaiting a response.

She wasn't playing this game.

She'd been born into a high-profile family—at least, high-profile in Range River—and starting somewhere around middle school, she'd encountered people who judged her and presumed things about her. About her values and how she saw herself and other people. Of course she'd wanted to fit in, wanted people to like her. And truly, despite their obsession with work and increasing the value of the family enterprise, her parents had raised Charlotte and Dinah to have respect for people who worked hard for their living, who may not have the physical comforts that the Halstead family had.

But trying to explain to people that she was not the clueless, pampered princess they assumed she was never worked. Didn't work in high school. Didn't work in college, either. She'd been tricked a few times, much to her humiliation, by people she'd thought were friends but who'd actually just wanted access to the meals and entertainments Charlotte had been able to pay for. And there had been a couple of boyfriends in college who'd eventually slipped up and exposed their true motivations for dating her—that they hoped to use Charlotte to weasel their way into the family business and get a piece of that fortune.

*I'm not doing this.* She broke her gaze away from Wade and shook her head slightly. She was not going to try to explain or prove herself to him. Convince him she was a decent person despite the situation she'd been born into. When she'd started attending Bible study in college, having come from a family that was nominally Christian but didn't really live in faith, she'd met the first people who weren't determined to judge her but were instead willing to accept her. And at a very dark time in her life, they'd helped her be able to accept herself.

She wasn't going to give that up just so Wade Fast Horse would accept or approve of her. Even though he was handsome in a rugged, intense kind of way. And yes, he was standing fast in support of her in a dangerous situation, and she appreciated that. But at the end of the day, he was doing it for money. This was his *job*. And the hard lesson she'd learned still held true: she couldn't rely on anyone but herself. Getting her hopes up that Wade could somehow be different was a sure road to disappointment and heartache, yet again.

"Welcome." A man who looked maybe ten years older than Wade, about forty or so, with coffee-colored eyes and military-cut dark hair, strode out from the direction of what she could now clearly see was a cozy room furnished like a den but also housing a heavy wooden desk and several pieces of office equipment in one corner. "I'm Connor Ryan," he added.

Charlotte reached for his extended hand. "Charlotte Halstead. Thank you for letting me stay here."

"I'm hoping we can do a lot more than that and we can help you find your sister." He ushered her toward a sofa and then dropped down into a chair across from her.

Wade took a seat with Charlotte on the sofa while Maribel excused herself to resume preparing dinner.

"I'm up-to-date with everything," Connor began, with a glance at Wade. "We've got a lot going on with various cases right now, but we're going to put all the resources we can into this." Now he focused on Charlotte. "Our legitimate direction, as bounty hunters, is to go after Brett Gamble because his bond has been revoked. Wade told me he has good reason to think Gamble is involved with the disappearance of your sister and I'm inclined to agree. Since we don't have any other specific leads for Gamble, we're going to try to find him by looking for your sister."

"Thank you." Charlotte knew the police were doing everything they could to find Dinah, but having these extra hands on deck in the search—people with experiences and connections that were different from the cops and who could supplement their efforts—made her feel a little better. But not much. Charlotte tried not to dwell on the thought that her sister might not even still be alive. But that was a real possibility.

*Lord, please protect her.* How could so much have happened, how could her world have changed so dramatically in such a short amount of time? It was just last night that she was meeting with the literacy committee members at dinner. Thinking that afterward she would go home and catch up on a couple of episodes of her current favorite TV program.

"Charlotte?"

Charlotte's eyelids fluttered open. "Sorry." Somehow she'd nearly fallen asleep. She hadn't been able to make herself eat much of anything today and she was exhausted from everything she'd been through over the last twenty-four hours. She reached up to rub her throbbing head where she'd been struck. Apparently the ibuprofen was wearing off.

"I'll get Maribel," Connor said quietly.

"You should probably rest for a little bit," Wade said. He started to reach over and touch Charlotte's hand, but for some reason he stopped himself.

"Let's head upstairs and get you settled." Maribel walked out from the kitchen ahead of Connor. She reached for Charlotte's suitcase, but Wade was already on his feet and he beat her to it.

"I wouldn't mind a little time to wind down." Charlotte found it took more effort than she'd expected to push herself up from the couch. Her energy was draining fast.

Along with Wade and Maribel, Charlotte headed up the stairs. Then she followed as Maribel led the way along the gallery to a bedroom door at the end of the hall. She was surprised to see a longhaired tabby cat curled up on the bed.

"I'll get her out of the way," Wade said.

"No." Charlotte held up a hand to stop him. "I love cats. And I wouldn't mind some company. Who is this?"

"Her name is Fluzzy. Connor says it's because she's fluffy and fuzzy. He found her in a storm drain a couple of years ago, in pretty bad shape, so of course he had to bring her home."

The story of Fluzzy brought a smile to Charlotte's lips. She needed the reminder that even though the world was cruel at times, there was some goodness and kindness in it. Including good and kind people, she thought, as she stole a glance at Wade.

"Dinner will be ready in an hour or so," Maribel said. "I'll check with you then to see if you want to come downstairs or if you'd rather have me bring you something up here."

"I don't want to trouble you."

Maribel glanced at her son. "I'm surrounded by people who trouble me. Why should you be any different?" She smiled and winked before turning to go.

Wade lingered in the doorway. "We're going to do everything we can to find Dinah," he said. "And we'll have both you and her in our prayers."

"You're a praying person?" Charlotte asked.

He nodded. "Yes. My mom, the Ryans, they're all people of faith, too."

Charlotte felt her eyes start to tear up. "Right now, faith is the only thing getting me through all of this."

Wade nodded somberly. "Faith can do that. You keep pressing in."

With that, he stepped out and closed the door.

Charlotte stretched out on the bed. Beside her, Fluzzy opened one eye and began to rumble a low purr.

Charlotte closed her eyes, hoping to catch some sleep. And also hoping she wouldn't have nightmares about what had happened and what might be yet to come. She had no idea what condition Dinah was in at the moment. And there was no way Charlotte could forget that she, too, was now a target for abduction. And possibly for murder.

"Charlotte's text says she'll be down here in a minute." Wade closed the message screen and slid his phone back into his pocket. "Let's give her a few minutes when she first gets down here, let her drink some coffee and maybe eat something before we spring the news on her."

A post on a local online newspaper had

something to say about the Halstead family, and Charlotte in particular, that was not especially flattering and was in some ways downright alarming.

"Are you sure she doesn't already know?" Connor asked.

Wade took a sip of coffee. "She didn't mention it in her text." Although, that didn't prove anything.

He glanced over at the two men he considered brothers, Connor and Danny Ryan, who stood near him as they'd gathered by the coffeepot in the kitchen. Danny was the same age as Wade and they'd been classmates in school. While Danny's facial features resembled his older brother somewhat, the younger brother had different coloring with blue instead of brown eyes and lighter-colored hair.

Danny's wife, Tanya, had shown up alongside him at the inn this morning. While not a bounty hunter like her husband, Tanya had been in danger and needed to take refuge at the inn not so long ago. When they'd arrived, she'd told Wade and Connor that she hoped to offer comfort and reassurance to Charlotte by keeping her company at the inn as well as relating her own experience of taking refuge with the Range River Bail Bonds crew and receiving Danny's help in the middle of a dangerous and volatile situation.

The fact that Danny and Tanya had fallen in love in the midst of that ordeal and later gotten married was not lost on Wade. But he was absolutely not looking for that with Charlotte.

She seemed like a kind person, and yes, maybe there was a little bit of a spark between them. Learning that she, like him, was a person of faith had admittedly set his heart beating a little faster when she mentioned it. Because *if* he were going to set aside common sense and get married someday, his bride would have to be a believer. That was important to him.

But in reality, he didn't intend to set aside common sense. So many marriages didn't work out. So many people were, ultimately, unreliable. Some people seemed to be able to put aside those facts and give in to starry-eyed romance anyway. Wade couldn't do that. He wouldn't.

He was five years old when his dad moved out of Range River, heading to California for work. At least, that was what he'd said. His dad had also claimed he was coming back home soon. He reassured Wade on sporadic phone calls that he was just going to work a little longer, save a little more money, and then head back home to Idaho.

Wade wasn't sure when his mom had stopped believing the empty promises. Probably much sooner than the hopeful boy who didn't understand that adults sometimes lied. That *dads* sometimes lied.

His dad sent money to them for a while. But eventually the money stopped, and then the phone calls became more erratic. Finally the calls stopped, too, and his dad filed for divorce. By then his mom was working at the Wolf Lake Resort. Long hours and not much money. Their friends and neighbors, the Ryans, were going through some rough times, too, after their parents died. So the Fast Horses and the Ryans backed each other up, shared resources with each other, prayed for each other, and eventually they all found themselves working and building a future together.

Things had turned out okay. But Wade had not forgotten his own disappointment in hoping his dad would come through and do the right thing. He hadn't forgotten the heartache his mother went through or his own heartbreak after being fed promises and reassurances from his dad that were just words.

Amazingly enough, his mom wasn't bitter. He'd asked her a few times over the years if she'd ever get married again and she'd just laughed and shaken her head in response and said something along the lines of "My life is full as it is."

Wade, admittedly, was bitter. He couldn't seem to let go of the anger and resentment and the sense of being a fool when he believed his dad's promises.

No, he and Charlotte would not be falling in love like Danny and Tanya. Wade simply wasn't willing to go there. But he did like Charlotte. And he did want to help her and keep her safe. For a short while. Until the case was resolved.

Wade knew Charlotte was coming down when he heard the sound of dog toenails skittering across the wooden floor near the bottom of the stairs in the great room as the pups ran to greet her. He could hear her talking to them as she headed toward the kitchen.

"Morning," she said, rounding a corner and tucking her light hair back behind her ears.

"Good morning." Wade grabbed a mug and filled it, dumping plenty of cream and sugar into the coffee because he'd learned yesterday that that was what she liked.

While she took a couple of sips, he noted

that her color was back to normal. Last night, she'd come downstairs just long enough to eat a little bit of dinner with him and Connor and Maribel. She'd looked pale then, and exhausted. She seemed more energetic now, but on the downside, a few of the light red marks that had been on the side of her face last night as a result of the kidnapping attempt had now darkened into significant bruises.

Wade introduced Charlotte to Danny and Tanya, and then everyone moved to the kitchen table, where places were set and a sausage breakfast casserole and cinnamon rolls were being kept warm in covered serving dishes.

Tanya grabbed a seat next to Charlotte, and after everyone plated their food and Maribel said grace, Tanya related her own experiences with having to be kept safe at the inn. Charlotte listened raptly and appeared to relax a little more.

Wade kept the news that he knew would disturb Charlotte to himself until everyone was finished eating. Then he realized he didn't know quite how to break it to her. She'd already been through so much, she'd gotten a small reprieve by relaxing over breakfast, and here he was, about to upset her again. He found himself stalling until Connor caught his eye and gave him a slight nod of encouragement.

Wade cleared his throat and turned to Charlotte. "So, have you looked at the local news yet today?"

She shook her head. "I haven't looked at the news, haven't read the zillions of texts people have sent me, and I definitely haven't listened to the voice mails from my parents and people calling from unfamiliar numbers. It's got to all be gossips wanting to know about Dinah's disappearance and everything that's been happening to me and I'm just not ready to deal with it all. I'll get caught up on it later." She stopped and lifted her brows. "Wait. Is there something in the news about Dinah?" She began to smile slightly. "Has she been found? Why would you make me wait until the end of breakfast to tell me?"

That dash of hopefulness in her tone made it that much worse to have to tell her the truth. "I'm sorry to say Dinah hasn't been found," he said evenly. "But what *has* happened is that someone anonymously leaked a story to the town's online newspaper that an internal auditor at the resort has discovered that *you* have been embezzling money since your return to Range River. And with Dinah missing, there's talk that she may have been involved in stealing money, as well."

Wade stopped talking and waited. His job often involved confronting people with the facts of unlawful things they'd done. If she immediately came up with an excuse or a belabored explanation, that would tell him what he needed to know. That she was guilty. Even if she didn't directly confess.

He steeled himself for the burn of disappointment if it turned out he'd misread her. That, like his dad, she'd been taking advantage of his trust.

Instead, she laughed. For kind of a long time, like she was either releasing stress or building up anxiety to a breaking point. Wade had no idea where it was going. Until she finally stopped, took a deep breath, shook her head and said, "You can't be serious."

"I am."

She crossed her arms, sat back in her chair and said, "Well, I didn't steal anything. The timing of this is bizarre. Maybe it's not coincidental that it's happening while Dinah is missing." She shook her head. "Once again, I have *no idea* what is going on. But I do know it's possible to hire someone to do a forensic computer audit and discover who actually played around with the accounts. If I have to pay for someone to do that and prove my innocence, I will."

"So you didn't do it?" Wade asked, encouraged by her confidence that her name would be cleared. "You didn't pilfer any money?"

"I did not. And if you don't believe me, I'll thank you for your hospitality and I'll leave."

"Not so fast." Connor held up a hand. "Just because we want to talk to you about this doesn't mean we're accusing you of actually doing it. But we had to ask. You must understand that."

Charlotte gave a sharp nod.

"We have a bounty hunting aspect to our business because we want to get dangerous fugitives off the streets," Connor continued. "But it's only part of our bigger bail bond business. We write bail bonds because the law presumes people are innocent until proven guilty. If bail is set, then arrestees have the right to post bail and walk free unless or until circumstances change. Being in this business for a few years, I've learned the innocent people do sometimes get arrested and charged. Their reputations are smeared and they're embarrassed. Sometimes their future careers are imperiled over something they didn't even do because news stories seem to live online forever and corrections and updates clearing a person's name aren't always issued."

Charlotte smiled faintly and sighed deeply. After a moment, she glanced at Wade.

"You say you didn't do it and I believe you." The words were out of Wade's mouth before he realized it. But what he said was true. His common sense might be inclined to remind him that he barely knew her. But some other part of him had come to the conclusion that she was the honorable woman that she appeared to be.

For reasons he didn't want to think about, that realization troubled him.

"Our sister, Hayley, and her husband, Jack, are tied up with a manhunt for Eagle Rapids Bail Bonds right now." Connor fixed his gaze on Charlotte. "Danny and I also have other cases we're working, but we'll still be able to put out the word to our own confidential informants in town and see what we can learn about Gamble and Murphy and anything else related to your sister."

"Thank you." Charlotte nodded. "I'll look into this embezzlement issue on my own."

"Jonah and Lorraine can do some deeper research on Gamble and Murphy and see if they can learn anything useful," Maribel suggested.

The trusted office assistants were often helpful in gathering background information. "Also, I believe Jonah's got connections at the online newspaper. He may be able to learn how the embezzlement story was delivered to the journalist there who posted it. Maybe we can find out who is feeding the lies and get some kind of lead from that."

"Good idea." Connor set his empty coffee cup on the table. He turned to Wade. "What do you have planned for today?"

"I figured we'd visit the coffee shop that Dinah manages on the resort property. Talk to the employees. See if anything unusual has been happening there lately. If anyone suspicious has been coming around. If Dinah seemed worried or fearful."

"That sounds reasonable." Charlotte set her napkin on the table and stood, a determined expression on her face. She picked up her plate and utensils to clear her spot at the table. "But before we go to the coffee shop, I intend to find my parents and talk to them face-to-face about this embezzlement issue." She shook her head. "I haven't done anything wrong and I'm not going to hide from this."

Wade watched her stride over to the kitchen to put her dishes in the dishwasher. Not exactly the type of behavior he'd expect from the daughter of wealthy resort owners. He'd assumed she was used to people cleaning up after her.

Beyond pondering that, he couldn't help worrying about her safety. Leaving the inn and going back into town could make her a target yet again. But the truth was he could benefit from her assistance in getting information that might help find her sister as well as his bail jumper.

Charlotte was willing to take a risk to do what she felt had to be done: find her sister and clear her own name. Wade was determined to do his best to protect her while she did that.

# SIX

"I don't think it's a good time for you to go in right now." Arthur Halstead's personal secretary stood behind her desk, apparently thinking her positioning might slow Charlotte down.

"Don't worry, Stella. I'll shoulder the blame for barging in." Charlotte continued past her, with Wade close on her heels, and shoved open the heavy wooden double door leading into her father's office. Thanks to Stella, she already knew her mother was in there with him. But she was surprised to see a third person there, as well.

"Mr. Deming." Charlotte managed to hide her surprise and gave the man a nod of greeting.

"Ms. Halstead." He smiled in return. Though the smile didn't appear to reach his eyes, which were cold and assessing.

Nolan Deming represented an investment

group out of Dallas that had been trying to outright purchase the resort, or at least purchase a percentage of it, for years. Her parents were adamant that they would never sell, but they took meetings with Deming once or twice a year because in return he sent business their way in the form of several large conferences run by Texans excited to get out of the Dallas heat in the summer and cool off beside a mountain lake.

Charlotte's parents—both appearing pale and worried, as would be expected since one of their daughters was missing—got to their feet and each of them gave her a weary hug. But, as was so often the case, it seemed to be mostly for show. She could tell they were annoyed by her interruption. Especially after she told them she wasn't there to give them news on the search for Dinah.

She told herself that her parents were themselves upset and traumatized by Dinah's disappearance and that it was unfair of her to expect a warmer reaction from them.

Still, she was disappointed. And a little sad.

She made a brief introduction between Wade and Deming, whose eyes widened when he heard the term *bounty hunter*. At the same moment, Kandace made a slight scoffing sound.

Charlotte heard it but she didn't care whether her mother approved of Wade or not. Let her mom have whatever opinion she wanted. The man had already helped Charlotte escape potentially lethal situations, twice. And yes, he was getting paid to hunt down the bad guys. But he'd already offered her and the Halstead family help and support beyond what could have been reasonably expected by a man just doing his job.

"Honey, why don't the three of us talk later." Her mom gave her a pointed look.

Of course her parents would want to keep a shiny gloss on things as much as possible. That was their default attitude on everything related to the Halstead public profile and the family business. And Charlotte agreed that there were plenty of situations that a family should keep private and quiet. But right now, when it came to Dinah's disappearance and the charges of business impropriety publicly leveled against Charlotte, they were way beyond that point.

"Mom, the story that I pilfered money from the resort has been published in an *online newspaper*. It's out there, whether we like it or not. And I want to make an equally public statement that I haven't taken anything. The story is an outright lie and I intend to find out who reported it. Meanwhile, tell me right now—do you believe you have actual evidence that I embezzled money?"

"That's enough!" Arthur Halstead's complexion had gone from pale to beet red. He was furious. After making eye contact with Charlotte, he glanced at Nolan Deming—who appeared enthralled by the drama unfolding in front of him—and then back at Charlotte again. The message was crystal clear: this shameful situation needed to be kept hidden and discussed out of earshot of witnesses.

"I don't have anything to hide," Charlotte said. Despite the feeling of heat in her cheeks and the increasing pounding of her heart, she fought to keep her voice calm. "Along with trying to find my missing sister and keep from getting *killed*, I now need to deal with this? Okay, I want to deal with it, head-on. I want to fight it. *Publicly*, because the accusation has been made public.

"And who knows?" she continued. "Maybe this fabricated story is related to Dinah's disappearance and the attacks on me. You know, Dad, there was another attack on me yesterday and it wasn't a case of those jerks Murphy and Gamble mistaking me for Dinah for a second time." Despite her best efforts, Charlotte found herself choking up, and tears of heartbreak and frustration pooled in the corners of her eyes. "Those criminals made it clear they knew who I was and that they were after *me*, personally."

"I'm sorry that happened to you," her father said, while her mother nodded in agreement.

She used the backs of her hands to impatiently wipe away the tears that were now rolling down her cheeks as a feeling of emptiness and abandonment hollowed out her chest. Some part of her had hoped for a more emotional response from her parents. Some words of warmth and expression of their faith in her. *Something* other than a response that made it clear their focus was more strongly on their business.

But really, what had she been thinking, expecting something like that? As her parents continued to simply look at her with sympathetic expressions, and Nolan Deming had a slight smile on his face—whether it was embarrassment or something else, she couldn't tell—Charlotte realized that this was how they were and they weren't going to change. And her thoughts flickered to Dinah, as she wondered how much her alienation from her twin had come from Dinah's decision to make their parents happy by hiding her *unappealing* emotions and just stamping down those feelings however she could.

Like with drugs, or alcohol, or compulsive spending.

Or in Charlotte's case, she'd dealt with them by doubting herself, being afraid to say how she truly felt, and ultimately running away to Seattle as soon as she could. All things she did before faith took root in her heart and she realized she truly was a cherished child of God. No matter what anyone else said or implied. And that had made her all the stronger.

The awkwardness of the moment began to sink in and Charlotte felt physically deflated. Almost like she could collapse. But Wade, who'd remained quiet for the last few moments, stepped closer to her side. While he didn't actually reach over to touch her, she could feel his presence nevertheless. And when she turned to him, the warmth and encouragement she saw in his eyes refilled her with confidence. Remembering their conversation about faith, she offered up a quick prayer and petition for support. *My help comes from the Lord, maker of heaven and earth.*

"If any evidence shows up that appears to prove I pilfered money from the resort, will you forward that to me?" Charlotte asked, shifting her gaze between both her parents.

"Yes," her father said tightly. When he didn't add anything further, and her mother didn't chime in with any kind of reassurance, Charlotte realized she'd been dismissed. There was nothing to be gained by staying.

"Let's go," she said to Wade.

"I'm with you."

As they both turned, he moved his hand slightly toward hers, brushing her fingers. He didn't take hold, but his touch was intentional, lasting longer than it would have if it had happened by accident. In that moment, when Charlotte was feeling so alone, it was nearly as powerful as a hug. It was a feeling that she'd craved for much of her life. A sense that someone understood what she was feeling and was offering their support. Even in an ugly situation. Maybe at a moment when she wasn't behaving as her best self.

Wade opened the door, and as Charlotte stepped past him and into the anteroom where Stella was stationed just outside the office, she was finally able to muster up a faint smile for him to express her appreciation. Instead of smiling back, the bounty hunter raised his eyebrows and shook his head slightly as if in disbelief. "That was rough," he said quietly.

*Finally*, someone understood that things were not always as rosy and enviable with the Halstead family as they appeared to be. *Wade* understood.

Or maybe he was just pretending to understand. Because he had a job to do and it would be easier for him if he got along with Charlotte. Like the resort staff had pretended to care about her because it was part of their job.

She sighed as fears and worries from her past came flooding back, and she fought to remind herself that right now she needed to focus on her missing sister and not on herself.

"Charlotte!" Ethan, looking haggard with dark circles under his eyes and uncharacteristic stubble visible on his chin and cheeks, rushed toward her and wrapped his arms around her in a tight embrace. "I heard you were in the building and I came to see for myself that you were okay."

He finally released her, his gaze appearing to linger on the bruises on her face that she'd tried to cover with makeup. Meanwhile, she took in the sight of him. While he might seem to have a reasonable appearance to anyone who didn't know him, Charlotte could see the toll

Dinah's disappearance had taken on her boyfriend. Normally, Ethan was clean-shaven and sharply dressed with every hair in place. At the moment, he looked like he might have slept in his suit, and his tie was slightly askew.

"Any word on Dinah?" he quickly asked.

Charlotte shook her head. "No. And I assume you already know that the police haven't offered an update beyond the assurance that they're still searching for her."

"Yes. I heard about the attack on you yesterday. It showed up on the police blotter of the online newspaper. Man, you've been through a lot."

"I've got a bodyguard alongside me." She smiled and gestured at Wade, attempting to lighten the mood a little.

Ethan and Wade exchanged nods.

"So," Ethan began, dragging out the word. "Have you seen the *other* news about you? Besides the attack yesterday?"

"You mean the anonymous report that I embezzled money? Yes, I've seen it. And it's a lie. I haven't taken anything. As a matter of fact, you could help me clear my name. Do you have any idea what the specific supposed evidence against me might be?" As the operations manager, he would be involved in investigating the claim.

"We're still looking into that. The newspaper refused to tell us who contacted them with the information or to show us specifically what evidence they had. If any. Actually, if you read the article closely, you'll see lots of terms like *reported* and *alleged*, which makes me wonder if they ran with a weak story just for the sake of a sensationalistic headline and getting people to click on the article while at the same time avoiding a potential libel lawsuit." He drew in a deep sigh. "We're doing an emergency audit right now." He winced. "And I'm sorry, but on your parents' orders, we retrieved your work laptop from your condo and we've got a tech taking a look at it."

"Well, they won't find anything damaging on that," Charlotte said firmly.

"Do you have any theories on why this accusation would come so close on the heels of Dinah's disappearance?" Wade asked.

Ethan shook his head. "I don't have any theories on *anything*. One minute life is going along like normal, and the next minute it feels like the whole world has gone off the rails."

Charlotte and Wade walked with Ethan back to his office, and then continued to the elevator for the trip down to the resort's ground floor. On the way, Charlotte filled Wade in on Nolan Deming and his company's yearslong attempt to purchase an interest in the resort or even the whole property outright. She also gave him a quick summary of Ethan's history with the Wolf Lake Resort and with Dinah in particular.

"Do you think there's a connection between this Deming guy showing up and the attacks on you and Dinah?" Wade asked as they reached the bottom floor.

Startled by the idea, Charlotte turned to him. "How so?"

He shrugged. "I don't know. I just find it pays to keep track of random bits of information and maintain an open mind about how those pieces might fit together. I don't have a specific theory or anything, I'm just thinking out loud."

Charlotte puzzled over the various *random bits of information*, as Wade called them. There was Dinah and her drug and alcohol issues. Gamble's claim Dinah owed him something. Money, presumably. And Wade's suggestion that Deming making a visit right now might somehow be connected to the kidnapping attempts.

"Ready to go talk to Dinah's coworkers at the resort's coffee shop?" Wade asked as the elevator doors opened and they stepped onto the highly polished lobby floors.

Charlotte nodded. The coffee shop was located in its own separate building on resort property beside the street so it could take advantage of drive-through customers. Wade had already mentioned the need to be extremely vigilant once they stepped outside, reminding her that she was a vulnerable target.

As they walked through the lobby toward the exit, Charlotte couldn't help noticing that staff members who were normally friendly were now avoiding eye contact with her. As with any workplace, the rumor mill at the resort was fast-moving. For a moment it seemed she could feel their suspicion, but then she shook it off. In the scheme of things, what difference did their opinion make?

What really mattered was finding Dinah, as soon as possible, alive and well. Charlotte willed herself to think only in those terms, that her twin was still alive and in decent shape. So many stories were told of twins *knowing* when one another was in trouble. Knowing if the other was alive or dead. Charlotte had no such sense when it came to her own identical twin. Which made the current situation all the sadder.

"Charlotte!"

For the second time this morning, she heard someone call out her name. This time it was a female voice, and she turned to see a woman waving her hand and hurrying toward her. Charlotte kept going.

"Who is that?" Wade asked.

"My cousin Kim Halstead Riggs."

"Aren't you going to stop and talk to her?"

"I suppose I have to." Charlotte made herself stop and offer the friendliest greeting she could muster given the stressful conditions of what her life had become over the last few days.

Her cousin took a long, lingering, head-to-toe look at Wade before turning to Charlotte and smiling expectantly. Charlotte made the introductions. Wade was impressively polite with the rude woman.

"I'm sorry, but we really don't have time to chat right now," Charlotte said before Kim could ask the questions she appeared to be dying to put forth. "We're doing our best to find Dinah and we've got to get going. I'm sure you understand."

"Of course," her cousin responded, appearing slightly put off. "I just wanted to offer my condolences."

"No one's dead," Charlotte snapped. And then immediately regretted her tone.

"Of course not. I'm sorry. Bad choice of words. But do let me know if there's any way I can help."

"I will. Thank you. Now, please excuse us." Charlotte turned and resumed walking. Wade stayed by her side.

"I take it you and your cousin aren't particularly close?"

Charlotte blew out a deep breath. "Oh, Kim drives me crazy with her drama and I just don't have time for it. Her dad inherited an interest in the resort and he sold it to my dad as soon as he turned twenty-one. He blew through all the money and Kim never stops lamenting that she should by rights still have a financial stake in the resort. That it's clearly what our great-grandfather who started the business would have wanted."

"Huh. So do you think she figures that if something happened to you and your sister, then after your parents are gone she'd inherit the resort?"

Charlotte sighed. "I know you want to consider every angle, just like the cops do, but I really think that's pushing it. Kim is annoying, but she's not deadly. Besides, once my parents are gone and Dinah and I have the property, we'll help Kim out with a little something extra financially. We've talked about it. My parents aren't willing to do that, but I say, why not? We don't have a very big family. Why shouldn't we share some of what we have? Plus, Kim has been working here for most of her life."

"Are there any people here that you *do* get along with?" Wade asked just before they stepped outside.

Charlotte turned to him. He offered her a teasing grin.

"There's tension between you and your parents, you and your sister, and you and your cousin," he continued. "Seems to me you must be kind of touchy."

"What do you think?" she asked. And she was serious. Because she did have a lot of tension with her family and maybe it really was her fault and she didn't realize it. She felt like Wade would tell her the truth.

"I don't know any of you well enough to have an opinion," he responded. "But maybe, after all of this is resolved, you could put a little more effort into understanding it all a little better. And maybe letting go of a few old grudges if you need to."

Her first instinct was to defend herself. But she'd asked his opinion, so she thought about it for a moment and then finally nodded. Ultimately, it was probably a fair response.

They stepped outside and immediately she felt her whole body tense. Especially when she saw Wade looking in every direction, head on a swivel and hand over the pistol she knew was tucked in a holster under his jacket. Her sister's life was in danger. Her own life was in danger. And, just by walking beside him, she was putting Wade's life in danger, too.

*Please, Lord, let Dinah be okay and let us both live through this. Please don't end either of our lives before we have a chance to revive the love and closeness we had when we were children.*

"Dinah would typically pop in and out of the shop several times a day. Occasionally, she'd give a reason for leaving. Like saying she had a hair appointment. But most of the time she'd just say she was stepping out for a while." The coffee shop's assistant manager offered Wade and Charlotte a slight shrug.

Wade nodded encouragingly, hoping the

young woman would keep talking and add a few helpful details. Instead, the manager, who'd stepped away from the busy counter to talk to them, simply looked at him. She'd expressed her concern for Dinah to Charlotte the moment they'd walked into the shop, and assured her she wanted to do everything she could to help Dinah get rescued.

Wade took a quick glance around the interior of the coffee shop. It was almost completely glass on three sides, offering beautiful views of the surrounding park, a section of the main resort building, a strip of Wolf Lake and the snow-dotted mountain peaks jutting skyward not too far away. It might make for a picturesque setting to sit and sip coffee, but with Gamble and Murphy intent on harming Charlotte for reasons that were still unknown, he didn't want to remain here very long. It would be too easy for anyone stalking her to get a clear view through the windows and fire an accurate shot. While prior efforts had been directed at kidnapping her, there was no telling when the situation might escalate to an intentionally lethal attack.

"It looks like business is good," Charlotte commented to the manager.

There were several patrons standing in line and sitting at tables.

The young woman nodded. "We stay pretty busy."

As they spoke, Wade again scanned the three window walls to keep an eye out for threats.

"We're obviously here because we're hoping to get a lead on finding my sister," Charlotte continued. "Maybe you could give us a little more help. Did you notice anything unusual going on around here? Or *anyone* unusual? Perhaps someone that seemed to make Dinah nervous?"

The manager shook her head. "Can't say that I have. Like I mentioned, she wasn't around all the time. Apparently she had other things going on that she thought were more important."

Wade heard the hint of disapproval in the assistant manager's voice. It sounded like she took her job seriously but her boss, daughter of the coffee shop's owners, did not.

"I'm going to be blunt because we can't afford to waste time," Charlotte said. "Do you have any ideas on what's going on? Any theories on who might be angry enough with my sister to endanger her? Thoughts on why she might owe money to a criminal?"

The manager's eyes widened on the phrase *owe money to a criminal*. "I show up every workday and do my job. And part of my boss's job." She gave Charlotte a meaningful look. "I stay busy. I mind my own business. I go home. That's it." She paused for a moment. "I vaguely remember a guy coming by and asking for her a couple of times. He didn't want to leave his name or tell me what it was regarding. I think he had brown hair. There wasn't anything particularly distinctive about him, and it wasn't like he seemed threatening or anything, so he didn't make that much of an impression." She shook her head. "Beyond that, I can't think of anything that could help you."

"That was disappointing," Charlotte said as she and Wade stepped out of the coffee shop a few minutes later.

He nodded. "Welcome to bounty hunting. Dead ends. Unanswered questions. People who don't know anything about your case, or at least won't *tell* you anything about it. Like Stuart at Club Sapphire. But if you keep at it, doggedly, eventually something turns up."

Well, one hoped and prayed that eventually something turned up. Some fugitives went missing for a very long time. Some cases had been open so long that it was only reasonable to assume that the fugitive had passed on without being found. But Wade didn't want to mention that reality right now. Not when Charlotte appeared so discouraged. Nevertheless, there genuinely was reason for them to hope that they would find her sister and Wade's bail jumper.

*Crack!*

"Gun!" Wade threw his body atop Charlotte's, sending them both tumbling to the ground outside the front of the coffee shop. Shredded glass flew in all directions as three more shots quickly followed.

He and Charlotte were partially hidden behind a bistro table and chair they'd knocked over on their way to the ground, but the table was lightweight and Wade knew it wouldn't offer much protection from bullets. Making the situation more worrisome, he could tell by the sound of the shots that the shooter was using a rifle, which would give the assailant better accuracy. Staying put, hunkering down and hoping for the best was not a good option.

"Are you hit?" Wade asked, still shielding Charlotte with his body.

"No. Are you?" Her voice was shaky.

Pressed so close to her, Wade could feel her pulse pounding in fear. "I'm okay." For her sake, he tried to sound calm even though he felt anything but that.

Screams and sounds of chaos spilled out from the coffee shop.

For the sake of their own safety, as well as the people inside the coffee shop, Wade and Charlotte needed to move to a better location as quickly as possible.

After a few beats of silence, Wade rose up slightly and crawled forward to peer around the tabletop. He looked in the direction the gunshot sounds had come from, but didn't see anyone. He assumed that Gamble and Murphy had come after Charlotte again and they'd changed their tactics. As Wade feared, they'd escalated from kidnapping to an outright attempt at murder.

Were the two perps working side by side? Or had they spread out, each of them targeting Charlotte and him from a different position and making it more difficult for them to take cover?

*Lord, please help me know what to do.*

He took a quick look around. They were too far from the main resort building to attempt a sprint in that direction. Going back into the coffee shop would be like walking into a trap. The shooters could follow them in there and finish the hit. Staying in position would get them killed. They *had* to move. And right now the best option was to race around to the back of the coffee shop, where they would at least have the concrete wall protecting their backs. Maybe get behind a metal trash bin and hunker down there until the cops showed up. Someone must have called them by now.

He did have his gun. But escalating the situation into an outright gun battle with Charlotte and so many other innocent people around was the last thing he wanted to do.

"We need to move." Wade took a deep breath. Staying crouched, he managed to get his feet underneath him and help Charlotte to do the same.

A volley of three more shots tore across the edge of the table they'd been hiding behind, the bullets pinging loudly and sending it wobbling before blasting into the window behind their intended targets.

"That was close," Charlotte said.

"Yeah. Their aim is getting more accurate. We've got to go."

"Where to?"

"We'll run to the back. There's got to be a large trash can or something we can hide behind." He drew his gun, hoping he wouldn't have to use it.

"You go first. I'll be right behind you." He intended to place his body between Charlotte and the shooters. "They'll expect us to stay pinned down. We've got an element of surprise by making a move, but we've got to use it aggressively. When I give the word, I want you to dart up and run around to the back of the building as fast as you can. Okay?"

She drew a deep breath, turned to him, her eyes wide with fear, and nodded.

"Okay," he said. *"Go!"*

They both took off running, away from the direction of the shooter and around the building to the back.

There was a delay of a few seconds before Wade heard shots fired. The tactic of taking the shooter by surprise when he and Charlotte broke cover and ran had evidently worked.

As he'd hoped, there was a large commercial trash can on a cement slab at the back of the shop. They dived behind it, curling up until they were completely hidden.

"At least Dinah's employees keep the area back here swept clean," Charlotte muttered. Her voice was still shaky. For good reason— she was still terrified. But she was trying to stay strong and Wade admired her for it. While getting shot at wasn't an everyday occurrence for him, he did have extensive training for dealing with violent situations. Charlotte did not.

*Crack!* The rifle shots began again, the bullet strikes making dull metallic thunking sounds as they struck the thick steel oversize trash can.

Wade's plan hadn't worked for long. *Where are the police?*

He peered around the corner, hoping to see which of the thugs was shooting at them and get a fix on exactly where the assailant was located. He saw movement between two parked cars, someone crouched down, but partially visible through the car windows.

And then, to Wade's surprise, the shooter moved around the car and headed straight toward him. To his greater surprise, the would-be assassin was neither of the two goons he and Charlotte had been dealing with up to this event. He'd seen the man before, but he couldn't think when or where.

Right now it didn't matter. The gunman was moving in for the kill and Wade had to take control of the situation. "Stay here," he said to Charlotte. Ignoring her protests, he moved away from their hiding place and ran for the row of parked cars on the edge of the street. His plan was to try to get behind the shooter and get him to give up and drop his weapon.

The shooter fired a couple of rounds at him, but Wade moved quickly in a zigzag pattern and managed to evade the shots. Crouched between two parked cars, he could see the industrial trash can that was shielding Charlotte and he could see the shooter. Staying bent down, he raced along the row of parked cars and was nearly at the point when he could attack the assailant from behind when the gunman began to run toward Charlotte's hiding place.

Wade raced toward him. "Stop! I'll shoot!"

The rifleman spun and fired at him before moving again.

Wade dropped to the ground. The slight hill now directly behind the assailant would prevent any bullets from striking an innocent bystander. Wade fired three rounds.

The attacker spun around and once again headed for cover behind the parked cars.

Seconds later, Wade heard the sound of a motorcycle engine growling to life in the direction where the shooter had disappeared. And then it sped away.

# SEVEN

"The shooter was a professional *hit man*?" Charlotte could barely speak the words. An hour had passed since the assailant disappeared. She was now sitting with Wade in the living room of her condo on the resort grounds as they were being interviewed by Detective Romanov. A couple of patrons had been cut by broken glass, but otherwise no one else in the coffee shop had been injured.

Fear and anxiety still held a tight grip on Charlotte's lungs. She was trembling—more so now than during the attack—as adrenaline swirled through her body, making her jittery and light-headed at the same time.

"I'm afraid so." Wade exchanged glances with the detective before turning back to Charlotte. "It took me a little while to realize why he looked familiar. His name is Paul Boutin. He skipped on a substantial bail bond a little over a year ago. Range River Bail Bonds didn't write his bond, but as a bounty hunter, I can still go after him."

"Who would want to *hire* someone to kill me?" Charlotte said softly, looking down at her feet and shaking her head. "And why?"

"Let's talk about that for a minute," Romanov said.

Charlotte and Wade had already given their statements on the specific actions that had happened at the coffee shop, both to the initial responding officers and to the detective.

"It's been over twenty-four hours since your sister was discovered missing, and in that time you've almost been abducted for a second time and now you're the target of a contracted hit. We haven't received a ransom demand for your sister, which is something I expected."

Charlotte gave in to a sob that she'd been struggling to hold back. She couldn't help it. That turned into a couple of minutes of her crying while repeatedly trying to collect herself, but her emotions were too far out of her control. She was scared for her sister, scared for herself, bewildered by what was going on and frightened by thoughts of what might happen next.

Beyond that, coming back here to her condo

to talk to the detective, where she'd thought the familiar surroundings would give her a feeling of normalcy and strength, had been a mistake. As soon as she'd stepped through the door, being back here had triggered horrible memories of how she'd felt the moment she realized her twin was missing and that something was terribly wrong.

Romanov waited patiently.

Wade spotted a box of tissues on an end table, walked over to get it, and then held it out toward Charlotte.

"Thank you." She grabbed a few tissues and began to dab at her eyes and wipe her nose.

After a moment's hesitation, Wade sat down on the sofa beside her and wrapped his arm around her shoulders.

Charlotte leaned into him, allowing herself to take momentary comfort in the warmth and strength he offered while warning herself not to think his gesture meant anything. Or that the support he offered was something that would last. So many times in her life when she'd been sad or upset about something and leaned on someone—typically one of her parents, and later, her twin sister—they'd quickly withdrawn. Maybe they hadn't wanted to share her burden. Or maybe they hadn't wanted to feel that closely connected to her. Either way, the sorrowful ache from the resulting feeling of abandonment had left her feeling worse than before.

She couldn't stand to have that feeling after letting herself depend too much on Wade.

She had to depend on *herself.* She had to be strong on her own. And through pressing into her faith. The idea that unwavering support could exist in the world around her was just an illusion. Something that people pretended. Just as her family pretended to be warm and close and cuddly for the sake of resort promotional photos back when she was a kid and a teenager.

Charlotte made herself push away from Wade's embrace even though she didn't really want to. It would be better, in the long run, to remember that he was a bounty hunter getting paid to do a job. Like the resort staff members around her when she was growing up. He was not actually her friend.

"We've got detectives and patrol officers covering varied aspects of this case," Romanov finally said, getting her interview back on track. "Surveillance video, credit card trails, phone records, all kinds of potential sources to develop leads. But right now I'd like to approach things from a different perspective and take a look at the possible motivation behind all of this. Specifically, money as a motivation. Do you have any theories?"

"Maybe Dinah has some kind of drug debt." Charlotte shook her head. "That's the only thing I can think of."

"There's a Halstead cousin who may ultimately have a claim to the resort property if something were to happen to Charlotte and Dinah," Wade interjected.

Charlotte laughed dismissively. She couldn't help it. "Kim? You think *Kim* is somehow involved." She shook her head at the ridiculousness of his suggestion.

"I think you might be so used to the wealth you grew up with that you don't realize the lengths many people would go to just to have a piece of it," Wade said grimly.

Ah, yes. Here it was again. The reminder that she'd grown up in a family with money and stature and therefore everything must have been perfectly smooth sailing for her. She couldn't possibly have any sense of what life was like for anyone else.

She itched to tell him a little bit more about herself. The lessons she'd learned both growing up here at the resort and when she went away to college. She'd experienced a lot of

things in Seattle that were new to her. She'd
learned some hard lessons about herself. She'd
also come to understand, through her faith
walk and by volunteering her time with people in dire circumstances, that people made
mistakes and deserved to be forgiven. And that
she needed to be a forgiver herself.

But explaining to people that she wasn't the
kind of person they'd presumed her to be felt
like she was begging for their approval. Her
sense of self-respect had finally demanded that
she stop doing that. In the end, people generally didn't want to believe her, anyway. Changing preconceived notions demanded too much
effort.

"There's also a man in town named Nolan
Deming you might want to check out," Wade
said to Romanov. "He represents an investment group that's looking to purchase the resort. Or at least an interest in it. I don't know
if that could somehow lead to an attack on the
Halstead twins, but it seems worth a look."

This time, Charlotte couldn't laugh at his
comment. Absurd as it seemed, maybe he was
right. Maybe these larger-than-life plots were
more realistic than she'd realized. Maybe, because she'd never been desperate for money,
she didn't really understand what other people

might do to get it. Or to get *more* of it. Even people she knew. Or thought she knew.

"Did you want to tell me anything about the embezzlement claims?" the detective asked.

Of course Romanov would know about that. Charlotte blew out a sigh.

"It's a complete fabrication," Charlotte replied, looking directly at the cop. "Take me down to the station and give me a lie detector test, if you want to. The *anonymous rumor* in the town's online newspaper has no validity whatsoever. Maybe it's related to all this other stuff that's going on. It could just be someone wanting to kick me while I'm down." She shook her head. "I'm angry and insulted about it. But right now I'm much more focused on finding my sister. And on keeping myself alive."

Sad and scary that she had to add that last bit, but it was true. Suddenly it was a fight just for her to make it through the day without some assailant trying to harm her. But she was not going to back down from the challenge.

"Okay." Romanov got to her feet. "This gives me enough to think about for now."

Charlotte and Wade also stood.

"I don't know if you were planning to move back home." The detective glanced around the condo. "But I suggest you continue to stay with Wade and the rest of his team at the inn. At least for now."

"Agreed," Wade said.

"Thank you." Charlotte let a glance flicker in his direction, but she didn't allow it to linger. She didn't need a reminder that the face she'd originally thought looked so harsh now appeared compassionate and handsome to her. And she definitely didn't want to dwell on how comforting it had felt for his arm to be wrapped around her.

There was enough danger coming at her from violent criminals—including paid assassins, apparently. It would be foolish to put her heart in danger, too. And it would be dangerous for her to care too much about Wade.

"Let me take you back to the inn so you can get some rest. You've been through a lot." Wade continually looked around while he spoke, hyperaware that there was a hit man at large who'd apparently been hired to take out Charlotte. Police were still on the resort property, a couple of them within view as he and Charlotte made their way to his truck, but that didn't mean she was safe. A skilled marksman could hit a target from very far away. And the shooter obviously took care to make sure he had a solid escape plan.

"What exactly are you going to do after you get rid of me?" Charlotte asked once they were in the truck and headed down the road.

"I'm not *getting rid* of you." He tried an amused tone to lighten the mood, but it didn't work. When he glanced over, she was looking at him with drawn brows and her arms tightly crossed at her chest. "I want you safe," he continued. "It was probably a mistake to let you work alongside me, anyway."

There was no *probably*. He was certain, now, that it had been a mistake.

"I want me to be safe, too."

From the corner of his eye, Wade could see her uncross her arms before she continued.

"*Believe* me. I've had nightmares about *both* attempts at kidnapping me. And the back of my head still hurts from getting smacked outside the diner." She reached up to touch it. "After this is over, I hope I never take safety and security for granted again. Ever. But we both know it isn't over yet. And I still believe I can help."

"Yeah, about that…" Wade could be diplomatic when he wanted to be. Especially in the pursuit of a fugitive, when finesse and manipulation were often required to get answers quickly from a reluctant witness. When it came to his personal life, he preferred being direct and honest. And he liked it when people were that way with him. He'd choose being insulted or having his feelings hurt over having someone hide what they were truly thinking any day. He supposed he could thank his unreliable dad for that.

"You haven't been able to get people to open up and give us information about Dinah like we thought you would," he finally said after a few moments of silence. "Turns out that tactic isn't paying off and it's too slow. Romanov did mention that the cops were contacting Dinah's friends. Maybe the intimidation factor of cops asking her associates questions might prove to have a better payoff than your influence due to being her sister. Or being the friend or acquaintance of the person being questioned. Or even being one of the famous Halstead twins."

*"Famous Halstead twins?"*

The anger in her words shocked him. "Well, you are a Halstead and your family is regionally well-known." Why was she overreacting? Was it because of a couple of the comments he'd made? About her family, their business, their status? But what he'd said was true. Or maybe it wasn't. He didn't know her. Not really.

But he'd like to.

"Look, I'm sorry—"

"Don't," she interrupted him. While she'd sounded angry before, now she sounded tired.

She'd been through so much, was still going through so much. And he'd been a jerk. Didn't matter that he hadn't realized the apparent depth of the sting of his words at the time he'd said them, that was no excuse. He knew better. And he didn't even want to think about how stressed and touchy and out of sorts he'd feel if Hayley or Danny or Connor Ryan were missing.

He wanted to apologize, but she'd just told him not to.

"I didn't think—"

"Let's focus on Dinah," she said, interrupting him again. "I have an idea, but first, tell me what you plan to do after taking me back to the inn."

"I intend to visit a few of my informants. Wave a little cash in front of them as incentive and see if I can motivate them to work harder to get information on Gamble and Murphy and, now, the hit man Paul Boutin. Get them to put their ear to the ground and find out what people are saying about your sister. I plan to get Hayley and the guys to press their informants harder, too. And my brother-in-law, Jack, and the bounty hunters at his bail bonds agency."

He glanced over and she gave him a tight nod. "That sounds like a good plan."

"So, how do you think you can help?"

"Turn right up here," she said as they approached an intersection near the center of town, "and I'll tell you."

Intrigued, Wade made the turn. He glanced in the rearview mirror to see if anyone turned behind them. He'd been watching to see if they were being tailed since they left the resort. So far, it looked as if they were in the clear.

"Slow down," Charlotte said after they'd gone a short distance. And then she directed him to park in front of a bohemian-looking shop with wind chimes hanging from the eaves in front of it. Flowers were painted on the window and there was a ceramic horse painted with a paisley pattern stationed by the front door.

"What's this?" Wade hadn't noticed the business before.

"I guess it's my last shot at trying to get information about Dinah from someone unexpected. Someone she's known for a long time. Maybe a confidante of sorts."

Continuing to keep an eye on their surroundings as they got out of the truck, Wade followed Charlotte toward the door, where he saw that the establishment was a hair salon. "Seriously?" he said as he pulled open the door and ushered Charlotte in ahead of him.

The place was busy. But it looked like a typical hair salon his mom or Hayley would go to, from what Wade could see. Not like a place that wealthy and stylish Dinah Halstead would patronize.

"Janelle and Dinah and I go way back," Charlotte said. "Although, she was really more of Dinah's friend than mine back when we were in high school. By the time Dinah quit college and moved back home, Janelle had opened this shop. Dinah originally came here just to visit an old friend. But she liked Janelle's work and kept coming back." Charlotte glanced around at the potted plants and eye-catching mixture of original artwork and photographs of exotic locations hanging on the walls. Then she drew in a deep breath through her nose. Wade had already noticed the scented candles burning throughout the shop, which didn't smell all that bad, in his opinion. Normally, he wasn't too wild about them.

"I think Dinah likes it here because she can let her guard down and be her true self. That's my guess, anyway. Janelle and the other stylists and clients aren't the people Dinah normally hangs around with. I think she feels like she doesn't have to prove anything to them. And I'm hoping that while she's here she opens up to Janelle. I think the cops are probably trying to talk to all of Dinah's regular friends, but I don't know that they'd think to talk to her hairstylist. Or that they'd realize she could turn out to be a true confidante."

"I'm impressed. You may be more of a natural at bounty hunting than either of us realized."

Charlotte gave him a slight smile before turning to a receptionist who was approaching them. Wade took the moment to type a quick text to Maribel asking her to get the word out to everyone that he really needed them to push their informants for reports on Dinah or any of the men he and Charlotte had already encountered while trying to find Dinah.

Wade finished the text as the receptionist was explaining that Janelle was in a storeroom taking inventory. He followed the women through a short hallway to an oversize storage closet. The receptionist left, and after greetings and exchanging a hug, Janelle directed them to her small office, where they could talk.

Charlotte introduced Wade and then wasted no time in explaining why they were there.

"What can you tell us about my sister that might help explain what's happening? Can you maybe give us a direction to start searching for information on people she knew or problems she was dealing with? I know she talked to you about everything. Any small detail could help. *Please*," she added when Janelle was hesitant to respond. "This is a life-or-death situation for Dinah. Her potentially being embarrassed, or getting caught doing something illegal, or being angry with you for betraying a confidence is the least of our worries right now. We *have* to find her and we need all the help we can get."

Janelle took in a deep breath, blew it out and let her shoulders slump. "Okay. There are a couple of things she told me in confidence that concerned me a little bit before, but they really concern me now that she's missing."

"You're doing the right thing," Charlotte assured her.

"She told me about going through some

pretty extensive rehab, going to a facility in Colorado, shortly after she left college. I know staying clean and sober was a battle. And I know it was a battle she was losing more often than not, recently. She came in obviously high a few times. I couldn't tell you on what, specifically, each time. But it didn't seem like she enjoyed it. Not really. She seemed sad and disappointed in herself."

There was no missing the fact that Charlotte was fighting back tears. Wade wanted to reach out and wrap an arm around her shoulders and offer her some kind of comfort so badly that the feeling was practically an ache. But he knew better than to give in to the impulse. Especially here and now, when she was working so hard to hold herself together. And when she might still be angry with him, anyway, for his assumption that she didn't understand the way people who weren't rich thought. And he deserved that.

"The other thing I know is that she was worried about money. Which seemed strange at first because, well, you know…" She gave Charlotte an embarrassed smile. "I figured the both of you had rivers of money coming your way all the time. I didn't know until Dinah told me that your parents gave you allowances from the time you were teenagers, but that you had to work at the resort to earn it. That you both had to work for your paychecks now. And that your parents had set up trust funds for you that you can't touch until you turn thirty-five."

Wade almost winced at hearing yet another confirmation that his assumptions about the Halstead twins—at least in terms of them living a spoiled and completely carefree life—had been wrong.

"So I guess Dinah had whatever income she was paid for managing the coffee shop. I think she said she got a combination of a salary and percentage of the profits. And it wasn't enough to cover what she wanted to buy. Clothes, especially. She liked expensive designer clothes. And jewelry. And luxury travel. You know that.

"She always paid me, which I appreciated. But she complained about money. I joked with her that maybe she shouldn't spend so much, but my comments didn't seem to have any impact. That went on for a while, but then about two months ago, it stopped. She still showed up in a new, very nice outfit whenever she came by to meet me for lunch. But she didn't seem worried. But then, all of a sudden, she was worried about money again."

Janelle shook her head. "That probably sounds scrambled, but I'm just telling you what I noticed, what I saw. I don't know any facts that could explain it."

Wade didn't know the facts, either, but a picture was becoming clearer. Addiction and accompanying bad judgment. Compulsive spending. He didn't want to say anything to Charlotte right now, but maybe it helped to explain how she'd come to be framed for embezzlement. It was possible that Dinah had pilfered money and set her twin up to take the fall. But how did all the assailants figure into this? And what about the resentful cousin and the aggressive investor? Could they have taken advantage of Dinah's issues for their own gain?

Wade felt his phone vibrate. He glanced at the screen while Charlotte and Janelle were saying their goodbyes. The text he read made his heart speed up. After politely offering his own goodbye to Janelle, he leaned in close to Charlotte as they headed for the door.

"I'm a terrible sister," Charlotte said before he could tell her about the text. "I should have been paying closer attention. Trying harder to understand Dinah."

"We do the best we can," Wade offered.

"And when we realize we've fallen short, we try to do better." He took her arm and stopped as they reached the doorway, pausing for a moment to scan their surroundings for signs of danger before they headed outside.

"I've got some news from an informant," he said as soon as they were inside the truck.

"What?" Charlotte asked, her eyes wide and brows lifted in a hopeful expression. "Has someone seen Dinah?"

"No. But we may have a solid lead. My informant works in a bar and grill. He says he's seen Gamble in there a few times with another guy who is presumably a friend. The *friend* was there last night. After eating his dinner and throwing back a couple of drinks, the man ordered some food to take out. Enough for about three or four people. Maybe it's nothing. But it could be something."

"You think Gamble and Murphy are hiding out somewhere with Dinah and this *friend* is bringing them food."

She really was good at thinking like a bounty hunter. "Yes. My informant says he'll call me if the guy shows up again this evening. I think it would be a good idea for both of us to head back to the inn right now. I'll need to organize a crew to be ready to go with us to the bar if I do get the call. We'll follow the guy and see where he goes."

"Please, Lord, let this be the lead that helps us find my sister," Charlotte prayed softly.

"Amen," Wade said in agreement.

He, too, hoped that this would turn out to be the helpful break they were both wishing for.

# EIGHT

"Your brother's home really does feel like a refuge," Charlotte said as she and Wade crossed the threshold of the Riverside Inn.

"Yeah, well, for the time being, let's not take safety for granted. Not even here." Wade turned and gave the parking area a quick visual scan before closing the door and engaging the heavy-duty lock. "Paul Boutin won't get paid until you're dead, so he's not going to quit coming after you. Aside from earning his pay, he's got a reputation to defend."

Charlotte drew in a deep breath and tried to settle her nerves. The shooting was the third time she'd been targeted for attack in just as many days. She was fairly certain her sister was in debt to some very dangerous men. And it was possible that Dinah had set things up to make it look like Charlotte had stolen money from the resort.

Happy barks and the sound of dog toenails tapping on the wooden floor greeted them as the resident canines bounded out of the first-floor office and hurried over to offer a boisterous welcome. That helped to lift Charlotte's spirits a little.

After the animals were settled down, she heard Maribel's voice coming from the office. She wore an earpiece and apparently spoke to someone on the phone while pacing in front of an open laptop on Connor's oversize desk. "I just found out that Miller has an ex-wife in that area. I'm texting you her address right now."

"Your mom is on the phone with Connor and Danny." A female voice came from the living room.

A woman with reddish-blond hair—who looked a lot like Danny Ryan—got up from one of the deep cushioned sofas, lifting an elderly-looking black cat from her lap as she stood. "The guys were going to help you out tonight if you got a call from your informant, but then they got a call on their own case and had to take off to hopefully catch their fugitive. So you've got me instead." She offered Charlotte a bright smile. "Jack would have come, too, but he got a call from Milo and Katherine requesting an assist, so of course he had to respond to that. The way things are going, maybe everybody will catch their fugitives today."

"That would be fantastic," Charlotte said.

"I'm Hayley Ryan Colter." She offered Charlotte another smile. "I understand you could use some help right now."

Charlotte nodded. "Yes. Thank you."

Hayley's smile settled into a more serious expression. "I know it can be horrifying to have someone trying to kill you. I *really* know. I've had it happen to me. At times it can look like they have the upper hand, that they have an insurmountable advantage because they skulk in the shadows and repeatedly take you by surprise. But most of them aren't as brilliant as they believe they are. And they can't skulk forever. When the pressure of trying to evade the cops—and us—gets them tired, they start to make mistakes."

"Most of them. You said *most* of them aren't so brilliant."

Hayley shrugged. "Some of them are quite intelligent. It's a shame they turned their talents to crime. But even the smart ones can get overconfident or just plain tired from being on the run. So they stumble. And that's when we pounce on them."

Hayley's words were intense, but also somewhat comforting. It was good to be reminded that the people Charlotte and her family were dealing with were not supervillains with special powers. They were just regular people who were criminals.

"Right now we aren't taking advantage of fugitives stumbling so much as getting hungry," Wade said to his sister. "We're hoping the friend of Gamble's who frequents my informant's bar and grill is bringing him food. And that when we follow the friend, he'll bring us to wherever Gamble and Murphy are hiding Dinah."

The reference to Dinah as a hostage set the pit of Charlotte's stomach squirming again. Fear and anxiety churned and twisted with the other dark emotions and thoughts that she'd tried to keep at bay. Was her assumption that the kidnappers had kept her sister alive based on a false hope?

She was excited by the thought of seeing Dinah again tonight. But that excitement was also tempered by the fear that instead of reuniting with her sister she would instead learn that her twin had perished. That they had been permanently separated before Charlotte ever had the chance to rebuild the strong connection that used to exist between them.

How would she live with that?

"Speaking of people being hungry," Wade said, "let me see if I can find us something to eat around here." He walked toward the kitchen.

Charlotte remained in place and gazed out the window at the deck jutting over the Range River. The sun had dropped low in the west and the view of the shadowy snowcapped mountains in the distance was dramatic and beautiful. Despite the fact that the temperature was dropping fast and it was cold, she would have loved to step outside and have a look around. Maybe shake off those dark thoughts and feelings, at least for a short while. But, as Wade had reminded her, she needed to be careful.

"Don't worry about me," she called out to Wade as he disappeared around a corner. "I don't need anything. I'm not hungry."

"You might want to rethink that." He stepped back around the corner. "If we get a call tonight and have to run, you'll need energy. You can't catch bad guys on just coffee and air."

"He makes a good point," Hayley said quietly to Charlotte. "Not that my *brother* needs to hear any woman telling him he's right." She offered a teasing grin. But then the grin faded.

"The call we're waiting for could come in the next few minutes, or it could come sometime after midnight. Maybe we won't get a call at all tonight. But just in case, we've got to be ready to go at the drop of a hat. That means eating enough to keep us going and resting when we can."

Wade strode back out from the kitchen with a package of deli turkey in one hand and a bowl of homemade potato salad in the other. "If we get a call from my informant tonight, you don't have to respond with us. You'd be safer if you stayed. That might be the better choice."

"Nice try at shaking me off, but if the informant calls, I want to go with you. That friend of Gamble's might look familiar to me. Maybe I've seen him around somewhere, and being able to tell the police about that could lead them to further information about what's going on and the rescue of my sister."

Charlotte paused for a moment, deciding that she would focus on helping rescue her twin instead of worrying that the worst possible outcome had already happened. "I changed my mind. I think I would like to have something to eat." She followed Wade into the kitchen.

"Don't forget about me," Hayley called out,

trailing behind them. "I'm always ready to eat."

"I know," Wade said without turning around. "That's why I didn't bother to ask."

He collected bread, lettuce and condiments to make the sandwiches while Hayley grabbed plates and cutlery. Not wanting to stand around and be waited on, Charlotte filled glasses with ice and grabbed a pitcher of tea from the refrigerator. She briefly checked in with Maribel, who was busy working on a laptop and said she'd eat later.

It felt good to do something so normal in the midst of everything that had been happening. Just a few short hours ago someone had been shooting at Charlotte and anyone else who got in the way. The hired assassin had escaped only to be able to come after her again.

Charlotte still felt shaky, despite her determination to toughen up so that she could help catch the criminals. When she carried glasses she'd filled with tea to the table, she could see the slight ripples form on the surface as her hands trembled.

*Lord, please give me the courage I need.*

When she looked up, Hayley caught her eye. The bounty hunter offered a sympathetic smile and then asked, "So, what do you like to do with your time when things are normal?"

*When people aren't trying to kill me, you mean.* Charlotte chewed her bottom lip for a moment. She appreciated that Hayley was trying to lighten the mood a little, so her first instinct was to make a joke or give some generic answer like hiking in the woods or going boating on the lake.

In the end, she gave in to the unexpected impulse to genuinely share something of herself. She glanced at Wade as he placed the prepared plates on the table and then sat down. After saying grace, they began eating.

"I actually work most of my waking hours these days," Charlotte began. "There was a time when I first moved away for college when I'd decided the family business wasn't for me. But then, things changed. I found a faith I didn't even know I was looking for." She smiled to herself, thinking about how puzzled she'd been at the beginning. How prayer and fellowship had given her insight into so many things that changed her perspective on life, on her family, on how she wanted to live.

"Eventually, I realized I could do a lot of good through working at the Wolf Lake Resort."

"And your parents were agreeable to the idea of focusing on doing good rather than making a profit?" Wade asked, raising an eyebrow. "That's pretty idealistic."

A stab of defensiveness made her regret saying anything. Maybe she should just change the subject. But after a moment, she realized that he wasn't attacking her so much as asking a reasonable question based on what he'd seen of the Halstead family. And what she'd said about them.

"Here's the thing," Charlotte said, setting down her sandwich for a moment. "My degree is in sales and marketing, and while earning it I learned quite a bit about the benefits of doing good when it comes to attracting customers. Supporting literacy programs or animal rescue or neighborhood litter pickups. The sorts of things that everyone can agree are worthwhile.

"When making a decision on where to spend their money, a significant number of people are more strongly drawn to companies that do something like that. So the company benefits, the community benefits and customers feel like they've spent their money wisely. There are also tax benefits for the company. My parents are willing to let me try this out and see where it goes. So I've started with a local literacy program."

Hayley made a sound of agreement. "It's good to have a job where you can be of service somehow."

"Yeah, well, I still have a lot to learn," Charlotte said after eating a bite of her sandwich. "I applied for an internship with a resort down in California, in San Diego, to get some hands-on experience with all of this plus international marketing, as well."

Wade, who'd been eating his potato salad, stopped chewing for a moment. He looked closely at Charlotte, and she braced herself for some sharp comment about her family or the resort or maybe her personally.

"I realize I'm fortunate to be able to go down to San Diego over the summer," she said, figuring that was what he was focusing on. She immediately gave herself a mental kick. She'd been determined not to fall into that old trap of explaining herself so that people would approve of her. Not think that she was spoiled and unappreciative.

"From what I've seen, San Diego is a beautiful city," he said flatly, before taking a sip of his tea. "Maybe you'll find you want to stay."

"Sounds like you're pretty committed to

staying here and working with your family," Hayley interjected. She turned to Charlotte. "You're just going for the summer?"

"It's for five months."

Wade nodded without saying anything, his expression shuttering. He continued eating his lunch, but his gaze stayed mostly settled on his food.

Charlotte's heart sank. She'd talked about something important to her and he apparently didn't think much of it. He'd obviously made up his mind about what kind of person she was. He'd probably kept the same opinion that he'd had from the beginning. Which meant those moments when she'd thought they were becoming friends must have only existed in her imagination.

He was helping her because it was his job.

Of course.

Not the first time she'd come up against that hard reality. Probably not the last.

The sinking disappointment in her chest turned edgier, until it felt like shards scratching her heart. So many old thoughts and emotions threatened to overtake and overwhelm her.

*No.*

She took a deep breath and forced herself to

set those feelings all aside. She'd worked too hard to move beyond them. To forge a new path in life where she was strong and pressed into her faith and directed her energy toward a greater good.

What she needed to do right now was focus on keeping herself alive and finding Dinah. She didn't have time for any new *friendships*, anyway. Later, she'd untangle the whole embezzlement accusation fiasco and prove to her family and to the public that she was trustworthy, so that all her plans wouldn't be ruined.

Even though her stomach felt leaden, she made herself continue eating. If all went well, she would be back in the battle to rescue Dinah tonight. After that, she and Wade Fast Horse could go their separate ways.

"Find a table and sit facing toward a wall," Wade said to Charlotte as he held open the door to the bar and grill and she walked past him to go inside. "We don't want this friend of Gamble's to recognize you."

"Understood."

Charlotte had her hair tucked into a beanie and the collar of her jacket flipped up to hide the lower part of her face. The last thing they needed was for the possible kidnappers' accomplice to look around and see someone who was the spitting image of the woman they'd abducted.

Hayley walked in behind Charlotte.

The three settled at a table with a low, flickering candle inside a bottle-shaped holder. A menu was propped up beside it offering a fairly extensive list of appetizers and burgers. Made sense that a lowlife looking for a place to throw down a couple of drinks before grabbing some food to take back to his fellow criminals would repeatedly come here.

Not that they had any proof the man Wade's informant had told them about—he said the guy's name was Larry—was legitimately a person of interest. He could just be a guy who happened to know Gamble and that was all.

Wade glanced toward the bar, where his informant, Shane, was working. The tall, skinny bartender caught Wade's gaze and gave him a slight nod before making a small gesture toward a patron sitting on a stool just a couple of feet away from him.

"Looks like we arrived in time and Larry is still here," Wade said quietly. They'd gotten the call a couple of hours after they'd eaten and hurried over from the inn as quickly as they could.

"I want to get a look at his face and see if I recognize him," Charlotte said.

Wade's gut tightened. It *felt* like a dangerous move, even though his brain told him it probably wasn't. With her pale blond hair covered and in the dim light of the bar, she wouldn't stand out so much. Still, she was a civilian, and if the guy made some kind of aggressive move, she wouldn't know what to do.

Or maybe she would. She'd managed to survive some pretty extreme events over the last couple of days.

Charlotte Halstead was strong, he'd learned. She was tough. She wasn't the pampered and entitled daughter of privilege he'd assumed she was. Charlotte had a lot more character than he'd initially given her credit for. More fight, more compassion, more concern for others.

But she was also going to be leaving town. Never to move back, most likely. San Diego was a big city with a lot going for it. She'd be offered good opportunities while she was working as an intern down there. She'd forget about her plans for her life in Range River, forget about the people in Range River she cared about and who cared for her.

Wade knew exactly how that would go.

Not that he believed *he* was someone in

Range River she cared about. Obviously not enough that she would come back for him. He'd thought there might have been a moment here or there when something significant had happened between the two of them, drawing them closer together.

Ridiculous. He shook his head slightly. What had he been thinking?

Besides, people moved on. He *knew* that. For a short while, fascinating Charlotte Halstead had made him want to forget that fact. But he'd come back to his senses.

She would establish her life in a beautiful Southern California beach town. He would remain in Range River.

"I'll go up to the bar with you so you can get a look at this Larry guy," Hayley said to Charlotte. "We'll go to the side where it wraps around so you can try to catch a quick glimpse of him without his noticing. I'll ask the bartender for a couple glasses of water. And then we'll come back to the table. Let's make this quick."

Charlotte nodded. "Okay."

"Try not to stare at him," Wade said as she stood.

"Right."

Wade watched them go. He knew that Hayley was more than capable of looking out for Charlotte should Larry recognize her and try to grab or attack her. But it still didn't make him feel more at ease.

They reached the bar, with Charlotte positioned so only her profile would be turned toward Larry. She and Hayley got their glasses of water and returned.

"I've never seen him before," Charlotte reported.

So much for the idea that he might have been someone connected to the resort. Abductions by complete strangers were relatively uncommon. That fact continued to stew in the back of Wade's mind.

"I've never seen him before, either," Hayley added. "He's not someone we've dealt with."

"All right. Well, let's follow him when he leaves and see where he goes."

"Should we call Detective Romanov?" Charlotte asked.

"Not yet. It could be this man has no connection to Dinah's disappearance and knows nothing about where Gamble is hiding out right now. Let's see where this takes us."

The fact that Larry had left the bar and grill with a bag of food and then driven to an old motor court on the edge of town had Charlotte's hopes up that they were about to find Dinah. "Seems to me this is the kind of place kidnappers would want to hide somebody."

Charlotte, Hayley and Wade sat in Wade's idling truck, watching as Larry parked at the room farthest from the main office and got out of his car. He walked up to the porch, visible in the light cast by a small fixture, glancing around for a moment before knocking and then being admitted inside.

"Time to let the police know what's going on." Wade grabbed his phone, tapped the screen and put it on speaker setting.

Romanov answered after a couple of rings. "Wade, what have you got for me?"

The bounty hunter explained where they were and what they'd seen.

"Sit tight. I'll be over with a couple of unmarked vehicles. Get the guy's plate number if he leaves. Don't engage with him." She disconnected.

Charlotte gazed out the window, thinking about her sister being held hostage just a few yards away, scared and miserable, having no idea that she was about to be rescued. Charlotte could only guess at the trauma Dinah had suffered through. She couldn't clearly imagine it, but then, she didn't really want to. A wave of guilt washed over her at that realization. At some point if she wanted to help Dinah cope in the aftermath, she would have to make a stronger effort to understand. She might have to sacrifice a bit of her own peace of mind to be of help.

"Breathe," Wade said quietly beside her.

Charlotte filled her lungs, held the air for a few seconds and then blew it out. The action brought her back to the here and now, away from those galloping thoughts of worry and fear for Dinah.

She turned to Wade. There was enough ambient light for her to see his face and those deep brown eyes that were such a fascinating combination of empathetic and assessing. Qualities that worked well together for anyone in his profession, she supposed. Probably beneficial for anyone. They certainly made her feel comforted and protected. At least for the moment.

"It will be all right," Wade said. "Things might happen quickly. If they do, duck down to the floorboard and stay out of sight. Or if you want me to take you away from here right now while things are still quiet, I will."

"I want to be here," Charlotte said. "If my sister is here, I want her to see me. I want her to know that I did everything I could to help find her." Her voice cracked and she blinked back tears. All manner of fear or worry and uncertainty struck her all at once. She was worried for Dinah's safety, for the bounty hunters' safety, and, perhaps selfishly, for her own safety and future. While she absolutely wanted to rescue her sister, and that was 100 percent her goal and priority, finding Dinah would also mean the end of spending time with Wade. And she would miss that. Very much.

She sniffed loudly.

Wade opened the center console and offered up a small box of tissues. She grabbed a few. "Thanks."

"How did you like living on the coast while you were in college?" Hayley asked from the back seat. "I've always thought that would be fun to live near the beach."

Charlotte smiled to herself, appreciating Hayley's effort at using small talk to ease Charlotte's anxiety. She conversed with the bounty hunter about coastal living until a work van pulled up nearby, followed by an older-model SUV.

Wade's phone chimed. "It's Romanov and a couple of plainclothes officers in undercover vehicles," he said after reading the text.

A few more rounds of messages went back and forth. "Okay, two undercover officers are going to knock on the door and pretend they're there to repair something. Romanov wants us to stay back but keep an eye on things in case anyone tries to make a run for it."

"Got it," Hayley answered.

Charlotte's heart raced as two men in jeans and heavy jackets got out of the van. One opened the back door and pulled out a tool kit. At the same time, the SUV that had arrived with them slowly moved forward and then stopped.

Appearing calm and easygoing, the officers chatted as they walked up to the door of the unit Larry had entered earlier, and they knocked.

Charlotte held her breath, waiting to see what happened.

The door opened, light spilled out, and then she saw sudden movement and heard shouting. The doors of the SUV flew open and Detective Romanov and two other cops got out and ran in to assist the undercover officers.

Charlotte's heart leaped into her throat as her whole body tensed, gripped by fear that she would hear gunshots or her sister's screams. But after a few moments, when it got quiet and she couldn't see anything happening, the fear morphed into impatience that practically pushed her out the door.

She reached for the handle, and Wade put his hand on her shoulder. "Wait."

"But I need to see if they found Dinah." Charlotte frantically rushed out the words. "I need to know she's finally okay."

"I know, but we need to hold off for a few minutes, give Romanov and her team time to secure the scene. Approaching officers unexpectedly right after a potentially deadly takedown is not a wise idea."

Charlotte nodded, and then let her chin drop down to her chest. *Dear Lord, please let my sister be okay.*

Wade's phone chimed a couple of minutes later. He looked down and sighed.

"What?" Charlotte demanded, perched on the edge of her seat, ready to leap out and race over to see her sister.

"They've got Gamble and Murphy. And they've arrested Larry for aiding and abetting criminal activity." He looked up. "I'm sorry, but they don't have Dinah. She's not there."

# NINE

"We won't stop searching for your sister. The police won't stop, either." Wade had spoken the same sentiment to Charlotte last night while Detective Romanov and her team were wrapping up the scene at the motor court and then again this morning at breakfast. There'd been no sign at all of Dinah, and the criminals had refused to talk. He understood why Charlotte was worried and it made his heart ache to see the sad, hollow expression on her face.

She gave him a distracted nod, as if only vaguely aware that he was in the room and speaking to her.

The two of them were seated on a sofa in the den that served as Connor's office at the Riverside Inn. Connor was there, as were Hayley and Danny. Connor stood by his desk, leaning against it, while Maribel sat in the desk chair with an electronic tablet, poised to take notes.

Breakfast had been quiet, with Charlotte moving her food around on her plate rather than eating it. Wade didn't blame her. Many times over the last two days he'd found himself imagining how he'd feel if one of his adoptive siblings were missing. Devastated, obviously. Just thinking about the very remote possibility tensed the pit of his stomach.

For Charlotte to have her hopes built up last night only to have them resoundingly dashed must have been gutting. He shook his head and took a deep breath. Caring about someone—Charlotte, in this case—and having to watch them suffer repeatedly while being unable to ease their pain or do anything to help them was a horrible feeling.

Wade had gone through a similar situation as a kid, watching his mom get hurt over and over again as his dad made promises of his imminent return from faraway California that never came through. Somewhere along the line Wade had made the decision to give up hope. Or at least give up hope when it came to his own personal relationships. The kind of relationships where you more or less handed your life to another person and trusted that they would take care of it.

Looking at Charlotte right now, recognizing the expression of someone on the verge of hopelessness, it struck him how utterly pointless that was. To give up hope in situations where possibilities for a good outcome still existed, even if they appeared only slightly probable at the moment.

Of course he had hope in terms of his faith, in terms of redemption and a better life to come. But did having that kind of hope get him off the hook for daring to have more hope in this lifetime? Right now, finding himself unexpectedly revisiting thoughts and feelings he hadn't considered in a while, he wasn't so sure.

This was certainly an awkward moment to realize that despite his concerns about Charlotte's social station in life, and his own, and about her plans to leave Range River for an internship down in California, he still dared to care about her. Enough to risk hoping that once this case was resolved, she might find that she cared about him, too.

"Still no word from Detective Romanov?" Charlotte asked him.

Wade shook his head.

"Romanov is a good interviewer." Danny sat in an upholstered chair beside Connor's desk. "She's highly motivated to solve cases and obtain convictions. It's early in the process. She'll get information out of Gamble and Murphy. Maybe their buddy Larry. Offer plea deals if she has to."

"What if Dinah wasn't there because they killed her and buried her somewhere?" Charlotte's voice sounded strangely monotone.

It was something Wade had already considered. He was fairly sure the rest of the bounty hunters had considered it, as well.

"That is a possibility," Connor acknowledged.

Wade cut him a dark glance. It was so like Connor not to sugarcoat things.

"But that doesn't strike me as likely," Connor continued. "What would be the point? There's obviously a conspiracy going on here—between Gamble and Murphy, plus a professional hit man, and possibly including several other people—and this clearly isn't some personal crime of passion sort of situation. Beyond that, to a criminal's way of thinking, your sister would be a person of value because she comes from a family with money. They'd need to keep her alive to get paid."

"But there's been no ransom demand," Hayley interjected.

Connor nodded at his sister. "Not that we know of. Maybe a demand was sent to her parents and they've kept it under wraps." He settled his gaze on Charlotte. "Or they could have sent a demand to her boyfriend. Any of them could be manipulated by threats to keep things secret."

"We have solid reasons to keep pushing forward," Hayley said to Charlotte.

"But we need to update our strategy." Wade had been pondering how to resume the chase and discover new leads. "Do deeper online dives into Gamble's and Murphy's backgrounds. Especially their criminal associates. Maybe we'll find someone with a history of extortion. We should increase the amount of cash we're offering our informants. See if that motivates them to look a little harder for information to give us. And, of course, we need to put energy in finding the hit man who came after us at the coffee shop. Paul Boutin. He's a legitimate target for us since he's a bail jumper. Beyond that, if we find out who hired him, that might lead us to whoever has taken Dinah."

"Looking into the embezzlement fiasco could help." Charlotte held up her phone. "There's a new *anonymously sourced* rumor in the online newspaper. I suppose acknowledging it as just a rumor protects them legally.

But the damage is done to my reputation, nevertheless."

"Jonah wasn't able to learn anything about the source of the original embezzlement rumors through his connections at the online newspaper, so I'll visit their offices and see if I can learn anything," Maribel said. "The arrest of Gamble and Murphy is a big, legitimate news story. If I offer them some previously unknown detail about how that went down in return for information on how they received the embezzlement rumors, maybe they'll go for it. With everything else that's been happening to Charlotte and Dinah, you'd think they'd take their reporting of all of this more seriously."

Charlotte made a scoffing sound. "They're just interested in sensational headlines that get clicks and make them money."

"It's easy enough to be flippant at a keyboard or over the phone," Maribel continued. "But having someone show up in person to talk to the managing editor might make them take things more seriously. Or I could mention that I'm willing to pay for information loudly enough that anyone in the office can hear. Somebody might contact me after that."

"I appreciate everything all of you are doing to help," Charlotte said, glancing around the room. "While you're trying to track down leads and information, I'm going to be at the resort talking with my parents."

Charlotte's words set off an internal alarm for Wade. Gamble and Murphy had been captured, but Boutin was still at large. Perhaps their arrest had led to the cancellation of the assassination order. But maybe not. It wasn't a chance worth taking. "Can't you just talk to your parents on the phone?" He really wanted Charlotte to remain safely hidden at the inn.

She held up her phone, a pinched expression on her face. "My dad messaged me about the news article regarding Gamble's and Murphy's arrests. I told him the police didn't get any new information about Dinah's whereabouts. He said that he and Mom want to see for themselves that I'm safe." She shrugged. "I'd say he wants to make sure I'm safe *and* he wants to talk about his missing money." She offered a sad smile. "I'm not sure which is the higher priority."

Wade's face heated as he thought about how Charlotte's parents seemed to undermine her sense of value. Maybe Dinah felt the same weak sense of support, and that was what drove her addiction issues. He obviously had no way of knowing anything about that. But

he did know that there were people in town—
or maybe from out of town—who wanted the
Halstead money and resort property. And anyone attempting to get to that wealth through
the Halstead twins would remain a serious
threat to Charlotte.

"The money was transferred into your personal account and yet you've said nothing
about it." Arthur Halstead let his words hang
in the air. It wasn't exactly a direct accusation,
but it felt like one. He stood in front of a window in his office, backlit by the bright sunlight outside so that it was hard for Charlotte
to see his face.

Charlotte's parents had hugged her when she
and Wade first arrived at the reception area
outside their office suite. They'd asked her if
she was okay, told her she looked like she'd lost
weight and expressed concern over the bruises
still visible on her face. Ethan had been there
as well, looking even worse than Charlotte felt,
practically begging for updates on the hunt for
Dinah. When Charlotte had to tell him she
didn't really have news about her sister at all,
he'd looked crushed.

Inside Arthur's office, with the door shut
and only Wade to witness the conversation be-

tween Charlotte and her parents, the communications from Arthur and Kandace to their daughter became cooler. Kandace had directed Wade to wait outside the office while they talked, but Charlotte had insisted he come along with her. She felt stronger with Wade by her side. Beyond that, he was sharp and attentive and might notice some detail she missed.

Charlotte shook her head in response to her father's insinuating comment. "I didn't realize the money was in my account."

"Don't you get notifications on your phone?"

"I have all kinds of messages on my phone that I haven't paid attention to because I've been busy and tired and had other things on my mind."

"And yet you saw your father's message about the news story this morning," Kandace said.

"Yeah, because we're *family* and that's supposed to mean something. And maybe that could be expressed by something like, oh, I don't know, prioritizing a response to messages from each other because it might be important."

Kandace tapped her lacquered fingernails on the armrest of her chair. "You don't need to get snippy, Charlotte. We're all under stress and worried about Dinah. And before you try to imply otherwise, no, the money is not more important than finding your sister. But it's the only situation we can do anything about."

Kandace's voice broke on the last few words and tears began to slide down her face.

Guilt hung around Charlotte's shoulders like an old weighted blanket. Her parents weren't completely unfeeling monsters, but they were so wrapped up in their business at times that they lost some of their capacity for a deeper connection and empathy when it came to their children. So much of their time was tied up in numbers and reports and scheduling and not wasting time on *silly* things. Never mind that those silly things—like hopes and dreams and a kid's desire to figure out who she was—were important to other people. To children. To the Halstead twins as they were growing up.

She glanced over at Wade, expecting to see judgment. He probably thought she was a jerk. The disconnect she oftentimes felt with her parents was such a subtle thing and they put on such a good front that no one else ever saw it. A circumstance that often made Charlotte feel very alone.

To her surprise, she saw acceptance in

Wade's eyes. He gave her a slight nod of encouragement. He *understood*.

Charlotte took a deep breath, reminding herself that her parents were as bewildered as she was by the events of the past few days. Even if they hadn't been forced to withstand the literal physical attacks that she'd faced. "If I had used my laptop to go into Accounting and used the payroll program to put money into my own account, don't you think I would have immediately moved it somewhere else to hide it? I haven't had anything to do with this, so it's probably still sitting there."

She took out her phone, tapped the screen a few times and pulled up her personal bank account. The balance remained way beyond normal. She showed the screen to her parents. "I don't have the necessary access to move it back into the corporate payroll account, but you can do that or have someone in Accounting do it." She looked up at them. "Am I right in assuming you're still looking into how this happened? You didn't simply assume I'd stolen it?"

Her father pursed his lips. "Well, we wanted to explore all possibilities before going further with the forensic audit."

"Just in case I'd had something to do with it?"

After a pause, her father nodded.

She was trying hard to be gracious, and finally decided that, in their own way, her parents were actually trying to be loving and protect her by potentially covering for her. And she supposed it was maybe sweet, in an odd kind of way. And that maybe, under their hard exterior, they had a tenderness she hadn't appreciated. Like anyone else, they could only be how they were.

"Mrs. Halstead, has anyone contacted you with a ransom demand?"

For a moment Kandace looked as if she'd forgotten Wade was in the room. "No," she finally said, wiping her eyes and recovering her controlled, professional expression. "If they had, we would have paid it." She exchanged looks with her husband. "We've expected that from the time Dinah went missing and we've made preparations to get cash quickly if we need to."

An awkward few moments of silence followed. There really wasn't much Charlotte's parents could do other than wait and do their best to be ready for anything. Charlotte, on the other hand, could keep working with Wade as they did their best to track down her sister.

"We should go." Charlotte got to her feet and Wade stood alongside her.

She gave both of her parents lingering hugs goodbye. And each of them seemed to melt their former defense stance while in her embrace.

A few minutes later Charlotte and Wade stepped out of the resort and walked to his truck. As usual, his head was on a swivel as he continually kept track of their surroundings. Having learned her lesson, Charlotte likewise remained vigilant. There was a payoff for being paranoid these days, she reminded herself, as she shifted her gaze and noticed the plants and trees beginning to put forth blooms and leaves. The weather had warmed up considerably over the last two days, and the bright sunshine was a welcome contrast to the dark gloom that felt like it had dropped over Range River since the night Murphy had kidnapped her.

"I'm going to take you back to the inn and then I'm going to go talk to a few informants," Wade said as they turned from the parking lot and drove down the road that would take them through town and beyond, to the open and undeveloped stretches of land near the inn.

"You don't believe I would be of any help," Charlotte said flatly.

"No, I don't. Not with what I have planned

for the rest of the day. The people I intend to visit will be *less* likely to talk in front of you. Or anyone else, for that matter. Their anonymity is important to them and I respect that."

"I understand," Charlotte said. There were things that were more important than Charlotte feeling like she was helping. This was probably a time where the most helpful thing she could do would be to stay out of the way.

He glanced over, like he needed to confirm that she meant it. So she summoned up a slight smile and nodded.

"I'm going to see if I can find out if Gamble and Murphy have any known enemies. If so, I'll try to track down those enemies and see what I can learn. Those are the kinds of people who would happily tell me everything I want to know. I'll do the same thing regarding Paul Boutin."

"That will be a lot of interviewing. I'm not complaining, but that will take a lot of time."

"I might be able to get Hayley's husband, Jack, at Eagle Rapids Bail Bonds, to help out."

Charlotte tried to push back against the sensation of chilly fear that was settling over her. Dinah had been missing for over forty-eight hours now and Charlotte had watched enough true crime stories on TV to know that was very, very bad. She could only hope that Detective Romanov and her team had some helpful information they hadn't shared with her and the bounty hunters.

*Bam!*

Charlotte heard a rifle shot. The truck shook and the front passenger side dropped down. The vehicle swerved to the side as Wade fought with the steering wheel to gain control.

"Get down!"

Charlotte scrambled down to the floorboard.

*Bam!* A second shot blew out the front tire on the driver's side, forcing Wade to stop.

*Bam! Bam! Bam!*

The added shots struck metal on the passenger side of the truck around the front and fender, making menacing thunking sounds as they moved toward the door beside Charlotte.

Sheer terror sent her shrinking down as far as she could go, curling up into a tight ball. Her heart nearly pounded out of her chest as she fervently prayed. *Please, Lord, help!*

The front windshield was struck twice, the bullets bursting through at the impact points while the surrounding safety glass shattered with a few splintery pieces breaking away.

"The truck's undrivable and we can't stay here." Wade was stretched across the bench seat, trying to stay out of view, his head toward Charlotte. "We have to get out. It looks like the shooter is on your side. I need you to get up and move in my direction."

Charlotte stared at him. Fear had locked most of her muscles tight. She'd barely been able to turn her head to look in his direction when he spoke to her. How could she possibly get up and out of the truck? Much less be able to run for cover?

"We can do this," Wade said, seeming to read her thoughts. His tone was urgent, but calm. He held his hands toward her. "We need to move while there's a lull in the shooting."

Charlotte imagined the assassin reloading. Or creeping closer to the truck until he felt the time was right to boldly step up and aim directly at her through the window before he finished her off.

A shudder passed through her body.

There seemed to be no safe option. She couldn't think of a way out of the situation that didn't involve taking a potentially fatal risk.

She looked at Wade's outstretched hands. Thought about her prayer, which she'd already silently repeated several times. Maybe this was a situation where she'd have to rely on another person to get the help she'd prayed for. Much as she disliked doing that, much as she wanted to resolve situations herself, much as she feared depending on someone and being bitterly disappointed, yet again, that was something she had to do. *Now.*

She reached for Wade's hands, let him help pull her up until he had to let go to open the door and back out. It was only for a few seconds, but his touch was enough to revive her, to break the hold of fear and get her moving and thinking again.

Wade hunkered down, using his open door as a shield. Charlotte climbed out until she was beside him.

*Bam!* The shot blasted through the passenger side window.

Wade grabbed her hand and they ran across the other lane in the street, heading for a cluster of trees with a dense thicket woven through them.

Charlotte heard a low rumble of traffic as cars approached from the direction of town. She moved slightly to look around the tree trunk she was hiding behind and saw the shadowy form of a man wearing a knit cap and dark glasses near the truck. He turned his head back and forth until he caught sight of her.

Paul Boutin. The hit man.

He holstered his pistol and reached around for the rifle that hung on a strap over his shoulder. When he lifted it and took a shooter's stance, Charlotte quickly ducked back behind the tree.

Seconds later, she heard the crack of a shot. At almost the same time, she heard a car whizzing by and the clank of a round striking metal. Charlotte took another look as the car veered off the side of the road, crashing into a tree. Her heart dropped at the realization the driver must be hurt.

A second driver rounded the curve, slowed and pulled to the side of the road by the crash site. That driver probably had no idea what had just happened and wasn't aware of the danger of being shot.

Meanwhile, the hit man had disappeared.

"Stay here in case Boutin is still lurking around and call 9-1-1," Wade said. "I'm going to go help the driver of that crashed car."

The occupants of the second car were already out of their vehicle and checking on the injured driver. Wade hurried over to assist. Together, the responders managed to force the driver's crumpled door open. It looked as if he was bleeding and trying to get out of the car.

Wade and the others encouraged him to stay put until an ambulance arrived.

By that time Charlotte had already punched in the emergency number and given the operator the specifics of what had happened. Emergency medical services appeared quickly, along with two police patrol cars. At that point, Charlotte reasoned it was safe for her to come out from hiding.

The driver of the wrecked car was not seriously injured by the gunshot or the crash, it turned out. The sound of the bullet striking his vehicle had startled him so badly that he'd swerved and struck the tree and been slightly cut by broken glass.

Meanwhile, officers had begun a search of the area for the gunman. Based on past experience and the fact that he was a professional, Charlotte had no doubt Paul Boutin had put an exit strategy in place ahead of time and was now long gone.

"Do you think Boutin saw us go to the resort and assumed we would come back along this route?" Charlotte asked Wade as they waited for a tow truck. "Could that be how he knew exactly where and when to find us?"

"Maybe. It's also possible that someone at the resort told him we were there. Knowing that gave him the information he needed to set up the ambush."

Charlotte sighed heavily. She didn't want to believe that someone at the resort had set her up for assassination. Didn't want to accept the possibility that someone she knew and trusted was behind every terrible thing that had been happening. Including the disappearance of her twin.

She'd tried to laugh off Wade's previous suggestions that someone close to her and her family was the one wreaking havoc on their lives. Now it looked like she had to seriously consider that possibility if she wanted to keep herself and her sister alive.

# TEN

After having his truck towed from the shooting scene, Wade called Maribel to give him and Charlotte a ride back to the inn. Then he borrowed a company vehicle and set out to locate the potential useful informants he'd mentioned to Charlotte.

When he arrived back at the Riverside Inn after being away most of the afternoon, the first thing he did once he walked through the front door was to go looking for Charlotte. He realized it was highly unlikely that she would have been in danger while he was gone, and if something untoward had happened, he would have been notified. Nevertheless, he wanted to see her.

Maybe it wasn't so much that he'd been worried, but rather that he'd felt something missing as he'd worked in town without her. And that was an odd experience for him. He had friends, he certainly wasn't antisocial, but letting a woman get close enough that he didn't feel quite 100 percent without her was not normal for him.

Nothing about this situation, or relationship, or whatever it was, was normal for him.

For one thing, while she wasn't exactly a client, this thing between them that had them spending so much time together *was* a business arrangement of sorts. And Wade did not mix business with his social life. And for another, despite how down-to-earth she seemed, she *was* one of the Halsteads. A fact he was reminded of several times today as he drove around to talk to various informants and constantly saw the resort tower on the edge of Wolf Lake.

He walked into the kitchen thinking Charlotte might be in there. Instead, he only saw Maribel, who was starting dinner. "Hi, Mom."

She turned to smile at him. "Did you drum up any good leads?"

He offered a half shrug in response. "You know how it is. People give you pieces of information. You can't see the big picture, so you don't know how to put it all together. Not until you learn that one specific detail that ties everything together."

"Well, keep pushing until you learn that detail." She picked up an onion and began peeling it.

"I handed out a fair amount of cash with the promise of more in return for some solid information. We'll see how that goes." He grabbed a bottle out of the refrigerator. "It seems odd to me that no one's been able to tell me anything so far. Lowlifes like to brag about their accomplishments as much as anybody else. Seems odd that nobody's overheard anything." He took a swig of water. "Or maybe they're just afraid to talk about it."

"It might be a very small number of people are involved and they're being smart about it," Maribel suggested as she started chopping the onion. "Or one of your earlier suspicions could be true. Maybe the Invaders motorcycle gang is involved. They're pretty tight-lipped."

"Could be an even tighter clique than that," Wade said grimly.

"What do you mean?"

"My gut instinct is telling me that a family member, a business associate or someone she believes is a friend is involved. Possibly involved in planning the whole thing. I've tried to talk to Charlotte about it a little. She wanted to dismiss the idea out of hand at first. But now she's starting to consider it." He took another drink of water. "I feel mean encouraging her to think about who might have betrayed her and her family. I know it's painful for her. But I also think it's possible if she considers the idea long enough she'll be able to point out someone we should spend more time investigating."

Betrayal by someone you knew and loved was the worst. Wade knew that from experience.

"Sounds like you're already on the follow-the-money trail." Maribel slid the chopped onion from the cutting board into a pan of warm oil and it started to sizzle. "Putting together a timeline is always a good idea, too. Sometimes it directs your attention toward something you hadn't thought of before."

While Maribel had never been an actual bounty hunter herself, she had spent plenty of time conducting interviews, doing online research and brainstorming with the bounty hunters. Over time, she'd developed a pretty sharp insight into how to find people.

Wade reached for a corn-bread muffin cooling on the countertop. "I need to talk to the others. Touch base and see what they've learned from their informants."

"Connor should be home in about an hour

or so. Danny and Hayley will be here for dinner tonight, too."

Wade nodded. "Good. Where's Charlotte?" He'd waited a while to ask, because he didn't want his growing interest in her to be obvious.

Of course, he didn't fool his mom, and the hint of a smile playing across Maribel's lips told him so. "Last I saw her, she was on the deck taking in some sun now that it's finally warmed up a bit."

Wade quickly finished drinking his bottle of water and then headed across the great room to open the slider to the deck.

Charlotte glanced over. "Hi."

For some dumb reason, he experienced a flutter of emotion that felt like, but couldn't possibly be, nervousness. "Hello."

"I came out to get a little bit of sun and try to cheer myself up."

"Is it helping?"

"Not much."

Tall, potted evergreen shrubs kept on the deck for purposes of providing security had been arranged to form a screen directly in front of Charlotte so that no one could see her and take a shot at her from the other side of the river.

Seeing that she was safely situated, he dropped into the chair beside her.

She had a novel in her lap, but before Wade opened the door he'd seen that she wasn't reading it. She'd been looking toward the end of the deck, where there was no evergreen barrier and the wide river was visible. The ground was fairly rocky in places, and depending on the weather and season, the waters could be flowing at a steady and smooth rate or they could be splashing in a swiftly raucous and unpredictable pattern. Either way, the view of the mountains in the distance was always calming. At least, that was his experience.

"I don't suppose you found Dinah while you were out today," Charlotte said dully.

"I'm sorry, but no, I didn't."

She turned to him, her face pale and her features appearing nearly statue-like in their stony fear. "Don't apologize. That came out sounding like I might be disappointed in you when I'm really disappointed in myself. I can't help thinking that all of this involves my family and that means I should have somehow seen it coming. I should have known Dinah was in some kind of trouble."

"We're going to have to agree to disagree on that one. Sometimes family members are the hardest people to understand. Even if you see them fairly often, you don't always pick up on the changes in them. Or maybe you just don't want to see them."

Her loyalty impressed him. Even under the immense stress of having repeatedly been attacked and having her sister missing, even with her parents believing she could have embezzled money from the family business, she still cared about them. Still wanted to protect them and still felt responsible to look after them to some degree. Loyalty was a trait Wade very much admired. Something that seemed to be in short supply in the world, at times.

"Were any of your informants able to tell you anything useful?"

"A few random bits of information. Where Gamble likes to hang out when he's not locked up. The part of town where Boutin has been seen fairly often recently."

"Well, that's something."

"After Connor gets home and Danny and Hayley show up for dinner, we'll compare notes and see if we get an idea of where to look next for Dinah and Boutin. Finding either one could help lead us to the other. But know that I realize finding Dinah is the priority."

"I'd hoped Detective Romanov would call

and tell me Gamble and Murphy finally started talking and gave her some information about my sister, but I never heard from the detective."

"I went by the police department and spoke with her. Gamble started to answer some of her questions, and in return the city prosecutor is putting together a plea deal so he'll be motivated to talk more. The stuff Gamble has been saying hasn't been investigated or confirmed, so it's not to be completely believed yet."

"What's he saying?"

"He's claiming that your sister really does owe him a significant amount of money. Apparently he's been expanding his burglary career into a loan-sharking enterprise. When he loaned Dinah the money and she stopped making any effort to pay him back, he figured he had to do something splashy. He wanted to scare her into paying him *and* he wanted to send a message. He wanted his other clients to see that it was dangerous not to pay him, plus he wanted the other goons in town to see that he wasn't a pushover. Otherwise, the criminals would come after him and his business."

"That all makes sense, but it doesn't explain why he came after me."

"He still claims that he and Murphy thought you were Dinah, originally. After that first kidnapping attempt fell apart, they figured Dinah would be extra vigilant and possibly surrounded by resort security staff because she knew he was after her. They decided to go after you because they thought you'd be easier to get to. The plan was to grab you and demand the money they were owed as a ransom. They figured Dinah would find a way to pay up. Get the money from your parents, if she had to."

"But what about Dinah's disappearance? Or the hit man trying to kill me? Or the embezzlement?"

Wade shook his head. "I don't know. Gamble isn't saying anything more until he gets his plea deal."

Charlotte tapped her fingers on the arms of her chair. "The men who started everything are locked up, and yet I'm still the target for assassination." She shook her head. "Someone hired a professional killer to come after me and Dinah's still missing." Her voice began to shake. "Instead of making progress, it feels like we're going backward. That things are getting *worse*."

"We'll find Dinah, we'll find Paul Boutin and we'll find whoever hired Boutin," Wade said, wanting to reassure himself as much as he wanted to reassure Charlotte. "The cops are on this. We're on this. At any moment we could get a break and wrap up this case."

The look in Charlotte's tear-filled eyes said it all. She wasn't buying his comforting words. And honestly, he was having a little trouble believing them himself.

Charlotte was sitting at the dinner table, moving her food around on her plate without eating much, when she heard her phone chime in her pocket, indicating an incoming call. Normally, she would ignore her phone at the dinner table. But with Dinah missing, she was desperate for any helpful information.

She froze in indecision, not wanting to be disrespectful to the people who had welcomed her into their home.

The main members of the Range River Bail Bonds team were seated at the table around her. Beside her, Wade offered an encouraging nod. "Go ahead and answer it if you want to."

Charlotte grabbed the phone and glanced at the screen. "It's from an unknown number." She looked up and locked gazes with Wade. It could turn out to be something inconsequential, like a wrong number or an automated sales call. Nevertheless, hope and fear warred within her. Could this be the good news she'd hoped for telling her that Dinah was okay? Or would it be yet another player in whatever weird game was going on, calling to make a ransom demand?

"Excuse me." Charlotte got up and stepped toward the living room to take the call. Behind her, she heard the scrape of Wade's chair as he got up to follow her.

Charlotte tapped the screen. "Hello?"

"You answered! I thought I was going to have to leave a message."

The connection wasn't great, but Charlotte still recognized the voice. *"Dinah?"*

"Put it on speaker," Wade said, standing beside her.

The rest of the crew quietly moved toward them from the dining room.

"Is it really you?" Charlotte said after tapping the screen. Her heart thundered in her chest and her pulse pounded in her ears as she waited for what felt like a very long time before hearing a reply.

"Hey, sis, how are you?"

It *was* Dinah. And she sounded so normal.

It was the last thing Charlotte expected. She shook her head to clear her confusion. "How am I? How are *you*? *Where* are you? What happened? Are you okay?" The questions poured out of her.

"I'm fine." There was a slight delay before she added, "I just needed to get away for a few days and clear my head."

*What?*

"Clear your head? Are you saying you just left? Of your own free will?" Anger and stunned disbelief battled in Charlotte's mind as she tried to understand what her sister was saying.

"Yeah. A couple of hours after you went to bed, I called Lyndsay Mercer. I wanted to slip away for a while. I didn't want to get into a big debate about it with Mom and Dad or Ethan or you. I just wanted to go. So I dressed in drab clothes and a hat so I wouldn't stand out in the dark. I left through the back door and kept my gaze turned downward so my face wouldn't show up on any security cameras. I didn't have to go far to reach the forested area of the property where I'd be hidden by trees, and then I crossed the half mile or so to the city road where Lyndsay was waiting for me. She picked me up and gave me a ride to the east end of the lake. Her parents have a pretty little summerhouse out there where it's quiet and I—"

*"We thought you had been kidnapped!"* Frustration flashed hot through Charlotte like

a wildfire. So many times her sister had been selfish and self-absorbed. And here she was, doing it again at a great cost, emotionally, and in terms of the dollar expense for the police and others to search for her. "You left everything behind. It looked like you'd left against your will."

"Oh sorry." Dinah cleared her throat. "I was kind of high when I realized I'd been playing around with drinking and a few other things way too much. I blamed myself for you getting kidnapped and decided I needed to get myself together. I wanted to go someplace quiet to do it."

*You're right to blame yourself for the kidnapping. It happened because of the foolish decisions you made.*

"I wanted to get away from the resort and everybody and everything going on there," Dinah continued. "Someplace kind of isolated seemed best and I knew Lyndsay's family had just inherited the house from her grandpa. I knew if I took my phone and credit cards I'd just give in to temptation again once my high wore off." There was a long pause and then she added, "I didn't want to say anything to Mom and Dad. Or Ethan. I couldn't stand to see the looks of disappointment on their faces."

*Please, Lord, give me patience and understanding.* Charlotte took a deep breath and looked up at the ceiling for a moment. Her cheeks were warm and she knew she was about to lose her temper.

"How is it that she's able to call now?" Wade asked quietly.

"Is someone there with you?" Dinah had apparently heard him.

Charlotte was about to unload all the details about the bounty hunters and the police and the attempts on her life and everything, when she caught Wade shaking his head. He held up a scrap of paper where he'd written, "Tell her I'm just a friend."

*Just a friend.* The truth was he was so much more. But Wade and all the other bounty hunters wore strangely reserved expressions. That didn't look happy or relieved that Dinah was okay. Obviously Charlotte felt a more tumultuous mix of emotions, but that was because her sister had behaved like a thoughtless jerk and Charlotte had a right to take more personal offense. She would have expected the bounty hunters to be glad this particular job was over.

"That's just a friend I met through the literacy project," Charlotte fibbed. By now Wade had scratched out a note saying "Ask her how she is able to call now," so she voiced his question.

"The second day I was here I discovered a prepay phone her family leaves up here just in case they need it. Turns out you have to stand in exactly the right spot to get connectivity."

"And you're just calling *now*?"

"Well, yeah," Dinah responded in a snippy tone. "The point was to *not* call anyone. To just dry out a little on my own. And I did."

"And now?"

"Now I need you to come get me."

"I'll do that. But first I need to call the police and let them know you're okay. And Mom and Dad. And Ethan. I need to tell them, too."

"No! Wait, please. I want you to come get me."

Wade reached for Charlotte's arm, and then leaned in to whisper directly into her ear. "We need to call the police. This could be some kind of trap."

Charlotte turned to stare at him. He thought Dinah would set her up to be hurt or killed? "My sister can be an idiot," Charlotte whispered into Wade's ear. "But she's not vicious."

"She could be doing this against her will. The hit man—or somebody—could have a gun pointed at her head."

He was right. The hired assassin had tried to kill Charlotte just a few hours ago. And, as a less substantial point but still one to be considered, there was the embezzlement situation. There was some kind of larger plot going on. Her main focus had been on finding her twin sister, but Dinah being missing was not the only danger at hand. There was something else going on, too. But it was all too shadowy for her to see it.

"Charlotte?" Dinah's voice carried through the phone.

She sounded worried, Charlotte thought. Scared.

"I'm here."

"Please don't call the police yet. Or Mom and Dad. Because they will call the police and I don't want that. Not just yet."

"Why?"

Dinah sighed. "Look, now that my mind has cleared, I realize what I did was stupid. But honestly, at the time, I thought it was the best thing. And I wanted to act fast, before I lost the will to do it." She sighed again, heavily. "I really, really want to get myself together. I'm sorry that what I did put you in danger. That will never, *ever* happen again."

Was that true? Would her sister never put

her in danger? Or was she in danger herself? Could it be that she was lying and she was under the influence right now?

"If you call the police, they'll send a car out here. Some wannabe photojournalist with a blog or their own gossip site or whatever will follow them. They'll end up getting pictures of me and posting them and I'll be humiliated and I just can't stand that." Dinah started to cry. "I really am doing my best here. And I'll answer for everything. Just…please help me with this."

"Okay. Where are you?"

From the corner of her eye, Charlotte could see Wade's expression darken with suspicion.

Dinah gave her an address. "You'll like it out here," she added hopefully, as if trying to lighten the mood of the conversation a little. "It's got a hippie vibe. There's a cute little gazebo in the front yard. Since the weather's nice, I'll wait for you out there. I'll be all packed up and I can just jump into your SUV and we can go."

"See you in a bit." Charlotte disconnected.

"This is not a good idea," Wade said gravely. "It has all the markings of an ambush."

Charlotte nodded. "I understand. And if you don't want to go with me, I understand that, too. But I'd really like all of you to help me with this." She took in everyone with a sweeping glance. "You know what? It's easy to be loving and forgiving to someone who looks like a victim. It's harder to be that way with someone who's made a mistake. A big one." She took a deep breath. "I'm angry with Dinah right now." She shook her head. "You can't imagine how angry."

She crossed her arms over her chest and hugged herself. "We can call the cops shortly after we get there, if you want. Bring Dinah to the police station if Detective Romanov asks us to. But first, I want to give Dinah a little bit of a chance. Let her hold on to a little bit of her dignity, if that is what this request is really about. Or let her confess to me first if she's done something illegal. Give her a chance to get it off her chest and explain before we go to the police. Because I don't intend to help her hide any wrongdoing."

They didn't need to hear her fairly lengthy, sad story about being alienated from her identical twin sister for so long. Or about how much she wanted to reforge that connection. If that reconnection had to happen in a situation like this, where Charlotte took the first step, maybe even the biggest step, or the most steps toward reconciliation, so be it. She'd prayed for the opportunity to repair her relationship with Dinah. Maybe this awkward, murky situation was part of the answer to that prayer.

Wade, Maribel, Danny, Connor and Hayley all exchanged glances with one another while Charlotte stood there waiting for their decision.

One by one, they each gave a slight nod.

"Looks like we're all going with you," Wade said. "But you have to agree not to take any chances with your own safety."

Charlotte offered what felt like a bleak smile. "I'll do my best."

# ELEVEN

"Looks like we're almost there." Charlotte turned her gaze from the GPS screen on the dash to glance at their surroundings. Wade was driving an SUV that belonged to Range River Bail Bonds while his truck was being repaired.

Darkness had fallen over the forested area at the eastern end of Wolf Lake. The terrain was much rockier than it was in town, and the narrow highway they were driving alternately dipped and rose, as well as curving back and forth, as it followed the edge of the lake.

"Don't get out of the vehicle the moment we arrive," Wade said, his voice tight with tension. "Even if you see Dinah, and she's alone, and everything looks fine. Wait. Give us a moment to make certain the location is secure and that this meeting isn't some kind of trap she's being forced to set against her will." He turned to her. *"Please."*

"Of course."

She meant to keep her word, though it would be a challenge. She wanted so much to hug her sister and know that she was okay. At the same time, she wanted to demand answers for the questions still swirling around in her mind. She was determined not to lose her temper, but she also wanted to make certain her twin truly understood the gravity of what she'd done. How many people she'd upset, how much time had been wasted by authorities as they'd searched for her. So many things needed to change in Dinah's behavior. For that matter, the whole way her family interacted needed to be adjusted in the wake of this string of horrible events. Charlotte offered a brief prayer for that to happen. Immediately, if possible.

The GPS indicated that they'd arrived at their final turn. It led them onto a private unpaved road with a wide curve shortly after turning off the highway. From there it continued downhill, around a couple of large rock outcroppings, toward the shore of the lake.

Lights flickered through the SUV's interior as the pickup truck following them passed over a bump in the road. Connor, Danny and Hayley Ryan were in there.

"I'm going to let Dinah know that we're here. Now that she knows about the attacks that have been launched on me, she might be scared when she sees unfamiliar vehicles driving up." She reached for her phone and tapped the screen to call the number Dinah had used earlier.

A recording told her the call didn't go through. She tried again, with the same result. "Well, she did say she had connectivity issues out here," Charlotte said, feeling uneasy even though there were plenty of locations around the lake where reception was spotty.

"Don't worry," Wade said. "We do this kind of thing all the time," he added easily, obviously trying to soothe her nerves. "Approaching people who are skittish while keeping the situation calm and friendly is a major part of our business. We'll smile and do our best not to appear threatening."

Charlotte thought about how she'd be feeling right now if she'd had to make the trip out here by herself. If she hadn't made these new friends. It was hard to believe she'd first met them just two days ago. It was three days ago that she'd met Wade. For so long she'd felt safer on her own and that trusting people would only leave her feeling disappointed and hollow. That the only way to truly feel safe, at least emotionally, was to not rely on anyone else.

She'd learned that from her parents and their obsession with their business.

And now look. Here she was, surrounded by people who took their business seriously but also knew how to keep their personal lives in perspective. She'd prayed for help. The Lord had sent her help. And to receive it, she'd had to trust and rely on other people.

She glanced at Wade's profile, visible in the light from the dashboard. She'd taken a chance relying on him. For physical protection, but even more, for emotional support. And she was glad she had. She'd let him into her heart, although she couldn't say the exact moment when she'd decided to do so, and taking that risk had healed a pretty jaded perspective when it came to her limited expectations from people.

This was an awkward moment for her to wonder how he felt about her, but she couldn't help it. He'd never said he'd changed his initial opinion of her. Not that he'd stated his prejudice toward her so blatantly, but the comments he'd made had expressed his thoughts quite clearly. He'd thought she was spoiled and entitled and clueless about how most people lived simply because of the family she'd been born into.

She hoped he didn't still feel that way about her.

They rounded the final curve in the road.

"There's your sister," Wade said. "She's in the gazebo."

To the left, across the narrow road and opposite the lake, was a fairly large rustic-style home perched midway up a low hill. There was a light on the front porch and one visible through a front window—otherwise, it was dark.

The gazebo was closer to the road. It was a small, white whimsical structure with fairy lights wrapped around the posts, surrounded by a wooden deck, outdoor furniture, a picnic table and a large grill. The perfect setting for outdoor parties in the summer.

Charlotte couldn't help smiling to herself and shaking her head. Of course her sister's quiet retreat had been at a nicely stylish location. An actual cabin, something simple and woodsy, would not have been Dinah's style. Even if her goal had been to sober up, get in touch with her emotions and clear her mind.

Charlotte couldn't see Dinah clearly inside the gazebo, but she could see her sister's shadowy figure as she stood from where she'd been sitting along the railing and looked toward the approaching vehicles with obvious hesitancy.

"Remember, we're going to take everything nice and slow," Wade said as he brought the SUV to a stop. "Things may not be as simple and safe as they look."

*It could be a trap.*

Charlotte nodded. She'd grown used to the feeling of muscles tightening in her stomach, and here it was again. Like Wade, she scanned their surroundings. The lights spilling from the house, the gazebo lights and the vehicle lights didn't illuminate nearly as much as she would have liked. There was still so much hidden in shadow. Thick trees covered much of the property. To her right, the inky waters of Wolf Lake lapped at the shoreline.

Danny Ryan drove his pickup past them and then made a U-turn before stopping. His headlights crossing with Wade's erased some of the shadows and gave a little clearer view of the expanse of lawn in front of the house and Dinah in the gazebo.

"There's no one in there with her," Wade said to Charlotte. "But that doesn't mean there isn't someone nearby watching. Let us go meet with her first. If everything's good, we'll bring her back here and you can talk all you want on the way back to town."

Wade opened his door. The bounty hunters in the other vehicle followed suit, all of them moving slowly, scanning their surroundings, a hand near the belts at their waists where they could grab pepper spray or a gun if they had to. They were wearing bulletproof vests and had insisted that Charlotte wear one, too.

Dinah appeared vulnerable and uncertain, and she began to back up and look around frantically as Wade and his fellow bounty hunters approached her.

Charlotte rolled down her window, hesitant to wave or call out until she was certain the situation was as safe as it appeared.

As promised, Wade approached Dinah with calm, measured movements. "Dinah Halstead? My name is Wade Fast Horse. I'm a friend of your sister." He managed to sound less like a cop approaching a person of interest and more like an engaging sort of person approaching a mutual friend.

"Where's Charlotte?" Dinah demanded, her voice shaky with uncertainty. She continued to back up until she was almost out of the gazebo. "Why isn't she here? She said she was going to come get me."

"I'm right here!" Charlotte called out through the open window, unable to wait any longer.

Dinah startled and then turned in her direction, squinting at the SUV's headlights and holding her hand up to her forehead as if trying to see past the glare. "Wh-what's going on?"

It took every bit of self-control Charlotte had not to dart out of the car. But nearly getting killed—more than once over the last three days—had taught her the value of keeping control of her emotions in an uncertain situation. "They're my friends and they're just making sure the situation is secure. They want to make sure you don't have someone nearby forcing you to draw me into a trap."

Dinah tilted her head slightly and was quiet for a moment. "How do I know this isn't some weird sort of trap for someone to get at *me*?" she called out. "I can't see you. Maybe somebody is beside you pointing a gun at *you* and making you say things to give me a false sense of security."

Charlotte felt a smile on her lips despite the seriousness of the situation. Her twin might behave like a fool at times, but she was not dumb. And considering that Gamble had meant to target Dinah in the beginning, and a hit man was being paid to come after Charlotte in the meantime, Dinah had a right to be suspicious.

"I think the situation looks secure," Charlotte called out, figuring Wade would know she was talking to him. "I'm going to get out so Dinah can see me."

Wade turned in her direction and gave a tight nod.

The other bounty hunters continued gazing around, keeping an eye on things.

Charlotte opened her door, suddenly feeling a bit nervous about doing it. It would be a relief to collect her sister and get back to the inn. Under different circumstances it would be nice to spend some time out here away from town and near the lake, but right now it felt creepy.

She stepped out onto the gravel drive. A breeze coming off the lake buffeted her hair. The same breeze sent tree branches swaying and creaking.

"Here I am," Charlotte called out. She began to move toward her sister. For the moment she set her frustration with Dinah aside, and let herself focus on the rush of emotions she felt as memories popped into her mind of their childhood when they were so close. It looked like she and Dinah were going to have that chance to rebuild their relationship. *Thank You, Lord.*

Dinah hesitated for a moment, watching her. And then she started moving toward Charlotte.

"You're alive!" Charlotte said when they reached each other and hugged. The emotion of the moment walloped her harder than she'd expected and tears collected in her eyes and then rolled down her cheeks.

"I'm so sorry," Dinah said. "For doing a thoughtless thing like disappearing without telling anyone what I was doing. For not making my loan payments and causing you to get kidnapped when they meant to take me." She started to cry and choke on her words. "For everything."

"Loan payments?" Charlotte asked.

"Yes." Dinah took a step back and wiped at her eyes. "Things weren't going as well at the coffee shop as they looked. Well, *I* wasn't doing a good job managing it." She looked down for a moment. "In some ways I wasn't managing it at all. I was gone a lot, visiting friends, just because I was bored. And when I got bored I went looking for something to ease that feeling and make the time pass faster."

"You mean you went looking for a drink? Or something else?"

Dinah nodded. "Things got out of control. I started to worry and things got worse. I'd leave more often, figuring I'd just have a quick drink or a smoke and come right back." She shook her head. "Stupid. I was so *stupid*. And embarrassed and I couldn't let Mom and Dad or Ethan know, because I was just so tired of messing things up and I didn't want to face them. Finally, I took out the loan, from a guy one of my friends knew."

"Brett Gamble."

"Yes." Dinah sighed heavily. "When I got the money from him, I told myself I would slowly add it to my deposits for the coffee shop, make my balance sheet look better, make it look like I was doing a good job managing it. And at the same time, I would work harder and smarter. I would get things into shape. I would be able to regain my self-respect."

"But that didn't happen?" Charlotte asked sadly.

Dinah shook her head. "I borrowed a little of the money to take my friends out to dinner and nightclubbing. We had fun and I was able to pay for everything. Because everybody loves a Halstead twin when we pick up the tab, right?"

Charlotte felt her heart break. "There are people who will love you for you," Charlotte said. "I do."

Dinah laughed bitterly and looked away.

"Yeah, well, I appreciate that, but I think you overestimate people." She drew herself up. "Anyway, I made some of the payments, but then I missed a few. Brett was fine with that. Said that he would just add it back to what I owed. Before I knew it, I was out of money and I hadn't made payments in a long time. Things at the coffee shop weren't getting any better, either.

"I ignored Brett's calls. People told me he came by the coffee shop looking for me, but of course I wasn't there. So I guess he hired someone to kidnap me, probably to scare me into getting the money to pay him somehow, but the guy grabbed you by mistake.

"I was so used to hiding everything, so used to putting up a false front by then, that I didn't tell you. I didn't tell anyone. I came here for a few days to try to untangle everything in my head."

Charlotte sensed Wade stepping up behind her. A moment later he leaned over her shoulder and said, "Let's get back in the SUV. You and your sister can talk in there." He glanced around. "I don't like standing out here like this. You're too exposed."

They'd found Dinah, but the contract killer was still at large.

Charlotte nodded. "Of course."

Before they started moving, Charlotte asked Dinah, "Why did you move that money from the payroll account into my personal account and make it look like I embezzled funds?" Since her sister seemed desperate to unburden herself with an admission of what she'd been doing, it seemed as good a time as any to ask her. "Were you trying to draw attention away from yourself? Did you intend to eventually move that money into your own account?"

Dinah stopped walking and gave her an odd look. "I didn't move any money into your account. What are you talking about?"

"Look, I know you're embarrassed—"

The sound of gunfire stopped Charlotte midsentence. At the same time, she felt the burning strike of a bullet hitting her body.

*"Everybody down!"* Wade leaped at Charlotte, knocking her off the steps of the gazebo and then quickly scooting with her until they were hidden behind a pile of large rocks. Shots continued to be fired at them by an unseen shooter hidden in the woods in the direction of Wolf Lake.

From the corner of his eye, Wade caught the quick movement of Hayley as she rushed toward Dinah. Charlotte's twin was already backing up in a panic. Hayley reached her and hurried her out the back of the latticework gazebo, where the two of them were able to hunker down behind a low wall at the edge of the wooden deck.

Connor and Danny likewise took cover, also sprinting beyond and flattening themselves behind the low wall.

Wade's heart thundered in his chest. He'd heard the first shot and seen Charlotte spin halfway around at the same time. He wasn't certain if she'd been struck, but stark fear that she might be critically injured washed over him. He was already shielding her body with his and he leaned even closer, his lips near her ear, in case the assailant was listening to find their location in the silence since the shooting had stopped. "Are you all right?"

"My right arm." Charlotte forced out the words through gritted teeth. She drew in a hissing breath. "I've been shot."

Being careful not to put pressure on her arm as he moved, Wade drew his gun. He had to be prepared in case the attacker came upon them. Then he moved again so he could see how badly she was injured.

It looked to him like she'd been hit twice. It

was hard to be certain because of the bulkiness of clothes. There was a fair amount of blood. "Doesn't look too bad," he said, trying to sound less concerned than he felt. "Looks like it did hit your upper arm." He leaned up enough to unfasten and remove his bulletproof vest and then shrug out of his flannel shirt. He wore a black T-shirt underneath. He folded the flannel, laid it over her wound and then set her hand atop it. "Hold that there," he said. "Makes for a bulky bandage, but we have to use what we've got."

"Wade." Connor's voice, quiet and confident, reached him from the other bounty hunters' position behind the gazebo.

"I hear you," Wade answered as he put the vest back on.

"We're okay over here. How about you?"

"Charlotte's been hit."

"But you said it wasn't bad," Charlotte muttered.

"I've got to get her out of here," Wade continued. "I want to get her to the hospital." He wasn't taking any chances.

"I can't get phone reception to call for help." This time it was Hayley's voice. "Can you?"

Wade pulled out his phone. No bars. He tried to call 9-1-1 a couple of times anyway, but it wouldn't go through. "I got nothing."

The shooting hadn't resumed. Maybe the gunman had left.

They couldn't hide here all night. Wade didn't want to stay any longer, not with Charlotte shot and bleeding. He needed to get her into the SUV and drive her into town. "We're going to try to get out of here," he said for Connor and the others to hear.

"Copy that," Connor replied. "Move quickly. We're ready to return fire if the assailant starts shooting again."

"I might not be able to move quickly," Charlotte said beside Wade. "I'm starting to feel a little dizzy."

That was not good.

*Lord, please protect all of us.*

"Let me make sure the coast is clear before we move. I'm just going to pop my head up for a moment to look around. Hopefully I won't get it shot off."

"Not funny," Charlotte muttered.

Wade leaned down to kiss her on the forehead. It felt like the most natural thing in the world to do. His lips were pressed to her soft skin before he even realized he was going to do it.

At the same time, Charlotte reached up to wrap her hand around his forearm. "Don't you get yourself shot, too, just because you want to show off."

He actually laughed a little. Charlotte's humor given the situation was unexpected. But so much about her was unexpected. Spending time around her, learning who she was under different circumstances, had been frustrating and maddening and charming all at the same time. She'd changed him without meaning to. Just by being herself, being loyal to her problematic sister, by having such backbone. By being a woman a man could trust.

He had to get her to the hospital, get her treated, get her to safety.

He moved slightly away from her, got his feet beneath him so that he was in a squatting position, and slowly rose up so that he could see beyond the boulders they'd been using as a shield.

All was quiet. He stood a little more.

*Bang! Bang! Bang!*

More shots! But this time coming from the opposite direction of the original gunfire. From an assailant up by the house.

Wade dropped back down.

"Two shooters," Connor called out.

Two shooters had them pinned down. *Now what?*

The shooters could have followed them from

the Riverside Inn. At night it was difficult to tell if you were being tailed. Or perhaps they'd already been hidden in place, waiting for Charlotte to arrive so they could launch their attack.

Beside him, Charlotte began to shiver. Wade worried she would go into shock.

"Are we still getting out of here?" she asked.

"I'm not sure if it's wiser to stay or go."

"Why don't you ask me what I think?"

He turned to her and gently ran a fingertip along the side of her face. Her skin was unexpectedly cool and clammy. Not a good sign. "I'm not sure you could make a good judgment call right now."

She locked her gaze on his. "I'm starting to feel really weird. I think I need to get to the hospital."

"Okay. Let's start by seeing if you can walk." Wade took a firm hold on her good arm and helped her get to her feet while they both still remained crouched. Her balance was unsteady.

"You ready to cover us?" Wade asked Connor. He wasn't thrilled to be moving Charlotte under these circumstances, but he had little choice.

"Ready," Connor responded.

Wade offered a quick prayer. And then he called out, "Now!"

Staying as low as they could, Wade and Charlotte moved from behind the rocks and headed for the SUV.

Shots rang out from the direction of the house, the bullets zinging in Wade and Charlotte's direction.

Seconds later, Wade heard return fire from the direction of the gazebo. Meanwhile, he and Charlotte stayed focused on their goal of reaching the SUV. As soon as they reached it, they crouched down and used it as a barricade.

The shooting stopped, and Wade heard Connor shout, "Clear! We got the guy who was shooting from beside the house!"

Rising up slightly to look over the SUV's fender, he saw Connor and Danny with the hit man Paul Boutin. The hired assassin had his hands raised and Danny was cuffing him while Connor stood by, gun in hand but at the moment pointed safely toward the ground.

"They got him," Wade said to Charlotte.

She remained crouched down. In the ambient illumination from the vehicle headlights, he could see that her face was drawn in pain. She looked unsteady and weak and exhausted. Wade's heart fell to his feet.

He needed to get her out of here *now*, before the second shooter started firing again. Hopefully, that assailant had seen Boutin get captured and had decided to run off.

Wade reached to open the SUV door so Charlotte could climb inside.

*Bang!*

The hidden second attacker shot out a tire. Wade and Charlotte weren't going anywhere.

Danny and Connor rushed into the darkness of the forest to escape the gunfire, pulling their prisoner with them.

Frantic, Wade's mind raced to consider the possible options he and Charlotte had. Maybe they could get to Danny's truck and use that, but they'd have to go out into the open and cross a significant distance to get to it. With the gunman sounding much closer now, that wasn't a reasonable option. Same with attempting to make for the house. Dinah had said it was possible to get reception if you were in the right spot up there, but again, it was too far. He glanced at Charlotte. She looked like she was fading more quickly. At this point maybe the best option would be for her to stay in as safe a spot as possible where she could rest and regain her strength.

They couldn't remain by the SUV. It didn't provide enough protection. "I think we need to go back to where we were," he said to Charlotte. "It'll be safer."

She nodded.

He reached for her hand.

They began to move, and in that same instant he heard an engine start up.

Bright headlights flicked on. The shooter from the lake side of the property must have used the cover of the dark woods to sneak to a vehicle he'd hidden. The engine roared and Wade grasped Charlotte's hand tighter. She obviously moved as quickly as she could, but it wasn't very fast, and she was unsteady on her feet.

The vehicle shot toward them, throwing up gravel behind it, the driver intending to mow them down.

Wade briefly slowed and slid behind Charlotte before speeding up again, half pushing and half carrying her forward. He propelled them around the pile of rocks where they'd hidden before and they both dropped to the ground. He drew his gun, prepared to defend her with every bit of strength he had.

The fast-moving driver slammed on the brakes, but it was too late and the vehicle crashed into the rock pile, the front end becoming stuck. Wade watched as the door flew open and the driver leaped out, hood pulled down low, collar flipped up, face hidden. Gun drawn, he raced toward Wade and Charlotte.

Wade stayed put until just the right moment, leaping up as the driver reached the rock pile and slamming his fist in the man's jaw. The attacker's upper body twisted under the impact, and he flailed his arms as Wade targeted a second punch to the man's gut. He was sent sprawling to the ground, hard.

From the corner of his eye, Wade saw Charlotte slowly stand up. Seeing that she was all right for the moment, he turned his attention back to the unconscious man in front of him. Then he rolled him over so that the assailant was faceup. He pulled up the attacker's hood and yanked down the collar of the jacket so the man's face was visible.

"Ethan," Charlotte said, disbelief making her voice sound hollow. She turned to Hayley, who was now standing and facing in her direction. "That's Dinah's boyfriend."

# TWELVE

Charlotte's safety—her *survival*—was all Wade cared about.

Flashing red and blue lights splashed across the gazebo, the trees, and the people talking in clusters or moving about purposefully on the road in front of the elegantly rustic home that had been Dinah's emotional refuge over the last few days.

The scene was relatively calm now. Paramedics continued to treat Charlotte while patrol officers marked the locations of spent bullet casings and any other physical evidence they could find. Detective Romanov spoke with Dinah while the three Ryan siblings gave their points of view regarding all that had happened to the additional detectives who'd arrived with Romanov.

Paul Boutin had already been arrested and driven away.

Ethan Frey had been revived, had refused medical treatment and was seated in the back of a patrol car.

Exactly how Ethan figured into everything remained unclear. So far he'd refused to talk. At the moment, that was the least of Wade's concerns. There would be plenty of time later to put the crime-spree pieces together and to see justice served. Right now, his focus was on Charlotte.

She lay on a gurney in the back of an ambulance with Wade holding her hand. She'd asked if he could be with her, and the paramedic, who happened to be a friend of Wade's, agreed. While the medic monitored her vitals and assessed her wound—she'd been struck by one bullet, not two, as Wade had feared— Wade prayed and thanked God. Everyone had made it through the violent attack and Charlotte's vitals were already improving. It turned out that Charlotte's symptoms, which Wade had feared were signs of blood loss, were actually psychological shock from the terrifying events unfolding around her. Now that the situation was stable and she felt safe, she was recovering from that fairly quickly.

The medic kept up a steady stream of conversation with Charlotte. Probably to assess her mental clarity. So Wade resisted the urge to talk with her for the moment. Instead, he and Charlotte took turns squeezing each other's hands at random moments. And they exchanged glances. Small gestures that gave the bounty hunter the sense of connection with her that he craved.

Wade realized that somehow, at some point, he'd given his heart to Charlotte. Feeling his own physical pain at seeing her in an injured condition confirmed it. It was as if he'd taken his heart from his chest and offered it to her for safekeeping, trusting her to take care of it. His realization that she was truly a trustworthy person had made that possible. The feeling was both terrifying and strengthening at the same time.

In the course of this whole experience with Charlotte, despite all of the terrible events, something inside him had healed. Some part of him that had not wanted to take the emotional risk of falling in love had decided it was worth the chance. And right now he absolutely knew it was worth it. Even with the fear for Charlotte's physical condition that remained over him despite the medic's reassurances.

"It might be a good idea for you to get out of here for a few minutes," the medic said to

Wade after asking Charlotte a question and getting no response from her because she was focused on the bounty hunter. "She's stable for right now, but she will need to have the wound taken care of at the hospital. I'll give you a heads-up before we roll out of here."

"I'll be fine," Charlotte said in a slightly creaky voice.

"Of course." Wade gave her hand one more squeeze and then climbed out of the ambulance.

Connor was waiting for him. "How is she?"

"She'll need surgery to repair the injury and X-rays to make certain there are no bullet fragments remaining in the wound. Other than that, she's doing pretty well." Wade was surprised to find his voice choke up a little.

Connor, always the big brother, gave him a strong one-armed hug and slapped him on the back several times.

Wade glanced toward Danny and Hayley, who were still talking to the police. They had both gotten married recently. Wade had been happy for them. Maybe even a little envious, though he would never have admitted to it. Because he'd been convinced that the type of happiness they'd found simply wasn't available to him.

Now? Well, now he was thinking a whole lot differently.

While Connor went to talk to an officer who'd waved him over, Wade headed toward the spot where Detective Romanov was interviewing Dinah. He figured he might as well be useful and see what he could learn and report back to Charlotte. Even when he could force himself to direct his focus toward the criminal case that had played out over the last few days, his mind still wanted to drift back to thoughts of her. He'd never had that problem before.

"How is Charlotte?" Dinah called out as Wade approached. Her arms were crossed over her stomach and she was bent slightly forward. She sounded as nervous as she looked.

Romanov sat with Dinah at the picnic table. In the glow from the fairy lights he could see the detective's stormy facial expression. Having learned from experience, Wade was grateful not to be the object of Romanov's wrath.

It was not a crime for an adult to disappear for a few days without letting anyone know what they were doing. But given everything that had happened, all of it tied back to Dinah, and Wade could understand the detective's frustration. And probably suspicion, too. Maybe Dinah had played everyone. Maybe she had more of a hand in everything than it appeared and that she admitted to.

What if the attacks weren't actually over? Charlotte might continue to be in danger after she was released from the hospital. Maybe even more so, since everyone would have let their guard down.

Anxiety twisted Wade's gut. His mind raced toward thoughts of the embezzled money, of Charlotte being framed and of a hit man being hired to kill Charlotte. Who exactly stood to gain by Charlotte's death? Her twin?

"She's stable," Wade said, realizing he hadn't answered Dinah's question. Right now, he wasn't sure he wanted to tell her much of anything. "Has your boyfriend started talking yet?"

She winced.

Maybe it was a genuine display of emotion and Wade had framed his question a little too harshly. Maybe she truly loved Ethan and had been as shocked as anyone by his behavior. Or maybe she was just a good actress.

Surprisingly, Romanov didn't tell him to go away while she conducted her interview. Instead, she remained quiet and kept her gaze focused on Dinah.

Charlotte and Dinah were identical twins,

but now that he knew them, Wade didn't think they looked identical at all. Of course their facial features were similar, but the warmth and compassion and determined good humor he often saw on Charlotte's face was absent from her twin. What he saw in front of him was someone spoiled and self-absorbed and anxious. That was sad. And potentially dangerous.

Dinah shook her head and sighed. "I know it looks bad. I know you think I'm involved with whatever Ethan had planned. But the only thing I did was borrow money from a loan shark and not pay it back." She turned to Romanov. "Like I told you." She returned her gaze to Wade. "Ethan is—*was*—my boyfriend," she corrected. "But obviously I didn't know him as well as I thought I did." She looked down for a moment before lifting her gaze. "I admit I didn't want to be alone and Ethan was, well, he was right there in front of me and I figured he was a stable kind of guy and my parents would approve of him. They've employed him for years. I guess he fooled them, too." Unshed tears collected in the corners of her eyes. "I thought he cared about me, but maybe he was just after the money. I have no idea what his plan was or what he thought he was doing."

She shrugged and the tears began to fall. "I don't know what else to say."

Romanov turned to Wade. "Ethan hasn't said a word since he asked for a lawyer."

Dinah offered Wade a weak smile. "Tell Charlotte I wasn't involved with any of this. That I would never hurt her."

"Why don't you tell her yourself? It might make her feel better to hear it directly from you."

She shook her head. "I've burned a lot of bridges with her over the years. She has reason not to believe me. But she'll believe you."

"What makes you so sure of that?"

"Well, she trusted you with her life tonight, didn't she?"

Wade's paramedic buddy called him over to the ambulance. "We're getting ready to transport Charlotte to the hospital," he said as Wade approached. "Before you ask, I don't want you riding in the back with her in case something happens and I need room to move around quickly."

Wade nodded and swallowed thickly, sending up a quick prayer that nothing would happen and that Charlotte's condition would remain stable. Then he popped into the back to tell her he'd be following her to the hospital.

"I spoke with Dinah. She says she had nothing to do with the attempts on your life and she knew nothing about them."

Charlotte sighed and smiled widely. "I'm happy to hear that."

Wade just hoped it was really the truth.

He bent over to kiss her forehead. In response, she reached up her hand that wasn't tethered to an IV to brush her fingertips across his cheek.

The shared moment wrapped around him like a warm embrace.

As he backed away, Wade noticed how pale she looked. Fear wriggled to life in his gut. What if the paramedic's assessment was wrong? Anxious to get her to the hospital, he hurried to the SUV and fired up the engine.

The feeling of her touch remained with him, along with the hope it offered that they truly might have a future together. As the ambulance started up the narrow road, he followed behind it, unable to remember when he'd ever felt so happy and so worried both at the same time.

"I guess it's a good sign that they aren't rushing me into surgery…" Charlotte said, her voice trailing off at the end.

Wade couldn't help smiling at the loopy expression on her face. He reached over to brush a few strands of hair from her face.

She wasn't being rushed into surgery, but she was going soon. Meanwhile, now that the adrenaline spike from the attack had subsided, she'd become very aware of the pain from her wound, and the emergency room nurse had given her some medication for that.

They were in a small curtained-off area in the ER with an officer standing guard in the hallway just outside the emergency unit's doors.

After he'd driven away from the crime scene, Romanov had called to let him know she'd be sending an officer to keep an eye on Charlotte until they got everything figured out and they were certain she was no longer in danger.

"Your bail jumpers Brett Gamble and Paul Boutin are both in custody now," she'd added firmly. "That means your job is done. You are not a detective. I know you're concerned for Charlotte, but if you involve yourself in this case going forward, I will arrest you for interfering in a police investigation."

"Understood."

He'd found himself annoyed with his adoptive siblings when he realized that Connor,

Danny and Hayley had all jumped into the truck and followed him to the hospital. While he appreciated their support, he'd been hoping for a chance to talk with Charlotte alone. Maybe it was a bad idea, but he wanted to tell her how he felt as soon as possible.

He loved her. He knew it beyond a shadow of a doubt.

He wanted her to know that he realized how foolish he'd been in judging her before he got to know her. And in assuming that because she was a Halstead that she would be self-absorbed and spoiled and shallow. He'd been wrong, and he was surprisingly anxious to admit it.

Maybe it was selfish of him, but he'd wanted to hear that she loved him, too.

He'd managed to ditch his siblings in the lobby, since patients in this section of the hospital were only allowed one visitor at a time.

Now, gazing at the sweet, groggy, loopy expression on Charlotte's face, he realized that he needed to get a hold on his emotions and wait until a better time to tell her how he felt.

He almost laughed aloud as the thought crossed his mind. Having to admonish himself to get a grip on his emotions seemed funny. That was never a problem for him before.

But now? He didn't care if the whole ER

staff could hear his declarations and could see how he felt. And given the layout of the place, they probably could.

But Charlotte needed calm and quiet now. And as far as he was concerned, everything was about what she needed. Not what he wanted.

The nurse told him they were about to take her into surgery and asked him to leave.

"I've got to go. They're going to fix you up and I'll see you soon after that."

"Okay." She nodded, sending strands of hair back across her face again.

After giving her a kiss on the cheek and squeezing her hand, Wade left.

He walked past the officer and toward the waiting room, where there seemed to be a crowd of people and something going on.

It turned out the people were there in response to the reports about Charlotte. That she had been shot and her identical twin sister was headed to the Range River police station for questioning.

Over the next hour Wade sat in the waiting area with his bounty hunter family beside him. He watched as Charlotte's parents arrived and reporters and online bloggers photographed them and asked them questions.

Well-dressed people who claimed to be good friends of Charlotte's also showed up and they were quick to chat with anyone who would give them a few moments of attention and then post whatever they'd said online.

Wade couldn't help wondering where these *good friends* had been over the last few days when Charlotte could have used their support. Maybe they'd reached out and she'd rebuffed them because she'd been focused on staying alive and finding her sister. Or maybe they weren't interested in getting involved until they could see something in it for them.

She hadn't mentioned friends, much. Wade had gotten the impression that while she had friends on the coast where she'd attended college and built up a church family, she hadn't really had so many that she was truly close to back here in Range River. Maybe the old friends had moved on and she hadn't been back in town long enough to make new ones.

Her parents aside, most of the people who showed up seemed to be there to grab their own piece of online celebrity or catch a little of the glitter from someone else's fame.

He'd almost forgotten that Charlotte had a bit of fame in this town as one of the Halstead twins. And her fame actually went beyond

Range River, since the resort had plenty of celebrity visitors and the Halsteads had made a name for themselves in the world of people who could afford to spend money on outdoorsy, north Idaho luxury.

As time passed, and Wade watched and listened to the other people waiting while Charlotte was in surgery, the reality of the gulf between his world and Charlotte's began to sink in.

She was a beautiful young woman from a wealthy family with goals and a future far different from his world of chasing bad guys down dark alleys or tracking them through the woods.

Of course she'd been caught up in the emotion of things. She'd been scared, and as a result she'd understandably been attracted to a man who'd helped to protect her.

Maybe Wade had gotten carried away with emotion, too. Perhaps he'd gotten too caught up in thinking about what she'd given him and hadn't thought enough about whether she wanted anything back. Or whether the connection they'd felt could possibly last once their lives went back to normal.

Perhaps he couldn't have the woman he loved. Maybe he should simply appreciate the blessing that had come as a result of spending time alongside her. Past wounds had healed and he'd found himself able to open his heart much wider than he'd thought possible. He was able to risk believing in someone, something he hadn't been able to bring himself to do in a long time.

A doctor finally came out to speak to Charlotte's parents. Wade hurried over, anxious to know that she was okay. To their credit, Arthur and Kandace Halstead did not send him away.

He learned that everything went well. That Charlotte would be staying overnight, possibly two nights, and that her parents would be allowed to see her soon.

Wade glanced over at the bounty hunters on the sofa, looking exhausted. It was time for all of them to go home. Life had taught him that when harsh reality showed up, it was best to accept it as quickly as possible and move on. And the harsh reality here was that he and Charlotte lived in different worlds. There was simply no option for them to be together as a married couple. He'd been foolish to think otherwise.

"She's in good shape," he said, walking up to the Ryan siblings. "Her parents will want to be with her for as long as she's able to have visitors tonight."

The bounty hunters got to their feet and they all headed for the exit.

Wade would get back to chasing fugitives and let Charlotte return to her normal life, as well. But he'd also be paying close attention to her case, feeling uneasy until Ethan Frey finally told the police everything he knew and Wade was certain that Charlotte was safe.

Detective Romanov had a right to warn Wade from trying to solve the case. Her position was understandable, and he was under no illusions that he could single-handedly unravel the series of connected attacks, anyway.

But if Charlotte found herself scared or in danger, she *had* to know she could call Wade for help and he would come running.

# THIRTEEN

Four days later, Charlotte's rideshare driver pulled up to a storefront office in a modest shopping mall near downtown Range River. Charlotte's doctor had recommended she not drive for at least a couple of weeks.

"We're here," the driver said cheerfully.

Charlotte didn't move. At first she just gazed at the gold lettering on the smoked-glass window: Range River Bail Bonds.

Maybe this was a mistake. Maybe she should have called first. Maybe Wade wasn't even here.

"Oh, let me help you," the driver said before hopping out and opening Charlotte's door for her.

The driver must have noticed her sore arm, with the recent injury being made obvious by the bandaging and the slow, careful way Charlotte moved. Or maybe the friendly woman had seen the news reports in the aftermath of the attack at the lake house and she recognized Charlotte.

There had been plenty of dramatic headlines and malicious bits of gossip and seemingly unending rumors swirling about online for the last four days. Specific facts—other than the reality that the attacks had happened and Dinah had voluntarily vanished for a few days—had remained in short supply. But people hardly seemed to notice. They didn't actually care as much as they'd wanted to be entertained. By somebody else's tragedy. By seeing someone with the aura of money and glamour take a spectacular public fall.

Wade Fast Horse had seemed to care. From the beginning. And Charlotte was about to find out if her impression was true. Maybe, as had been the case for so much of her life, his *caring* was something he'd been paid for. Like the nannies who'd been around when Charlotte and Dinah were growing up. Or the *friendly* employees who'd been friendly because they'd wanted to keep their jobs.

Charlotte got out of the car even though she was a little bit afraid to. Because what if the care and concern Wade had shown wasn't real? What if those warm, light touches and the gentle kisses on her face were impulses of the moment and nothing more? Maybe the man had a brief romance with every damsel in distress that he helped.

*You don't really believe that about him.* The thought came in an instant.

No, she didn't. But she was afraid, nevertheless.

She'd let herself rely on him and trust him. Something she'd thought she would never be able to do after leaning on people—her parents especially—and having them refuse to help hold her up. Even for a short while. Because they had *important things to do*.

Money to make.

What if now that it wasn't part of his job, Wade didn't want to be someone she could lean on when she needed strength? And what if he wouldn't let her be there for him when he was in need of support? That was something she really, *really* wanted to do. Be the support that someone else needed. Have that kind of close relationship.

The driver shut the car door, gave a cheery wave and drove off.

Charlotte still hesitated.

She'd only managed to drum up the courage to come here because Detective Romanov had given her an excuse. In response to Charlotte's daily inquiry on the status of the ongoing investigation, Romanov had messaged her that there had been a break in the case. But she was in the middle of something, couldn't talk now, and Wade knew the details and he could fill her in.

Not that she was in such a hurry to hear the details. She was afraid of what she might learn about members of her family or other people she knew. Maybe someone close to her had planned it all.

Nevertheless, it provided an excuse for Charlotte to see the bounty hunter again. But she didn't know what to expect. He hadn't called her since she'd last seen him in the hospital emergency room. He hadn't texted her. He hadn't reached out at all.

She remembered seeing Wade in the emergency room, although the details of that were a little fuzzy. Her mother had mentioned that he and three other bounty hunters had stayed in the waiting room until her surgery was over. But after that, nothing.

Nerves fluttered in the pit of her stomach as she took a deep breath and headed for the door, determined to play it cool when she saw him.

She stepped inside, where she saw a reception area with a sofa and padded chairs in the front. Farther back, beyond a low wooden wall with a swinging door, were office desks and visitor chairs.

"Charlotte!" Hayley Ryan called out and smiled broadly.

Connor and Danny, who'd each been sitting at a desk and talking to one another, turned to look at her.

"Hi," Charlotte said, walking toward them as Hayley hurried forward to greet her. Connor and Danny likewise got up to say hello.

Wade remained at a desk, focused on a computer screen while typing in information with a phone pressed to his ear.

"He picked up a new case this morning," Hayley explained to Charlotte.

Charlotte figured her disappointment at his lack of attention toward her must have been written on her face. Well, that was embarrassing.

Hayley walked to Wade and gave his shoulder a light shove. He looked up at her and she gestured toward Charlotte.

As soon as he saw her, she heard him say, "Let me get back to you," and he disconnected the call.

He stood up and took a deep breath.

"I didn't mean to interrupt your work," Charlotte said awkwardly.

"It's all right. I can finish that call later." His gaze shifted from her face to her injured upper arm. "How are you?" His gaze traveled back to her face. "You look good."

"I'm doing well." It took an effort to settle her nerves so her voice wasn't shaky. Now that she was actually here with Wade, she had that feeling again. That sense of being shored up by his presence. Of feeling connected.

Of feeling stupidly giddy and giggly because there was just something about those dark eyes, brown skin with a warm, red undertone and raven hair that made her a little bit light-headed. Especially when he smiled that boyish smile. And he smiled at her right then.

Her response was a grin so wide that her cheeks started to hurt.

So much for playing it cool and not scaring him away.

Not that he was a man who was easily scared away from anything. She knew that from experience.

After they stood and stared at each other for a moment, she finally gathered her thoughts. "I'm glad you weren't out chasing down a bad guy. I guess I should have called first. But Detective Romanov said you could fill me in on the latest details in my case."

Wade raised an eyebrow slightly. "Romanov told you to come see me?"

Charlotte nodded.

He exchanged glances with the Ryans, who were lingering nearby, obviously eavesdropping.

Wade chewed his bottom lip for a moment. "It will take me a few minutes to explain everything. Do you want to grab a coffee from next door? Maybe walk across the street to the park?" He glanced at her arm. "That is, if you feel up to it."

"Sure," Charlotte answered, feeling relieved and keyed up at the same time. "I'd love some coffee. Fresh air is always good."

After a quick round of goodbyes, which included a moment when Danny Ryan smiled widely at his best friend and Wade gave him a menacing look in return, they stepped outside.

Wade held the door for Charlotte as she exited the coffee shop carrying a huge espresso drink, and then he followed her out. "You sure that much caffeine is good for you?" he asked with a nod toward the cup in her hand.

"Oh, I *need* this. Besides, compared to all

the surges in adrenaline I've had over the last week as people tried to kill me, the little boost from this drink is nothing."

Wade's laugh in response was partly from her joke and partly from nervous energy. Being away from Charlotte the last four days had been miserable. Instead of getting over her, he'd missed her *more*. And now here she was. Her face more beautiful than he'd remembered. Her smile making him feel like *he* was the one who needed to cut back on caffeine. The sound of her voice soothing and invigorating at the same time.

"How are things with your family?" he asked as they crossed the street. The sky was clear, the sunlight shining down was warm, and the mixture of evergreens and deciduous trees with newly sprouting leaves offered a nice, lacy mixture of light and shadow in the park.

"Things around the resort have been a little tense." Charlotte sat on the top of a picnic table, her feet on the bench seat. Wade stood across from her, wanting to drink in the sight of her. To finally see her fairly relaxed and happy rather than anxious and fearful. Whatever tension she felt at the resort wasn't visible on her face right now.

"Everyone is on pins and needles waiting for the full story to come out," she continued. "The resort tech team finally confirmed that I didn't attempt to embezzle any money. The transactions made to move resort payroll funds into my personal account were done on a work laptop assigned to me. Security video inside the management offices showed Ethan taking my laptop into his office during the time frame when the transactions were made. It's obvious he was trying to set me up and I can only hope that he'll confess to it at some point. Meanwhile, all the money is back where it belongs." She sighed. "My parents have been supportive of Dinah and me after all we've been through, but at the same time, that support is measured." She shrugged. "What else is new? It's always been that way. And Dinah is researching rehab and counseling facilities. Maybe she'll find something that appeals to her and give it a sincere try."

Wade nodded. "I hope so."

"Me, too." She fixed her gaze on him. "I don't know how you deal with potentially life-or-death situations for a living. But I know this has taught me a lot. The most important thing I have is my faith. And I'm leaning into that more than ever now."

"That's the way I get through the dangers and snares of life, too."

She sat up a little straighter. "So, I haven't pressed you to hurry up and tell me the details you've learned about the case because I'm not sure I want to know them." She shrugged. "I guess I'm afraid to learn that Dinah was more criminally involved than she admitted."

"That's not the case. Thanks to a combination of Detective Romanov's excellent interrogation skills and plea bargain offers from the prosecutor, Ethan finally started talking. Gamble and Boutin did, as well. Turns out there were a couple of different things going on at once."

Wade took a deep breath and blew it out. "Dinah was telling the truth. She wasn't doing a good job of managing the coffee shop. She borrowed money from Gamble and stopped making payments. He hired Murphy to grab her and bring her to him so he could scare her into figuring out a way to pay him his money."

"That's when Murphy mistakenly kidnapped me."

"Right. Gamble was just starting out in the loan-sharking business, and he knew if people got away with not paying him back, he was sunk. In his mind, if he didn't get paid, he had to seriously harm or kill someone to maintain a reputation that would keep him in business.

That's why he and Murphy were so recklessly willing to shoot at you.

"Once Gamble realized they'd grabbed the wrong person, he figured the police would be keeping a close eye on Dinah. Rather than making a second attempt to grab her, he planned to kidnap you and ransom you back to your parents. That's why they started targeting you."

"Did they hire the hit man?"

"No. Ethan hired him."

Charlotte shook her head. "Why? He seemed so enamored of Dinah. He'd worked for the family for so long. My parents thought so much of him."

"All of that helps to explain why. He hoped to, well, own the resort one day. He figured he'd marry Dinah and eventually inherit half the value of it through her when your parents died. But then he realized Dinah was going off the rails. He knew about her poor management of the coffee shop. Knew she was having substance abuse issues. He was afraid he would become her husband only for your parents to disinherit her and then he would never have his dream come true. Apparently he tried to switch his affections to you and it failed."

"Me?" Charlotte's voice nearly squeaked. "If he tried to make the moves on me, I never even noticed." She shook her head. "I've never been interested in Ethan. Not my type, at all."

"Well, maybe he was insulted by that and it played into what followed. Dinah disappeared, and apparently he honestly knew nothing about that. He thought she might not be found alive and he got the idea that if both Halstead twins were dead, your grieving parents might look to him as the son they never had and he might actually inherit the resort after all. So he hired the hit man to kill you and figured if Dinah reappeared he'd either convince her to marry him since she would be sure to inherit, being the only surviving child, or if she wouldn't marry him, he'd just wait a bit and have her killed, too."

There was nothing else to add, so Wade just waited quietly.

"I've thought about walking away from it all," Charlotte finally said in a quiet but strong voice. "I've prayed about it. A lot. I get the feeling that I should keep working at the resort and push my parents to use some of the money to the benefit of other people."

"Does that mean you're still planning to go to California for that internship program in San Diego?" Wade asked. *Please say no.* It was a selfish thought, but he'd had a lifetime of remembering the cold fact that people often left, said they'd return, but never did.

She nodded. "Yeah, I'm going." She gave him a shy smile. "But I'll be coming back."

So this was probably the moment he needed to speak up. "I wish you would stay."

Her blue eyes appeared to pick up a bit of a sparkle at that. "Do you?" she asked in a teasing tone. "Why?"

Feeling emboldened, Wade moved a little closer. "Because I got used to seeing you every day and I liked it." He reached out to rub a finger along the line of her jaw and she leaned into it. Maybe the fears that had crept into his mind in the hospital waiting room about the two of them not being able to build a life together had been baseless. Perhaps he hadn't given her enough credit. Or perhaps he hadn't given the both of them enough credit. Each had proved that they could grow and change and they could face difficult situations. Like coming from different backgrounds and different social worlds.

He moved even closer toward her, while sliding his fingertips down the delicate skin until they were under her chin. "I think you might have gotten used to being around me, too." He smiled. "You didn't have to make the trip here to the office to ask me about your case. You could have called."

"I didn't know if what we'd shared was just a working relationship. I thought maybe with your fugitives captured, everything between us would be over. I wanted to see you for myself and find out." She looked flustered and her cheeks turned a pretty shade of pink.

Wade closed the gap between them, brushing his lips across her cheeks and the side of her neck and then finally kissing her until he felt her sigh and relax in his arms. He felt the seriousness of the trust she was placing in him, and he meant to honor it. "So you think there's room for a bounty hunter in your life?"

"Absolutely, yes." She looked at him with eyes filled with love and a hint of mischief. "I can't wait to spend time with you when there isn't someone trying to kill or kidnap me."

He reached for her hands and gave each of them a kiss. "Charlotte Halstead, you have been nothing but trouble since the moment I met you." He leaned in to press another kiss to her lips. "It's a good thing I love trouble."

In that moment, he knew he loved her enough to accept the risk of her leaving town for several months. During that time, he would hope and pray that she would come back.

# EPILOGUE

*One year later*

"It's okay, Mom. Everything doesn't have to be perfect." Wade looked into the mirror where his gaze connected with his mother, who was standing behind him.

His eyes started to sting a little, and he looked away. The happiness in his heart was so strong and sharp that it almost hurt.

Maribel resumed straightening his suit collar, tugging the back of his coat to make sure it hung correctly and brushing his shoulders. As if dust could have landed there in the three or four minutes since she'd last brushed them.

"Let me do this," Maribel said with a slight sniff. As if she were holding back tears. "I want my big bad bounty hunter son to look good on his wedding day."

*Wedding day.*

Wade Fast Horse was about to get married and he couldn't quite believe it.

"Mom, do you think you'll ever get married again?" He'd asked her that more times than he could count since he was young, starting when his dad had finally initiated the divorce. Her response had always been a laugh, maybe a head shake and a firm answer along the lines of *Not a chance*.

This time, she simply shrugged.

Wade read that as a *maybe*.

"I guess you never know," she added.

Wade's already overwhelmed heart felt like it could burst. The love he felt for Charlotte just kept growing. His bride-to-be had given him courage enough to dare to hope again, and seeing that must have inspired his mom.

What women he had in his life. What a blessed man he was.

Shortly after Wade and Charlotte had become a couple, Charlotte had left for California.

And then she'd come back. Just like she'd promised.

Wade had been anxious while she was gone. Of course, they had talked on the phone and texted. Still, he'd been irritable. So moody that he could hardly stand himself during the long days when he wondered what she was doing.

But at the same time he had prayed, had healed and had remembered that the true source of his strength would never leave him nor forsake him. Based on that promise from the Lord, he could take the risk of loving Charlotte.

And, man, was he ever glad he had.

"Hey, do you think you look pretty enough yet?" Danny Ryan knocked lightly on the partially open door and walked in.

"Dude, I will always be prettier than you," Wade joked with his best man. "Try not to be jealous."

They were in the bedroom Wade typically used at the Riverside Inn. The wedding ceremony would be taking place outside, under a white pavilion decorated with flowers and with the river—made sparkly by the bright midday sun—flowing along in the background.

Charlotte had said she wanted a ceremony that was simple and heartfelt. Wade was determined that she would get what she wanted, and Connor had been more than happy to help out by offering the use of the grounds at the inn.

There was another light knock on the door. "Are you dressed?" Hayley called out.

"You can come in," Maribel answered.

Hayley walked into the room with Connor right behind her. "It's time," she said.

Surrounded by his mom and the family that was truly as much his family as the one he had been born into, Wade headed out of the room and downstairs.

A couple of Connor's dogs joined them, both animals wagging their tails and trotting happily as if they understood that this was a very special occasion.

Outside, Wade stopped for a moment to take in the beautiful view in front of him. The flowers and decorations. Nature, stunningly displayed by the view of the river and the forest and mountains in the distance. Friends and family here to help Charlotte and him celebrate their marriage.

He and Danny took their positions in front of the assembled guests, exchanging nods with the pastor.

The music started up, and moments later, Charlotte appeared. She wore a lacy ivory-colored dress with a veil and carried a bouquet of pink and yellow roses.

Her beauty as she approached him took his breath away.

For so long, he wouldn't have even been able to imagine a moment like this.

God truly was the God of the impossible.

And Wade was so very grateful.

\* \* \*

The kiss Wade gave Charlotte to mark the end of the ceremony was a little more enthusiastic than she'd anticipated.

Not that she was complaining.

But it was a good thing her brand-new husband was strong enough to hold her up. Because her knees went weak. And for a moment, it felt like every bone in her body had melted.

Of course, their guests laughed and hooted and hollered. The Ryans, most notably. Wade's family. Now *her* family, too.

And this would be her new home. Connor had invited Charlotte and Wade to move in and reside there. Apparently the self-possessed owner of Range River Bail Bonds had decided he liked having a little company on a regular basis. Lots of things were changing, and that was good.

As she and Wade started back down the aisle together, she glanced over at her parents. They looked slightly more relaxed than normal. That was something. And Dinah was looking well, too. She had shown an interest in faith and Charlotte was encouraged by that.

The happy couple made a beeline for the cake, where they served each other first bites, and then got busy serving guests. Because they felt like they had already been given so much. They worked as a team, chatting with guests as they served the cake and doing their best to make everyone feel valued and included.

During their many, many long talks while they were getting to know each other better, Charlotte and Wade had discovered that those were two feelings they'd both always wanted. Feeling valued and included. Now that they had each other, as a married couple they wanted to extend those feelings, and true support, to others.

Faith and love could do so much. They'd both learned that. And they were looking forward to spending the rest of their lives together, sharing that lesson with others.

\* \* \* \* \*

*If you enjoyed this*
*Range River Bounty Hunters story*
*by Jenna Night, pick up these previous*
*books in the series:*

Abduction in the Dark
Fugitive Ambush

*Available now from Love Inspired Suspense!*

Dear Reader,

Thank you for coming along on yet another race to capture the bad guys!

Family stories are interesting to me because no family is perfect, no matter how things look from the outside. Good thing we don't have to be perfect to be lovable.

I'm gearing up to write the story of the final member of the Ryan family, the owner and founder of Range River Bail Bonds, Connor Ryan. This man has some secrets that are about to be exposed. I hope he's ready!

I invite you to visit my website, jennanight. com. You can also keep up with me on my Jenna Night Facebook page or get alerts about upcoming books by following me on Book-Bub. My email address is Jenna@JennaNight. com. I'd love to hear from you.

*Jenna Night*

# Get 4 FREE REWARDS!

**We'll send you 2 FREE Books plus 2 FREE Mystery Gifts.**

**FREE** Value Over **$20**

Both the **Love Inspired®** and **Love Inspired® Suspense** series feature compelling novels filled with inspirational romance, faith, forgiveness and hope.

# Get 4 FREE REWARDS!

**We'll send you 2 FREE Books plus 2 FREE Mystery Gifts.**

FREE
Value Over
$20

Both the **Harlequin® Special Edition** and **Harlequin® Heartwarming™** series feature compelling novels filled with stories of love and strength where the bonds of friendship, family and community unite.

**YES!** Please send me 2 FREE novels from the Harlequin Special Edition or Harlequin Heartwarming series and my 2 FREE gifts (gifts are worth about $10 retail). After receiving them, if I don't wish to receive any more books, I can return the shipping statement marked "cancel." If I don't cancel, I will receive 6 brand-new Harlequin Special Edition books every month and be billed just $5.49 each in the U.S. or $6.24 each in Canada, a savings of at least 12% off the cover price, or 4 brand-new Harlequin Heartwarming Larger-Print books every month and be billed just $6.24 each in the U.S. or $6.74 each in Canada, a savings of at least 19% off the cover price. It's quite a bargain! Shipping and handling is just 50¢ per book in the U.S. and $1.25 per book in Canada.* I understand that accepting the 2 free books and gifts places me under no obligation to buy anything. I can always return a shipment and cancel at any time by calling the number below. The free books and gifts are mine to keep no matter what I decide.

Choose one: ☐ **Harlequin Special Edition**
(235/335 HDN GRJV)
☐ **Harlequin Heartwarming Larger-Print**
(161/361 HDN GRJV)

Name (please print)

Address                                                                                          Apt. #

City                                        State/Province                                Zip/Postal Code

**Email:** Please check this box ☐ if you would like to receive newsletters and promotional emails from Harlequin Enterprises ULC and its affiliates. You can unsubscribe anytime.

Mail to the **Harlequin Reader Service:**
**IN U.S.A.:** P.O. Box 1341, Buffalo, NY 14240-8531
**IN CANADA:** P.O. Box 603, Fort Erie, Ontario L2A 5X3

Want to try 2 free books from another series! Call 1-800-873-8635 or visit www.ReaderService.com.

# THE 2022 LOVE INSPIRED CHRISTMAS COLLECTION

## Buy 3 and get 1 FREE!

May all that is beautiful, meaningful and brings you joy be yours this holiday season...including this fun-filled collection featuring 24 Christmas stories. From tender holiday romances to Christmas Eve suspense, this collection has it all.

## William Graham Summer

## THE MORES *

*Folkways is almost universally acknowledged to be one of the few top-drawer classics in the American sociological tradition. Its author, William Graham Sumner, was a professor in the Divinity School at Yale. His "research" consisted of a collection of reports by travelers and writers of the customs of far away peoples. He formulated, however, a considerable amount of theory concerning these collections of data. He also formulated some of the basic concepts which are still central in sociological thinking, among them the mores. The following excerpts are part of the development of his ideas and contain some of his theory about the mores.*

*66. More exact definition of the mores.* We may now formulate a more complete definition of the mores. They are the ways of doing things which are current in a society to satisfy human needs and desires, together with the faiths, notions, codes, and standards of well living which inhere in those ways, having a genetic connection with them. By virtue of the latter element the mores are traits in the specific character (ethos) of a society or a period. They pervade and control the ways of thinking in all the exigencies of life, returning from the world of abstractions to the world of action, to give guidance and to win revivification. "The mores are, before any beginning of reflection, the regulators of the political, social, and religious behavior of the individual. Conscious reflection is the worst enemy of the mores, because mores begin unconsciously and pursue unconscious pur-

* William Graham Sumner, *Folkways* (Boston, Ginn & Co., 1904), paragraphs 66, 68, 80 and 83. Used by permission.

54

sistent and clearcut. Nothing could be further from the truth. Actually all cultures, including our own, are fraught with innumerable ambiguities, inconsistencies, and contradictions. Part of this built-in chaos for Americans is due to what is called "cultural pluralism," that is, the people in our society, having come from a variety of cultures, still retain a considerable amount of the imported culture and hence there is a plural, rather than a single, set of cultural norms. But cultural inconsistencies and contradictions are also indigenous to each of the separate sub-cultures. Two papers are addressed to this problem, the first, "Our Schizoid Culture" by Read Bain, deals with the question in a general way (Page 69). The second paper, by Robert S. Lynd (page 78), narrows the focus somewhat and concentrates chiefly on ideological elements to show that the themes by which we live, which comprise the "American Creed," form by no means a coherent unity.

One of the recent emphases in the study of human behavior has been the emergence of a specialization called the study of "national character." A number of works, such as Ruth Benedict's *The Chrysanthemum and the Sword* [2] and Geoffrey Gorer's *The American People*,[3] are widely known. A great deal of work of a technical and precise nature has gone into this field of endeavor. The objective, however, has been essentially the same, namely to try to discover the central ideologies and deeper "character structures" of the "typical" personality in a given society (or culture). Obviously this involves a high level of generality and it is precisely at this point that some of the studies have proved less than convincing. The resultant picture is so generalized that to many people in the society which is being described, the emergent portrait does not seem quite real. Nor does it often make much difference if the portrait is fashioned from the inside, that is, by someone indigenous to the culture, or by an outsider, that is, a visiting social

[2] (Boston, Houghton-Mifflin & Co., 1946.)
[3] (New York, W. W. Norton and Company, Inc., 1948.)

scientist who may have the advantage of less ethno-centrism but also has less experience. The excerpt from Don Martindale on American character (page 82), from the preface to his book *American Social Structure*, presents a portrait of Americans with which probably some Americans won't agree. But the perceptions of the people recorded therein, one a poet and the other a social scientist, can hardly be dismissed as not at least worthy of thoughtful consideration. Some of these "slants" on American society are sure to provide inter-est, even if accepted with reservations.

All culture is not ideological. Or, as some theorists prefer to put it, some of the ideology becomes embodied in material things, hence the familiar phrase, "material culture." Particularly in contemporary Western society there is a pervasive phenomenon which has become so much a part and parcel of life that it is taken for granted —technology. The late William F. Ogburn, a lifelong student of technology and social change, discusses (page 88) how persons in different positions in society "come at" technology. The meanings which it has not only vary but they vary with respect to the *function* of technology to persons in various positions.

Perhaps the most important aspect of culture, though not discussed directly in any of the readings in this section, is treated in a number of others (for ex-ample, pages 229, 242, 248, 274, 284, 288, and 300), namely the cardinal and ever baffling fact of *cultural change*. Some theorists have gone so far as to define culture as "a set of problem solving devices" for the human. Putting the matter in this way, the inevitability of change is better understood. So often, change is re-garded as a defeat for the time-honored way of doing or thinking. This leads to the unfortunate consequent view that the normal condition of human existence is constancy. To the tradition-minded this point of view may be comfortable psychologically and may serve cer-tain practical ends in politics or economics or morality, but the proponents of traditional orientation always fight a losing battle. They win some skirmishes now an[d] to be sure, and the tactics for delaying action are times quite ingenious, but, as the cliche goes, [ ] has for long held back the hands on the clock o[ ]

So here we have a curious paradox—the inevi[ ] of change and the widespread prejudice against i[ ] is this so? Why do human beings spend so muc[ ] and effort and suffer so much heartache trying[ ] the impossible? One can identify many reasons [a ] gether they may answer our question. Perhaps t[ ] something inescapable about the psychology of [ ] habit. Then, of course, there is vested interest—fo[ ] there seems to be more to gain by retaining t[ ] rather than embracing the new. There is also an i[ ] conflict between the nature of culture and the [ ] of society. The latter requires orderliness in ord[ ] it exist. In fact, social structure (or society its[ ] often defined, as Robin Williams, Jr.[4] does, as [ ] current and therefore predictable uniformities in [ ] behavior. Now, if culture is a set of problem-[ ] devices and man is an intelligent animal, he will p[ ] ably devise new, not necessarily better, ways of [ ] problems, and he will also find new problems [ ] solved. Thus, built into his life is an inescapable[ ] between the practical requirements of the social [ ] which dictates stability and continuity and predict[ ] and active intelligence which is the perpetual [ ] of innovation in thought and deed. Man can t[ ] no automaton, despite the efforts of some to ma[ ] so, and the "social order," about which some wri[ ] dripping sentimentality, can at best be only a [ ] and partial measure of man's condition.

[4] *American Society* (New York, Alfred A. Knopf, Inc.

poses, which are recognized by reflection often only after long and circuitous processes, and because their expediency often depends on the assumption that they will have general acceptance and currency, uninterfered with by reflection." [1] "The mores are usage in any group, in so far as it, on the one hand, is not the expression or fulfillment of an absolute natural necessity and, on the other hand, is independent of the arbitrary will of the individual, and is generally accepted as good and proper, appropriate and worthy." [2]

68. *The ritual of the mores.* The mores are social ritual in which we all participate unconsciously. The current habits as to hours of labor, meal hours, family life, the social intercourse of the sexes, propriety, amusements, travel, holidays, education, the use of periodicals and libraries, and innumerable other details of life fall under this ritual. Each does as everybody does. For the great mass of mankind as to all things, and for all of us for a great many things, the rule to do as all do suffices. We are led by suggestion and association to believe that there must be wisdom and utility in what all do. The great mass of the folkways give us discipline and the support of routine and habit. If we had to form judgments as to all these cases before we could act in them, and were forced always to act rationally, the burden would be unendurable. Beneficent use and wont save us this trouble.

80. *The mores have the authority of facts.* The mores come down to us from the past. Each individual is born into them as he is born into the atmosphere, and he does not reflect on them, or criticise them any more than a baby analyzes the atmosphere before he begins to breathe it. Each one is subjected to the influence of the mores, and formed by them, before he is capable of reasoning about them. It may be objected that nowadays, at least, we criticise all traditions, and accept none just because they are handed down to us. If we take up cases of things which are still entirely or almost entirely in the mores, we shall see that this is not so. There are sects of free-lovers amongst us who want to discuss pair marriage. They are not

[1] v. Hartman, *Phänom. des Sittl, Bewusstseins,* 73.
[2] Lazarus in *Ztsft. für Völkerpsy.,* I., 439.

simply people of evil life. They invite us to discuss rationally our inherited customs and ideas as to marriage, which, they say, are by no means so excellent and elevated as we believe. They have never won any serious attention. Some others want to argue in favor of polygamy on grounds of expediency. They fail to obtain a hearing. Others want to discuss property. In spite of some literary activity on their part, no discussion of property, bequest, and inheritance has ever been opened. Property and marriage are in the mores. Nothing can ever change them but the unconscious and imperceptible movement of the mores. Religion was originally a matter of the mores. It became a societal institution and a function of the state. It has now to a great extent been put back into the mores. Since laws with penalties to enforce religious creeds or practices have gone out of use any one may think and act as he pleases about religion. Therefore it is not now "good form" to attack religion. Infidel publications are now tabooed by the mores, and are more effectually repressed than ever before. They produce no controversy. Democracy is in our American mores. It is a product of our physical and economic conditions. It is impossible to discuss or criticise it. It is glorified for popularity, and is a subject of dithyrambic rhetoric. No one treats it with complete candor and sincerity. No one dares to analyze it as he would aristocracy or autocracy. He would get no hearing and would only incur abuse. The thing to be noticed in all these cases is that the masses oppose a deaf ear to every argument against the mores. It is only in so far as things have been transferred from the mores into laws and positive institutions that there is discussion about them or rationalizing upon them. The mores contain the norm by which, if we should discuss the mores, we should have to judge the mores. We learn the mores as unconsciously as we learn to walk and eat and breathe. The masses never learn how we walk, and eat, and breathe, and they never know any reason why the mores are what they are. The justification of them is that when we wake to consciousness of life we find them facts which already hold us in the bonds of tradition, custom, and habit. The mores contain embodied in them notions, doctrines, and maxims, but they are facts. They are in the present tense. They have nothing to do with what ought to be, will be, may be, or once was, if it is not now.

83. *Inertia and rigidity of the mores.* We see that we must conceive of the mores as a vast system of usages, covering the whole of life, and serving all its interests; also containing in themselves their own justification by tradition and use and wont, and approved by mystic sanctions until, by rational reflection, they develop their own philosophical and ethical generalizations, which are elevated into "principles" of truth and right. They coerce and restrict the newborn generation. They do not stimulate to thought, but the contrary. The thinking is already done and is embodied in the mores. They never contain any provision for their own amendment. They are not questions, but answers, to the problem of life. They present themselves as final and unchangeable, because they present answers which are offered as "the truth." No world philosophy, until the modern scientific world philosophy, and that only within a generation or two, has ever presented itself as perhaps transitory, certainly incomplete, and liable to be set aside to-morrow by more knowledge. No popular world philosophy or life policy ever can present itself in that light. It would cost too great a mental strain. All the groups whose mores we consider far inferior to our own are quite as well satisfied with theirs as we are with ours. The goodness or badness of mores consists entirely in their adjustment to the life conditions and the interests of the time and place. Therefore it is a sign of ease and welfare when no thought is given to the mores, but all cooperate in them instinctively. The nations of southeastern Asia show us the persistency of the mores, when the element of stability and rigidity in them becomes predominant. Ghost fear and ancestor worship tend to establish the persistency of the mores by dogmatic authority, strict taboo, and weighty sanctions. The mores then lose their naturalness and vitality. They are stereotyped. They lose all relation to expediency. They become an end in themselves. They are imposed by imperative authority without regard to interests or conditions (caste, child marriage, widows). When any society falls under the dominion of this disease in the mores

it must disintegrate before it can live again. In that diseased state of the mores all learning consists in committing to memory the words of the sages of the past who established the formulae of the mores. Such words are "sacred writings," a sentence of which is a rule of conduct to be obeyed quite independently of present interests, or of any rational considerations.

*John Gillin*

# CULTURE IS LEARNED *

*John Gillin is a well-known anthropologist whose career has been devoted not only to theoretical work but to extensive field work and also to the application of behavior science materials to such widely varied practical matters as the education of medical students and advice to governments on anthropological matters. His book,* The Ways of Men, *from which this short excerpt is taken, is a very readable, student-oriented presentation of many ideas in cultural anthropology.*

. . . We sometimes have difficulty in convincing ourselves that the customs which we practise are actually acquired or learned. They seem so much a part of our nature that we are sometimes inclined to regard them as inherited, in the biological sense.

There are three types of data which convince us that the customs of mankind are *not* inherited biologically, either by the species or by any subgroup within it. *First,* we have the investigations on new-born infants, already mentioned, which indicate the extreme paucity of inborn goal-directed activity patterns of any type. This material still leaves open a question, however. Someone may say, "O.K., human babies don't come into the world already equipped with adaptive behavior. But, how do you know that they may not develop inherited tendencies as they mature? Possibly the patterns carried in the germ plasm don't emerge until certain stages of development are reached, just as age-linked dark hair often does not appear until the child is half-grown." At this point we bring in our *second type*

* From John Gillin *The Ways of Men* (New York, Appleton-Century-Crofts, 1948), pp. 190-191. (Italics by the editors.) Used by permission.

*of evidence,* consisting of various carefully controlled studies of identical twins who have been reared apart from each other and have grown up developing different custom patterns. In these cases the individuals were identical in inheritance and differed only in the type of experience and training accorded them. If they grew up to exhibit different culture patterns we can hardly assign the culture to heredity.

*Finally,* and perhaps most convincing for anthropological purposes, we have the evidence of the variability of human culture itself. We have already seen that all qualified experts agree that the species is one, biologically speaking. Yet the cultures practised by diverse groups within the species vary enormously among themselves. Likewise there is no uniformity or regularity in the types of culture to be found within a single race or other subgroup of the species. Many a full-blood Negro is culturally North American, whereas genetically he is practically identical with his relatives still practising cannibalism in West Africa. World War II convinced most Americans that soldiers of Japanese ancestry when brought up as Americans, can be culturally as American as anyone else, and entirely different from their and our [then] enemies under the influence of Tokyo. When we are acquainted with the great variety of cultures it is impossible to believe that culture is carried in the germ plasm. There are only two other alternatives: either it descends upon people in some mysterious, unknown fashion, or it is learned. The first hypothesis has no data to support it, while the second seems to fit the facts.

## Peggy B. Harroff

# ON LANGUAGE

*There are many excellent books on linguistics, several of which are cited in the footnotes to this reading. In the ordinary course of training, students of sociology receive little if any formal training in this highly important area. Most sociology textbooks treat the subject inadequately, if at all. Accordingly, it was decided to present a synopsis of several works on language. This reading has been prepared by the junior editor of this book on the assumption that this is the first exposure of students to the implications of language for social organization and the socialization process.*

## I

Of all Promethean gifts we must surely count among the most important the "gift of tongues." That Greek demi-god who brought culture to mankind, fire from the heavens, and all manner of arts that men might travel on "the road of dark and riddling knowledge" provides us with the "origins" of culture. But this is only in the world of *mythology;* in the world of *science* origins are lost in antiquity and have eluded scholars who have searched in vain for the beginnings of culture, language, and human society.

If the search has been in vain, the efforts have not. In seeking to satisfy his curiosity about his own beginnings, man has learned much about the conditions necessary for the attainment of culture and the inter-relationships of language, culture, and personality.

Language has been called "the storehouse of culture" and

as a prerequisite to the development and transmission of culture its study and some understanding of its structures and workings are essential.

The problem of the origin of human language is inseparable from that of the origin of human society. Neither could exist without the other. Certain obvious conditions are necessary for the development of language. There must be continued relationships of individuals having enough common experiences and having the necessary biological factors—adequate vocal and mental capacity—to devise a means of communicating. These conditions obtain, however, for species other than man, and if we are to use the term language to refer to the strictly human phenomenon then some distinctions must be made.

## II

Weston LaBarre's discussion of language in *The Human Animal* [1] gives considerable detail concerning the contrasting as well as the shared features of the communicative systems of man and some of his near relatives. The primitive communication systems of some of the higher primates, the gibbon for example, are quite different from the semantic systems of man. The calls of the gibbon "are at best vague 'phatic' communications, which convey no detailed information about the structure of the universe; they are actually no more than unclassified intelligence concerning the individual ape's physiological or emotional state. All that is conveyed, quite literally, is a 'tone of voice'." [2]

In contrast to this, man's communication is mostly by means of abstract *symbols,* the semantics of which enable him to express himself in a wide range of subjects, emotions, and degrees of precision. "Human speech, unlike the cry of an animal, does not occur as a mere element in a larger response. Only the human animal can *communicate abstract ideas and converse about conditions that are contrary to fact.*" [3]

[1] Weston LaBarre, *The Human Animal* (Chicago, The University of Chicago Press, 1954), chapters 10 and 11.

[2] LaBarre, *Ibid.,* p. 165.

[3] Clyde Kluckhohn, *Mirror for Man* (New York, McGraw-Hill Book Co., 1949), p. 145. (Italics by the editors.)

While the gibbon has some fourteen calls and can warn his band of immediate danger, man can communicate his anticipation of a danger not yet encountered, can discuss objects and situations as yet unmet, and speculate on the future or reminisce about the past. "Man is apparently almost unique in being able to talk about things that are remote in space and time (or both) from where the talking goes on. This feature—'displacement'—seems to be definitely lacking in the vocal signaling of man's closest relatives . . ." [4]

This is not meant to imply that man, in the process of evolving semantic speech, has completely left behind the "phatic" communications of sub-humans. Sighs and grunts, and physical attitudes—a way of striding into a room, tossing the head, or clenching the fist—can communicate much. In more subtle and significant ways, man still depends upon phatic communication. In family life, LaBarre refers to the "acute phatic prescience" of a mother when her infant child is concerned and to the phatic closeness of lovers which "commonly reaches fantastic extremes of precision." [5] But it is safe to assume that man would not have travelled far along that "road of dark and riddling knowledge" to culture, if this type of communication had been the *sole* means of building and transmitting ideas and ways of life.

Nor should the specificity of human speech as compared to the communications of sub-humans be overdrawn. The pitfalls of symbolism are such that even the most cautious statements may be met with misunderstanding and frustrating uncertainty. The shared meanings of symbols are always imperfect and our communications suffer to the degree that the message *intended* differs from the message *received*. Edward Sapir, one of the "great men" in American linguistics, points out that "communication, which is the very object of speech, is successfully effected only when the hearer's auditory perceptions are translated into the appropriate and intended flow of imagery or thought or both combined . . ." [6]

[4] Charles F. Hockett, "The Origin of Speech," *Scientific American*, Vol. 203, No. 3 (Sept., 1960), p. 90.

[5] LaBarre, *op. cit.*, p. 167.

[6] Edward Sapir, *Language: An Introduction to the Study of Speech* (New York, Harcourt, Brace & Co., 1921), p. 17.

## III

There is nothing simple about meeting this condition for effective communication. Even in the most simplified situation of one speaker and one listener there is the choice of words, delivery of the words with intended inflection, and knowledge of the meanings of the words—denotative and connotative. On the other hand, the words must be *received* attentively, perceptively, and with like knowledge of the meanings—denotative and connotative. At any step in the process there is ample room for error. Under the best conditions human communications are only approximate. Any student who has been exposed to the difficulties of learning a foreign language appreciates the problems involved in attempting to communicate ideas and feelings, and to understand the ideas and feelings of others. The difficulty is one of degree and not of kind. Even when speaking in one's native tongue the complexities are there, although speech habits become so automatic that we are unaware of them. It is well to realize that all learning has been imperfect, incomplete, and often biased, and whether in the role of speaker or listener, each brings his potential for error to the situation.

The problem of meanings associated with symbolic language has been the special province of the *semanticists*, who constantly make the point that "the symbol is not the thing." Although this would seem elementary, a closer look at some typical speech and action patterns shows that Americans generally are *not* aware of the independence of the two. In *Language in Thought and Action*,[7] S. I. Hayakawa gives many examples of such faulty reasoning, among them that of the use of the word *snake* which many people consider a "nasty, slimy *word*" since they identify snakes as "nasty, slimy *creatures*." He also makes note of the propensity for Americans to go into debt to buy *symbols* of prosperity and then as "owners" of shiny new gadgets, cars, or houses to *feel* prosperous. Such reasoning carried over into all aspects of society, and at all levels of decision making, can understandably add to our problems. "The habitual confusion of symbols with things symbolized . . . is serious

[7] S. I. Hayakawa, *Language in Thought and Action* (New York, Harcourt, Brace & Co., 1949), p. 30.

enough at all levels of culture to provide a perennial human problem. But with the rise of modern communications systems, there arises with peculiar urgency the problem of confusion of verbal symbols with realities." [8]

# IV

The idea that language is significant as more than a communications system has received much attention in recent decades due in part to the writings of such men as Sapir and Benjamin Lee Whorf. "Language and our thought-grooves are inextricably interwoven, are, in a sense, one and the same" [9] was written by Sapir in 1921. Whorf has gone a step further with this idea in his hypothesis that *the structure of the language spoken by a people determines their world view.* He referred to language as "the lens through which we see" the world and "the shaper of ideas" and said that we dissect nature along lines laid down by our native languages. Since the structures of languages vary, the rationalizations of different peoples also vary, and people are not led by their languages to the same picture of the universe. In discussing the scientific work of linguists in a number of languages he states, "It was found that the background linguistic system (the grammar) of each language is not merely a reproducing instrument for voicing ideas but rather is itself the shaper of ideas, the program and the guide for the individual's mental activity, for his analysis of impressions." [10]

The use of symbolic language has enabled man to *structure his universe.* Man does not merely "react" to his surroundings; he contemplates, speculates, and *organizes his world* into a system of "understandable" entities. His capacity for conceptual thought is the essence of culture and in the structure of his language he has a whole set of assumptions concerning the "universe." Even though there is constant interplay between language and experience, speech habits become so automatic and uncritical that man is incapable, according to Whorf, of consciously molding

[8] *Ibid.,* p. 30.

[9] Sapir, *op. cit.,* p. 232.

[10] Benjamin Lee Whorf, "Science and Linguistics," *The Technology Review,* 1940, XLIV, p. 231.

his thoughtways along lines other than those prescribed in his established language.

Most students who have struggled with a foreign language have waged their battles not in truly "foreign" ideas but in various dialects of the Indo-European languages—French or German, Spanish or Latin, or the like. The structures of the languages are similar and the ideas of the universe presented are not "foreign." "We must learn Navajo and Nootka and Nam —or some other non-Indo-European language—to have any legitimate sense of how alarmingly variable and arbitrary a thing a given language is, and how little it mirrors the structures of reality." [11]

Whorf's hypothesis has not been universally accepted by linguists and remains yet to be tested. Carrol calls this the "Weltanschauung" (world-view) problem and states that "a more conservative hypothesis is that linguistic structure *predisposes* the individual to pay attention to some things more than others, or to perceive things in one mode rather than in others, even though with respect to his general perceptual capacities he is no different, on the average, from users of other languages." [12] [13]

However, Whorf convincingly illustrates his theory by reference to the Hopi language, which he compared to English to demonstrate how differently we "dissect nature," pointing out that this is only one of many languages which approach nature quite differently from the ways in which we do. Our use of verbs and nouns gives us a bipolar division of nature. "But nature herself is not thus polarized. If it be said that strike, turn, run, are verbs because they denote temporary or short-lasting events, . . . why then is fist a noun? It also is a temporary event. . . . It will be found that an 'event' to *us* means 'what our language classes as a 'verb'. . . ." [14] Many of our nouns are verbs in the Hopi language—such words as *lightning* and

[11] LaBarre, *op. cit.*, p. 175.

[12] John B. Carroll, *The Study of Language* (Cambridge, Harvard University Press, 1953), p. 46 (Italics by the editors).

[13] Linguists have recently developed a synthetic "logical language" for the purpose of testing Whorf's hypothesis. See James Cooke Brown, "Loglan," *Scientific American,* Vol. 202, No. 6 (June, 1960).

[14] Whorf, *op. cit.*, p. 231.

*wave* are verbs because of their brief duration. The Hopi classifies events by duration of time in nature, while what we call verbs, often can be defined as such only by falling back on the "rules of grammar."

While our verbs have tense and we speak of an act as past, present, or future, the Hopi verb has *validity*, that is, from the form used the listener knows whether the speaker is *reporting* an event, is *expecting* an event, or from his actual experience *knows* of the event as a regular thing. Thus the Hopi language is based on the *objective* and the *subjective*, the manifest and the unmanifest.

There are numerous other examples of grammar systems which contrast with ours. It has been pointed out that many of the Indian languages with their concepts of *process* as opposed to ours of cause-and-effect have languages more suited to the understanding of current concepts in physics. Our built-in notions of time as kinetic and space as static hamper our understanding of relativity—in contrast to the Hopi whose events always include *both* space and time. That these ways of thinking give us different views of the world is now apparent and "There is no reason to suppose that English, French, Spanish, or any other Western language, with its two-valued logic, its subject-predicate form, and its law of identity, is the ultimate in a communication system." [15]

The arbitrary dissection of the spectrum into eight "colors" provides another example of how our language "structures our perceptions." "Our language thus provides certain verbal symbols in terms of which we habitually classify colors. It is quite possible to conceive other languages (and there are such languages) which break the spectrum into different groupings of wave lengths." [16] Some Indian tribes have another system of dissecting the spectrum and the shadings which for us range from yellow to violet and are known as green and blue, are known by only one name to the Indians. That is, they do not differentiate in this color range but consider them all shades of the same hue.

[15] Stuart Chase, *Power of Words* (New York, Harcourt, Brace and Co., 1954), p. 109.
[16] Carroll, *op. cit.*, p. 44.

The idea that if we do not have the word in our language, then we can have no notion of the conception is difficult to grasp. But our thinking is in the words and thoughtways of our language and each society's language is a cultural phenomenon incorporating the necessary and important views of that society. That eskimos have many words for snow and the Trobriand Islanders have many words for sweet potatoes is generally well known and merely demonstrates that the language of each society is suited to its own needs. It is not necessarily commensurable with any other. ". . . Social organization represents diverse ways of life which must be surrounded by verbal scaffoldings if they are to endure. This interdependent relationship between language and group life and its numerous implications for human conduct constitute one of the most promising pursuits of the social sciences." [17]

## V

There is probably no other single item of culture which is embraced more fiercely than one's native language. Man identifies with the mother tongue "as the tangible manifestation of each culture's uniqueness." [18] At times of crisis most intense feelings are aroused with regard to one's language—as demonstrated poignantly by the final words of Daudet's Alsatian schoolmaster to his "Last Class"—he speaks of the beauty of the French language, and pleads with them to retain it always among themselves, and never forget it, "because when a people falls into servitude, so long as it clings to its language, it is as if it held the key to its prison." Feelings such as these come from no mere habit or wish for convenience, but rather from deep-seated and entrenched ways of thinking, of coming at life, and of capturing the future.

[17] Joseph Bram, *Language and Society* (Garden City, New York, Doubleday & Co., Inc., 1955), p. 48.
[18] Kluckhohn, *op. cit.*, p. 151.

*Read Bain*

# OUR SCHIZOID CULTURE *

*Read Bain, who spent much of his professional career at Miami University (Ohio), has been a formidable critic, and also a forceful and cogent writer. Unlike some of his colleagues, he has not been reluctant to express himself colorfully and dramatically, even if the case is thereby slightly overstated. Schizophrenia, a mental disease term used to characterize persons whose behavior is fragmentized into inconsistent parts, is used in this article as the model for the analysis, or at least description, of some of the more dramatic incongruities in American culture. Most of us will readily recognize that our own thinking is characterized by these inconsistent assumptions and our behavior likewise. This should serve as a strong antidote to those beliefs which grow out of an overstatement of the consistency principle in culture, which is also, of course, to a degree correct.*

## I

Our culture contains a great deal of irrational, contradictory behavior. When an individual exhibits similar symptoms, the psychiatrist calls him neurotic, or if he lacks "insight" into his difficulties, psychotic. Since most of us possess only partial insight concerning these cultural confusions, this paper may be regarded as a study of neurotic and psychotic societal behavior.[1]

* From Read Bain, "Our Schizoid Culture," *Sociology and Social Research*, 19 (January-February, 1935), pp. 266-276. By permission.

[1] There is an enormous literature from which this thesis might be documented. Some of the more general discussions only are cited. E. Carpenter,

These conflict-complexes are not characteristic of the entire culture, but are segmental in nature, i.e., certain practices and "attitudes" are representative of most members of certain groups, but, since there is seldom complete unanimity in any group and all men are multi-group members, the confusion is geometrically confounded. Only social scientists, and not all of them, are likely to attain the scientific knowledge of these societal contradictions analogous to the psychiatrist-patient relation. Whether sociologists shall be able to create a body of societal science sufficient to provide therapeutic and preventive techniques remains to be seen. When we consider the amount of societal infantility, imbecility, and violence in our culture, the immediate outlook is not very encouraging.[2]

Space prohibits more than a sketch of the divisive societal behavior in our culture. The material has been organized roughly under institutional categories and is thrown into antithetical form. This does not imply that *all* people are victims of *all* these confusions, but it is contended that sufficient numbers are affected by them, frequently in groupal conflict-patterns, so that none of us can wholly escape their impact. Adequate treatment would require a monograph for each heading.

*Sex—Family—Children.* The confusion in our culture on sex is notorious. There is scarcely any official recognition of the reproductive system by church, school, or home. Birth control is widely condemned but more widely practiced. Venereal disease is still more of a moral than medical problem. The "double standard" still flourishes. Sex-attitudes oscillate from the "romantic-holy" to the "prosaic-evil." We eulogize sex and love in the

*Civilization: Its Cause and Cure,* New York, 1921 (first printed, 1891); T. Veblen, *Theory of the Leisure Class,* New York, 1899; W. F. Ogburn, *Social Change with Respect to Culture and Original Nature,* New York, 1922; L. Stoddard, *The Revolt Against Civilization: The Menace of the Under-Man,* New York, 1923; O. Spengler, *The Decline of the West,* New York, 1926-28, two volumes; R. H. Lowie, *Are We Civilized? Human Culture in Perspective,* New York, 1929; C. M. Case, *Social Process and Human Progress,* New York, 1931; E. D. Martin, *Civilizing Ourselves: Intellectual Maturity in the Modern World,* New York, 1932; S. D. Schmalhausen, editor, *Our Neurotic Age,* New York, 1932; Ortega y Gasset, *The Revolt of the Masses,* New York, 1932.

[2] See Case, *op. cit.,* Ch. VII and VIII and *Our Neurotic Age,* pp. 434-52, "We Americans: A Study in Infantilism" by E. S. Bates.

abstract, but there is a great deal of furtiveness, shame, and sense of sin connected with the facts and acts of sex.

We glorify parenthood, but provide little education for prospective parents. Declining birth rate, child care outside the home, and technological specialism have largely defunctionalized women. Monogamous marriage is our ideal, but infidelity, marital maladjustment, and divorce abound. Marriage and divorce laws are anarchic and are frequently violated with impunity. Legal grounds for divorce are seldom the "real" reasons and the courts wink at collusion.

Our reliance upon mother love and maternal "instinct" results in personality distortions of both parents and children. If we would, we could cut maternal and infant death rates in half. We still control children by fear and force, but many parents, fearful of Freudian complexes and represions, abjure all discipline and control. This is the age of the child, but we still have child labor, malnutrition, remediable defects, and preventable diseases. We have school health examinations but little treatment. We "love" children too much and too little; frequently the same child is a victim of this emotional polarity, indulged and frightened in almost the same breath.

*Economic Confusion.* Yes, we starve in the midst of plenty. We are thrifty, but also extravagant, conspicuous spenders. We praise competition, but practice merger and monopoly. Everybody has equal economic opportunity, except Negroes, immigrants, women, and the unemployed. Honesty is the best policy, but there is more graft and chicanery in business than in politics. We build irrigation projects, drain swamps, and teach scientific farming while we hire farmers to let land lie fallow. We "maintain prices" by dumping vegetables into the ocean and milk into sewers. We praise business organization but condemn and prevent labor organization. We extol quality and service, but through high pressure salesmanship and blatant advertising we sell people "cheap and nawsty" goods and services which they do not need and do not want for prices they cannot afford to pay. We pour billions into productive plants when what we already have must lie idle half the time because men cannot work unless other men can make profit out of their labor. Public service corporations are conscienceless exploiters of the public

. . . We waste and exploit human and natural resources. We give heavier and more certain sentences to bank robbers than to bank wreckers. We boast of business ethics but we give power and prestige to business buccaneers.

*Political and Legal Patterns.* We profess respect for law and order, but we tolerate racketeering gangs, lynching, race riots, and privately paid industrial "police." Policemen are supposed to protect society, but they are frequently found in collusion with crooks—and the same goes for some judges. Everybody is equal before the law, except Negroes, women, immigrants, poor people, and economic "radicals." Our penology is largely punitive and produces more recidivism than it does re-education. We value our jury system, but most juries are composed of the senile, illiterate, and dull-witted. Lawyers are trained largely at public expense to serve the public, but many of them spend most of their time with considerable success in aiding individuals and corporations to evade the law and escape its penalties. A large proportion of lawyers are more concerned with making money than with promoting justice.

We ridicule politicians in general but honor all officeholders in particular and most of us would like to be elected to something ourselves. We think of voting as the basis of democracy, but we buy and sell and miscount votes, stuff ballot boxes, prevent Negroes from voting, and seldom find more than fifty per cent of eligible voters actually registering their "will." We glorify government by the people, but corrupt machines still exist in many of our largest (and smallest) political units. We hate and fear the state, but progressively increase and centralize its functions. We condemn "entangling alliances," but we practice "dollar diplomacy" all over the earth. We are a peaceful people, but we spend ten times as much for military purposes as for all other federal functions, enforce compulsory military training, laud and reward military heroes, glorify our military history, thrill at military music and uniforms, treat war profiteers as respectable citizens. . . .

*Democratic Dogmas.* Democracy is one of our most cherished ideals, but we speak of upper and lower classes, "look down on" many useful occupations, trace our genealogies, sport our coats-of-arms, marry our daughters to indigent scions of nobility, join snob societies, and shout "What we need is a Mussolini!" We are contemptuous of all things European, but we kowtow to Europe in a thousand ways as the real seat of "culchaw." Men and women are socially equal, but they are paid unequally for the same services, the laws of every state discriminate against women, while the "unwritten laws" "keep women in their place" along with Negroes and servants. We believe in the brotherhood of man, but we are full of racial, religious, economic, and numerous other prejudices and invidious distinctions. We value equality, but tolerate greater inequality of wealth and income than has ever existed in any other society. We believe freedom of speech and opinion is the very foundation of democracy, but we prevent economic radicals from speaking and even discharge teachers for expressing "dangerous" ideas.

*Philanthropy and Social Work.* Despite sound theory, our care of the socially inadequate is still dominated by almsgiving and the spirit of Lady Bountiful. We advocate rehabilitative social work, but must fight continually (and not very successfully) to keep social work from degenerating into mere relief. We possess a "poverty complex" which demands that relief recipients must grovel and be "thankful" for their mere-subsistence doles . . . It is disgraceful to receive charity, but it is noble to give to "worthy causes," and we continue to cherish the myth of "private charity" even in the face of its almost complete breakdown. The state spends more per capita for idiots, imbeciles, paupers, and habitual criminals than it does for college students and four or five times as much as for grade school pupils. We emphasize character, but in hard times the character building agencies are first to be cut. We honor great economic exploiters who "rob widows and orphans to build homes and hospitals for widows and orphans." We pay social workers poorly on the theory that they are sufficiently rewarded by their consciousness of good work well done. Social workers should be highly skilled, but we permit almost anyone to practice (or malpractice) social work. We are justly proud of our juvenile and domestic courts, but many of them are in the hands of incompetents, politicians, legalistic pedants, and social ignoramuses.

*Art and Recreation.* Modern art reflects the confusion, triviality, inner tension, and lack of integration in our culture. Many artists are clearly damaged souls and those who are not deal chiefly with the doings of damaged souls. The sex complex referred to above is present on almost every page of modern literary art. The rest is not silence, but the hectic cries of cultural neurotics struggling to bring some semblance of order out of their cultural chaos. We drape nude statues and supress noble books like *Ulysses, Desire Under the Elms,* and *The Well of Loneliness* as obscene, while lubricious burlesques run wide open and pornographic periodicals purvey their pruriency. In spite of our pride in the "higher things," most of our "art appreciation" is on the Mickey Mouse comic-strip, jazz music, and sloppy-sentimental-risqué song level. Cinema, stage, and reading are for millions of people chiefly used as a means of escape from reality into a soul-sick world of daydreams and wishful reverie.

We try to foster participative recreation, but most of it is passive, much of it vicious, and almost all of it, flagrantly commercialized. We love animals and birds and plants, but we glorify hunting and fishing and ravage the countryside of flowers and shrubs. We spend millions for flowers and S. P. C. A.'s in communities where children are being starved and beaten. We spend a great deal of money on education for recreation, frequently emphasizing games that are never played in later life but that chiefly promote the professional careers of coaches and players and provide a doubtful prestige for schools.

*The Muddle of Medicine.* Doctors are trained largely at public expense but many charge what the traffic will bear and excuse themselves by treating many people free—they say. They generally oppose public medicine even though they . . . cannot collect their bills, and millions of people cannot pay for much-needed medical care. We grow lyric over the triumphs of science in medicine, but we spend millions with medical fakers and more millions for nostrums and faith cures. We prize health above everything, but we gourmandize, turn night into day, live in city slums, smother our lungs with carbon monoxide and tobacco fumes, and try to pay the national debt by drinking booze. We support millions of cats and dogs while millions of mothers and children lack food and medical care, to say nothing of decent education and recreation. We are proud of our numbers, but we practice birth control, commit over a million abortions a year and allow millions of people to die from preventable causes. We still have moral reactions to mental illness while the average doctor knows little and cares less about mental hygiene and psychotherapy.

*Religion.* We are a Christian nation, but half of us belong to no church; half of those who do, seldom attend; and half of those who attend do not believe the creed. We still pray for the sick even though we call the doctor. Many who have faith in the afterlife weep at death instead of rejoicing. Whether or not we believe in spiritual immorta!˙ y, our graveyard complex is equally illogical and enormously costly. We honor religion, but make fun of "Sunday School boys," "Y. M. fellows," and even ministers. The ministry is a noble, learned profession, but we see many priests who are willing to live fat, lazy, ignorant lives, preaching to wealthy pewrenters in palatial churches sedative sermons in praise of the God-of-things-as-they-are. No wonder social revolutions have always slaughtered the priests! We believe in a God of peace and love, but all nations pray to Him for victory in war and most denominations furnish army chaplains. This is the age of science, but there is more belief in miracles, spirits, occultism, and providences than one would think possible.

*Education and Science.* Education and science are the particular pride of our culture, but we sneer at the Brain Trust and "book larnin'" and generally regard teachers and scientists as childish, impractical theorists. We are proud of our free public education, but about two thirds leave school at fourteen; even though the census figure is about four per cent for illiteracy, the army draft was about twenty-five per cent unable to read and write in any functional manner. We pay teachers very little and still have thousands who are poorly trained, socially unintelligent, and emotionally maladjusted. We assume that people go to college for professional training or love of learning, but some educators have called the college a country club, mating ground, kindergarten, and snob-factory.

Our scientific system produces a specialism that gives great prestige and great technical skill, but not always great wisdom. Especially is this true of the nonsocial scientists who are frequently quite willing to advise and lead in societal affairs even though they are quite ignorant and contemptuous of social science. We use the findings of science to destroy each other physically, to exploit each other economically, and to produce all sorts of irrational behavior. The very triumphs of science produce an irrational, magic-minded faith in science so that "science" becomes a stereotype with which fakers, quacks, demagogues, advertisers and half-baked fanatics can and do mislead, confuse, and exploit the uncritical populace.

## II

Such contradictions and confusions as have been sketched briefly here, or their analogues, are found in all cultures. They are almost always evaded by usage, rationalization, and imperative repression into the "unconscious." Neurotic and psychotic behavior frequently results from individual failure to build up a sufficiently coherent (socially acceptable) system of such escape mechanisms.[3]

Hence we find ourselves in this peculiar situation: Our personalities are formed by cultural conditioning, a large part of which we must irrationally escape in order to remain "rational." Our culture is rent with internal divisions and conflicts which erupt into group behavior patterns which in their turn produce societal counterparts of all sorts of schizoid symptoms. It is not difficult to think of societal behavior similar to sadism, masochism, persecution, grandeur delusions, paranoias, abulias, phobias, manias, regressions, fixations, symbolisms, fetishisms, over-and-under compensations, and so on. All of us, even sociologists, carry these antithetic action-emotion patterns deeply embedded

[3] T. Burrow, *The Social Basis of Consciousness*, New York, 1927; B. Malinowski, *Sex and Repression in Savage Society*, New York, 1927; F. M. Keesing, "The Changing Life of Native Peoples in the Pacific Area: A Sketch in Cultural Dynamics," *American Journal of Sociology*, 39:443-58, 1934; and Freud, of course. See also John Dollard, "The Psychotic Person Seen Culturally," *American Journal of Sociology*, 39:637-48, 1934. My paper, written in December, 1933, attempts to make explicit the same theory that is implicit in Dollard's paper. He is dealing with the personal results of such cultural confusion as is set forth here. R.B.

in our personalities like tubercular scar tissue in our lungs. We are all Mr. Facing-Many-Ways; the nearest we can approach rationality is to recognize that we are inescapably irrational,—that much of our behavior is sheer rationalization.

Why is this? Is the human mind fundamentally alogical, ambivalent, irrational? Or is it merely culture lag? Do the fantasy and reality principles oppose each other in irrepressible and insoluble conflict? If so, is it realistic to try to be rational? Is it possibly an aspect of the growth principle? Perhaps these phenomena are the very source of "consciousness" and hence have a survival value. If so, the so-called "genuine" cultures, those harmoniously integrated, are defective for survival and hence should be called "spurious." [4] Such cultures may be like the so-called superior men who are outbred and hence outlived by their so-called inferiors. The dynamic, culture-creating (and destroying) men are the zealots, the frenetic enthusiasts, the symbols of cultural confusion and conflict,—the Hitlers, Lenins, Carnegies, Napoleons. . . .

[4] E. Sapir, "Culture—Genuine and Spurious," *American Journal of Sociology*, 29:401-29, 1924. The questions are of course suggested by the specific writings of Lévy-Bruhl, Freud, Ogburn, B. Russell, J. B. Watson, *et al.*

## Robert S. Lynd

# THE PATTERN
# OF AMERICAN CULTURE *

*Robert S. Lynd, professor at Columbia, is probably best
known for his classic studies of* Middletown *(New York,
Harcourt, Brace and World, 1929) and the follow-up
study,* Middletown in Transition *(New York, Harcourt,
Brace and World, 1937). Lynd has also addressed himself to some theoretical questions in sociology and his*
Knowledge for What? *is one of these efforts. The following excerpt which deals with the use of cultural ideologies
in the day-to-day thinking of people in our society has
helped many students to appreciate (a) their reliance
upon ideologies entrenched in the culture for "their own
views," (b) the standardized repetitive nature of what
passes for "individual thinking," and (c), as in the excerpt
from "Our Schizoid Culture," the coexistence of contradictory ideas in a given culture.*

As one begins to list the assumptions by which we Americans
live, one runs at once into a large measure of contradiction and
resulting ambivalence. This derives from the fact that these
overlapping assumptions have developed in different eras and
that they tend to be carried over uncritically into new situations
or to be allowed to persist in long diminuendos into the changing
future. Men's ideas, beliefs, and loyalties—their non-material culture—are frequently slower to be changed than are their material tools.[1] And the greater the emotional need for them, the

* From Robert S. Lynd, *Knowledge for What?* (Princeton, N.J., Princeton University Press, 1939), pp. 59-62. By permission.

[1] See W. F. Ogburn, *Social Change* (New York, Huebsch, 1922).

longer men tend to resist changes in these ideas and beliefs. These contradictions among assumptions derive also from the fact that the things the mass of human beings basically crave as human beings as they live along together are often overlaid by, and not infrequently distorted by, the cumulating emphases that a culture may take on under circumstances of rapid change or under various kinds of class control. In these cases the culture may carry along side by side both assertions: the one reflecting deep needs close to the heart's desire and the other heavily authorized by class or other authority.

Wherever, therefore, such dualism in assumptions clearly exists, both assumptions are set down together in the following listing. The juxtaposition of these pairs is not intended to imply that they carry equal weight in the culture. One member may be thrown into the scale as decisive in a given situation at one moment, and the other contrasting assumption may be invoked in the same or a different situation a few moments later. It is precisely in this matter of trying to live by contrasting rules of the game that one of the most characteristic aspects of our American culture is to be seen.

The following suggest some of these outstanding assumptions in American life:

1. The United States is the best and greatest nation on earth and will always remain so.

2. Individualism, "the survival of the fittest," is the law of nature and the secret of America's greatness; and restrictions on individual freedom are un-American and kill initiative.

*But:* No man should live for himself alone; for people ought to be loyal and stand together and work for common purposes.

3. The thing that distinguishes man from the beasts is the fact that he is rational; and therefore man can be trusted, if let alone, to guide his conduct wisely.

*But:* Some people are brighter than others; and, as every practical politician and businessman knows, you can't afford simply to sit back and wait for people to make up their minds.

4. Democracy, as discovered and perfected by the American people, is the ultimate form of living together. All men are created free and equal, and the United States has made this fact a living reality.

*But:* You would never get anywhere, of course, if you constantly left things to popular vote. No business could be run that way, and of course no businessman would tolerate it.

5. Everyone should try to be successful.

*But:* The kind of person you are is more important than how successful you are.

6. The family is our basic institution and the sacred core of our national life.

*But:* Business is our most important institution, and, since national welfare depends upon it, other institutions must conform to its needs.

7. Religion and "the finer things of life" are our ultimate values and the things all of us are really working for.

*But:* A man owes it to himself and to his family to make as much money as he can.

8. Life would not be tolerable if we did not believe in progress and know that things are getting better. We should, therefore, welcome new things.

*But:* The old, tried fundamentals are best; and it is a mistake for busybodies to try to change things too fast or to upset the fundamentals.

9. Hard work and thrift are signs of character and the way to get ahead.

*But:* No shrewd person tries to get ahead nowadays by just working hard, and nobody gets rich nowadays by pinching nickels. It is important to know the right people. If you want to make money, you have to look and act like money. Anyway, you only live once.

10. Honesty is the best policy.

*But:* Business is business, and a businessman would be a fool if he didn't cover his hand.

11. America is a land of unlimited opportunity, and people get pretty much what's coming to them here in this country.

*But:* Of course, not everybody can be boss, and factories can't give jobs if there aren't jobs to give.

12. Capital and labor are partners.

*But:* It is bad policy to pay higher wages than you have to. If people don't like to work for you for what you offer them, they can go elsewhere.

13. Education is a fine thing.

*But:* It is the practical men who get things done.

14. Science is a fine thing in its place and our future depends upon it.

*But:* Science has no right to interfere with such things as business and our other fundamental institutions. The thing to do is to *use* science, but not let it upset things.

15. Children are a blessing.

*But:* You should not have more children than you can afford.

16. Women are the finest of God's creatures.

*But:* Women aren't very practical and are usually inferior to men in reasoning power and general ability.

17. Patriotism and public service are fine things.

*But:* Of course, a man has to look out for himself.

18. The American judicial system insures justice to every man, rich or poor.

*But:* A man is a fool not to hire the best lawyer he can afford.

19. Poverty is deplorable and should be abolished.

*But:* There never has been enough to go around, and the Bible tells us that "The poor you have always with you."

20. No man deserves to have what he hasn't worked for. It demoralizes him to do so.

*But:* You can't let people starve.[2]

[2] In Chapter XII of *Middletown in Transition* (New York, Harcourt, Brace, 1937), dealing with "The Middletown Spirit," the author has attempted to set down a more extended list of these "of course" assumptions relevant to that particular city. With allowances for the heavily native-born, Protestant, small-city, Middle Western character of Middletown's population, most of the assumptions there set down would probably apply widely throughout the country.

## Don Martindale

# IMAGES OF AMERICANS *

*Probably every student knows or soon will learn that what passes for "sociology" in America today consists of two quite different kinds of "research." One consists of very factual, usually statistical, thorough study of a rather circumscribed problem, such as those discussed in the article, "Sociologists Invade the Plant." The other kind of effort is more like that which the historian writes—empirically based to be sure, but the generalizations being derived from a less formalized kind of integration. The latter is deceptively easy and many amateurish efforts are made from time to time. These are often called "journalistic accounts" by social scientists. This is quite unfair in many instances because journalism, like any other profession, can be practiced either badly or well. Nevertheless, the resultant product often seems like journalism, even though it may be compounded of a great deal of hard work and careful analysis, and reflect unusual talent and maturity. The following portrait of the American character, circa 1960, by Don Martindale (University of Minnesota) is taken from the preface of his book on* American Social Structure. *How many people who have lived their lives as part of American society would see these things about themselves and their contemporaries?*

There is a curious contradiction between the first and the second impressions which the United States tends to give its observers.

* From Don Martindale, *American Social Structure* (New York, Appleton-Century-Crofts, 1960), pp. vii-xi. Used by permission.

To foreign observers, America is at first most striking for its bustling energy, its intellectual inferiority, and its hunger for culture. The foreign lecturer is given a reception in the United States accorded nowhere else. The array of types attracted by America is described by Dylan Thomas in inimitable terms.[1]

There they go, every spring from New York to Los Angeles: exhibitionists, polemicists, histrionic publicists, theological rhetoricians, historical hoddy-doddies, balletomanes, ulterior decorators, windbags and bigwigs and humbugs, men in love with stamps, men in love with steaks, men after millionaires' widows, men with elephantiasis of the reputation (huge trunks and teeny minds), authorities on gas, bishops, best-sellers, editors looking for writers, writers looking for publishers, publishers looking for dollars, existentialists, serious physicists with nuclear missions, men from the B. B. C. who speak as though they had the Elgin marbles in their mouths, pot-boiling philosophers, professional Irishmen (very lepricorny), and, I am afraid, fat poets with slim volumes.

The foreign lecturers, in Thomas' opinion, are attracted to America like flies to a honey jar. Where else can they find audiences so eager to treat them as authorities, so pathetically concerned with the foreign visitor's opinion of themselves, so ready to pay to be informed of their own cultural inferiority? But, according to Thomas, the observer finds that the American, so eager to be possessed, in the end eludes possession; although he is ever so ready to be generalized about, he is forever incapable of being comprehended in any set of generalizations.[2]

"At first, confused and shocked by shameless profusion and almost shamed by generosity, unaccustomed to such importance as they are assumed, by their hosts, to possess, and up against the barrier of a common language, they write in their notebooks like demons, generalizing away, on character and culture and the American political scene. But, towards the middle of their middle-aged whisk through middle-western clubs and universities, the fury of the writing flags; their spirits are lowered by the spirit with which they are everywhere strongly greeted and which, in ever increasing doses, they themselves lower; and they

[1] Dylan Thomas, *Quite Early One Morning* (New York, New Directions, 1954), pp. 234-235.
[2] *Ibid.*, pp. 232-233.

begin to mistrust themselves, and their reputations—for they have found, too often, that an audience will receive a lantern lecture on, say, Ceramics, with the same uninhibited enthusiasm that it accorded the very week before to a paper on the Modern Turkish Novel . . ."

It is not simply the amazing wells of American energy that have daunted the poet; these he could have taken. Nor is it the irrepressible naïveté, for what poet cannot feel kinship with that? It is the peculiar way in which America so openly invites and so stubbornly resists generalization. Beneath the same colossal uniformity of chewing gum, toothpaste, hamburgers, hot dogs, soft drinks, automobiles, maiden-form bras, and cigarettes that scream at one from the billboards, there is a veritable ocean of differences. Where else will so many genuinely spiritual themes be cast into the disguise of pure materialism? Where else will religion be run on a business basis, with Christ conceived as a kind of super-Rotarian, while the most statesmanlike political addresses assume the form of a sensitive religious sermon? Where else will the so-called serious movies constitute pure fantasies in which the good guys always win and are rewarded by wealth and sex galore? Meanwhile the comic cartoons (Mickey Mouse and Donald Duck) cheerfully portray clear strains of unretouched meanness and outright violence.

It is little wonder that foreign observers, for all their contemptuous superiority about the American lack of culture, are sometimes baffled. In America one finds some of the finest religious sermonizing in politics, some of the clearest examples of cynical business organization and smugness in religion, some of the best forms of entertainment in political campaigns and the poorest in what passes as entertainment, some of the purest fantasies in the so-called serious movies, some of the best morality tales in the presentations of nature, and some of the most remarkable insights into the violence of nature and human nature in the cartoon comics.

One's first impression of the United States tends to fasten on the amazing surface uniformity. The images that most quickly leap forth are those of mass production, the interchangeable part, mass arts, mass man, and standardized taste. However, if one cuts below the surface uniformity, he touches a deeper level of American experience that seems to reverse all this. In its local forms, America presents an almost unbelievably diverse fermenting fluidity. Holding the whole together is the ever-bubbling fountain of American dynamism.

There are two fundamental kinds of errors that can be made in the interpretation of America: (1) assuming that the only important property of America is derived from its characteristics as a mass culture, and (2) assuming that the standardization everywhere evident in American life is superficial and the only true key to America is its diversity. America is not either; it is both. Neither property is trivial or superficial. The one property sums up the integration of the United States as a whole. The other property phrases the amazing fluidity of America in all local situations. . . .

. . . All major observers agree that American character tends to manifest great practicality, considerable anti-intellectualism, a genius for organization, a strong materialism, a tendency to conceptualize social and political affairs in moralistic terms, a manifestation of great faith in individual initiative, and a sense of civic responsibility. These are the major clues to American character, and the Yankee emerges as the central and unique American type.

In all local situations, however, America presents an amazing array of community forms. A community is a complete way of life and the system of institutions that makes it possible. The community arises out of the ever-present forces in human action for stability, consistency, and completeness. In addition to these principles, various secondary principles may come into being as well.

As a product of these forces at local levels, American society tends to form into regional, rural, urban, ethnic, and status community forms. The two major properties of American life, its general integration and its local ferment, are anchored at different points. The background for the general themes manifest in American character is provided by the nation; the ferment is provided by the tendency of local society to crystallize into stable forms.

By taking account of both major features of American life, one can arrive at new insight into a phenomenon that has disturbed some of the most sensitive students of America—its re-markable dynamism. The traditional explanation of the volcanic industry of Americans has usually been in terms of the role of the Protestant ethic in its social history.

Protestantism broke with the sacramental theory of the church and shifted the point of gravity of religious experience from observations of the sacraments and the ministrations of the priesthood to exemplary behavior—in whatever position pre-destination had cast one—and behavior in accord with the dic-tates of conscience. Protestantism reconceptualized everyday behavior as a religiously relevant sphere. One's position was his "calling." By one's behavior in it, he demonstrated his religious worthiness. This did not guarantee his salvation, but it at least offered some evidence to the individual that he could be among the elect that God had chosen to save. The individual could never be completely certain, however, and all his life long had to reassure himself continually by proper behavior. In some respects the more correct the individual was in his life conduct, the more intense his anxiety. The more correct, the greater pos-sibility that he was actually one of the elect, hence the greater anxiety to be completely certain. And of course it goes without saying that the good work done by exemplary performance in one's occupation could not be undone by frivolity in one's leisure time.

Individuals raised on the Protestant ethic were a surprising group. They insisted with almost unbelievable stubbornness on their individuality and freedom, their right to run their own lives. They stood up and defied kings. At their height they were incorruptible by the powers of this world. They paid a fantastic individual price for their autonomy.

While casting off all external controls, the Protestants im-posed upon themselves a most intensive system of personal con-trols. In their work they drove themselves unsparingly. They spent their leisure time on activities as grim in Spartan discipline as their work. They exercised to improve their bodies. They studied zealously to improve their minds. They ate simple and nourishing foods, scorning anything that looked like gluttony; they took long constitutionals. They walked when they could have ridden; they did not spend their money on frivolous things, but processed it back into the business; they did not retire at the normal time, but merely went to work with greater vigor.

There is little doubt that the early forms of individual dynamism in America are in good measure to be accounted for by the role of the Protestant ethic in its experience. The powerful restrictions of Protestantism dammed up the energies of these men and channeled them into an intensified business and civic activity. Beacon Hill is one such American community where these factors remain powerful into the present.

However, the peculiar properties of the Protestant theology (belief in predestination, original sin, and election) did not correspond to the realities of American experience. As time went by, it was not easy to persuade Americans—with an entire continent lying open before them—that they were sinful people who ought to be racked by pangs of conscience. Far more akin to American experience was an optimistic view of individuals and groups. The idea soon developed that the individual was perfectable and his society progressive. Education became the secular vehicle of these ideals.

A strong confidence in individualism has remained and tends to reserve the local group as an inviolate sphere. However, because Americans have confidence in the progress of the group and because they formed their own state, they also continue to have considerable faith in that state. Americans tend simultaneously to maintain the inviolability of the local unit while turning for help in every crisis to the federal government, not even hesitating to try to legislate their own drinking habits on a national basis.

As a result of these policies, local life in America shows the continuous operation of community formation. At the same time, the promotion of the nation continually decrystallizes such local formations. American life thus shows continuous mobilization of energy into communities and the release of energy therefrom: This organization and release of energy in the intersection of the claims of the nation and of local society are two of the primary foundations of the new dynamism of American society.

*William F. Ogburn*

# THE MEANING OF TECHNOLOGY *

*William F. Ogburn spent most of his life studying social change, particularly in its technological aspects and consequences. He originated the concept "culture lag," which by now has acquired a number of meanings as well as having become a somewhat controversial concept in social science. (See, for example, the excellent treatment of the subject by Delbert C. Miller in Francis R. Allen, et al.* Technology and Social Change *(New York, Appleton-Century-Crofts, Inc., 1957), Chapter 5.) Professor Ogburn is also well known for his contributions to the epoch-making study* Recent Social Trends, *prepared in the 1930's, probably the most thorough collection of factual material on many aspects of social change in the United States. In the reading below Professor Ogburn directed himself to an analysis of the meaning of technology from various viewpoints. With a little reflection most persons will find it interesting to find themselves in this collective portrait.*

Technology is like a great mountain peak. It looks different according to the side from which one views it. From one vantage point only a small part may be seen, from another the outlook is clouded; yet we may get a clear view from still another side. Few of us see it from all its sides; so each of us is likely to have a very limited conception of its nature. It is desirable, then, to look at technology from various points of view; for in this way we get a less narrow picture.

* From Francis R. Allen, Hornell Hart, Delbert C. Miller, William F. Ogburn, and Meyer F. Nimkoff, *Technology and Social Change* (New York, Appleton-Century-Crofts, 1957), pp. 3-10. Used by permission.

## DIFFERENT VIEWPOINTS TOWARD TECHNOLOGY

*Technological schools.* To many young students who have not thought very much about it, technology is understood as something that is taught at an institute of technology or something they learn about in a technological high school. It has to do with engineering, mechanics, electricity, chemistry, laboratories, shop work, and various studies that one does not find in the curriculum of a liberal arts college or an ordinary secondary school. Graduates of these technological schools get jobs with engineering companies in construction work, or go out to develop new countries, or are associated with architectural firms. To them, technology is very definitely not a social science such as history, economics, or politics.

*Gadgets and push buttons.* An even more narrow view is found among those who think of technology only as the source of the many gadgets that are finding their way into our homes, offices, restaurants, automobiles, and other places frequented by the mass of the people. These gadgets may be radio sets, pipes for radiant heat, deep-freeze lockers, automatic gear shifts, microfilm readers, tape recorders, copying machines, electric blankets, automatic door openers, or ultraviolet-ray lamps. Hundreds of such gadgets are being placed at our disposal for our convenience and comfort. These are the products of technology with which we come in daily contact, their newness forced upon our attention by advertisements. Thus it is natural that we should think of technology as something that furnishes the mechanical devices which appeal to us as aids; although sometimes they may appear to some of us as nuisances.

*Destroyer of artistic skills.* The great flowering of technology as we know it today, based on metals and mechanical power, succeeded an era of handicrafts based upon wood and muscle. The age of handicrafts was one of great individual skill, and it resulted in productions of charm and artistic merit. A single craftsman would fabricate a whole product—a chair, a clock, a costume, or a curtain. We may suppose that he derived a certain joy in his creation, much as an artist does in painting a picture. But as the machine age replaced handicrafts, the individual worker created only part of a product. His skill and the joy that went with it were destroyed. In their place came routine, monotony, and toil, with a workman assigned only a fragment of a complete job, for example, sawing a piece of wood, winding a wire, sewing a buttonhole, or unfolding a bolt of cloth. This repetition daily, monthly, and yearly meant utilizing only a minute part of man's great capabilities. Thus the workman and the artist tend to view technology as the destruction of an artistic and humanly wholesome way of life and a replacement of these by long hours of monotonous toil in a factory.[1]

*Technological unemployment.* To some observers, technology suggests unemployment and little else. To them the social implications of technology, particularly in the 1920's and the 1930's in the United States, were the loss of a job and the replacement of men by machines.[2] There was a good deal of unemployment in these decades, and the idea that it was caused by technological innovations was widely spread in writings and discussions in newspapers, magazines, and books. Other influences of technology were only dimly seen at the time, and technology came to signify this social problem of unemployment. Since the prosperous years of the 1940's and 1950's, marked by a scarcity of labor, little has been heard of technological unemployment. [The problem in this form is with us again in the early 1960's.]

*Aid to non-industrial peoples.* Another aspect of technology has been introduced to the popular mind in the 1940's and the 1950's. It is that technology will raise the standard of living of peoples who are as yet without much industrialization.[3] This idea was presented to the general public as the fourth point in a program submitted by President Truman to the Congress. "Point Four" came to symbolize technological aid to less-developed countries. World War II made Americans more familiar with many distant peoples. Soldiers and travelers were impressed with the rudimentary nature of the tools used, for example, in

---

[1] John Ruskin, *The Crown of Wild Olive* (Philadelphia, H. Altemus, 1895).

[2] Corrington Gill, *Unemployment and Technological Change*, Report to the Temporary National Economic Committee (Philadelphia, Work Projects Administration, 1940).

[3] "Factors of Economic Progress," *International Social Science Bulletin*, Vol. VI, No. 2 (1954), Part I, pp. 159-294.

parts of the Far East, as compared with those in the United States and in Western industrial countries. If an iron plow could replace the wooden one, the productivity of a farm worker could be increased, and his labor lessened. To do something to help the so-called "backward" peoples appealed to the imagination of Americans who had been forced by war to kill and destroy. The exportation of machinery and tools no doubt appealed to our businessmen, for raising the incomes of these peoples would create a better market. But experience had taught that it was not enough to export equipment to peoples who would not know how to make the best use of it or repair it. So there arose the necessity of exporting "know-how" as well as the implements. Thus was technology to be exported. The idea was also in line with the ameliorative aims of other organizations such as UNESCO. Teams of technicians were, therefore, sent to the different peoples to teach them the best ways to use these new tools and machines. In this manner, then, Americans began to learn another influence of technology: its capability of raising the standard of living of slightly-industrialized peoples.

*Maker of wealth.* Technology can not only improve the material well-being of peoples with low per capita incomes, but it can also raise the standard of living of highly industrialized peoples. The standard of living of the people of the United States in 1950 is twice as high as it was in 1900. This doubling of per capita income in dollars of the same purchasing power is due largely to developments in technology and applied science.[4] There are valid reasons to think that, short of destructive war, the already high incomes in the United States will be increased even more during the second half of the twentieth century as a result of continued inventions and discoveries in science. A mechanical cotton picker now exists which can do the work of twenty-three laborers picking by hand. Today we are discussing the coming of automatism in industry when only a few will be needed in a factory to push buttons, to run the machinery that will manufacture products without further assistance from human beings. Nearly automatic factories will

---

[4] W. F. Ogburn, "Technology and the Standard of Living in the United States," *American Journal of Sociology,* Vol. LX, No. 4 (January, 1955), pp. 380-386.

greatly increase productivity per worker and our standard of living will be raised, for national income is a function of the rate of production. Technological development, thus, may be seen as the force which raises the standard of living of peoples of any level.

*Materialization versus spiritualization.* The peoples who were to benefit from "Point Four" programs in material wages and standards of living generally had a set of values which emphasized religion, the life of the spirit, or such human values as happiness. New and better tools brought material advantages, but they did little or nothing to help the human spirit in its search for sustaining philosophies.

In the highly industrialized countries of the West, technology brought about an increased emphasis on material things that seemed relatively to de-emphasize spiritual values. Many religious and moral groups see this aspect of technology, namely, that it is a force seemingly antagonistic to the life of the spirit. To them, technology stands for the secularization of life. One goes to a school of technology now instead of to a school of theology as in former times. To these followers of the spirit, technology is a false god. They resent the sight of our young people with no higher aim than material success.

*Machine the master.* The view of technology as a tempter which leads us away from the true values of the good life changes rather readily into the view that technology is a dictator that controls our lives. When the factory whistle blows, we must be up and at work. The railroad runs on a time table that we must follow and obey. The automobile maims and kills. We listen to the radio and watch television, but we seem to be unable to do anything to improve their programs.[5] Factories close down in a business depression, and we lose our jobs. The assembly line moves by, and the workers must keep up with its speed. The typist works for a typewriter which makes her sit before it for eight hours a day. To those groups of people whose temperament is tinged with rebelliousness, or who love the open road or the ways of nature, technology dictates a schedule that takes away freedom and makes daily life a routine.

[5] Siegfried Giedion, *Mechanization Takes Command* (New York, Oxford University Press, 1948).

*Technology as a worker of miracles.* By contrast, technology appears as a mechanical slave to do our bidding. It helps us do the things we want to do. It makes for us the things we want.[6] An automobile is ours to command, to take us anywhere at any time we wish. The airplane enables us to fly over mountains and over seas, and with it we can travel around the world in two or three days. By means of radio we can speak instantly to millions of people on the other side of the world. We can measure the distance to the sun and tell the composition of distant stars. A block of wood can be made into silken stockings, and one element can be changed into another. A lump of coal will yield dyes of more colors than are found in nature. We can record a symphonic concert on coiled wire no bigger than a spool of thread. From this viewpoint technology is a servant, but it is more. With its aid we can work miracles undreamed of by the ancients. It will continue in the future to give us power to do things that we now cannot even imagine. To these observers, technology is a great boon because it extends the capabilities and powers of men.

*A precipitator of change.* A banker once defined an invention as that which made his securities insecure. The securities of the railroads fell with the invention of the motor truck and the airplane, and the nitrate industry of Chile lost its market in the United States when nitrate was made from the nitrogen of the air. Inventions in technology bring profits and prosperity to some, woe and destruction to others. Technology is seen, at any rate, as a cause of changes for better or worse.[7]

The range of inventions is wide, and changes are occurring in many different phases of life.[8] To agriculture, oil and electricity have brought the power revolution. Warfare is mechanized and the great powers among nations are reranked. Science is changing the forms and nature of religious beliefs. These changes may or may not be progress, but the new replaces or is added to the old. So to many, technology is viewed as a disturber of

[6] Waldemar Kaempffert, *Modern Wonder Workers: A Popular History of American Invention* (New York, Blue Ribbon Books, 1931).

[7] Lewis Mumford, *Technics and Civilization* (New York, Harcourt, Brace, 1934).

[8] M. D. C. Crawford, *The Influence of Invention on Civilization* (New York, World Publishing Company, 1942).

the status quo, a destroyer of peace and quiet by precipitating unanticipated changes. These changes may offer prospects for new business or opportunities to make the world a better place in which to live, or they may bring threats that we feel we should oppose.

*A changing environment to which we adjust.* Like other animals, man adjusts to his environment; otherwise he does not live. Man's material environment, however, unlike that of the lower animals, does not consist only of land, water, air, fauna, flora, temperature, and pressure. It also consists of buildings, tools, clothing, fire, vehicles, books, schools, clocks, churches, munitions, writing materials, medicines, contraceptives, machines, prime movers, and the various objects that we call material culture. These are the products of technology and applied science.[9] The natural environment in any one place is quite stable except for diurnal and seasonal changes, but the technological environment in recent years is a whirling mass of change. This change in modern material culture is partly owing to inventions and scientific discoveries. Technology may thus be viewed as a changing environment of mankind.

The natural environment changes from winter to summer, to which a man must adjust as he also does when he goes from, say, the arctic to the tropics. Likewise, man has had to adjust as his technological environment changes. The life of a farmer differed from that of a hunter. The way of life in a city is different from life in the open country. In recent years we have changed our habits as we use television. We read less; we stay at home more; we go to motion pictures less frequently; our children play at athletic sports less. We make similar adjustments to the automobile and the airplane. And just now we are concerned with what adjustments we must make to the atom bomb and the thermonuclear bomb. The harnessing of atomic energy for peaceful purposes will occasion still other adjustments. We have, then, a technological environment which is changing rapidly and to which we must make continuous adjustments.

*Creator of cultural lags.* Adjustment to a changing environment is difficult for many reasons. One is that the change in the

[9] Stuart Chase, *Men and Machines* (New York, Macmillan, 1929).

technological environment is seldom foreseen, and preparation for it is rarely ever made. The automobile was first thought not to be practical; and the railroads, much of whose business was taken away by automotive vehicles, made no prior adjustment to it. City streets were not widened in anticipation; nor were through highways constructed in time. That airplanes carrying bombs would bring war to the civilian population and would find great cities ideal targets was not foreseen, nor have adjustments to this yet been made. That the hydrogen bomb would change international relations, make alliances more difficult, and increase the tendency toward neutrality was not anticipated.

There are delays and lags in adjusting to new technological developments, and during this period of lag man's adjustment is generally worse than it was before the technological change.[10] Thus cities in a farming area draw families to higher-paying jobs, and mothers leave crowded quarters to work away from home. Their unsupervised children join city gangs of youngsters with thieving and juvenile crime as a result, a worse adjustment for children than on the farms and in the villages. There are some groups who make a quick adjustment and profit thereby. Such are the business groups who make money out of new inventions, for instance, motion pictures, metals, and mowing machines. However, in some situations, adjusting is more difficult than inventing. Thus making atomic bombs was quicker and less difficult than is the abolition of war, the dispersal of cities, the formation of a one-world government, or the effective prohibition of the manufacture and use of atomic bombs. From this standpoint, technology is seen as the generator of social problems because of lags in adjustments to new mechanical inventions.

## Technology as a Broad Concept: Its Interrelations with Sociology

From the foregoing it is apparent that "technology" may be variously conceived by different observers. We shall, however, use the term in a very broad sense. A strict definition of technology is that it is the study of technics. Technics, though, covers

10 W. F. Ogburn, *Social Change* (New York, The Viking Press, 1950).

a very great range of material objects. Indeed, it is so comprehensive as to include all the objects of a material culture. Technology would thus encompass the making of a great variety of objects, such as bows and arrows, pottery, harness, plows, dynamos, engines, jewelry, and nylon. Technology therefore goes far beyond the curriculum of an institute of technology, which necessarily is limited.

Exploring further the concept of technology, we may inquire into the relationship of science to technology. Is technology different from applied science? It may be said that the making of mechanical objects rests upon the application of science, though in cases the science may be very crude and simple, as in the making of a trap or a spear by primitive hunters. Technology may therefore include the applied science that aids in making material objects. A good deal of applied science, for instance, goes into the making of a radio receiving set.

In popular language we often find word symbols that are roughly equivalent to the term *technology*. The word *machine* is an abbreviated symbol that stands in a rough way for technology. So also is *factory* or the *factory system* as a referent for the technology that has developed since the invention and use of the steam engine.

. . . The significance of technology lies in what it does. For example, we are interested in a telephone only for what it does. The wires, the current, the transmitter, the receiver are of no concern in themselves. Their significance lies in their use in transmitting sounds for long distances between persons. It is the function of the structure that gives it importance, and the function of the products of technology is use by human beings. Technology is therefore essentially social.

We do not ordinarily think of technology as sociological. Rather we consider it as mechanical and belonging to the physical sciences. To the degree that technology is concerned with the making of physical objects, it lies in the realm of the physical sciences. The curricula of colleges of technology are largely devoted to the physical sciences and deal little with the biological or the social sciences. Producing the objects of technology is, then, not in the field of social science. But since the meaning of these technological objects lies in the field of the social sciences, it is strange that the social sciences are treated as if they have no concern with technology. They discuss behavior, motivations, relation of the individual to the group, and institutions such as the family, the church, and government as if they existed independently of a material culture. So, too, teachers in technological schools instruct their students in how to make this and construct that; and though these fabrications are to be used by society and have an effect upon social life, such matters appear to be of no concern to technologists. It is as if there were a great wall separating technology and sociology. . . .

The interrelationship of sociology and technology is of two kinds. One is in the sociological situation that gives rise to invention and discovery and to their uses by society. The other is in the effects upon society of the uses of invention and discovery.

It is true that technological work does not take place in a vacuum but generally in response to a social demand. So the origin is sociological. Yet those who learn the techniques of fabrication or apply them in construction are essentially concerned with physical properties of the materials used and not with the social conditions that originated the work. The men who make a prime mover are concerned mainly with making one that is more efficient or less costly or more durable or that occupies less space. They do not think very much about the reasons for this demand. . . .

Sociology deals with the interrelationship between the individual and the group, and between one group and another, as they are manifested in habits and institutions. Groups, habits, and institutions are all being altered by technological developments. The technology of early agriculture increased the size of groups from small wandering bands of hunters to larger stabilized villages. Domesticated animals and plows brought about communities with larger populations, making possible many kinds of small organizations not possible in a hunting culture. The steam engine changed the large family which was an economic institution producing a variety of goods into a small one producing little or nothing, with the members of the family becoming producers in other economic institutions. The invention of contraceptives had the effect of lowering the birth rate, of reducing the number of children in a family, and hence of affecting the personality of children; for a child with no brothers or sisters to play with, or with only one, has a personality different from a child reared with many playmates. Inventions in communication and transportation, coupled with conquest, have made possible larger governments, and made them more centralized. The practice of war has been changed frequently by inventions: when gunpowder replaced arrows and lances, when tanks replaced cavalry, and when Flying Fortresses brought destruction to civilians. So the materials with which sociology deals—groups, habits, institutions—are being changed from time to time, indeed in modern times continuously, by technology. So it is proper that the fences which separate technology and sociology be removed.

*Part Three*

# PERSONALITY
# IN SOCIAL PSYCHOLOGY

reprehensible, for instance, to set up an experiment to see what a person would be like if he were reared without any human contact. Fortunately for the development of social science, however unfortunate for the victims, a few instances of such isolation have actually occurred. Some have been shrouded in antiquity and reports concerning them have possibly been unreliable. Two cases, however, have occurred recently and have actually been studied by behavior scientists. Kingsley Davis, who has had first hand personal contact with both these cases, has summarized what study of these isolated children has taught us (page 113).

The relationship of personality and culture is by no means as close as over-simplified accounts in some textbooks have made it appear to be. No personality is a simple carbon copy of any other, and no culture has ever succeeded in molding men exactly to specifications. Yet the imprint of culture upon personality is one of the cardinal discoveries of social science. What are the limits to the cultural imprint? In a way, the whole of social science, especially social psychology, is necessary for a complete answer to our question. But special insight into the matter is provided in a very recent paper by Dennis H. Wrong. Professor Wrong takes his more naive colleagues to task (page 121). He accuses them of holding to an "*over*-socialized conception" of man. While not denying that socialization produces conformity, he shows that the impact is often less completely successful than we claim. This is an important paper. While a mastery of this idea may be a taxing exercise for some college students, it should also be a very rewarding one for those who wish to move beyond the pedestrian level of "taking soc."

The concept of "personal identity" is becoming an increasingly prevalent one in seeking understanding of human behavior in the modern world. Along with "anxiety," sometimes placed in juxtaposition to it, it focuses, many of us think, on the cardinal problems of human adjustment in the twentieth century. The "quest for identity," as some put it, is a very complex quest and very likely no one knows all about it, or even enough about it to be confident about even his own identity. His identity emerges and is manifest by interaction with others. In a mass society this "presentation of self" takes on forms little understood. The article by Don Martindale (page 146), indebted to the work of Erving Goffman, seems to us to be a lucid opening-up of an important and difficult aspect of personality structure in contemporary society.

It is doubtful whether there is any more widely known social scientist in America today than David Riesman. His *The Lonely Crowd* is a contemporary classic and his phraseology and insights (for example the concepts, inner-direction and other-direction) are part of the everyday language of even moderately literate people. Regrettably, it must be reported that Riesman would probably shudder at the way in which his concepts are sometimes bandied about, but that they are known and respected, no one can seriously deny. The reading on page 150, consisting of two excerpts from *The Lonely Crowd*, is an attempt to present briefly in the words of Riesman and his colleagues, exactly what he had to say about the three types of character and about the way other-direction works as a prevailing syndrome in American society today.

Everyone, it seems, professionals and laymen alike, are plagued with the Aristotelian dichotomy, "normal" and "abnormal." If most people are sure about anything, it is that there are somehow two kinds of behavior—the kind which we approve and assume to be in harmony with the universe, and the kind which we disapprove and judge to be somehow disharmonious with the inherent order of things. This is a naivete which should have been dispelled long ago, but alas, seems ever with us. Perhaps the clear logic and persistence of presentation of the reading on page 159 may do something to dispel the old idea. And those who may possibly not want to go the whole way with Brown may get some comfort out of a related view of the matter in the selection by John Gillin (page 167); although very likely the reading by J. S. Wallerstein and C. J. Wyle (page 170) will properly raise doubts again.

Nobody wants to be prejudiced, but everybody is, at least to some degree. Gordon W. Allport, in his *The Nature of Prejudice* has written one of the more significant books of our time. He has probed the subject to a degree to which few behavioral problems have been researched. For those who have not yet discovered *The Nature of Prejudice*, perhaps the substantial excerpt, "The Prejudiced Personality," should whet the appetite (page 175).

Most textbooks, and teachers also, "harp all the time" as students often say, on the research basis for knowledge in sociology. But seldom is it possible, because of the mechanics of class-room instruction, to show how actual studies are done with sufficient concreteness to convince a skeptical student. Such phrases as "research design," "hypothesis," and "levels of confidence" are more than analogies lifted from the more respectable sciences. Sometimes they have been misused to achieve a kind of flattery of self, to be sure, but there is a demonstrable license to the claim for a "science" of human behavior. After consideration of a number of possible researches, we have chosen two. The reasons for our choice ought, we think, to be shared, since certain features of the process have educational implications.

The two research studies selected are not presented as paragons of technical excellence. We regard them as typical of the better efforts of sociologists, rather than as models. Moreover, we have chosen studies, which our experience has indicated, are within the comprehension level of most students (probably not all) who study beginning sociology. On the other hand, we have tried to avoid using studies which are too simple, so as not to present an inaccurate conception of what is involved in sociological research. We begin with a study by Arnold M. Rose (page 192) because in his paper the research procedures are carefully spelled out and virtually all of the data presented in tables, so that the student can make comparisons himself and, if he is so inclined, check the text against the tabular material. The question researched is admittedly not of great import, but it is a competent piece of work and it concerns a question which ought to be of interest to a group of people typically a year or two removed from the subject matter studied.

The second study (page 208) involves, we feel, a second, and more advanced step. While all of the procedures may not be as precisely spelled out as in the first, there is less need so to do since some sophistication in reading research may be presumed to have been gained through the first study. In this study two constructs are used instead of one—"occupational aspiration" and "family interaction." Both are abstract, but the authors concretize the abstraction sufficiently so that it can be "felt." The study is also set into a tradition of research by citing related studies. Some discussion of measurement of concepts is introduced. Finally, the findings are presented and attention given to the question of levels of significance. We doubt, of course, that most students will understand without guidance from the teacher what, for example, is meant by $X^2 = 7.87$, or $df = 1$, or $P < .01$, but most of them have studied enough algebra that the teacher will be able to make at least an elementary explanation as to what these mean. And even if one does not comprehend all that is involved in the "significance of difference" concepts, at least he will come to appreciate that sociological research as currently being carried out has gone considerably beyond "counting the privies in Pittsburgh." And if he should still be under the illusion that "sociology is the study of what is already known," he is at least likely to wonder whether he already knew anything about the relationship between occupational aspiration and antecedent family interaction.

Thus, in this unit on social psychology we have tried

to sample both theory and research. In so doing we have used excerpts from the professional literature, editing rather liberally to aid student comprehension at this level, and have also used some especially lucid secondary sources. The extent to which we have been successful will undoubtedly vary from person to person, and itself be dependent, as we sociologists say, on other "significant variables," like the teacher, the ability level of the student, motivation—and possibly also the humidity and the proximity to holidays!

*Lawrence Guy Brown*

# THE INTERACTION HYPOTHESIS *

*Lawrence Guy Brown wrote one of the first textbooks in social psychology. He has been a particularly careful analyst, even if some might judge him too precise and thorough a writer. This statement of the interaction hypothesis is, we think, particularly thorough and should go a long way toward correcting some naivetes about the behavior of people generally, naivetes which, unfortunately, are sometimes reinforced by certain professional writings and teachings.*

The idea of cause and effect is dropped from thinking in the frame of reference here presented. No element is seen as a causative factor, since there is not an element in life that has its meaning within itself. Everything plays its role and gets its meaning in interaction; hence interaction becomes a chief concept in every explanation.

Heredity and environment, instead of being causative factors in human nature, are seen as interactive factors, having their meanings in terms of other elements. They function not as heredity and environment *per se* but as they are shaped in an interactive relationship. Any element in either the organic or the social heritage is an abstraction that becomes definite not in terms of its own nature alone but in terms of the interactive whole already in existence.

It is easy enough to see that this is true when an environ-

* From Lawrence Guy Brown, *Social Pathology* (New York, Appleton-Century-Crofts, 1942), pp. 9-12. (Title by the editors). Used by permission.

mental factor is involved, but it is not quite so obvious to many when a physical factor is considered. This is because thinking is still colored by the old theory of organic motivation which came into existence under a doctrine of causation. This theory assumed that human nature and society became the outward consequences of biological forces, of native instincts and other organic units. Many have been reluctant to abandon this point of view, since it is so simple to use.

Apart from this frame of reference, individuals talk about glands of internal secretion as causative factors. Within this frame of reference, before the case has been studied, it is not known whether the glandular condition started as a social maladjustment, a mental disorder, a physical disorder, or as all three.[1] Hypochondria shows the close interactive relationship in this frame of reference by revealing the ease with which human-nature disorders or social maladjustments may masquerade as physical disorders. In any case it is impossible to draw lines and say that here the organic ends and the social and human nature begin.

Had the idea of interactive factors preceded the idea of cause and effect there would have been a very different explanation for the behavior of the adolescent individual. There would not have been an explanation of adolescence in purely biological terms. The interactive relationship between the human nature brought from childhood, the social situation with its definition, the unique experience of the adolescent in a particular culture, and the organic maturity in the sex and other processes make up the frame of reference.

Had thinking been done in this frame of reference and in terms of interactive factors instead of cause and effect, the "individual-group controversy" would never have appeared and consumed so much time in the development of philosophy, social psychology, and sociology. "A separate individual is an abstraction unknown to experience, and so likewise is society, when

[1] Professor A. J. Carlson [a distinguished physiologist] of the University of Chicago has said: "We do not know whether these histopathological endocrine changes found in persons with mental disorders are causative factors in the disorders, contributory factors, sequellae, or merely parallel phenomena." (*The Problem of Mental Disorder* (New York, McGraw-Hill Book Co., 1934), p. 239.)

regarded as something apart from individuals." [2] It is a waste of time to try to establish the individual or society as the unit through which all human nature can be explained when the two have no separate existence but are two interrelated aspects of a total situation. It was outside the frame of reference discussed above that the futile conflict over a basic science had its origin. There is no basic science in this frame of reference. In this frame of reference, thinking could not have achieved the ecclesiastical view of man that separated mind from body, nor would the early philosophizing and biological study have produced so many confusing dichotomies such as "structure and function," "heredity and environment," and the like.

Certain erroneous life philosophies that have affected the political, economic, religious and cultural lives of a whole population for generations have resulted from the thinking that has been done outside of the interactive relationships in this frame of reference. The philosophy of individualism is an important example. It has ignored the fact that there has never been and never will be an individualist who is not also a "collectivist." [3] An individual cannot become human apart from a collectivity. Human nature is the phenomenon that ties the individual and his social heritage together; thus to be a human being is to be both a collectivist and an individualist. The nature of the collectivity determines the nature of the individualism and the character of the individualism determines the form of collectivism. After all, even the philosophy of individualism is a philosophy of a collectivity. If it were not, it could not exist. The "individualist" found this philosophy a widely accepted belief in the social heritage into which he was born. He is not even an individualist in the selection of his philosophy of individualism. It was passed on to him along with his language, his religion, his mode of dress, and other patterns.

Had thinking been done in terms of interactive factors rather than in terms of cause and effect, particularistic theories would never have gained academic status. The instinct theory,

[2] Charles H. Cooley, *Human Nature and the Social Order* (New York, Charles Scribner's Sons, 1922), p. 33.

[3] The term is not used in its narrow political sense but in its broad connotative meaning.

the division of insanity into organic and functional categories, the explanation of personality in biochemical terms, the doctrine of physical stigmata—none of these could have come to actualization had cause and effect not been the guiding principle.

In the same way there would not have been so much emphasis on "social determinants" if there had not been a search for cause and effect relationships. If the idea of interactive factors regulates the thinking, it is obvious that any social factor in a certain interactive relationship could be significant in either delinquency or nondelinquency, for instance, or in any other pathological behavior. Had there been an acceptance of the idea that nothing is important apart from interaction, the concept of free will would not have colored thinking for so long. "Will," to have importance, would necessarily be in interaction and would, therefore, not be free. Will, *per se,* is an abstraction. Like everything else, its nature is determined by the other interactive factors.

Many of the most important misconceptions concerning human behavior have materialized through thinking in terms of cause and effect. The idea that the first five years of a child's life are the most important is one of these. Too much emphasis has been placed on childhood experiences *per se.* In reality, subsequent experiences determine the importance of these early activities. They can have meaning in adulthood in no other way. The individual is not a product of his childhood but is the result of what adolescence, youth, and adulthood do to childhood experiences. Each subsequent period becomes a testing place for the human nature developed in a preceding period. Childhood experiences, like the experiences of any other period, must be viewed as an interactive part of a process. Each new experience makes childhood reactions a part of a new totality. These new experiences may continue the childhood patterns but they may also change them. If childhood patterns reach adulthood it is because the experiences of youth and adulthood were of a nature to foster rather than change them.

Many treatment programs would never have been instituted had thinking been done in terms of interactive factors rather than cause and effect. Treatment, to be successful, must be of a nature to become an interactive factor in a life organization that already exists. Consequently, therapeutic methods must vary with each personality. Quite as important is the fact that an interactive factor (such as drug addiction, alcoholism, perversion, etc.) has to be removed. The same difficulty arises if a socially approved interactive factor has to be eliminated; an interactive whole is broken up which by its nature tends to persist.

These illustrations could be extended to cover the entire field of social relationships, but since most of these will be discussed later in the text, these few will suffice to show the importance of this frame of reference and the necessity of thinking in terms of interactive factors rather than of cause-and-effect relationships.

*Kingsley Davis*

# ISOLATED CHILDREN:
# WHAT THEY SHOW *

*Kingsley Davis has been an extremely competent general practitioner in American sociology. Unlike the life-long devotee of some narrow specialization, he has from time to time tilled the academic soil on quite different terrain—but always competently. One of his lines of endeavor has been the study of isolated children. This excerpt summarizes somewhat briefly the more extensive treatment of the subject in two professional papers cited in the footnote below.*

One line of evidence showing the role of socialization in human mentality and human behavior and demonstrating how utterly limited are the resources of the organism alone, is afforded by extremely isolated children. Since with these individuals physical development has proceeded to an advanced point with practically no concomitant social influence, they reveal to what degree the stages of socialization are necessarily correlated with the stages of organic growth. They enable us to see what an unsocialized mind (and body) is like after developing beyond the point at which normal minds have been socially molded.

Two such cases have been seen by the writer.[1] The first was the case of an illegitimate child called Anna, whose grand-

---

* From Kingsley Davis, *Human Society* (Copyright © 1948, 1949 by The Macmillan Company, New York, and used with their permission), pp. 204-208.

[1] The material that follows is condensed, with permission of the publisher, from two papers by the writer: "Extreme Social Isolation of a Child," *American Journal of Sociology*, Vol. 45 (January, 1940), pp. 554-564; and "Final Note on a Case of Extreme Isolation," *ibid.*, Vol. 50 (March, 1947), pp. 432-437. The literature on feral and extremely neglected children has

father strongly disapproved of the mother's indiscretion and who therefore caused the child to be kept in an upstairs room. As a result the infant received only enough care to keep her barely alive. She was seldom moved from one position to another. Her clothing and bedding were filthy. She apparently had no instruction, no friendly attention.

When finally found and removed from the room at the age of nearly six years, Anna could not talk, walk, or do anything that showed intelligence. She was in an extremely emaciated and under-nourished condition, with skeleton-like legs and a bloated abdomen. She was completely apathetic, lying in a limp, supine position and remaining immobile, expressionless, and indifferent to everything. She was believed to be deaf and possibly blind. She of course could not feed herself or make any move in her own behalf. Here, then, was a human organism which had missed nearly six years of socialization. Her condition shows how little her purely biological resources, when acting alone, could contribute to making her a complete person.

By the time Anna died of hemorrhagic jaundice approximately four and a half years later, she had made considerable progress as compared with her condition when found. She could follow directions, string beads, identify a few colors, build with blocks, and differentiate between attractive and unattractive pictures. She had a good sense of rhythm and loved a doll. She talked mainly in phrases but would repeat words and try to carry on a conversation. She was clean about clothing. She habitually washed her hands and brushed her teeth. She would try to help other children. She walked well and could run fairly well, though clumsily. Although easily excited, she had a pleasant disposition. Her improvement showed that socialization, even when started at the late age of six, could still do a great deal toward making her a person. Even though her development was no more than that of a normal child of two to three years, she had made noteworthy progress.

been summarized by J. A. L. Singh and Robert M. Zingg, in *Wolf-Children and Feral Man* (New York, Harper, 1942). This source contains a full bibliography up to the date of publication. Since that time several articles have appeared, mostly devoted to the question of whether or not so-called "wolf-children" have actually existed. This aspect of the subject has been, in the writer's opinion, magnified beyond its importance.

A correct interpretation of this case is handicapped by Anna's early death. We do not know how far the belated process of socialization might ultimately have carried her. Inevitably the hypothesis arises that she was feebleminded from the start. But whatever one thinks in this regard, the truth is that she did make considerable progress and that she would never have made this progress if she had remained isolated. Of course, she was not completely isolated. Had she been, she would have died in infancy. But her contact with others was almost purely of a physical type which did not allow of communicative interaction. The case illustrates that communicative contact is the core of socialization. It is worth noting that the girl never had, even after her discovery, the best of skilled attention. It took her a long time to learn to talk, and it is possible that once she had learned to talk well the process of socialization would have been speeded up. With normal children it is known that the mastery of speech is the key to learning.

The other case of extreme isolation, that of Isabelle, helps in the interpretation of Anna. This girl was found at about the same time as Anna under strikingly similar circumstances when approximately six and a half years old. Like Anna, she was an illegitimate child and had been kept in seclusion for that reason. Her mother was a deaf-mute and it appears that she and Isabelle spent most of their time together in a dark room. As a result Isabelle had no chance to develop speech; when she communicated with her mother it was by means of gestures. Lack of sunshine and inadequacy of diet had caused her to become rachitic. Her legs in particular were affected; they "were so bowed that as she stood erect the soles of her shoes came nearly flat together, and she got about with a skittering gait." [2] Her behavior toward strangers, especially men, was almost that of a wild animal, manifesting much fear and hostility. In lieu of speech she made only a strange croaking sound. In many ways she acted like an infant. "She was apparently utterly unaware of relationships of any kind. When presented with a ball for the first time, she held it in the palm of her hand, then reached out and stroked my face with it. Such behavior is comparable

[2] Francis N. Maxfield, "What Happens When the Social Environment of a Child Approaches Zero," unpublished manuscript.

to that of a child of six months." [3] At first it was even hard to tell whether or not she could hear, so unused were her senses. Many of her actions resembled those of deaf children.

Once it was established that she could hear, specialists who worked with her pronounced her feebleminded. Even on non-verbal tests her performance was so low as to promise little for the future. "The general impression was that she was wholly uneducable and that any attempt to teach her to speak, after so long a period of silence, would meet with failure." [4] Yet the individuals in charge of her launched a systematic and skillful program of training. The task seemed hopeless at first but gradually she began to respond. After the first few hurdles had at last been overcome, a curious thing happened. She went through the usual stages of learning characteristic of the years from one to six not only in proper succession but far more rapidly than normal. In a little over two months after her first vocalization she was putting sentences together. Nine months after that she could identify words and sentences on the printed page, could write well, could add to ten, and could retell a story after hearing it. Seven months beyond this point she had a vocabulary of 1,500-2,000 words and was asking complicated questions. Starting from an educational level of between one and three years (depending on what aspect one considers), she had reached a normal level by the time she was eight and a half years old. In short, she covered in two years the stages of learning that ordinarily require six.[5] Or, to put it another way, her I.Q. trebled in a year and a half.[6] The speed with which she reached the normal level of mental development seems analogous to the recovery of body weight in a growing child after an illness, the recovery being achieved by extra fast growth until restoration of normal weight for the given age. She eventually entered school where she participated in all school activities as normally as other children.

Clearly the history of Isabelle's development is different from that of Anna's. In both cases there was an exceedingly low,

[3] Marie K. Mason, "Learning to Speak after Six and One-Half Years of Silence," *Journal of Speech Disorders*, Vol. 7 (1942), p. 299.

[4] *Ibid.*

[5] *Ibid.*, pp. 300-304.

[6] Maxfield, *op. cit.*

or rather blank, intellectual level to begin with. In both cases it seemed that the girl might be congenitally feebleminded. In both a considerably higher level was reached later. But Isabelle achieved a normal mentality within two years, whereas Anna was still markedly inadequate at the end of four and half years. What accounts for the difference?

Perhaps Anna had less innate capacity. But Isabelle probably had more friendly contact with her mother early in life, and also she had more skillful and persistent training after she was found. The result of such attention was to give Isabelle speech at an early stage, and her subsequent rapid development seems to have been a consequence of that. Had Anna, who closely resembled this girl at the start, been given intensive training and hence mastery of speech at an earlier point, her subsequent development might have been much more rapid.

Isabelle's case serves to show, as Anna's does not clearly show, that isolation up to the age of six, with failure to acquire any form of speech and hence missing the whole world of cultural meaning, does not preclude the subsequent acquisition of these. Indeed, there seems to be a process of accelerated recovery. Just what would be the maximum age at which a person could remain isolated and still retain the capacity for full cultural acquisition is hard to say. Almost certainly it would not be as high as age fifteen; it might possibly be as low as age ten. Undoubtedly various individuals would differ considerably as to the exact age.

Both cases, and others like them, reveal in a unique way the role of socialization in personality development. Most of the human behavior we regard as somehow given in the species does not occur apart from training and example by others. Most of the mental traits we think of as constituting the human mind are not present unless put there by communicative contact with others. No other type of evidence brings out this fact quite so clearly as do these rare cases of extreme isolation. Through them it is possible "to observe *concretely separated* two factors in the development of human personality which are always otherwise only analytically separated, the biogenic and the sociogenic factors." [7]

[7] Kingsley Davis, in a foreword in Singh and Zingg, *op. cit.*, pp. xxi-xxii.

## Ralph Linton

# CULTURE AND PERSONALITY *

*It would be difficult to find a more distinguished anthropologist than the late Ralph Linton. His book,* The Study of Man, *is a classic. This excerpt comes from a small book in which a series of lectures on culture and personality has been published. Linton is a very lucid writer, and his original contributions to anthropological theory are many. Several of them will be found in this collection of source materials. This excerpt concerns some of the problems that have induced anthropologists, sociologists, and psychologists to make an attempt to work together.*

One of the most important scientific developments of modern times has been the recognition of culture. It has been said that the last thing which a dweller in the deep sea would be likely to discover would be water. He would become conscious of its existence only if some accident brought him to the surface and introduced him to air. Man, throughout most of his history, has been only vaguely conscious of the existence of culture and has owed even this consciousness to contrasts between the customs of his own society and those of some other with which he happened to be brought into contact. The ability to see the culture of one's own society as a whole, to evaluate its patterns and appreciate their implications, calls for a degree of objectivity which is rarely if ever achieved. It is no accident that the modern scientist's understanding of culture has been derived so largely from the study of non-European cultures where observa-

* From Ralph Linton, *The Cultural Background of Personality* (New York, Appleton-Century-Crofts, 1945), pp. 125-128. By permission.

tion could be aided by contrast. Those who know no culture other than their own cannot know their own. Until very recent times even psychologists have failed to appreciate that all human beings, themselves included, develop and function in an environment which is, for the most part, culturally determined. As long as they limited their investigations to individuals reared within the frame of a single culture they could not fail to arrive at concepts of human nature which were far from the truth. Even such a master as Freud frequently posited instincts to account for reactions which we now see as directly referable to cultural conditioning. With the store of knowledge of other societies and cultures which is now available, it is possible to approach the study of personality with fewer preconceptions and to reach a closer approximation of the truth.

It must be admitted at once that the observation and recording of data on personality in non-European societies is still fraught with great difficulty. It is hard enough to get reliable material in our own. The development of accurate, objective techniques for personality study is still in its infancy. Such appliances as the Rorschach tests and Murray's thematic apperception tests have proved their value, but those who have worked with them would be the first to recognize their limitations. In the present state of our knowledge we still have to rely very largely upon informal observations and upon the subjective judgments of the observer. To complicate matters still further, most, although by no means all, of the information which we have on personality in non-European societies has been collected by anthropologists who had only a nodding acquaintance with psychology. Such observers, among whom I include myself at the time that I did most of my ethnological field work, are seriously handicapped by their ignorance of what to look for and what should be recorded. Moreover, there is a lamentable lack of comparative material on the various non-European societies which have been studied. The rapidity with which primitive societies have been acculturated or extinguished during the last hundred years has led to the development of a particular pattern of anthropological investigation. Since there were always far more societies available for study than there were anthropologists to study them and since most of these societies had to be investigated immediately or not at all, each investigator sought a new and unknown group. As a result, most of the information which we have has been collected by one investigator per society. The disadvantages of this are obvious in any case, but especially so in connection with personality studies. In a field where so much depends upon the subjective judgment of the observer and upon the particular members of the society with whom he was able to establish intimate contacts, the personality of the observer becomes a factor in every record. It is to be hoped that with the increasing number of anthropologists and the dwindling number of unstudied societies this pattern of exclusiveness will be broken down and that personality studies will benefit accordingly.

# Dennis H. Wrong

# THE OVERSOCIALIZED CONCEPTION OF MAN *

*Professional criticism, everyone should understand, is the lifeblood of every field of knowledge, whether from the tradition of the humanities or from that of science. Periodically there arise within the ranks of every professional group people who see things differently, or who become particularly perceptive, or who simply focus more sharply on matters which others take for granted. Often the task of criticism is made more easy because of the exaggerations or simple carelessness on the part of other practitioners of the profession. But easy or difficult, their role is indispensable, and everyone,* especially those criticized *are eternally in their debt.*

*This important paper by Dennis Wrong can well become a milestone in the presentation of the sociological point of view, not only for instructional purposes but for research endeavors as well. There seems little doubt that textbook writers especially, this editor no exception, have been something close to naive in the way in which they have overstated the role of society and culture in human behavior and in the way in which they have talked about conscience, the control of behavior, conformity, and the like.*

*Much more will probably be heard in the future concerning the ideas contained in this paper.*

* From Dennis H. Wrong, "The Oversocialized Conception of Man in Modern Sociology," *American Sociological Review* (April, 1961), Vol. 26, No. 2, pp. 187-193. (Italics by the editors.) Used by permission of the author and the *American Sociological Review.*

The relation between internalization and conformity assumed by most sociologists is suggested by the following passage from a recent, highly-praised advanced textbook: "Conformity to institutionalized norms is, of course, 'normal.' The actor, having internalized the norms, feels something like a need to conform. His conscience would bother him if he did not." [1] What is overlooked here is that the person who conforms may be even more "bothered," that is, subject to guilt and neurosis, than the person who violates what are not only society's norms but his own as well. To Freud, it is precisely the man with the strictest superego [conscience], he who has most thoroughly internalized and conformed to the norms of his society, who is most wracked with guilt and anxiety.[2]

Paul Kecskemeti, to whose discussion I owe initial recognition of the erroneous view of internalization held by sociologists, argues that the relations between social norms, the individual's selection from them, his conduct, and his feelings about his conduct are far from self-evident. "It is by no means true," he writes, "to say that acting counter to one's own norms always or almost always leads to neurosis. One might assume that neurosis develops even more easily in persons who *never* violate the moral code they recognize as valid but repress and frustrate some strong instinctual motive. A person who 'succumbs to temptation,' feels guilt, and then 'purges himself' of his guilt in some reliable way (e.g., by confession) may achieve in this way a better balance, and be less neurotic, than a person who never violates his 'norms' and never feels conscious guilt." [3]

Recent discussions of "deviant behavior" have been compelled to recognize these distinctions between social demands, personal attitudes toward them, and actual conduct . . .[4] They

[1] Harry M. Johnson, *Sociology: A Systematic Introduction* (New York, Harcourt, Brace and Co., 1960), p. 22.

[2] Sigmund Freud, *Civilization and Its Discontents* (New York, Doubleday Anchor Books, 1958), pp. 80-81.

[3] Paul Kecskemeti, *Meaning, Communication, and Value* (Chicago, University of Chicago Press, 1952), pp. 244-245.

[4] Robert Dubin, "Deviant Behavior and Social Structure: Continuities in Social Theory," *American Sociological Review*, 24 (April, 1959), pp. 147-164; Robert K. Merton, "Social Conformity, Deviation, and Opportunity Structures: A Comment on the Contributions of Dubin and Cloward," *Ibid.*, pp. 178-189.

represent, however, largely the rediscovery of what was always central to the Freudian concept of the superego. The main explanatory function of the concept is to show how people repress themselves, imposing checks on their own desires and thus turning the inner life into a battlefield of conflicting motives, no matter which side "wins," by successfully dictating overt action. So far as behavior is concerned, the psychoanalytic view of man is less deterministic than the sociological. For psychoanalysis is primarily concerned with the inner life, not with overt behavior, and its most fundamental insight is that the wish, the emotion, and the fantasy are as important as the act in man's experience.

Sociologists have appropriated the superego concept, but have separated it from any equivalent of the Freudian id. . . . Deviant behavior is accounted for by special circumstances: ambiguous norms, anomie, role conflict, or greater cultural stress on valued goals than on the approved means for attaining them. Tendencies to deviant behavior are not seen as dialectically related to conformity. The presence in man of motivational forces bucking against the hold social discipline has over his is denied.

Nor does the assumption that internalization of norms and roles is the essence of socialization allow for a sufficient range of motives underlying conformity. It fails to allow for variable "tonicity of the superego," in Kardiner's phrase.[5] The degree to which conformity is frequently the result of coercion rather than conviction is minimized.[6] Either someone has internalized the norms, or he is "unsocialized," a feral or socially isolated child, or a psychopath. Yet Freud recognized that many people, conceivably a majority, fail to acquire superegos. "Such people," he wrote, "habitually permit themselves to do any bad deed that procures them something they want, if only they are sure that no authority will discover it or make them suffer for it; their anxiety relates only to the possibility of detection. Present-day society has to take into account the prevalence of this state of

[5] Abram Kardiner, *The Individual and His Society* (New York, Columbia University Press, 1939), pp. 65, 72-75.

[6] C. Wright Mills, *The Sociological Imagination* (New York, Oxford University Press, 1959), pp. 39-41; Ralf Dahrendorf, *Class and Class Conflict in Industrial Society* (Stanford, Calif., Standford University Press, 1959), pp. 157-165.

mind." [7] The last sentence suggests that Freud was aware of
the decline of "inner-direction," of the Protestant conscience,
about which we have heard so much lately. So let us turn to
the other elements of human nature that sociologists appeal to
in order to explain, or rather explain away the problem. . . .

The insistence of sociologists on the importance of "social
factors" easily leads them to stress the priority of such socialized
or socializing motives in human behavior.[8] It is frequently the
task of the sociologist to call attention to the intensity with which
men desire and strive for the good opinion of their immediate
associates in a variety of situations, particularly those where received theories or ideologies have unduly emphasized other

---

[7] Freud, *op. cit.*, pp. 78-79.

[8] When values are "inferred" from this emphasis and then popularized,
it becomes the basis of the ideology of "groupism" extolling the virtues of
"togetherness" and "belongingness" that have been attacked and satirized so
savagely in recent social criticism. David Riesman and W. H. Whyte, the
pioneers of this current of criticism in its contemporary guise, are both
aware, as their imitators and epigoni usually are not, of the extent to which
the social phenomenon they have described is the result of the diffusion
and popularization of sociology itself. See on this point Robert Gutman and
Dennis H. Wrong, "Riesman's Typology of Character" (forthcoming in a
symposium on Riesman's work to be edited by Leo Lowenthal and Seymour
Martin Lipset), and William H. Whyte, *The Organization Man* (New
York, Simon and Schuster, 1956), Chapters 3-5. As a matter of fact, Riesman's
"inner-direction" and "other-direction" correspond rather closely to the
notions of "internalization" and "acceptance-seeking" in contemporary
sociology as I have described them. Riesman even refers to his concepts
initially as characterizations of "modes of conformity," although he then
makes the mistake, as Robert Gutman and I have argued, of calling them
character types. But his view that all men are to some degree both inner-
directed and other-directed, a qualification that has been somewhat neglected by critics who have understandably concentrated on his empirical
and historical use of his typology, suggests the more generalized conception
of forces making for conformity found in current theory. See David Riesman,
Nathan Glazer, and Reuel Denny, *The Lonely Crowd*, New York: Doubleday Anchor Books, 1953, pp. 17 ff. However, as Gutman and I have observed: "In some respects Riesman's conception of character is Freudian
rather than neo-Freudian: character is defined by superego mechanisms and,
like Freud in *Civilization and Its Discontents*, the socialized individual is
defined by what is forbidden him rather than by what society stimulates him
to do. Thus in spite of Riesman's generally sanguine attitude towards
modern America, implicit in his typology is a view of society as the enemy
both of individuality and of basic drive gratification, a view that contrasts
with the at least potentially benign role assigned it by neo-Freudian thinkers
like Fromm and Horney." Gutman and Wrong, "Riesman's Typology of
Character," p. 4 (typescript).

motives such as financial gain, commitment to ideals, or the effects on energies and aspirations of arduous physical conditions. Thus sociologists have shown that factory workers are more sensitive to the attitudes of their fellow-workers than to purely economic incentives; that voters are more influenced by the preferences of their relatives and friends than by campaign debates on the "issues"; that soldiers, whatever their ideological commitment to their nation's cause, fight more bravely when their platoons are intact and they stand side by side with their "buddies."

It is certainly not my intention to criticize the findings of such studies. My objection is that their particular selective emphasis is generalized—explicitly or, more often, implicitly—to provide apparent empirical support for an extremely one-sided view of human nature. Although sociologists have criticized past efforts to single out one fundamental motive in human conduct, the desire to achieve a favorable self-image by winning approval from others frequently occupies such a position in their own thinking. . . .

But there is a difference between the Freudian view on the one hand and both sociological and neo-Freudian conceptions of man on the other. To Freud man is a *social* animal without being entirely a *socialized* animal. His very social nature is the source of conflicts and antagonisms that create resistance to socialization by the norms of any of the societies which have existed in the course of human history. "Socialization" may mean two quite distinct things; when they are confused an oversocialized view of man is the result. On the one hand socialization means the "transmission of the culture," the particular culture of the society an individual enters at birth; on the other hand the term is used to mean the "process of becoming human," of acquiring uniquely human attributes from interaction with others.[9] All men are socialized in the latter sense, but this does not mean that they have been completely molded by the particular norms and values of their culture. All cultures, as Freud contended, do violence to man's socialized bodily drives, but this in no sense means that men could possibly exist without

[9] Paul Goodman has developed a similar distinction. "Growing up Absurd," *Dissent,* 7 (Spring, 1960), pp. 123-125.

culture or independently of society.[10] From such a standpoint, man may properly be called as Norman Brown has called him, the "neurotic" or the "discontented" animal and repression may be seen as the main characteristic of human nature as we have known it in history.[11]

But isn't this psychology and haven't sociologists been taught to foreswear psychology, to look with suspicion on what are called "psychological variables" in contra-distinction to the institutional and historical forces with which they are properly concerned? There is, indeed, as recent critics have complained, too much "psychologism" in contemporary sociology, largely, I think, because of the bias inherent in our favored research techniques. But I do not see how, at the level of theory, sociologists can fail to make assumptions about human nature.[12] If our assumptions are left implicit, we will inevitably presuppose of a view of man that is tailor-made to our special needs; when our sociological theory over-stresses the stability and integration of society we will end up imagining that man is the disembodied, conscience-driven, status-seeking phantom of current theory. We must do better if we really wish to win credit outside of our ranks for special understanding of man, *that plausible creature* [13] *whose wagging tongue so often hides the despair and darkness in his heart.*

[10] Whether it might be possible to create a society that does not repress the bodily drives is a separate question. See Herbert Marcuse, *Eros and Civilization* (Boston, The Beacon Press, 1955); and Norman O. Brown, *Life Against Death* (New York, Random House, Modern Library Paperbacks, 1960). Neither Marcuse nor Brown are guilty in their brilliant, provocative and visionary books of assuming a "natural man" who awaits liberation from social bonds. They differ from such sociological Utopians as Fromm, *The Sane Society* (New York, Rinehart and Company, 1955), in their lack of sympathy for the de-sexualized man of the neo-Freudians. For the more traditional Freudian view, see Walter A. Weisskopf, "The 'Socialization' of Psychoanalysis in Contemporary America," in Benjamin Nelson, editor, *Psychoanalysis and the Future* (New York, National Psychological Association For Psychoanalysis, 1957), pp. 51-56; Hans Meyerhoff, "Freud and the Ambiguity of Culture," *Partisan Review*, 24 (Winter, 1957), pp. 117-130.

[11] Brown, *op. cit.*, pp. 3-19.

[12] "I would assert that very little sociological analysis is ever done without using at least an implicit psychological theory." Alex Inkeles, "Personality and Social Structure," in Robert K. Merton and others, editors, *Sociology Today* (New York, Basic Books, 1959), p. 250.

[13] Harry Stack Sullivan once remarked that the most outstanding characteristic of human beings was their "plausibility."

## Lawrence Guy Brown

# HUMAN NATURE *

*"Human nature" is something that we are irresistibly impelled to think and to talk about. Probably by the time any adult is able to read material of this sort, he has learned the hard lesson that concepts from everyday language, and buttressed by common sense perceptions, are likely to be in need of substantial re-examination in the light of professional knowledge and experience. Human nature has been variously defined, even by the experts, and the formulation in the following excerpt is not presented as necessarily any more defensible than some other one. It is, however, a widely held concept of the matter and is quite consistent with the Interaction Hypothesis discussed in an earlier reading. The subordinate concept of the behavior reserve is somewhat unique to the writings of Professor Brown and is an added refinement, we think, to the ordinary discussions of the subject.*

In considering any type of personal disorganization one is dealing with human nature, so that it is necessary to understand this part of the frame of reference. Human nature is everything that results from the interaction of the human-nature potentialities in the organic and social heritages through the unique experience of an individual. It is the way in which heredity and environment are incorporated into a life organization, the way the organic and social processes are brought into a life organization. Each experience of any type produces human nature. Human

* From Lawrence Guy Brown, *Social Pathology* (New York, Appleton-Century-Crofts, 1942), pp. 43-48. Used by permission.

nature gives the individual and society their inextricable relationship and is the phenomenon that ties the organic and social heritages together, making them a functioning unity. . . .

## The Origin of Human Nature

There have been many erroneous ideas concerning the origin of human nature in the life of an individual. The present view on the subject, which has tended to supplant earlier conceptions, is that the individual does not possess human nature at birth. At the present time few, if any, students of social behavior look into the biological process alone for the origin or the explanation of human nature. No modern student talks about human behavior being congenitally predetermined. A few, however, are tending to go to the opposite extreme, turning away from the organic heritage to the social heritage to find the inception of human nature. Others have recognized the importance of both these heritages and have discovered the origin of human nature in the interaction of these two heritages. This is the point of view in this text. Human nature in the life of any individual, whether normal or abnormal, has its inception in the unique experience of the person as these two heritages interact.

Human nature, then, is something that has to be achieved after the birth of the individual. No individual of any racial or nationalistic affiliation is born human, nor is he born to be either normal or abnormal so far as a life organization is concerned. Normality or abnormality in human nature has to be achieved in a social order through the unique experience of the person.

## All Behavior Is a Manifestation of Human Nature

Repulsive acts have been called animal nature, but this is a false conception. All behavior, whether normal or abnormal, is a manifestation of human nature. Insanity is just as much human nature as sanity. Delinquency is human nature, as are likewise the behavior patterns of the law-abiding citizen. Dishonesty must be classed with honesty as human nature. Sex pathologies of all types are human nature along with sex normalities. Lying and veracity are human nature. Any adjustment is human nature, whether it is socially approved or disapproved. Degradation on the lowest known level is human nature quite as much as manifestations that are called noble and sublime.

In the penal institutions throughout the world the life organizations of criminals are human nature. A murderous mental organization is human nature; so likewise is any criminal pattern. The behavior of every person in the insane institutions of the world is a manifestation of human nature. Human nature works for war and peace. Inhumane cruelties, so-called, are, after all, human cruelties. Vulgarity, suicidal intentions, drug addiction, alcoholism, vice, etc., are evidences of human nature.

## Reserve Potentialities in Human Nature

One never sees a total life organization in action. Each person has behavior reserve potentialities that are both conscious and unconscious and are both normal and abnormal. When a student of behavior speaks of unconscious elements in human nature, he is not thinking of some metaphysical entity or a phenomenon that is so different from conscious elements. Behavior reserve is human nature that can be used in the same way that one uses his conscious life organization. As a matter of fact, the human nature that ties the two heritages together and becomes an interactive factor in every adjustment is both conscious and unconscious. One aspect is no more important than the other. Both are involved in personal organization and disorganization, since both contain adjustment assets and liabilities. The two regions of a life organization have many more characteristics in common than they have differentiating them from each other.

It is the belief of some that these hidden elements in human nature are more significant than the recognized factors; but this is not the case. An unknown in a chemical solution is no more consequential than the known elements in the interactive relationship, and the same is true of the unconscious factors in one's behavior reserve. Unconscious elements in human nature are not expressed apart from known elements. They have their meaning in terms of perceptible traits. They cannot exist apart from them or influence behavior except in an interactive relationship with them. A person cannot be explained by an un-conscious trait. The discovery of a hidden experience in the unconscious mind merely gives a more complete picture of the individual and enables him to have a better understanding of his own complex nature. Hidden experiences may lead to happi-ness and normality quite as often as to misery and abnormality. If a person is interested in treatment, he must look for hidden assets quite as much as for concealed liabilities.

Although each and every experience is integrated into the life organization of the individual, it is often recorded there without the individual's recognizing this registration. A person does not say to himself, each time he has an experience, "This has become a part of me." He does not always notice the day-by-day changes in his human nature. He is not always aware that he is going step by step toward an adjustment end. He is surprised eventually, and does not understand the accumulated result. The step-by-step procedure may have been unconscious, since life is an unconscious process until some definite thwarting is experienced. The dynamic role of unrecognized integrations is not weakened merely because the person does not know that he has certain human-nature characteristics. Furthermore, self-deception is one of man's outstanding accomplishments.

When a new interactive factor from the organic or the social heritage enters the adjustment life of an individual, it is likely that human-nature potentialities never used before will be disclosed and utilized. A person discovers himself and reveals himself to others only in adjustment situations. Thinking, day-dreaming, philosophizing, and similar activities are adjustment situations, along with more overt behavior. When a behavior specialist asks a client questions, these queries are new inter-active factors that may reveal conscious and unconscious poten-tialities, but it is possible that these questions will not have that function in a complete sense. There seem to be many potential attitudes in each life organization that lack maturity or lack a social situation that will make them functional. An individual may have immature murderous attitudes that may be released when his honor or that of someone dear to him is endangered.

Most individuals have unconscious attitudes that could easily throw them into the category of the pathological. There are probably few individuals without delinquent attitudes. Most people have unconsciously considered, at least, the violation of the mores of their groups. Murders of passion have back of them a long history of attitudes, habits, emotions, and desires just as do any other murders. People would be frightened if they realized the potentialities that exist in their unconscious minds.

Some of these unconscious factors reveal themselves under various circumstances. An alcoholic depressant releases some of them and the person behaves in a way strange to his sober role. The drinking did not suddenly implant new complex patterns of behavior but released some that were already there in the unconscious organization of past experiences. Anger, fear, and other emotions reveal many unconscious patterns. Mental ill-health opens up the unconscious hidden potentialities, also. Indecent exposure in senile dementia is evidence of a desire that has been present, perhaps, since childhood. The person may not have been aware that it was there or had not admitted its existence to himself. Every day people are surprising themselves with attitudes that they did not know they had. The sudden overt expression of attitudes of bravery, cowardice, jealousy, selfishness, abnormality, etc., often occasions surprise to the person who evidences them. There is no sudden change in the life of the trusted citizen who absconds with the funds of the bank. For years he has been developing slowly in that direction. In the life of each individual there are many potentialities carefully concealed in the unconscious. The behavior specialist is not surprised at the unconventional behavior of a conventional person though the individual's friends may refuse to believe that he is guilty. This discussion only hints at the complexity of human nature in its conscious and unconscious aspects.

Impulsive behavior, so-called, is a part of the unconscious mental organization of the individual. The attitudes and potentialities were there as an essential part of his human nature. The person excuses himself if he has behaved badly in so-called impulsive demonstrations and says that his actions were not a part of him. Actually, this behavior was a part of the human nature of the individual even though he feels sure that it was not. It is quite as much a product of his unique experience as are the factors of which he is aware. Apologies are accepted for "impulsive" behavior, since it is believed that the individual was not himself. But a person is always what he does. Perhaps he was not his customary self, but he was his unconscious self, at least. A part of concealed human nature was revealed. In reality, there is no impulsive behavior as the term is frequently used. Impulsive behavior is like all other behavior. It is an expression of the life organization of the person and is quite as much a part of him as are his usual activities.

The chief function of the unconscious aspect of a life organization is to prepare the individual for situations that do not arise day after day. It gives the individual adjustment potentialities not demanded by daily activities. Nature has not made the mistake of limiting an individual to his conscious personality, the one demanded by the habitual world. A conscious life organization is not adequate for all the exigencies of a complex or even of a simple cultural heritage. The unconscious personality is just as vital, just as necessary as the conscious aspects of a life organization. The unconscious aspect can be organized for pathological behavior, normal behavior, or both. A weak-willed person, so-called, is often behaving in terms of a strong unconscious life organization that makes it possible to go contrary to the wishes of friends and relatives.

Behavior reserve in a life organization may prepare the person to meet a crisis with hysteria, mental ill-health, suicide, alcoholism, crime, sex abnormalities, escape mechanisms, compensatory distortions, hypochondria, or any of the great number of pathological adjustments. A crisis like the First World War revealed a great variety of life organizations: conscientious objectors, some who married to escape service, others who maimed themselves, a great many who sought service in noncombative branches; there were suicides, mental ill-health, hypochondria, and the stressing of all physical disabilities. On the other hand, many took the war in their stride, showing courage where it was supposed not to exist, revealing on all occasions reserve forces from unconscious life organizations that made these individuals ready for the exigencies of war. This happened even when these persons were opposed to war.

Many unconscious life organizations have been revealed by

the economic depression, by marriage, by transition from rural to urban life, by loss of many values—occupation, position, wealth, health, dear ones. All of these factors reveal personal organization as well as personal disorganization.

Individuals escape from private conventional worlds by using the reserve potentialities found in the unconscious aspects of their life organization. Part of this procedure is in terms of a conscious pattern of life, but often the individual is able to go further in his escape from his private world than his conscious attitudes would permit. The conscious life organization may give an individual a strong repugnance for an activity, but once in a situation his reserve human nature seems to have a tolerance. There are many cases where individuals have gone into a situation prepared to criticize but remained to participate. Many persons, critical in their daily attitudes concerning pathological behavior, have themselves engaged in similar pathological behavior under certain conditions. The explanation is to be found in reserve potentialities.

The crowd, the mob, secret organizations like the Black Legion, underworld retreats, and many other situations offer individuals opportunities to express conscious and unconscious aspects of their human nature. Wars, revolutions, strikes, conflicts between minority and majority, bring out human nature that would not be revealed in daily life. Associations with many different classes of people reveal the many-sided nature of a single life organization.

It is important to remember that the conscious and unconscious aspects of a life organization are not separate entities in a functional sense, though we have been inclined to think of them as distinct from each other. The nature of each is determined by the other. If the unconscious life organization were different, then the conscious would be different.

## Hadley Cantril

# DON'T BLAME IT
# ON "HUMAN NATURE"! *

*Professor Cantril is a psychologist well known for numerous empirical studies as well as for more generalized writings such as the following. This discussion of human nature will be interesting to compare, in its implications, with the previous reading.*

. . . Tastes, standards and values vary from one culture to another. And if you have walked on the other side of the tracks, visited other parts of your city, mingled at all with people not in your own social class or your own customary groups, you will also know that tastes, standards and identifications vary a great deal even within a single [society].

If "human nature," then, means anything at all, it must include not only the innate biological characteristics that make you not only a human being but a unique human being; it must also include the direction of your individual or your group effort as learned or formed through the identifications you have made in your particular process of becoming a member of society.

An important and necessary part of the psychologist's account of human motivation is found in the individual's identification with a specific group. For it is this that gives him his status, that builds in him his ego-satisfaction. Thus he strives to maintain or enhance his status; he strives to place himself as far up as he can in that social hierarchy whose values have become his.

* From Hadley Cantril, "Don't Blame It on 'Human Nature'," *The New York Times Magazine* (July 6, 1947), pp. 5, 32-33. (Italics by the editors.) By permission.

If we could get firmly into our minds this distinction between those characteristics of man that are biologically determined and those directions of his activity that are learned according to the particular ideas of the particular social and economic groups with which he has lived, a great deal of the vagueness surrounding the phrase "human nature" would disappear.

Examine, for instance, the statement that "human nature can't be changed." Obviously, we cannot change the genetic characteristics of man (except perhaps experimentally). We cannot create people with three eyes; we cannot create a third sex; we cannot so change people that none of them has an I.Q. of less than 180. But this has nothing whatever to do with the potentiality of changing the *direction* of man's efforts.

Whether a man is going to be "competitive" or "cooperative"; whether he is going to be a Catholic, a Protestant, a Mohammedan, or an atheist; whether he is going to be a Republican or a Democrat—such things are almost entirely determined by the particular set of conditions and values the man has learned. These identifications, these modes of behavior, even if diametrically opposed to each other, all serve the same basic psychological function for the individual. We do not need to drag in any instinct of gregariousness or any innate drive for status to account for man's activities. Group identifications emerge inevitably because man lives, not in complete isolation, but with other men.

"Human nature," then, is anything but static and unchangeable. It can and does change with conditions. In fact, it is always changing. And not only is there gradual change, but frequently there is the sudden emergence of new qualities and characteristics formed when a single individual or group of individuals find themselves in a new set of conditions. Technological developments, for example, such as the steam engine, the airplane, the harnessing of atomic energy, at first provide some means to a specific end. Generally, however, they soon begin to affect and modify the ends themselves.

Take, for example, the following case of a complete "reversal" of "human nature" effected by a war-created situation in a normal American boy who was not "cruel" or "pugnacious" by disposition. The case was reported to me by one of my Princeton students who knew the captain he describes:

"The captain was a Southerner in his mid-twenties. He had been a rifle company commander on the Western Front. He was very well liked by both his fellow-patients and by the hospital personnel. His outstanding personality traits were modesty and the friendliness and kindliness of his disposition. As a boy he had been fond of duck-hunting but had given up the sport because, as he said, 'I didn't see much fun in killing.' Once, during a discussion of war experiences, he told the following story:

"He had commanded a company during the disastrous Battle of the Bulge, when the German Army had broken through the American lines in the Ardennes Forest. The captain found himself cut off from the rest of our forces and surrounded by the enemy. His situation was desperate. He had only about forty men left, no food, little ammunition and no idea where the American lines were. In addition to these difficulties, his company had a large number of German prisoners on hand. There was no way to get rid of the prisoners by sending them to a camp in the rear area. Guarding them with his depleted forces was out of the question.

"Therefore, he determined to kill the prisoners. He and the sergeant took them out in the woods in small groups and shot them. Among the captain's group was a young boy, only about 15 or 16 years old. The captain concluded his story with this remark: 'He was crying and begging me to save him and I was kind of sorry I had to kill him.' "

Hundreds of illustrations of this type could be given, with respect not only to individuals but to the changed direction of group activities such as occur in revolutionary situations. People are not gangsters or law-abiding citizens, Fascists or Communists, agnostics or believers, good or bad, because of innate dispositions. People's actions do not take the directions they do because people are blessed or cursed with a certain kind of "human nature." People's actions take the directions they do because a certain set of conditions has provided status, meaning and satisfaction, or, in critical times, because status, meaning and satisfaction must be sought in new ways.

Hence conflicts between one individual and another, between one group and another, are inevitable so long as conflicting identifications and conflicting purposes, springing from social conditions, persist.

These conflicts will never be resolved by compromises or attempts to "change human nature" on any individualistic basis. They will be solved finally only when social, economic and political relationships are so arranged that an individual, while retaining his own purposes, his own status and his own ego-strivings, can identify these with the larger, all-inclusive goals of the whole society. Personal goals must become socially valuable goals and social goals must become personally valuable.

It should be stressed that this idea of a common purpose does not mean a leveling off of taste, interest, or performance with respect to the inherent and unique capacities and temperamental characteristics of the individual. For these differences in abilities and temperament will determine the specific role an individual can fruitfully play within his group and within the larger interests of society.

Someone is sure to ask the psychologist why, if he thinks he knows so much about human nature, can't he do something about it? Why must we endure unending conflict? Why can't the social psychologist tell people—especially those in power—what should be done? . . .

In casually patterned societies such as ours is today, the psychologist and the social scientist are apt to be laughed off by the "man of affairs" as impractical and starry-eyed dreamers. We need not argue the claim that the physical scientists are ahead of the social scientists. It is difficult to know what measuring rod one should use. It might, however, be pointed out that the problem of man and his relationships are probably even more complex than the problems of nuclear physics and not so amenable to controlled experimentation.

*But the main point is that we already know a great deal more about man and his social relationships than most people in our casually patterned society are willing to use.* And we also know why people aren't willing to pay attention to scientists who deal with people. Apparently we have to wait until people learn the hard way that real democracy and real world peace can come about only when human beings recognize their common purposes as human beings. Further, they must see that the dignity and uniqueness of every individual (pathological cases aside) can be preserved and enhanced without in any way running head-on into the common purposes of all men.

We can say, then, that there is nothing fixed, or static, or immutable about human nature. We can say that there is no one single accurate characterization of it. We can say that it is fluid, constantly changing, that occasionally, under a new set of conditions, it exhibits new and heretofore undreamed-of possibilities. When conditions are changed, human nature is changed.

Human nature as it characterizes any group at any given time is what it is because of the conditions under which the individuals in that group have matured. And the only way to bring about the human nature we want is to plan scientifically the kind of social and economic environment offering the best conditions for the development of human nature in the direction we would specify—a direction that spells freedom from group conflict and freedom for personal development.

# Ralph Linton

# STATUS AND ROLE *

*It is doubtful whether there is any more widely diffused
confusion in sociological and anthropological writing
than that between status and role. This article is the
classic statement of the case to which everyone refers
in footnotes whether or not his own usage is consistent
with that of Linton. This is not meant to imply that the
distinction is a trivial one or that the difference is one
of hair splitting at which admittedly some academicians
are particularly adept. To the contrary, the distinction
is an important one and the discussion of achieved and
ascribed statuses essential to any adequate understanding of socio-cultural conditioning.*

The term *status*, like the term *culture*, has come to be used with
a double significance. A *status*, in the abstract, is a position in
a particular pattern. It is thus quite correct to speak of each
individual as having many statuses, since each individual participates in the expression of a number of patterns. However,
unless the term is qualified in some way, the *status* of any individual means the sum total of all the statuses which he occupies.
It represents his position with relation to the total society. Thus
the status of Mr. Jones as a member of his community derives
from a combination of all the statuses which he holds as a
citizen, as an attorney, as a Mason, as a Methodist, as Mrs.
Jones's husband, and so on.

A status, as distinct from the individual who may occupy it,
is simply a collection of rights and duties. Since these rights and

* From *The Study of Man* (New York, Appleton-Century-Crofts, Inc.,
1936), pp. 113-119. Used by permission.

duties can find expression only through the medium of individuals, it is extremely hard for us to maintain a distinction in our thinking between statuses and the people who hold them and exercise the rights and duties which constitute them. The relation between any individual and any status he holds is somewhat like that between the driver of an automobile and the driver's place in the machine. The driver's seat with its steering wheel, accelerator, and other controls is a constant with ever-present potentialities for action and control, while the driver may be any member of the family and may exercise these potentialities very well or very badly.

A *role* represents the dynamic aspect of a status. The individual is socially assigned to a status and occupies it with relation to other statuses. When he puts the rights and duties which constitute the status into effect, he is performing a role. Role and status are quite inseparable, and the distinction between them is of only academic interest. There are no roles without statuses or statuses without roles. Just as in the case of *status,* the term *role* is used with a double significance. Every individual has a series of roles deriving from the various patterns in which he participates and at the same time a *role* in general, which represents the sum total of these roles and determines what he does for his society and what he can expect from it.

Although all statuses and roles derive from social patterns and are integral parts of patterns, they have an independent function with relation to the individuals who occupy particular statuses and exercise their roles. To such individuals the combined status and role represent the minimum of attitudes and behavior which he must assume if he is to participate in the overt expression of the pattern. Status and role serve to reduce the ideal patterns for social life to individual terms. They become models for organizing the attitudes and behavior of the individual so that these will be congruous with those of the other individuals participating in the expression of the pattern. Thus if we are studying football teams in the abstract, the position of quarterback is meaningless except in relation to the other positions. From the point of view of the quarter-back himself it is a distinct and important entity. It determines where he shall take his place in the line-up and what he shall do in various plays. His assignment to this position at once limits and defines his activities and establishes a minimum of things which he must learn. Similarly, in a social pattern such as that for the employer-employee relationship the statuses of employer and employee define what each has to know and do to put the pattern into operation. The employer does not need to know the techniques involved in the employee's labor, and the employee does not need to know the techniques for marketing or accounting.

It is obvious that, as long as there is no interference from external sources, the more perfectly the members of any society are adjusted to their statuses and roles the more smoothly the society will function. In its attempts to bring about such adjustments every society finds itself caught on the horns of a dilemma. The individual's formation of habits and attitudes begins at birth, and, other things being equal, the earlier his training for a status can begin the more successful it is likely to be. At the same time, no two individuals are alike, and a status which will be congenial to one may be quite uncongenial to another. Also, there are in all social systems certain roles which require more than training for their successful performance. Perfect technique does not make a great violinist, nor a thorough book knowledge of tactics an efficient general. The utilization of the special gifts of individuals may be highly important to society, as in the case of the general, yet these gifts usually show themselves rather late, and to wait upon their manifestation for the assignment of statuses would be to forfeit the advantages to be derived from commencing training early.

Fortunately, human beings are so mutable that almost any normal individual can be trained to the adequate performance of almost any role. Most of the business of living can be conducted on a basis of habit, with little need for intelligence and none for special gifts. Societies have met the dilemma by developing two types of statuses, the *ascribed* and the *achieved*. *Ascribed* statuses are those which are assigned to individuals without reference to their innate differences or abilities. They can be predicted and trained for from the moment of birth. The *achieved* statuses are, as a minimum, those requiring special qualities, although they are not necessarily limited to these. They are not assigned to individuals from birth but are left open to be filled through competition and individual effort. The majority of the statuses in all social systems are of the ascribed type and those which take care of the ordinary day-to-day business of living are practically always of this type.

In all societies certain things are selected as reference points for the ascription of status. The things chosen for this purpose are always of such a nature that they are ascertainable at birth, making it possible to begin the training of the individual for his potential statuses and roles at once. The simplest and most universally used of these reference points is sex. Age is used with nearly equal frequency, since all individuals pass through the same cycle of growth, maturity, and decline, and the statuses whose occupation will be determined by age can be forecast and trained for with accuracy. Family relationships, the simplest and most obvious being that of the child to its mother, are also used in all societies as reference points for the establishment of a whole series of statuses. Lastly, there is the matter of birth into a particular socially established group, such as a class or caste. The use of this type of reference is common but not universal. In all societies the actual ascription of statuses to the individual is controlled by a series of these reference points which together serve to delimit the field of his future participation in the life of the group.

The division and ascription of statuses with relation to sex seems to be basic in all social systems. All societies prescribe different attitudes and activities to men and to women. Most of them try to rationalize these prescriptions in terms of the physiological differences between the sexes or their different roles in reproduction. However, a comparative study of the statuses ascribed to women and men in different cultures seems to show that while such factors may have served as a starting point for the development of a division the actual ascriptions are almost entirely determined by culture. Even the psychological characteristics ascribed to men and women in different societies vary so much that they can have little physiological basis. Our own idea of women as ministering angels contrasts sharply with the ingenuity of women as torturers among the Iroquois and the sadistic delight they took in the process. Even the last two generations have seen a sharp change in the psychological patterns for women in our own society. The delicate, fainting lady of the middle eighteen-hundreds is as extinct as the dodo.

When it comes to the ascription of occupations, which is after all an integral part of status, we find the differences in various societies even more marked. Arapesh women regularly carry heavier loads than men "because their heads are so much harder and stronger." In some societies women do most of the manual labor; in others, as in the Marquesas, even cooking, housekeeping, and baby-tending are proper male occupations, and women spend most of their time primping. Even the general rule that women's handicap through pregnancy and nursing indicates the more active occupations as male and the less active ones as female has many exceptions. Thus among the Tasmanians seal-hunting was women's work. They swam out to the seal rocks, stalked the animals, and clubbed them. Tasmanian women also hunted opossums, which required the climbing of large trees.

Although the actual ascription of occupations along sex lines is highly variable, the pattern of sex division is constant. There are very few societies in which every important activity has not been definitely assigned to men or to women. Even when the two sexes cooperate in a particular occupation, the field of each is usually clearly delimited. Thus in Madagascar rice culture the men make the seed beds and terraces and prepare the fields for transplanting. The women do the work of transplanting, which is hard and back-breaking. The women weed the crop, but the men harvest it. The women then carry it to the threshing floors, where the men thresh it while the women winnow it. Lastly, the women pound the grain in mortars and cook it.

When a society takes over a new industry, there is often a period of uncertainty during which the work may be done by either sex, but it soon falls into the province of one or the other. In Madagascar, pottery is made by men in some tribes and by women in others. The only tribe in which it is made by both men and women is one into which the art has been introduced within the last sixty years. I was told that during the fifteen years preceding my visit there had been a marked decrease in the number of male potters, many men who had once practised the art having given it up. The factor of lowered wages, usually advanced as the reason for men leaving one of our own occupations when women enter it in force, certainly was not operative here. The field was not overcrowded, and the prices for men's and women's products were the same. Most of the men who had given up the trade were vague as to their reasons, but a few said frankly that they did not like to compete with women. Apparently the entry of women into the occupation had robbed it of a certain amount of prestige. It was no longer quite the thing for a man to be a potter, even though he was a very good one.

The use of age as a reference point for establishing status is as universal as the use of sex. All societies recognize three age groupings as a minimum: child, adult, and old. Certain societies have emphasized age as a basis for assigning status and have greatly amplified the divisions. Thus in certain African tribes the whole male population is divided into units composed of those born in the same years or within two- or three-year intervals. However, such extreme attention to age is unusual, and we need not discuss it here.

The physical differences between child and adult are easily recognizable, and the passage from childhood to maturity is marked by physiological events which make it possible to date it exactly for girls and within a few weeks or months for boys. However, the physical passage from childhood to maturity does not necessarily coincide with the social transfer of the individual from one category to the other. Thus in our own society both men and women remain legally children until long after they are physically adult. In most societies this difference between the physical and social transfer is more clearly marked than in our own. The child becomes a man not when he is physically mature but when he is formally recognized as a man by his society. This recognition is almost always given ceremonial expression in what are technically known as puberty rites. The most important element in these rites is not the determination of physical maturity but that of social maturity. Whether a boy is able to breed is less vital to his society than whether he is able to do a man's work and has a man's knowledge. Actually, most puberty ceremonies include tests of the boy's learning and fortitude, and if the aspirants are unable to pass these they are left in the child status until they can. For those who pass the tests, the ceremonies usually culminate in the transfer to them of certain secrets which men guard from women and children.

The passage of individuals from adult to aged is harder to perceive. There is no clear physiological line for men, while even women may retain their full physical vigor and their ability to carry on all the activities of the adult status for several years after the menopause. The social transfer of men from the adult to the aged group is given ceremonial recognition in a few cultures, as when a father formally surrenders his official position and titles to his son, but such recognition is rare. As for women, there appears to be no society in which the menopause is given ceremonial recognition, although there are a few societies in which it does alter the individual's status. Thus Comanche women, after the menopause, were released from their disabilities with regard to the supernatural. They could handle sacred objects, obtain power through dreams and practise as shamans, all things forbidden to women of bearing age.

The general tendency for societies to emphasize the individual's first change in age status and largely ignore the second is no doubt due in part to the difficulty of determining the onset of old age. However, there are also psychological factors involved. The boy or girl is usually anxious to grow up, and this eagerness is heightened by the exclusion of children from certain activities and knowledge. Also, society welcomes new additions to the most active division of the group, that which contributes most to its perpetuation and well-being. Conversely, the individual who enjoys the thought of growing old is atypical in all societies. Even when age brings respect and a new measure of influence, it means the relinquishment of much that is pleasant. We can see among ourselves that the aging usually refuse to recognize the change until long after it has happened.

## Don Martindale

# THE FORMALIZATION
# OF PERSONAL IDENTITY *

*Most of the writings on the self, social roles, and self-
other behavior found in standard text books have been
derived from the writing of Charles Horton Cooley and
George Herbert Mead. In both instances the point of
reference which they seem to use is that of a primary
group orientation, that is, they assume that the interaction takes place between people who know each other
more or less totally and the opportunities for systematic
manipulation and deception of the other are minimized
if not extirpated. Contemporary mass society, however,
presents a very different picture. Much, if not the major
part, of interaction between people is fragmentized, or
"secondary" as sociologists tend to call it, and the individual interacts with others in a much more fragmentized and potentially deceptive way. This notion
has been grasped effectively by Erving Goffman on
whose work the following summary and interpretation
by Martindale has been based.*

. . . The language of social roles seems to be unusually appropriate to the problem of the social presentation of the self in
modern society. The description of self in its everyday social
affairs in these terms has been carried out with unusual economy
and insight by Erving Goffman.[1]

* From Don Martindale, *American Society* (Copyright 1960, D. Van
Nostrand Company, Inc., Princeton, New Jersey), pp. 61-64. [Italics by the
editors]. Used by permission.

[1] Erving Goffman, *The Presentation of Self in Everyday Life* (Edinburgh, University of Edinburgh Social Sciences Research Center, 1956).

Goffman maintains that when an individual appears before others he has motives for trying to control the impression they receive of the situation. Interaction is the reciprocal influence of individuals on one another's actions during social contacts. A *performance* is all the activity of a given participant serving to influence other participants. The pre-established pattern of action unfolded during the performance is a "part" or a "routine." When an individual plays a part he implicitly requests his observers to take seriously the impression that is fostered. The actor's attitude toward the impression he fosters varies from his belief in it, sincerity, to his disbelief in it, or cynicism. *Front* is the expressive equipment of a standard kind, intentionally or unwittingly employed during the performance. The "setting" is the same scenic parts of expressive equipment. *Manner* consists of those stimuli which warn the audience of the attitude the performer expects to bring to the situation. The tendency for a large number of different roles to be presented behind a small number of fronts is a natural development of social organization. Since fronts tend to be selected to fit the task to be performed, trouble arises when those who perform a given task are forced to select a suitable front from several dissimilar ones. Tasks may arise that do not fit the standard array. In military and medical hierarchies, for example, tasks arise which fall between the spaces of existing ranks.

Goffman maintains that while in the presence of others the individual infuses his activity with signs which dramatically highlight acts that might otherwise remain obscure. Sometimes dramatization constitutes a problem for practical reasons, as when merchants must charge high prices for things that look expensive to pay for the insurance, slack periods, and things of the sort that do not appear before the public eye. Sometimes the management of appearance is so complex that it becomes a special function of some members of an organization while the real work is done by others.

According to Goffman, since the performance of a routine through its front makes claims upon the audience, the individual's performance tends to incorporate and exemplify the officially accredited and accepted values of the society. There is thus a constant difference between appearance and reality. One of the richest sources of data on the presentation of idealized performances is the literature on social mobility. Upward mobility involves presentation of performances proper to the strata above one's own in the efforts to move upward and keep from moving downward. In American society Goffman thinks such upward mobility is most frequently expressed in status symbols of material wealth. Idealized performances are not confined to status movements, but also appear defensively, as when southern Negroes present the stereotype of ignorant shiftlessness or when the junk peddler maintains an image of abject poverty.

In appearances before the public, economies and pleasures and profits and errors tend to be repressed. The urbane style affected in some scholarly books contrasts with the feverish drudgery the author may have endured in earlier drafts; and many performers foster the impression that they have only ideal motives for acquiring the role or that they have ideal qualifications for it (suppressing the indignities, insults, and humiliations and deals entering into its acquisition). Medical schools, according to Goffman, often recruit students partly on the basis of ethnic origin, while they publicly sustain the myth that the students occupy their position by merit alone.

Nor must one assume that the audience wants the truth. The audience may experience a great saving of time and emotional energy if it accepts the performance at face value. For example, it saves wear and tear on the emotions if one accepts the myth in relation to the medical doctor that the general practitioner sends the patients to a specialist on the basis of merit rather than because of college ties or fee splitting arrangements.

The performer can therefore rely on his audience to accept minor clues as a sign that something is important about the performance. The audience may, however, misunderstand such clues. Moreover, unintended gestures occur, incompatible with the impression being presented: by accident, because of self-consciousness or embarrassment, or lack of dramaturgical direction. Performances, in fact, differ in the degree that expressive consistency is required. It is usually greater in sacred performances, but may be present in secular performances as well. The expressive coherence required in a performance often reveals the discrepancies between the social and real self.

While it is necessary for the audience to accept signs to orient itself to the performance, this puts the performer in the position of misrepresenting and may lead the audience to examine with special care those properties of the performance that cannot easily be feigned. The reaction to impersonation is ironically strongest when it most nearly approximates the real thing. The social definition of impersonation is, however, not very consistent. It tends to be rigid with regard to such sacred status as that of doctor or priest, but weak with regard to others. Organizations such as real estate bodies develop codes specifying the degree to which doubtful impressions (by overstatement, and omission) may be conveyed. In American law intent, negligence, and strict liability are distinguished, but there are no universal rules to guide socially approved amounts of misrepresentation. The possibilities range from the barefaced lie to the white lie that may accomplish a humanistic purpose.

As Goffman sees it, the performance of an individual always accentuates some matters and hides others. The restrictions placed on confidence and maintenance of social distance may generate awe, holding the audience in a state of mystification. The audience often cooperates in a respectful fashion with awed regard of the sacred integrity imputed to the performer. Frequently the only real secret is that there is no secret.

Goffman urges that some performances serve mainly to express the characteristics of the task rather than of the performer. A number of individuals cooperating in staging a single routine is a team. A routine which requires a team often centers in a member of the team who becomes a star, forming the lead or hub of attention. A team always has something of the character of a secret society.

David Riesman, Reuel Denny
and Nathan Glazer

# THREE TYPES OF CHARACTER STRUCTURE *

*Few collegians have not heard about inner- and other-
directed character or do not know that a David Riesman wrote a book on* The Lonely Crowd *which many
people regard as important. The book and its senior
author rated a cover story in* Time. *This in itself is no
mean achievement. In the bandying about of Riesman's
ideas there is ample evidence that we should all go
back and read our lesson again. What did Riesman say?
First he said that his study enabled him to differentiate
three "character types," which many others would
probably simply call "personality types"—tradition-
directed, inner-directed, and other-directed. He did not
say that every person is in all of his behavior clearly one
or the other of these; quite to the contrary he speaks of
"mixed types" and in other ways warns against a too-
naïve taking over of his trichotomy.*

*The three types compared.* One way to see the structural differences between the three types is to see the differences in the
emotional sanction or control in each type.

(1) The tradition-directed person feels the impact of his
culture as a unit, but it is nevertheless mediated through the
specific, small number of individuals with whom he is in daily
contact. These expect of him not so much that he be a certain

* Reprinted from David Riesman, Reuel Denny, and Nathan Glazer,
*The Lonely Crowd* (Copyright, 1950, by Yale University Press, New Haven,
Conn.). By permission. pp. 40-42, 36-38 (Doubleday Anchor Edition).

type of person but that he behave in the approved way. Consequently the sanction for behavior tends to be the fear of being *shamed*.

(2) The inner-directed person has early incorporated a psychic gyroscope which is set going by his parents and can receive signals later on from other authorities who resemble his parents. He goes through life less independent than he seems, obeying this internal piloting. Getting off course, whether in response to inner impulses or to the fluctuating voices of contemporaries, may lead to the feeling of *guilt*.

Since the direction to be taken in life has been learned in the privacy of the home from a small number of guides and since principles, rather than details of behavior, are internalized, the inner-directed person is capable of great stability. Especially so when it turns out that his fellows have gyroscopes too, spinning at the same speed and set in the same direction. But many inner-directed individuals can remain stable even when the reinforcement of social approval is not available—as in the upright life of the stock Englishman isolated in the tropics.

(3) Contrasted with such a type as this, the other-directed person learns to respond to signals from a far wider circle than is constituted by his parents. The family is no longer a closely knit unit to which he belongs but merely part of a wider social environment to which he early becomes attentive. In these respects the other-directed person resembles the tradition-directed person: both live in a group milieu and lack the inner-directed person's capacity to go it alone. The nature of this group milieu, however, differs radically in the two cases. The other-directed person is cosmopolitan. For him the border between the familiar and the strange—a border clearly marked in the societies depending on tradition-direction—has broken down. As the family continuously absorbs the strange and so reshapes itself, so the strange becomes familiar. While the inner-directed person could be "at home abroad" by virtue of his relative insensitivity to others, the other-directed person is, in a sense, at home everywhere and nowhere, capable of a rapid if sometimes superficial intimacy with and response to everyone.

The tradition-directed person takes his signals from others, but they come in a cultural monotone; he needs no complex receiving equipment to pick them up. The other-directed person must be able to receive signals from far and near; the sources are many, the changes rapid. What can be internalized, then, is not a code of behavior but the elaborate equipment needed to attend to such messages and occasionally to participate in their circulation. As against guilt-and-shame controls, though of course these survive, one prime psychological lever of the other-directed person is a diffuse *anxiety*. This control equipment, instead of being like a gyroscope, is like a radar.[1] . . .

If we wanted to cast our social character types into social class molds, we could say that inner-direction is the typical character of the "old" middle class—the banker, the tradesman, the small entrepreneur, the technically oriented engineer, etc.—while other-direction is becoming the typical character of the "new" middle class—the bureaucrat, the salaried employee in business, etc. Many of the economic factors associated with the recent growth of the "new" middle class are well known. They have been discussed by James Burnham, Colin Clark, Peter Drucker, and others. There is a decline in the numbers and in the proportion of the working population engaged in production and extraction—agriculture, heavy industry, heavy transport—and an increase in the numbers and the proportion engaged in white-collar work and the service trades. People who are literate, educated, and provided with the necessities of life by an ever more efficient machine industry and agriculture, turn increasingly to the "tertiary" economic realm. The service industries prosper among the people as a whole and no longer only in court circles. . . .

These developments lead, for large numbers of people, to changes in paths to success and to the requirement of more "socialized" behavior both for success and for marital and personal adaptation. Connected with such changes are changes in the family and in child-rearing practices. In the smaller families of urban life, and with the spread of "permissive" child care to ever wider strata of the population, there is a relaxation of older patterns of discipline. Under these newer patterns the peer-group (the group of one's associates of the same age and class) becomes much more important to the child, while the parents

[1] The "radar" metaphor was suggested by Karl Wittfogel.

make him feel guilty not so much about violation of inner standards as about failure to be popular or otherwise to manage his relations with these other children. Moreover, the pressures of the school and the peer-group are reinforced and continued—in a manner whose inner paradoxes I shall discuss later —by the mass media: movies, radio, comics, and popular culture media generally. Under these conditions types of character emerge that we shall here term other-directed. To them much of the discussion in the ensuing chapters is devoted. *What is common to all the other-directed people is that their contemporaries are the source of direction for the individual—either those known to him or those with whom he is indirectly acquainted, through friends and through the mass media. This source is of course "internalized" in the sense that dependence on it for guidance in life is implanted early. The goals toward which the other-directed person strives shift with that guidance: it is only the process of striving itself and the process of paying close attention to the signals from others that remain unaltered throughout life.* This mode of keeping in touch with others permits a close behavioral conformity, not through drill in behavior itself, as in the tradition-directed character, but rather through an exceptional sensitivity to the actions and wishes of others.

Of course, it matters very much who these "others" are: whether they are the individual's immediate circle or a "higher" circle or the anonymous voices of the mass media; whether the individual fears the hostility of chance acquaintances or only of those who "count." But his need for approval and direction from others—and contemporary others rather than ancestors— goes beyond the reasons that lead most people in any era to care very much what others think of them. While all people want and need to be liked by some people some of the time, it is only the modern other-directed types who make this their chief source of direction and chief area of sensitivity.[2]

[2] This picture of the other-directed person has been stimulated by, and developed from, Erich Fromm's discussion of the "marketing orientation" in *Man for Himself,* pp. 67-82. I have also drawn on my portrait of "The Cash Customer," *Common Sense,* XI (1942), 183.

# Don Martindale

# SELF DEVELOPMENT LITERATURE *

*It will be recalled from reading Martindale's "The Formalization of Personal Identity" (p. 146) that Goffman uses the language of the theater to characterize much of the interaction in the mass society. It is almost as if there is a tacit understanding of all this, and that this understanding may account for the tremendous popularity of what Martindale calls the "self development literature" which Americans devour by the carload. Presumably we do this in order to play the required role, we hope, more adroitly.*

The approach to personality by the practical students of personal relations, seems to flow naturally into the language and categories of merchandising. The contemporary self improvement literature is by and for people with something to sell. Perhaps the most famous "how to" book on socially effective personal relations is Dale Carnegie's *How to Win Friends and Influence People.*[1] Carnegie rose from the obscurity of a Missouri farm to international fame by skillfully exploiting a widespread demand for effective self-presentation. The book was first published in 1936, selling a million copies the first year. It has been printed abroad in fourteen languages. It was on the *New York Times'* best seller list for ten years. It has sold over 5,000,000 copies, and continues to sell over 250,000 a year.

* From Don Martindale, *American Society,* copyright 1960, D. Van Nostrand Company, Inc., Princeton, New Jersey, pp. 72-75. By permission.

[1] Dale Carnegie, *How to Win Friends and Influence People* (New York, Pocket Books, Inc., 1958).

It was Carnegie's opinion that there are some fundamental techniques for "handling" people. The first principle is never to criticize, for it only puts a man on the defensive, makes him strive to justify himself, wounds his pride, and hurts his sense of importance. Rather than criticize—this is the second principle —praise him. On the other hand, we should not use flattery, for, Carnegie tells us, everyone would catch on to it and we would all be experts in human relations, but give honest, sincere appreciation.[2] Moreover, it is only possible to influence others by getting them to talk about what they want and showing them how to get it.

To put them into the terms of Goffman, Carnegie's formulations could, perhaps, be stated somewhat as follows: A most crucial set of roles in everyday life are those intended to get the other person to do one's bidding. For all such roles there are three basic techniques of self-presentation that will go far toward achieving one's objective. (1) Never attack other persons, at least not directly; it only puts them on guard—in fact sometimes they counter-attack when they are wounded. (2) Soften them up with a little praise; that is, "honest, sincere appreciation." (3) Always disguise the form of influence you wish to exercise as something the other man wants.

With respect to the second principle, Carnegie warns that one should not use flattery, for if that were all there were to influencing others, all persons would be experts in social relations. If one really does not like the other person or persons, however, this is not a condition that can be changed by fiat. It may be assumed, then, that the difference between "flattery" and "honest, sincere appreciation" in this context is the subtlety and effectiveness of the latter.

While there are three principles for influencing people, the task of making them like you appears to be a bit more complicated, for this is said to require six rules:

Rule 1. Become genuinely interested in other people.
Rule 2. Smile.
Rule 3. Remember that a man's name is to him the sweetest and most important sound in any language.
Rule 4. Be a good listener. Encourage others to talk about themselves.

[2] *Ibid.*, p. 38.

Rule 5. Talk in terms of the other man's interest.
Rule 6. Make the other person feel important—and do it sincerely.[3]

Above all, Carnegie urges, if you wish to make people like you, or if you wish to manipulate them, avoid doing what comes naturally. "Hesitate about doing the natural thing, the impulsive thing. This is usually wrong." [4] Moreover, it is wise to practice constantly one's newly won arts. "Apply these rules at every opportunity. If you don't, you will forget them quickly." [5]

It appears somewhat more difficult to win people to one's own way of thinking than it is to make them feel friendly, for it requires no less than twelve rules for this:

Rule   1. The only way to get the best of an argument is to avoid it.
Rule   2. Show respect for the other man's opinions. Never tell a man he is wrong.
Rule   3. If you are wrong, admit it quickly and emphatically.
Rule   4. Begin in a friendly way.
Rule   5. Get the other person saying "yes, yes" immediately.
Rule   6. Let the other man do a great deal of the talking.
Rule   7. Let the other man feel that the idea is his.
Rule   8. Try honestly to see things from the other person's point of view.
Rule   9. Be sympathetic with the other person's ideas and desires.
Rule 10. Appeal to the nobler motives.
Rule 11. Dramatize your ideas.
Rule 12. Throw down a challenge.[6]

The kinds of things one can expect to gain out of life is not inconsiderable if one will only observe these rules.
"If you can be sure of being right only 55 per cent of the time, you can go down to Wall Street, make a million dollars a day, buy a yacht, and marry a chorus girl." [7]
Carnegie expresses enthusiastic agreement with J. Pierpont Morgan's opinion that a man usually has two reasons for doing a thing—the one that sounds good, and a real one.[8] Under these circumstances, if one intends to persuade another to one's way

---

[3] *Ibid.*, p. 107.
[4] *Ibid.*, p. 56.
[5] *Ibid.*, p. 56.
[6] *Ibid.*, p. 176.
[7] *Ibid.*, p. 114.
[8] *Ibid.*, p. 165.

of thinking, it behooves him to exploit the reasons that sound good.

As one's skill develops in manipulating people, making them like you, and persuading them to accept your way of thinking, one approaches the time when he is able actually to change people's opinions without giving offense or arousing resentment. There are, it seems, nine rules for this:

Rule 1. Begin with praise and honest appreciation.
Rule 2. Call attention to people's mistakes indirectly.
Rule 3. Talk about your own mistakes before criticizing the other person.
Rule 4. Ask questions instead of giving direct orders.
Rule 5. Let the other man save his face.
Rule 6. Praise the slightest and every improvement. Be "hearty in your approbation and lavish in your praise."
Rule 7. Give the other person a fine reputation to live up to.
Rule 8. Use encouragement. Make the fault seem easy to correct.
Rule 9. Make the other person happy about doing the thing you suggest.[9] . . .

Many persons have criticized Carnegie for the development of rules for a kind of pseudo-*Gemeinschaft*—developing a kind of imitation of family attitudes into a strategy of business success. Actually, he turns the flank on all such critics and proposes the transformation of family behavior into a personal relations strategy. There are seven lucky rules for success in marriage:

Rule 1. Don't nag.
Rule 2. Don't try to make your partner over.
Rule 3. Don't criticize.
Rule 4. Give honest appreciation.
Rule 5. Pay little attentions.
Rule 6. Be courteous.
Rule 7. Read a good book on the sexual side of marriage.[10]

It is not unfair to describe this most famous of all self-improvement books as extending the rules for successful personal behavior in the market place to the sphere of the family. Here and there Carnegie gives some idea of what he really thinks about people. He feels that about 85 per cent of personal

[9] *Ibid.*, p. 203.
[10] *Ibid.*, p. 238.

success is due to skill in manipulating people.[11] People are primarily motivated by an inflated sense of self-importance.

If some people are so hungry for a feeling of importance that they actually go insane to get it, imagine what miracles you and I can achieve by giving people honest appreciation this side of insanity.[12]

People are not particularly complicated; in fact, in Carnegie's universe their sexual maladjustments can be cleared up by reading a good book on the sexual side of marriage. Moreover, in the end, people are bores. . . .

Bores, that is what they are—bores intoxicated with their own egos, drunk with a sense of their own importance. . . .

Remember that the man you are talking to is a hundred times more interested in himself and his wants and his problems than he is in your problems. His toothache means more to him than a famine in China that kills a million people. A boil on his neck interests him more than forty earthquakes in Africa.[13]

The unvarnished truth, according to Carnegie, "is that almost every man you meet feels himself superior to you in some way." [14] This is true even in life's most intimate spheres, and he quotes with approval Dorothy Dix's view that "matrimony is no place for candor. It is a field for diplomacy." [15]

[11] *Ibid.*, p. 13.
[12] *Ibid.*, p. 34.
[13] *Ibid.*, pp. 91-92.
[14] *Ibid.*, p. 99.
[15] *Ibid.*, p. 105.

*Lawrence Guy Brown*

# THE NORMAL
# AND THE ABNORMAL *

*In this excerpt Professor Brown comes to grips not only
with the semantics of "normal and abnormal" but with
a great deal of empirical evidence which bears upon
the notion. The person who wants quick answers to
quick questions will find this tedious; the one who wants
to ask the better question so that he can get more reliable answers will find this exceptionally illuminating.
The research-minded person will find it indispensable.*

## INTRODUCTION

Both normal and abnormal behavior are manifestations of human
nature. This fact places the normal and the abnormal in the
same broad category and makes them, in general, the same type
of phenomenon; it also makes it possible to establish unifying
principles that will apply to all social phenomena. Furthermore,
the research student or the treatment specialist will never find
a single situation where the abnormal is isolated from the normal. There are not two classes of people in society, the normal
and the abnormal, but persons with varying degrees of normality
and abnormality.

The research students and the treatment specialists who
are interested in social control have abandoned the idea of
studying or dealing with an abnormality alone. When explana-

* From Lawrence Guy Brown, *Social Pathology* (New York, Appleton-
Century-Crofts, 1942), pp. 57-62. Used by permission.

tions and treatment are in order, the person rather than the pathology is the center of attention. Just as the modern doctor deals with the patient rather than with the disease alone, so the student of behavior deals with the total person rather than the pathology. The study of the total person is always a study of normality and abnormality. Personal disorganization never functions apart from personal organization, and one cannot be explained apart from the other in the life of any person. If the normal characteristics were different, then the abnormal traits would be different. If one wishes to understand and rehabilitate a pathological person, he has to study his assets as well as his liabilities, since one has no meaning apart from the other. In treatment, the assets serve as the basis for the program of re-habilitation. In a course in social pathology, one can talk about the abnormal and differentiate it from the normal, but the student must realize that normality and abnormality have many things in common and do not exist apart from each other. A delinquent, for instance, has many nondelinquent attitudes that help, quite as much as any other factor, to determine the nature of his delinquencies. If his socially approved attitudes were different, his misdemeanors would be different.

Knowledge of the close relationship between the normal and the abnormal has more than a research value. It is significant for the adjustments of individuals. Ignorance concerning this relationship has led people to believe they are abnormal when they are not. Likewise, abnormal persons may regard themselves as normal. Medical students have fears concerning the diseases that they study because they have had symptoms similar to those disclosed. Students in courses in abnormal psychology see in themselves rudimentary traits of the various insane types, little realizing that every insane mental process has its sane prototype. Similar feelings are the experience of all who dis-cover in themselves traits that are like those in the abnormal. Many persons are convinced that such processes as rationaliza-tion, escape mechanisms, and introspection are definitely ab-normal; we shall see later that these processes are as much a part of normal behavior as they are a part of abnormal adjust-ments.

## DEFINITION OF THE ABNORMAL

It is customary to define the abnormal in a course in social pathology and differentiate it from the normal. This, however, is not at all necessary for understanding and explaining behavior. The research specialist can study a unit of behavior without waiting for labels. All behavior, normal or abnormal, arose in interactive living and can be studied as the same type of phenomenon. If one is interested in treatment, he wants to know what is abnormal so that he may select cases for a therapeutic program. Even then he must realize that abnormal behavior is modified in precisely the same manner in which normal behavior is modified.

The important thing in the field of human adjustments is to be able to explain the behavior of an individual or a group. A research specialist studies the unique experiences of all individuals in the same way, whether they are normal or abnormal. His frame of reference is the same, his approach is identical, his attitude is objective, and he finds the same principles applying in all cases. He uses connotative labels to locate a problem but becomes interested in denotative labels only after he has completed his research. In one case he finds abnormal characteristics in the overt activities of the person and in another he discovers the abnormal only in the behavior reserve potentialities. In the first case, the necessary interactive factor has been experienced in the organic or social heritage to release the abnormal; in the other case, the proper interactive factor has not been experienced, so the abnormality remains only a potentiality. In the second case, the preparation for abnormality may be quite as adequate as it was in the first one where the pathology is a part of overt behavior. While the interest here is in personal rather than social disorganization, the same can be said about group behavior. One group may be at war while another is at peace, yet in the social organization of the second group all the potentialities for aggressive war may exist.

In the definition of the normal and the abnormal there will have to be a broad, general, connotative meaning that can be used for theoretical discussions. This definition will have to be made specific in each individual case since no two persons are normal or abnormal in the same way. An interactive factor can be normal in one totality and abnormal in another. This is easily observed in the physical aspect of the totality when there is an allergy for some food that causes distress for the allergic person but may be eaten without ill effect by another. In the social area of life, education can be a factor in either normal or abnormal behavior. In human nature, an emotional attitude of love can be normal or abnormal. So there is need for a connotative definition that permits many denotative usages.

Since a person always has normal and abnormal characteristics and potentialities, the abnormal life organization must be one that contains more abnormal potentialities than normal in certain characteristics. Two so-called abnormal persons are not alike. They differ from each other in many respects. Consequently the abnormal is not an absolute. It is an abstraction, since it varies with every person. The normal person, from the standpoint of human nature and social behavior, may be regarded as one whose behavior is not injurious to himself or to members of his group. This definition applies equally well to any phase of the social-organic-psychological unity.

A tentative, connotative definition designed for theoretical discussion of the behavior of a hypothetical individual could read as follows: The abnormal refers to behavior in which characteristics injurious to the individual or to members of his group predominate over those which are beneficial. One is abnormal when any organic or social process is integrated into his life organization in a way to be injurious to the social, physical, or mental welfare of the individual or the group. This may include such deviations as over- or under-development or perversions of any type. This definition has no functional denotative meaning but can be made specific in actual cases in the hands of the expert. A usable concept must be both theoretical and functional; that is, it must lend itself to both connotative and denotative usages.

Then comes the problem of deciding what is injurious to the individual and the group. It is obvious that what is injurious to one person or to one group may not be harmful to the adjustment health of others. Excessive behavior is injurious in most cases, but that which is excessive behavior for one is not excessive behavior for another. This difficulty arises whether one is considering the organic individual, the psychological individual, the social individual, or the functioning unity that includes all three. Two persons with the same physical malady are not equally ill. In both cases there is a pathological condition but the pathology is not the same in both cases.

The whole problem of defining the abnormal seems even more complex when it is realized that any factor in life can be important in either normality or abnormality. Religion, for instance, can be a factor in either normality or abnormality, in sanity or insanity; so, likewise, can education, marriage, or any other factor. A person can be a religious fanatic or one who does not stress this aspect of life at the expense of other phases. If the matter is measured by the value-judgments of the layman the question is still more complicated. What would be considered religious fanaticism in one group would be regarded as normal in another.

So far as overt behavior is concerned, the same person is not equally abnormal day after day. A person may be fairly normal so far as his conscious potentialities are concerned but he may have many well-developed abnormal potentialities that have never been expressed. In most discussions, the terms *normal* and *abnormal* never refer to a total person but to segments of a life organization. The normal and the abnormal are often so close together that it is difficult to tell where one merges into the other. The abnormal may be little more than the normal exaggerated, which is the case in certain types of insanity. The real interest here is not in definitions but in the process through which a person acquires human nature that may be personal organization or personal disorganization; the study of this process is essential so that unifying principles may be established. As we have seen, the study of the process through which human nature is achieved does not demand such categories as normal and abnormal. In all cases, the research student is dealing with the same general phenomenon. It is in treatment that he needs these definitions. Even in treatment he deals with the normal and the abnormal in the same way if he expects to be successful.

## THE PROCESS BY WHICH ABNORMALITY IS ACHIEVED

More important than a formal definition of the abnormal is knowledge concerning the process by which an individual becomes abnormal and the process through which he can be made normal. We have already seen that the individual is not born human; but, more than this, he is not destined to be either normal or abnormal so far as human nature is concerned. He is an unbiased candidate for either. The organic and social heritages of any individual lend themselves to both normal and abnormal behavior. If an individual becomes abnormal, he does so through his unique experience in bringing his organic and social heritages into human nature.

An individual develops human nature by forming attitudes, ideas, desires, interests, and habits. This is true whether the human nature is normal or abnormal. It is through his unique experience in achieving these characteristics that he becomes normal or abnormal. The social conformist can meet the nonconformist with the realization that he became what he is in exactly the same way that the nonconformist became what he is. This fact does not make social variants less abnormal but does help in understanding them; and it should offer a clue to those who have selected the responsibility of changing patterns of behavior. It does not make abnormal behavior as desirable as normal behavior. It merely points out the fact that social variants are normal for their experiences but are abnormal by social definition or according to norms established in research.

In reality one learns to be normal or abnormal, learns to be a delinquent or a nondelinquent, learns to be sane or insane, achieves his philosophy of life through learning, learns to desire morality or immorality, learns to be a radical or a conservative, an atheist or a religionist. Some of these adjustments are not so desirable from the standpoint of group and individual welfare, but they are just as natural so far as the nature of organic and social processes is concerned. Abnormal behavior is a naturalistic phenomenon and must be dealt with in the same way as all other material in this category.

## Processes Are Neither Normal
## Nor Abnormal

Until recently only abnormal behavior was studied, so it was believed that many of the processes connected with pathological adjustments were peculiar to them. Now that abnormal behavior is being studied in relation to normal behavior it has been discovered that these processes in human nature are neither normal nor abnormal. Most of the vocabulary concerning these processes connotes abnormal behavior because the terminology was accepted and given popular usage while only abnormal people were being studied.

Negativism, considered as part of a pathological adjustment, often saves an individual from an environment with great potentialities for maladjustments. Thus there can be nondelinquents in delinquency areas, or moral persons in vice districts, or honest persons where graft and corruption abound. There can be negativistic reactions to socially disapproved patterns as well as to socially sanctioned activities. Mental ill-health can result from either case.

The pathological person uses rationalization to convince himself that he has a right to behave as he does. The normal person forgets his mistakes and makes his lot in life bearable by the same process. Though some writers talk about the harmful effect of introspection, it is just as necessary for an ordered mind as it is important in a disordered mind. Escape mechanisms, in themselves, are not abnormal. After a person has gone into some business occupation, he may feel the limitations imposed on him by his ignorance of certain things, and use a further education as an escape mechanism. A person may be dissatisfied with his field of work and seek an adjustment elsewhere. These facts do not lessen the significance of these processes in abnormal behavior but the normal person should not be led to believe that he is abnormal merely because he uses these processes.

There is considerable evidence that deficiencies in learning in certain fields are really escape mechanisms. If one cannot learn to spell, or work arithmetic problems, or master a foreign language, then he escapes certain responsibilities and considerable hard work. He ignores the fact that he started life with undefined intellectual processes and now has learning habits not suited to mastering certain types of data. Failure in these tasks may be an unconscious negativistic reaction. Compensatory behavior may involve delinquencies and other adjustments not approved by society, but it can lead to socially sanctioned behavior as well. Repressed ideas may be evidence of normality. Secrets are kept until certain plans are mature. Repression does not necessarily denote abnormality.

Pathological adjustments, disorganized minds, socially maladjusted patterns of behavior do not postulate any processes outside of normal behavior. So one cannot speak of these processes as normal or abnormal. As processes *per se* they function as the same phenomena in all human nature. No process in human nature necessarily leads to abnormality.

We shall see later that many of the mental processes associated with mental ill-health can be found in the adjustments of normal persons. False beliefs, self-pity, ideas of reference, disorders of judgment, disturbed train of thought, flight of ideas, incoherence, retardation or inhibition of thought, disturbance of consciousness, dream states, confusion, emotional indifference, inaccessibility, impulsive behavior, obsessions, fears, phobias, mental conflict, repression, projection, regression, and many more adjustments can be found in varying degrees in the activities of both normal and abnormal persons.

In most cases, the abnormal is merely an exaggeration of the personality trends found in normal individuals. There is no way of telling in social-psychological terms or in any other terms where normality leaves off and abnormality begins. It has been pointed out that it is possible to arrange a series among the sane, semi-insane, and insane, in which the insane mental process would be the outcome of the pre-existent sane prototype, the exaggeration of mental trends found in normal persons. In most social adjustments it is possible to arrange a series of cases beginning with the normal person and ending with the person with marked abnormalities. In this series the common components of human nature are found in each case existing in varying degrees of normality and abnormality.

## John Gillin

# CULTURAL DEVIANCY
# AND ABSOLUTE DEVIANCY *

*Due to reasons cited in the preceding reading, social
scientists these days talk less and less about abnormal
and more and more about something they call deviancy.
The difference is not simply a preference for one word
over another. If "normality" is simply a word for adherence to a norm which in the accident of time and
circumstance happens to be preferred, then the person
or behavior which conforms to that norm has no intrinsic
merit; it simply has the characteristic of adherence. It
should be obvious, then, that there are some people and
behaviors which do not correspond to the model; to
these the term deviant is ascribed. It is obvious that
deviancy is a matter of cultural proscription. If Solomon
lived today in our society and practiced the mode of
life attributed to him by history, he would be a criminal
deviant 499 times over! But is that all there is to the
question?*

In the first type the individual happens to be in the wrong culture, but if placed in another situation is able to make a satisfactory adjustment. Much of the treatment of neurosis as practised by psychiatrists consists in "situational readjustment," that
is, finding a cultural and social atmosphere in our own society
which the maladjusted individual finds congenial—a change of
job, a change of mate, a new neighborhood, and the like. . . .
On the other hand there are undoubtedly certain types of

* From John Gillin, *The Ways of Men* (New York, Appleton-Century-
Crofts, 1948), pp. 589-591. Used by permission.

individuals incapable of adjusting satisfactorily to any type of culture or to any social situation. The feeble-minded, particularly those of the grade of idiot or imbecile, are obvious examples. Some societies on the other hand, do make places permitting social interaction for certain types of psychosis or mental illness. It has been pointed out that tribes of Siberia and California, for instance, select out for the status of medicine man or woman individuals who are subject to epileptoid and cataleptoid seizures. Medicine men among the Tembu and the Fingo (Bantu) tribes of South Africa are often, according to Laubscher, schizophrenic. The accepted role of homosexuals in certain North American Indian tribes has already been mentioned, while from the Lango, of East Africa, to cite only one other instance, we hear of men who publicly live with other men and simulate menstruation.

Yet when we admit that certain cultures apparently find places for some types of psychotics, there are other types of mental illness which apparently unfit the individual for any type of culture. We mention only a few examples by way of illustration. In advanced and profound catatonia the patient withdraws completely from the outer world and frequently lies for days rigidly immobile. Although such an individual may be an object of veneration or of idle curiosity in some societies, he is still an *object* rather than a person; he is incapable of interacting and adjusting to any pattern of social activity. In advanced general paresis the personality is frequently so destroyed or disorganized that the patient is unable to control elimination, to feed himself, and to speak a coherent sentence or even to pronounce words. So far as the present writer is aware, no culture has developed a social status, role, or personality type into which such cases could be fitted.

We may, therefore, speak of individuals of this short as suffering from *basic or absolute psychosis*. At present, all the causes of such conditions are not known; in our society progress is being made in achieving remission of the symptoms so that some such basic psychotics can be restored to at least a limited social role. Taken together, the low-grade feeble-minded and the basic psychotics may be considered the type of persons who are *absolutely abnormal* regardless of the cultural or social circumstances in which they find themselves. In essence, absolute abnormality implies an inability of the person to interact socially and to learn culture, or an inability to perform cultural patterns sufficiently consistently and meaningfully for other individuals to interact with him according to any known type of cultural system.

*Cultural influences in maladjustment.* If we understand that a culture may provide opportunities and patterns of interaction for individuals who, because of their personal characteristics, would be unable to function in certain other circumstances, it follows that a culture may also have the effect of creating conditions conducive to maladjustment in certain types of persons. We have already alluded to the maladjustment resulting in some individuals in our society by reason of our incessant cultural harping on ambition and success. It is also significant that the cultural structuralization of different situations in our society seems to set up distinctive patterns of strain and pressure upon the individual.

## J. S. Wallerstein and C. J. Wyle

# OUR LAW-ABIDING
# LAW-BREAKERS *

*Everyone, to be sure, knows that there is a certain amount of undetected crime in this or any other society, but few suspect how much, who the offenders are, and what kinds of offenses go undetected. This well-known study published by the National Probation Association is a vivid, if somewhat disconcerting, index to our "respect for law and order."*

We have no accurate gauge of the extent of delinquency and crime in the United States. What we know comes to our attention through admittedly inadequate statistical data gathered by some police departments, juvenile and adult courts, and correctional institutions. There are no comprehensive figures which cover the entire country even for this imperfect measure.

We can only hazard guesses at the incidence of hidden delinquency and crime. Most law violations are probably unknown to juvenile and adult courts, and hundreds of thousands of offenses never are reported to the police. In a paper given at the annual conference of the National Probation Association in June of 1946, Fred J. Murphy, speaking of "delinquency off the record" on the basis of findings of the Cambridge-Somerville Youth Study, reported that of a total of some 6000 offenses admitted by youths who were subjects in the study, a scant 1.5 per cent were actually brought to public attention by arrest or juvenile court hearing.

* J. S. Wallerstein and C. J. Wyle, "Our Law-abiding Law-breakers," *Probation* (National Probation Association, now National Council on Crime and Delinquency, April, 1947). By permission.

Another slant on this subject appears in the report of a study made in Fort Worth, Texas, by Austin L. Porterfield of Texas Christian University. Mr. Porterfield's interest was in the social factors which may be back of this hidden delinquency. He compared a group of college students with a group of delinquents who came to the attention of the local juvenile court for commission of one or more of 55 specific offenses ranging in seriousness all the way from making a disturbance in church to homicide. The 237 students (both men and women) received little or no attention from the public authorities. (One ministerial student got by with 27 and one with 28 of the listed offenses.) The delinquent acts of these students were apparently as serious though not as frequent as those which brought other young people into court. Why did they enjoy relative immunity? Mr. Porterfield states that their behavior is an expression of the same fundamental wishes—for new experiences, adventure, recognition, for instance—which motivated the court group. The varying socioeconomic status of the family is undoubtedly important, as is family disorganization which was notably higher in the court cases.

## Concealed Crime

What similar ratios might be revealed among adults? The authors, interested in Mr. Porterfield's study, set out to get some descriptive data by distributing questionnaires listing 49 offenses under the penal law of the state of New York. All of these offenses were sufficiently serious to draw a maximum sentence of not less than one year; fourteen were felonies, seven might be felonies under certain conditions, the rest were misdemeanors. Replies were returned anonymously to insure frankness. The study was not a rigidly scientific one, but was carefully and critically prepared and tabulated. Some effort was made in distributing the questionnaires to secure a balanced racial and religious community cross-section, although this could not be done with precision. Economically the group was probably weighted on the upper income side. . . .

## Vocations of the Sample of 1698 Individuals

| Occupations | Men | Women |
|---|---|---|
| Business and law | 13 | 12 |
| Teachers and social workers | 80 | 117 |
| Scientists and doctors | 63 | 15 |
| Writers and artists | 80 | 55 |
| Ministers | 17 | – |
| Sales clerks and office workers | 59 | 71 |
| Military and government employees | 53 | 11 |
| Mechanics and technicians | 239 | 32 |
| Farmers | 44 | – |
| Laborers | 100 | 10 |
| Housewives | – | 276 |
| Students | 148 | 79 |
| | 1020 | 678 |

## What Crimes Were Committed

Replies were received from 1698 individuals, 1020 men and 678 women. Geographically most of the responses came from the metropolitan area of New York, Westchester and Long Island, but there was a scattering from upstate New York, Pennsylvania, Ohio and California. Ninety-nine per cent of those questioned answered affirmatively to one or more of the offenses. The percentage of individuals admitting to these offenses, excluding those committed as juvenile delinquencies, is shown in the following partial list [See table on next page]:

The high rate for assault may be explained by the inclusion of such episodes as fist fights and the more violent shoving in the subway. Probably most males don't mind admitting this type of offense. The low rate on election frauds suggests that New Yorkers may be more conscientious citizens in exercising the ballot than one would expect. However, interpretation of these figures is necessarily speculative.

Businessmen and lawyers were highest in perjury, falsification, fraud and tax evasion; teachers and social workers in malicious mischief; writers and artists in indecency, criminal libel and gambling; military and government employees in simple

| Offense | Per cent Men | Per cent Women |
|---|---|---|
| Malicious mischief | 84 | 81 |
| Disorderly conduct | 85 | 76 |
| Assault | 49 | 5 |
| Auto misdemeanors | 61 | 39 |
| Indecency | 77 | 74 |
| Gambling | 74 | 54 |
| Larceny | 89 | 83 |
| Grand larceny (except auto) | 13 | 11 |
| Auto theft | 26 | 8 |
| Burglary | 17 | 4 |
| Robbery | 11 | 1 |
| Concealed weapons | 35 | 3 |
| Perjury | 23 | 17 |
| Falsification and fraud | 46 | 34 |
| Election frauds | 7 | 4 |
| Tax evasion | 57 | 40 |
| Coercion | 16 | 6 |
| Conspiracy | 23 | 7 |
| Criminal libel | 36 | 29 |

larceny; mechanics and technicians in disorderly conduct; farmers in illegal possession of weapons; laborers in grand larceny, burglary and robbery; students in auto misdemeanors.

The number of offenses per person ran high. The mean [average] number of offenses committed in adult life (over sixteen) for men, classified according to occupation, ranged from 8.2 for ministers to 20.2 for laborers, with a mean of 18 for all men. For the women, excluding again acts committed under the age of sixteen, the range was from a low of 9.8 for those classed as laborers to a high of 14.4 for those in military and government work, with a mean of 11 for all women. In addition, the men reported a mean of 3.2, the women 1.6 of juvenile offenses. . . .

## WHAT MIGHT HAVE HAPPENED

Under New York law conviction of a felony is ground for deprivation of citizenship rights. Analysis of the replies on the fourteen felony offenses brought out the fact that the felony rate for the group as a whole was 64 per cent for men and 29 per cent for women, that is, considerably more than half of the men and nearly one-third of the women admitted to committing at least one felony. If we can envisage law enforcement machinery which could detect all law violations, the ultimate result would be loss of franchise for a substantial proportion of our citizens, and deprivation of other civil rights such as special licenses for business operations. While this carries us somewhat into the realm of fantasy, the solid truth remains that there is a large chance element in our administration of justice and it's the unlucky ones who are caught. . . .

## The Point of View

Perhaps the principal conclusion to be drawn from this study is the revelation of the prevalence of lawlessness among respectable people. It is perhaps less important to show that good citizens are not always good than that these same citizens can commit crimes and still become eminent scientists, intelligent parents, leading teachers, artists and social workers, or prominent business executives. The absence of a police record for many citizens arises not from their individual virtue but from sheer accident and from less than one hundred per cent law enforcement. From this angle the punitive attitude of society toward the convicted offender becomes not only hypocritical but pointless. In time to come men may be rated not by their past mistakes but by their assets and potentialities.

*Gordon W. Allport*

# THE PREJUDICED PERSONALITY *

*Everyone knows that something called "prejudice" exists. There is a pervasive tendency, however, to explain it away as simply personal idiosyncrasy, a nuisance at worst. A careful look, however, at the accumulated research on the subject of prejudice presents a far more ominous picture. Prejudice is not superficial; it is not trivial; it is, indeed, one of the most fruitful constructs within which human behavior may be scrutinized. The following is an excellent synthesis of a good deal of research written by a man who has done a good deal of the research himself.*

Prejudice, as we have seen, may become part of one's life tissue, suffusing character because it is essential to the economy of a life. It does not always act in this way, for some prejudices are merely conformative, mildly ethnocentric, and essentially unrelated to the personality as a whole. But often it is organic, inseparable from the life process. This condition we shall now examine more closely.

## METHODS OF STUDY

Two methods have proved fruitful in the study of character-conditioned prejudice, the *longitudinal* and the *cross-sectional*.

In the longitudinal approach the investigator attempts to trace back through a given life-history factors that might account for the present pattern of prejudice. . . .

* From Gordon W. Allport, *The Nature of Prejudice* (Reading, Mass., Addison-Wesley, 1954), pp. 371-376 (Doubleday Anchor Edition). Used by permission.

The cross-sectional method attempts to find out what the contemporary prejudice pattern is like, asking especially how ethnic attitudes are related to other social attitudes and to one's outlook on life in general. Using this method, we uncover some interesting relationships. For example, Frenkel-Brunswik reports that highly prejudiced children tend to endorse the following beliefs (not one of which deals directly with ethnic matters): [1]

There is only one right way to do anything.
If a person does not watch out somebody will make a sucker out of him.
It would be better if teachers would be more strict.
Only people who are like myself have a right to be happy.
Girls should learn only things that are useful around the house.
There will always be war; it is part of human nature.
The position of the stars at the time of your birth tells your character and personality.

When the same method is applied to adults, similar results occur. Certain types of propositions are endorsed by highly prejudiced more often than by tolerant adults. [2]

The world is a hazardous place in which men are basically evil and dangerous.
We do not have enough discipline in our American way of life.
On the whole, I am more afraid of swindlers than I am of gangsters.

At first sight these propositions seem to have nothing to do with prejudice. Yet it is proved that all of them have. This finding can only mean that prejudice is frequently woven firmly into a style of life.

## FUNCTIONAL PREJUDICE

In all cases of intense character-conditioned prejudice a common factor emerges which Newcomb has called "threat orientation." [3] Underlying insecurity seems to lie at the root of the per-

[1] Else Frenkel-Brunswik. "A Study of Prejudice in Children," *Human Relations,* 1948, 1, 295-306.
[2] G. W. Allport and B. M. Kramer, "Some Roots of Prejudice." *Journal of Psychology,* 1946, 22, 9-39.
[3] T. M. Newcomb, *Social Psychology,* (New York, Dryden, 1950), p. 588.

sonality. The individual cannot face the world unflinchingly and in a forthright manner. He seems fearful of himself, of his own instincts, of his own consciousness, of change, and of his social environment. Since he can live in comfort neither with himself nor with others, he is forced to organize his whole style of living, including his social attitudes, to fit his crippled condition. It is not his specific social attitudes that are malformed to start with; it is rather his own ego that is crippled.

The crutch he needs must perform several functions. It must give reassurance for past failures, safe guidance for present conduct, and ensure confidence in facing the future. While prejudice by itself does not do all these things, it develops as an important incident in the total protective adjustment.

An essential feature of this pattern is *repression*. Since the person cannot in his conscious life face and master the conflicts presented to him, he represses them in whole or in part. They are fragmented, forgotten, not faced. The ego simply fails to integrate the myriad of impulses that arise within the personality and the myriad of environmental presses without. This failure engenders feelings of insecurity, and these feelings engender, in turn, repression.

Thus an outstanding result of studies of bigoted personalities seems to be the discovery of a sharp cleavage between conscious and unconscious layers. In a study of anti-Semitic college girls they appeared on the surface to be charming, happy, well-adjusted, and entirely normal girls. They were polite, moral, and seemed devoted to parents and friends. This was what an ordinary observer would see. But probing deeper (with the aid of projective tests, interviews, case histories), these girls were found to be very different. Underneath the conventional exterior there lurked intense anxiety, much buried hatred toward parents, destructive and cruel impulses. For tolerant college students, however, the same cleavage did not exist. Their lives were more of a piece. Repressions were fewer and milder. The *persona* they presented to the world was not a mask but was their true personality.[4] Having few repressions, they suffered no ego-

[4] Else Frenkel-Brunswik and R. N. Sanford. "Some Personality Factors in Anti-Semitism," *Journal of Psychology,* 1945, 20, 271-291.

alienation, and facing their own calamities frankly, they needed no projection screen.

This study, as well as others, reveals that the consequences of such repression are likely to be the following:

Ambivalence toward parents
Moralism
Dichotomization
A need for definiteness
Externalization of conflict
Institutionalism
Authoritarianism

All of these characteristics can be regarded as devices to bolster a weak ego unable to face its conflicts squarely and unflinchingly. They are accordingly the earmarks of a personality in whom prejudice is functionally important.

## AMBIVALENCE TOWARD PARENTS

In the study of anti-Semitic women students cited above, the authors found that "without exception these girls declared that they liked their parents." Yet in their interpretation of pictures (Thematic Apperception Test), a preponderance of responses to parental figures accused them of meanness and cruelty, and betrayed jealousy, suspicion, and hostility on the part of the daughter. By contrast, the unprejudiced subjects in the same test were much more critical of their parents when they discussed them openly with the interviewer, but showed less animosity in the projective tests.[5] The sentiments of these latter girls toward their parents was more *differentiated*. That is to say, they saw their parents' faults and openly criticized them, but they also saw their virtues, and on the whole got along pleasantly enough with them. The prejudiced girls were torn: on the surface all was sweetness and light, and this view was held up to public gaze; but deeper down there was often vigorous protest. The sentiment had become bifurcated. The anti-Semitic girls had more fantasies of their parents' death.

[5] *Ibid.*

## Moralism

This anxiety is reflected in the rigidly moralistic view that most prejudiced personalities take. Strict insistence on cleanliness, good manners, conventions is more common among them than among tolerant people. When asked the question, "What is the most embarrassing experience?" anti-Semitic girls responded in terms of violations of mores and conventions in public. Whereas non-prejudiced girls spoke more often of inadequacy in personal relations, such as failing to live up to a friend's expectation. Also, anti-Semitic girls tend to be harsh in their moral judgments of others. One said, "I would sentence any striker to 50 years in the penitentiary." Tolerant subjects, by contrast, show much greater lenience toward transgression of the mores. They are less condemnatory of social misdemeanors, including violations of sexual standards. They tolerate human weakness just as they tolerate minority groups.

The Nazis were noted for their emphasis upon conventional virtues. Hitler preached and in many respects practiced asceticism. Overt sex perversion was violently condemned, sometimes punished with death. A rigid protocol dominated every phase of military and social life. The Jews were constantly accused of violating conventional codes—with their dirtiness, miserliness, dishonesty, immorality. But while pretentious moralism ran high, there seemed to be little integration with private conduct. It was sham propriety, illustrated by the urge to make all expropriation and torture of the Jews appear "legal." . . .

Moralism is only surface compliance; it does not solve the conflicts within. It is tense, compulsive, projective. True morality is more relaxed, integral, and congruent with the life pattern as a whole. . . .

## Authoritarianism

Living in a democracy is a higgledy-piggledy affair. Finding it so, prejudiced people sometimes declare that America should not be a democracy, but merely a "republic." The consequences of personal freedom they find unpredictable. Individuality makes for indefiniteness, disorderliness, and change.

To avoid such slipperiness the prejudiced person looks for hierarchy in society. Power arrangements are definite—something he can understand and count on. He likes authority, and says that what America needs is "more discipline." By discipline, of course, he means *outer* discipline, preferring, so to speak, to see people's backbones on the outside rather than on the inside. When students were asked to list the names of great people they most admired, prejudiced students usually gave names of leaders who had exercised power and control over others (Napoleon, Bismarck) whereas the unprejudiced listed, more typically, artists, humanitarians, scientists (Lincoln, Einstein).[6]

This need for authority reflects a deep distrust of human beings. Earlier in this chapter we noted the tendency of prejudiced people to agree that "the world is a hazardous place where men are basically evil and dangerous." Now, the essential philosophy of democracy is the reverse. It tells us to trust a person until he proves himself untrustworthy. The prejudiced person does the opposite. He distrusts every person until he proves himself trustworthy.

The same suspicion is seen in responses to the following question: "If I were to express a greater fear of one of the following types of criminals I would say that I am more afraid of (a) gangsters, (b) swindlers." About half of the respondents choose one, and half the other alternative. But those who are more afraid of *swindlers* have higher prejudice scores in general. They feel more threatened by trickery than by direct physical attack. Ordinarily it might seem that fear of gangsters (physical threat) is a more natural and normal type of fear—and it is this that unprejudiced people report.[7]

To the prejudiced person the best way to control these suspicions is to have an orderly, authoritative, powerful society. Strong nationalism is a good thing. Hitler and Mussolini weren't so wrong. What America needs is a strong leader—a man on horseback!

[6] *Ibid.*, 271-291.
[7] G. W. Allport and B. M. Kramer, *op. cit.*

## DISCUSSION

Our portrait of the prejudiced personality (called by some authors "the authoritarian personality") is based largely on the results of recent research. While the outlines of the pattern are clear, the weighting and interlocking of evidence are not yet complete. Contrasting with the authoritarian type, investigators report an opposite pattern of correlated qualities that comprise what is sometimes called a "democratic," a "mature," a "productive," or a "self-actualizing" personality.[8] . . .

. . . Our picture may be oversharp and may later need modification and supplementation, but the basic fact is firmly established—prejudice is more than an incident in many lives; it is often lockstitched into the very fabric of personality. In such cases it cannot be extracted by tweezers. To change it, the whole pattern of life would have to be altered.

[8] The fullest and most standard comparison of these two basic types of personality is contained in T. W. Adorno, E. Frenkel-Brunswik, D. J. Levinson and R. N. Sanford, *The Authoritarian Personality* (New York, Harper, 1950). Likewise relevant are the discussions in E. Fromm, *Man for Himself* (New York, Rinehart, 1947); and in two articles by A. H. Maslow, "The Authoritarian Character Structure," *Journal of Social Psychology*, 1943, 18, 401-411; "Self-actualizing People: A Study of Psychological Health," *Personality Symposium*, 1949, 1, 11-34.

## Hans Sebald

# DISCONTINUITY
# AND ADOLESCENT SUB-CULTURE *

*Since most of the people reading this book will know
that they are just emerging from an uncomfortable and
much maligned category called "adolescence," this original paper by Hans Sebald may have more than academic
interest. Regardless of this prospect, however, this paper
is a careful integration of a voluminous literature on
the subject of adolescence in contemporary American
society. Much research is summarized and integrated
around two central interpretations, both of which are
defined, and the relationship between them documented
and explained—cultural discontinuity and the formation
of a sub-culture.*

The focus of this inquiry is the social situation of the American
*middle class* adolescents of today. The qualification, *middle class*,
is not always spelled out throughout the study; however, it should
be kept in mind as the focus of the study.

According to opinions of a number of sociologists and anthropologists, life in the modern American society provides little
continuity between the role of the child and the role of the
adult.[1] The period of adolescence may be described as the time
when the role and the status of the child vanish and the role
and the status of the adult are not yet available. This situation
has been conceptualized as *discontinuity*. Discontinuity may ap-

* Hans Sebald, an unpublished manuscript edited for this book.
[1] Ruth Benedict, "Continuities and Discontinuities in Cultural Conditioning," *Psychiatry*, 1:161-167, 1938.

proach a degree of disruption of life-conditions that justifies the application of the concept *crisis*.

A number of anthropological studies, which compared American adolescence with other cultures, arrived at the conclusion that the phenomena which we call adolescence does not exist in most other societies.[2] There is enough evidence concerning adolescent problems in historical and anthropological accounts of contrasting societies to justify the conclusion that in comparison with other cultures the American culture exhibits an exceptional amount of parent-youth conflict and of discontinuity. In some cultures the outstanding fact is generally not the rebelliousness of youth, but its docility. Especially in primitive tribal cultures the young willingly submit to the customs of their society.

What, then, can we recognize as the features of American society which are responsible for the wide-spread maladjustment, alienation, confusion, or whatever negatively loaded term we want to apply, of "the teenagers"?

This quest leads us to the dimension of discontinuity. The assumption is made here that this is the responsible variable, making for the typical adolescent problems—or we might say for adolescence as such.

*Discontinuity.* The definition of discontinuity could be introduced by first considering the question of what *continuity* means. This paper accepts Benedict's general definition which describes continuity as the "cultural way of dealing with the cycle of growth from infancy to adulthood." The life cycle of a human being considered in its entirety may be visualized as general continuity. But this entirety is interspersed with very definite discontinuities. It is a universal fact that the child becomes a man—but the way in which this transition is effected

[2] Margaret Mead, "Adolescence in Primitive and Modern Society," in V. F. Calverton and S. Schmalhausen, eds., *The New Generation* (New York, Bacon, 1930).

Bronislaw Malinowski, *The Family Among the Australian Aborigines* (London, University Press, 1913).

Bronislaw Malinowski, "Parenthood—The Basis of Social Structure," in V. F. Calverton and S. Schmalhousen, eds., *The New Generation* (New York, Bacon, 1930).

H. Ian Hogbin, *Law and Order in Polynesia* (New York, Harcourt, Brace, 1934).

varies from one society to another. Within the cultural premises of the American society, and judged from a comparative point of view, American life goes to great extremes in emphasizing *contrasts* between the child and the adult.

## ANTECEDENTS WITHIN THE
## SOCIAL ORGANIZATION OF AMERICAN LIFE

### 1. *The Modern American Family: Nuclear Versus Extended Family System*

In a typical familistic society where there are a number of adult female and male relatives within the kinship group to whom the child may turn for affection and aid, and where there are many members of the younger generation in whom the parents have a paternal interest, there appears to be less intensity of emotion for any particular kinsman and consequently less chance for severe conflict. The cohesive kinship group also provides related playmates. Adolescents do not have to step outside of their kinship group in order to find companions of the same age group. A significant implication may follow: there is no need or desire for the adolescent to join or to inaugurate a separate subculture. His feeling of loyalty and belonging is contained in the larger "family" group.

### 2. *Rapid Social Change*

The extremely rapid change of American society, in contrast to most societies, accentuates adult-youth conflict. Inevitably, youth is reared in a milieu different from that of the parents'. Some of the specific aspects of discontinuity brought about by rapid social and cultural change are the following:

(a) *Disputed Parental Authority.* The parents are charged with the obligation and the privilege of controlling and training the child in conformity with the mores of the cultural structure. This privilege gives them great authority. But since the rapid social change puts the parents in a kind of "cultural lag" position, their authority is constantly questioned by the younger generation.

(b) *Conflicting Norms.* Rapid change has given old and young a different social content, so that they possess conflicting norms.

(c) *Confusion Within each of the Generations.* In addition to the cultural discrepancy between the two generations, social complexity has confused the standards within the generations. Faced with conflicting goals, parents become inconsistent with one another and even with themselves at different times.

(d) *Competing Authorities.* Education is largely in the hands of professional specialists. They are teaching and informing the high-school aged students in correspondence with the diverse insights and products of the rapid social change. So, frequently the adolescents have ideas in advance of the parents. This fact widens the gap between parents and children and, in effect, deprives parents of the function of helping the young in their transition from childhood to adulthood.

## 3. *Lack of "Rite de Passage"*

The roles of the adolescent change rather suddenly in the American culture. Anthropologists have found that in other cultures, e.g. Samoa, there are clear and definite rituals which mark and define stages in the life .cycle of the member of their society. Puberty as such is regarded as a joyful symptom which is not kept secret and unknown. Mead described the consequences of the "rite de passage" as a feeling of self-importance, acceptance in society, clear self-image, and clear role definition.[3] On the other side, Mead thought that puberty in the American society is often accompanied with embarrassment and circumlocution. It causes self-consciousness and is regarded as an unlovely symptom.

## 4. *"Momism"*

The phenomenon labelled as "momism" is frequently, if not exclusively, found in the American middle class. Basically, the term is used in describing the deprivation of the child's independence on account of mother domination. It includes the "bargain-

[3] Mead, *op. cit.*, pp. 174-176.

ing process" where mother offers love in return for obedience. Additional significance for the male child arises from the fact that in mom-dominated families the female is the authority image.

## 5. The Complexities of Industrialized and Urbanized Life

(a) *Long period of education.* The complexity of American culture requires a long training for full participation. During such long training, the adolescent is prevented from occupying any longer the status of child, nor is he given the status of the adult.

(b) *Late marriage.* This is due to the need for long economic preparation for married life. Thus a conspicuous discrepancy exists between sexual maturity and social maturity. The lack of the latter presupposes a period of sex restraint and of sexual inequality compared with the "adults." Such discrepancy and inequality typically cause conflicts, uncertainties, and role confusion.

(c) *High mobility.* Disemphasis upon family continuity and tradition is sometimes blamed on high mobility in two ways: geographical (migration) and social. In either instance it may mean for the families involved shifting points of reference, changing social milieu, and fluctuating socio-cultural orientation. The growing child experiencing such irregularities may encounter difficulties in his orientation as to role and status—and thereby accentuate adolescent discontinuity.

(d) *Separation of home and work.* For most urban families it is a long cry since son learnt his occupation from father and the daughter from mother. The place of work and the place for child rearing are completely separate. When the adolescent's time has come to step out into serious vocational activities, he is received into a completely new surrounding.

(e) *Multi-specificity of division of labor.* Modern American life does not give the individual a chance to do a "whole" job. In an age of assembly-line production, it is a most common practice that a man does only one specific detail in a longer process. In the urban situation, there is very rarely the chance that the child can follow so holistically the occupation of a parent that one could speak of occupational continuity.

## ANTECEDENTS WITHIN THE CULTURAL VALUES: DICHOTOMIZED PATTERNS

1. *The All American Dichotomies.* Numerous polarities complicate role definitions and prevent the smooth flow of an uniformly patterned life cycle. On an abstract level, these polar ingredients of American culture have evidenced themselves in the history of the nation; such as (a) pious vs. free thinking; (b) individualistic vs. standardized norms; (c) competitive vs. cooperative effort; (d) religious principles of puritanical quality vs. a set of shifting slogans, which indicate that, at a given time, one may get away with just about anything if in pursuit of the all American goal of success.

2. *Child-Adult Dichotomies.* Benedict recognized this problem when she stated that dogmas of American culture ascribe to the child and to the adult the following qualities or expectations, respectively: sexless—sex; obedience—dominance; protection from the facts of life—facing responsibility; etc.[4] From a comparative point of view, the American culture goes to great extremes in emphasizing contrasts between the child and the adult—a fact which makes continuity very difficult. Thus, one may see that various cultural institutions and dogmas contribute to adolescent discontinuity.

## THE CONSEQUENT OF DISCONTINUITY

### *The Formation of the Adolescent Subculture*

The crucial conditions for the emergence of a new cultural form is the existence of a *number of* persons seeking a solution of *common problems* and who effectively *interact* with one another. The membership in such a group not only ideally works as a problem-solving circumstance, but it develops into a reference group relationship. This emergence of group standards and shared frames of reference means the emergence of a *subculture.*

[4] Benedict, *op. cit.*

Adolescent subculture as dealt with in this paper comprises mainly the teenage culture of the ordinary and "normal" high school population.

Adolescents as a collectivity are marginal: A segment of the population occupying a wavering intermediate position between child culture and adult culture. In this marginal state it is of vital importance to the adolescents to be secure and to have a belonging to something. In other words, the relative unstructuredness of marginality cannot be endured. Restructuring and redefining behavior develops. There is a need for models, for acceptance into a community, for definitions of roles and statuses, for a sense of being someone (search for identity), for a sense of social worth. The adolescent needs a bridge to the adult world—and this bridge is the adolescent subculture with its dogmas and standards. The fads may change, but the social structure of the subculture remains. A more analytical and useful study should recognize fads and crazes as expressions and efforts to restructure and redefine the situation. Or, in an advanced phase of subcultural formation, they may more accurately be described as normative behavior within an established culture.[5]

## LIFE IN THE ADOLESCENT SUBCULTURE

Morgan has called the adolescent subculture the Teen-Land of America [6] which is "struggling" toward identity, or, actually, has already achieved a certain level of identity. Because the members of it have to live at home, go to school, shop for supplies, and appear in court, the "teen-agers' colony is attached to the American mainland and carries on foreign relations with it. . . . They feel and they are made to feel that they are a race apart, a minority in an alien land. Thus they cling with fierce pride to a private set of folkways that seem mysterious and confounding to the outsider." These folkways create pressures to conform and inhibit the individual as insistently as those in the adult world. Teen-Land is built on insecurity and its greatest concern is for safety. What are those safety symbols, safety values, safety

[5] Ralph H. Turner and Lewis M. Killian, *Collective Behavior* (Englewood Cliffs, N.J., Prentice-Hall, 1958), p. 208.

[6] B. Thomas Morgan, "Teenage Heroes: Mirrors of a Muddled Youth," *Esquire* (March 1960), pp. 65-73.

norms, etc.? In order to gain insight into this, a look at the teen-agers' heroes might be of help. The heroes directly or indirectly reveal much about the hero-worshippers' values and social condition.

## 1. *Heroes and Crazes*

When Frankie Avalon, a rock-and-roll ballad singer doing his performance at the Steel Pier Music Hall in Atlantic City, stepped on the stage, about 200 well-fed, well-enough-dressed girls in the first six rows and in the side balconies shrieked in the typically violent and mechanical way we have come to know from TV shows. "A number of the screamers were not looking at their hero, but at each other, to make sure that they were being seen screaming—i.e. belonging." [7] The report mentioned that the back rows did not scream, but only applauded conventionally. The inferential explanation for this spelled out that they were outside of the bright glow of the footlights and thus outside the field of observation.

Other teen-age heroes are Ricky Nelson, who earned in 1959 $400,000 for teen-age song recordings and is interpreted as representing the value of "sincere sex"; Edd "Kookie" Byrnes sold 2,000,000 records of "Kookie, Lend me your Comb" and is thought of as modelling the teen-agers' reproach of "I'm young, so they blame it on me."

## 2. *Communication*

Morgan reported that 18 million teen-agers spent $10 billion to support their cult: They have publications written in their own language, like *Dig, Ingenue, Seventeen, "16", Teen,* etc., which instruct them in custom, propriety, sex mores, and proper-thinking with the purpose of inculcating group values.

". . . Youth is consuming mass media in unprecedented quantity . . . Children spend on the average from 17 to 20 hours each week watching TV; teen-agers particularly spend eight or more hours per week listening to their radios and go to movies

[7] *Ibid.,* p. 65.

once a week to once every other week. They spend about seven hours weekly reading out of school. This total of some 37 hours each week is more time than the youngsters spend in school." [8]

## 3. *Values*

It is difficult, without careful research, to make any valid inferences concerning the values which such behavior exemplifies. It has been noted that the first-class teen-age hero is typically a recording star, and *not* an athlete, politician, businessman, or intellectual. Morgan established that these are types standing out from the crowd or from the mass: "The ideal athlete is admired for *courage*, the politician for *principles*, the businessman for *enterprise*, and the intellectual for devotion to *hard truths;* all represent values that tend to separate the individual from the crowd, that expose him, and that lead him into an uncertain future" [9]—even into possible unpopularity.

And this is exactly the situation from which the teen-agers are trying to escape. They seek the warmth and security of the crowd and not the open exposure of individuality. Such exposure or such values are not congruent with their demand for safety. They make, rather, virtues of conformity, mediocrity, and "sincerity." Through their heroes, through their songs and dances, they can express themselves without leaving the warmth and the security of the crowd or mass. Their expressions reflect a certain violence against the adult world from which they are yet excluded.

Instead of considering values and norms per se, there is need to understand them in their function of filling a vacuum, of bridging an unorganized period; in short: as restructuring and redefining endeavors.

Various research findings state that the favorite leisure-time activity is group-centered and conformity-oriented. The criteria for membership in the leading crowd were found in one study to be in the following order of importance: Good personality, being friendly, being accepted by the right people,

[8] "Mass Media—Powerful Educational Tool?", *OSU Monthly*, May, 1960, p. 14.

[9] B. Thomas Morgan, *op. cit.*, p. 70.

good looks, nice clothes, money, and the lowest item was "being smart." [10]

Remmers, who is known for his nation-wide polling of adolescents, definitely corroborated such findings. This report showed that in many decisions and choices the opinions and the feelings of the teen-agers' friends were of greater importance than the opinion of their parents. Quite clearly, the essence of the findings suggested the following attributes: highest desire for popularity, far-reaching conformist attitude, valuing others' opinions above their own.[11]

## SUMMARY

1. *Adolescence* is basically an expression of discontinuity, a *disruption of life conditions.*

2. The disruption represents a collective *crisis* for which *no definite social mechanism* is provided by the larger American society.

3. Since this crisis is *common* to a collective segment of the society, namely to the adolescents, a process of collective problem-solution develops: *interaction* (especially on high school campuses), *communication* (mainly through mass media), *organizing tendency* (clubs, gangs, fan clubs, etc.) develop. There is, mostly unconscious, the assumption that a collective approach will bring about a solution to the problem.

4. Evolving new values, norms, and symbols produces a *subculture.* The original unstructured situation attains structure; new roles and statuses are defined. This brings about a collective entity: heroes and followers, key-noters and supporters, etc.

5. The *over-all situation* has now been changed for the adolescent from one of social unstructuredness to one of social structuredness, the result being the juxtaposition of the larger adult culture with the adolescent culture.

6. A cycle has now been concluded: from social organization (childhood) to social unorganization (adolescence) to social organization again (subculture).

[10] James S. Coleman, "Academic Achievement and the Structure of Competition," *Harvard Educational Review,* 29:330-351, 1959.

[11] Herman H. Remmers and Ben Shimberg, *Problems of High School Youth,* Purdue Opinion Poll For Young People, Report No. 21, April, 1949.

*Arnold M. Rose*

# REFERENCE GROUPS
# OF RURAL HIGH SCHOOL YOUTH *

*This reading has been included for two reasons. The major one is that it is a sample of a certain type of research which sociologists frequently perform. The author selects a concept, in this case "reference groups," which occurs in the theoretical literature about personality. He then uses this concept to find out something not already known about somebody—in this case rural high school students. But he can't study all rural high school students, so he chooses a sample—four high schools in Minnesota. He then asks them some questions—in writing—and proceeds to analyze their answers. He finds out that there are certain similarities among these students and he finds that these similarities relate in various ways to one another. This is one kind of statistical research of a somewhat elementary type of which there are innumerable examples in the professional literature.*

The hypotheses of this paper are the ones long held in sociology that, in a pluralistic society such as our own, an individual is moved to rank the groups to which he belongs or which he otherwise knows about and that his attitudes and behavior reflect the dominant values of the top groups in this hierarchy more than those of the lower groups. Recently this concept of the highly-valued groups has been given the label "reference

* Arnold M. Rose, "Reference Groups of Rural High School Youth," *Child Development,* Vol. 27, No. 3 (September, 1956), pp. 351-363. Reprinted with the permission of the author and the publisher, Society for Research in Child Development, Inc., Purdue University, Lafayette, Indiana.

groups," a term apparently used first by Herbert Hyman (1). This paper considers only those reference groups which are also membership groups (that is, groups to which the individuals studied themselves belong).

The data consists of answers to questionnaires filled out by all students (except for those absent on the typical school day when the survey was taken) in four rural high schools, representing widely different areas in Minnesota. The questionnaires were administered in classrooms by an advanced graduate student at the University of Minnesota, who assured the subjects of anonymity and of the legitimate purposes of the study.

The main question used to ascertain reference groups was "In your life which is most important?" and permitted checking of the following: (a) school chums; (b) relatives (uncles, aunts and cousins); (c) social clubs; (d) work groups; (e) church groups; (f) immediate family (father, mother, brothers, sisters). Of the 582 students filling out the questionnaire, 18 provided no answer to this question and 54 gave more than one answer; both of these categories of individuals were excluded from the analysis. Only four students gave "relatives" as their reference group; the small number precluded any analysis of this category. Those indicating church groups (42 cases), work groups (16 cases), and social clubs (4 cases) were combined into a single category hereafter labelled "organized groups."

## Factors Associated with Choice of Reference Group

Table I indicates some background characteristics of the boys and girls, as they report them themselves, which might be thought to direct the selection of the different reference groups. These background traits probably existed before the reference group was chosen and hence could have influenced the choice. There is no consistent association of the degree of life satisfaction or happiness of the parents and the tendency to choose the immediate family as the reference group. Only a slightly larger percentage of boys who indicated "immediate family" as their reference group said their fathers were very happy, as compared to those who chose other reference groups, but these same boys

## TABLE 1

## Background of Choice of Reference Groups

| | PERCENTAGE GIVING INDICATED ANSWER AMONG: | | | | | |
| | Boys for whom following groups are most important | | | Girls for whom following groups are most important | | |
| | School Chums | Immediate Family | Organized Groups | School Chums | Immediate Family | Organized Groups |
|---|---|---|---|---|---|---|
| *Reported life satisfaction of father* | | | | | | |
| Very satisfied ....... | 29.4 | 41.0 | 39.6 | 46.7 | 42.6 | 31.6 |
| Satisfied ........... | 53.0 | 38.5 | 43.7 | 30.0 | 30.2 | 47.3 |
| Average ........... | 17.6 | 13.9 | 12.5 | 13.3 | 12.9 | 15.8 |
| Dissatisfied ........ | 0.0 | 0.6 | 0.0 | 0.0 | 2.7 | 0.0 |
| Very dissatisfied ..... | 0.0 | 0.0 | 2.1 | 3.3 | 0.0 | 0.0 |
| No answer ........ | 0.0 | 6.0 | 2.1 | 6.7 | 11.6 | 5.3 |
| *Reported happiness of mother* | | | | | | |
| Very happy ........ | 41.2 | 34.9 | 33.3 | 35.7 | 33.8 | 36.8 |
| Happy ............ | 29.4 | 49.5 | 41.7 | 44.3 | 46.2 | 42.1 |
| Average ........... | 29.4 | 10.2 | 14.6 | 13.3 | 16.0 | 10.5 |
| Unhappy ........... | 0.0 | 3.0 | 2.1 | 6.7 | 1.3 | 5.3 |
| Very unhappy ...... | 0.0 | 0.6 | 0.0 | 0.0 | 0.0 | 0.0 |
| No answer ........ | 0.0 | 1.8 | 8.3 | 0.0 | 2.7 | 5.3 |
| *Father's participation in voluntary associations* | | | | | | |
| Yes .............. | 58.8 | 48.2 | 37.5 | 30.0 | 43.1 | 42.1 |
| No .............. | 41.2 | 45.8 | 58.3 | 63.3 | 49.3 | 52.5 |
| No answer ........ | 0.0 | 6.0 | 4.2 | 6.7 | 7.6 | 5.4 |
| *Mother's participation in voluntary associations* | | | | | | |
| Yes .............. | 58.8 | 62.0 | 47.9 | 43.3 | 40.9 | 47.4 |
| No .............. | 41.2 | 35.5 | 47.9 | 56.7 | 57.3 | 47.4 |
| No answer ........ | 0.0 | 2.5 | 4.2 | 0.0 | 1.8 | 5.2 |
| *Number of siblings* | | | | | | |
| None or one ........ | 17.6 | 10.3 | 10.4 | 20.6 | 12.5 | 16.0 |
| Two or three ....... | 17.6 | 37.9 | 31.3 | 41.0 | 29.5 | 5.3 |
| Four to seven ....... | 53.0 | 37.9 | 35.4 | 31.6 | 42.6 | 57.4 |
| Eight or more ...... | 11.8 | 13.9 | 22.9 | 6.8 | 15.4 | 21.3 |
| *Estimation of popularity with other students* | | | | | | |
| Very popular or popular .......... | 29.4 | 18.7 | 14.6 | 26.7 | 16.9 | 10.6 |
| Average .......... | 65.6 | 76.5 | 79.1 | 56.6 | 76.9 | 73.6 |
| Unpopular or very unpopular ........ | 0.0 | 2.4 | 4.2 | 0.0 | 3.1 | 15.8 |
| No answer ........ | 5.0 | 2.4 | 2.1 | 16.7 | 3.1 | 0.0 |
| N .................. | 17 | 166 | 48 | 30 | 225 | 19 |

reported their mothers to be slightly less happy, on the average. Among the girls, even these differences did not appear. If happiness of parents does not help to direct the choice of reference group, it might be thought that this important background variable is blunted in its influence on children possibly because it stems from, and reflects itself in, activities of the parents outside the home rather than within it. But data on the parents' participation in voluntary associations also show no consistent relationship to the children's choice of reference group.

The number of siblings, however, does show a relationship to the choice of reference group: In families where there are few or no siblings, children are more likely to choose school chums as their reference groups, whereas in large families, children are more likely to choose organized groups as their reference groups.

Concerning the child's estimation of his popularity with his schoolmates, it is difficult to say whether this is possible cause or possible effect of his choice of reference group. There is a significant association between these two, however: Children who choose school chums as a reference group are more likely than other children to consider themselves popular. On the other hand, children who choose organized groups as their reference groups are least likely to think of themselves as popular with their schoolmates. These relationships are found among both boys and girls and are statistically significant at the 90 per cent level of confidence, which criterion of significance is used throughout this paper.

## The Influence of the Reference Group on Social Participation and Career Plans

We turn now to some of the expected *consequences*, in behavior and attitude, of choice of certain reference groups by our rural high school youth. There seems to be no reliable and consistent pattern of differences among the youth who have chosen the three different kinds of reference group in regard to two important matters raised in our survey (Table 2): (1) the number

## TABLE 2

### Attitudes and Behavior Associated with Reference Groups

| | PERCENTAGE GIVING INDICATED ANSWER AMONG: | | | | | |
| | Boys for whom following groups are most important | | | Girls for whom following groups are most important | | |
| | School Chums | Immediate Family | Organized Groups | School Chums | Immediate Family | Organized Groups |
|---|---|---|---|---|---|---|
| *Number of organized activities ° youth participating in* | | | | | | |
| None | 11.8 | 4.2 | 6.2 | 3.3 | 12.0 | 0.0 |
| One | 0.0 | 8.4 | 18.7 | 13.3 | 8.4 | 15.8 |
| Two | 29.4 | 13.3 | 14.6 | 6.7 | 10.2 | 10.5 |
| Three or four | 17.6 | 23.5 | 29.3 | 26.7 | 29.9 | 36.8 |
| Five or six | 23.5 | 29.0 | 14.6 | 30.0 | 21.3 | 26.3 |
| Seven or eight | 11.8 | 10.2 | 10.4 | 6.7 | 9.3 | 5.3 |
| Nine or more | 5.9 | 11.4 | 6.2 | 13.3 | 8.9 | 5.3 |
| *Desire to quit school now* | | | | | | |
| Yes | 11.8 | 6.6 | 6.2 | 3.3 | 4.0 | 5.3 |
| No | 88.2 | 82.6 | 87.6 | 93.4 | 88.9 | 84.2 |
| Undecided | 0.0 | 10.8 | 6.2 | 3.3 | 7.1 | 10.5 |
| *Expect to do when finish high school †* | | | | | | |
| Go farming | 35.3 | 24.7 | 27.1 | 3.3 | 1.8 | 0.0 |
| Get full-time job | 29.4 | 33.1 | 25.0 | 30.0 | 39.6 | 47.4 |
| Vacation 3-4 mos. & then get full-time job | 11.8 | 8.4 | 6.2 | 0.0 | 4.0 | 5.3 |
| Get part-time paid job | 17.6 | 10.2 | 8.3 | 23.3 | 14.7 | 15.8 |
| Vacation 3-4 mos. & then get part-time job | 0.6 | 1.2 | 2.1 | 0.0 | 2.7 | 0.0 |
| Go to college or vocational school | 17.6 | 25.3 | 25.0 | 36.7 | 35.6 | 26.3 |
| Misc: Housework, loaf, armed serv. | 0.0 | 12.7 | 14.6 | 6.7 | 12.4 | 5.3 |
| Don't know | 0.0 | 0.6 | 2.1 | 3.3 | 0.0 | 0.0 |
| N | 17 | 166 | 48 | 30 | 225 | 19 |

° The list does not include church affiliation, which explains why a few of the boys could indicate that they participated in no organized activities and yet say that their reference group was an organized group: these boys indicated more specifically that their reference group was the church.

† Percentages add up to more than 100 as some respondents gave more than one answer.

of organized activities the youth participates in, both in and out of school, and (2) the desire to quit school (at the time of the survey).

There is some difference, however, in regard to plans for after high school graduation. Among the boys, a slightly larger proportion expected to go into farming, or get a part-time job, or vacation for several months and then get a full-time job, if their reference group was "school chums." If their reference group was their immediate family, however, they were more likely to be planning to get a full-time paying job immediately or to go to college. If their reference group was an organized group, they were also more likely to be planning to go to college or into the armed services or to loaf.

Among the girls whose reference group was their school friends, a disproportionately large number expected to get a part-time job or go to college. Girls whose reference group was some organized group were distinctive in their tendency to expect to get a full-time paying job and not go to college.

## FACTORS ASSOCIATED WITH INTIMACY OF FAMILY LIFE

By far the most frequently mentioned reference group is the immediate family, and because the degree of intimacy with the immediate family seems so important, it is analyzed further. Tables 3 and 4 present cross-tabulations with answers to the question "How close (intimate) a family life do you have with your parents and brothers and sisters?" There is a very high correlation, as might be expected, between intimacy of family life and fondness for the parents, although the correlation is not quite as high as was found to prevail among a sample of University of Minnesota students (3). The correlation is higher among boys than among girls, especially in regard to fondness for father, in spite of the fact that more girls than boys claim to be very fond of their parents.

Both a very large number and a very small number of siblings seem to be associated with intimacy of family life: The boys who have between three and seven siblings, and the girls who

## TABLE 3

### Conditions Associated with Intimacy of Family Life

| | PERCENTAGE GIVING INDICATED ANSWER AMONG: | | | | | |
| | Boys who say their family life is | | | Girls who say their family life is | | |
| | Very Close | Close | Not very Close or Not Close at All | Very Close | Close | Not very Close or Not Close at All |
|---|---|---|---|---|---|---|
| *Indicated fondness for father* | | | | | | |
| Very fond | 87.4 | 54.5 | 22.2 | 82.1 | 56.7 | 44.4 |
| Moderately fond | 9.9 | 32.2 | 38.9 | 9.7 | 36.9 | 55.6 |
| No particular feeling either way | 0.9 | 7.0 | 27.8 | 0.7 | 2.8 | 0.0 |
| Rather dislike him | 0.9 | 0.0 | 5.6 | 0.0 | 0.0 | 0.0 |
| No answer | 0.9 | 6.3 | 5.5 | 7.5 | 3.6 | 0.0 |
| *Indicated fondness for mother* | | | | | | |
| Very fond | 91.9 | 69.2 | 38.9 | 94.5 | 73.8 | 50.0 |
| Moderately fond | 7.2 | 24.5 | 38.9 | 2.8 | 22.7 | 44.4 |
| No particular feeling either way | 0.9 | 3.5 | 16.7 | 0.7 | 2.1 | 5.6 |
| Rather dislike her | 0.0 | 0.0 | 0.0 | 0.7 | 0.0 | 0.0 |
| No answer | 0.0 | 2.8 | 5.5 | 1.3 | 1.4 | 0.0 |
| *Number of siblings* | | | | | | |
| None or one | 12.6 | 11.2 | 11.1 | 18.6 | 12.7 | 11.1 |
| Two | 20.7 | 11.9 | 11.1 | 10.3 | 12.1 | 16.7 |
| Three to five | 34.2 | 44.1 | 44.4 | 38.7 | 44.8 | 44.4 |
| Six or seven | 15.3 | 14.7 | 16.7 | 18.0 | 16.3 | 0.0 |
| Eight or more | 17.2 | 17.5 | 16.7 | 13.7 | 14.1 | 27.8 |
| No answer | 0.0 | 0.6 | 0.0 | 0.7 | 0.0 | 0.0 |
| *Indicated popularity with classmates* | | | | | | |
| Very popular | 3.6 | 0.7 | 0.0 | 5.5 | 4.3 | 0.0 |
| Popular | 24.3 | 14.7 | 5.6 | 16.6 | 11.3 | 5.6 |
| Average | 64.9 | 81.8 | 83.3 | 71.0 | 77.4 | 94.4 |
| Unpopular or very unpopular | 1.8 | 2.1 | 11.1 | 4.9 | 3.5 | 0.0 |
| No answer | 5.4 | 0.7 | 0.0 | 2.0 | 3.5 | 0.0 |
| *Training for certain (specified) occupation* | | | | | | |
| Yes | 50.5 | 55.2 | 72.2 | 57.9 | 62.4 | 66.6 |
| No | 26.1 | 23.1 | 0.0 | 19.3 | 14.2 | 5.6 |
| Not training for occupation | 20.7 | 19.6 | 11.1 | 20.7 | 21.3 | 22.2 |
| No answer | 2.7 | 2.1 | 16.7 | 2.1 | 2.1 | 5.6 |
| N | 111 | 143 | 18 | 145 | 141 | 18 |

## TABLE 4

## Expectations for Future Associated with Intimacy of Family Life

| | PERCENTAGE GIVING INDICATED ANSWER AMONG: | | | | | |
| | Boys who say their family life is | | | Girls who say their family life is | | |
| Expectations | Very Close | Close | Not very Close or Not Close at All | Very Close | Close | Not very Close or Not Close at All |
|---|---|---|---|---|---|---|
| *For activity after high school graduation* | | | | | | |
| Farming | 23.4 | 28.0 | 33.3 | 2.1 | 2.8 | 5.6 |
| Full-time paid job | 32.4 | 30.1 | 33.3 | 40.0 | 42.6 | 27.8 |
| Vacation then full-time job | 7.2 | 9.8 | 5.6 | 4.8 | 4.3 | 11.1 |
| Part-time paid job | 9.9 | 8.4 | 11.1 | 16.6 | 11.3 | 16.7 |
| Vacation then part-time paid job | 0.9 | 2.1 | 0.0 | 2.1 | 3.5 | 0.0 |
| College | 34.2 | 16.1 | 16.7 | 29.0 | 35.0 | 38.9 |
| Misc: Housework, loaf, armed serv. | 12.6 | 14.7 | 27.8 | 11.7 | 12.8 | 16.7 |
| Don't know | 0.9 | 0.7 | 0.0 | 0.7 | 0.0 | 0.0 |
| *For staying or leaving community* | | | | | | |
| Stay | 42.3 | 39.9 | 33.3 | 31.7 | 31.9 | 22.2 |
| Leave | 46.9 | 46.8 | 61.1 | 62.1 | 61.0 | 72.2 |
| Don't know | 8.1 | 12.6 | 5.6 | 5.5 | 5.0 | 5.6 |
| No answer | 2.7 | 0.7 | 0.0 | 0.7 | 2.1 | 0.0 |
| *For age of marriage (in years)* | | | | | | |
| Under 20 | 0.0 | 1.4 | 0.0 | 7.6 | 7.8 | 11.2 |
| 20–21.9 | 13.5 | 9.8 | 33.3 | 37.2 | 40.4 | 27.8 |
| 22–24.9 | 37.9 | 29.3 | 33.3 | 32.4 | 35.5 | 27.8 |
| 25–27.9 | 23.4 | 25.9 | 16.7 | 6.9 | 5.7 | 11.1 |
| 28 or over | 3.6 | 8.4 | 5.6 | 4.2 | 2.1 | 11.1 |
| Don't want to marry | 4.5 | 5.6 | 11.1 | 2.1 | 2.1 | 5.5 |
| Don't know or no answer | 17.1 | 19.6 | 0.0 | 9.6 | 6.4 | 5.5 |
| *For future number of children (wanted)* | | | | | | |
| None | 4.5 | 9.1 | 22.2 | 4.1 | 6.4 | 5.6 |
| One or two | 17.1 | 24.5 | 33.3 | 22.1 | 20.6 | 16.7 |
| Three to five | 44.2 | 40.6 | 22.3 | 51.7 | 53.2 | 55.6 |
| Six to eight | 8.1 | 4.2 | 0.0 | 9.0 | 9.2 | 16.7 |
| Nine or more | 9.9 | 4.2 | 16.7 | 6.2 | 2.1 | 0.0 |
| Don't know or no answer | 16.2 | 17.4 | 5.5 | 6.9 | 8.5 | 5.4 |
| N | 111 | 143 | 18 | 145 | 141 | 18 |

have between two and five siblings report having the least intimate family life. While few students consider themselves unpopular with their schoolmates, the lowest relative popularity was found among those who have the least intimate family life. We have already seen that these are the youth whose reference group tends to be an organized group, especially a church group.

Intimacy of family life is also negatively correlated with definiteness of selection of a future occupation: Especially among the boys with the most intimate family life there are the largest proportion who are not training for any definite occupation. (There is no status differential in the occupations toward which the youth in the three categories of family intimacy are aiming, except that a larger proportion of boys with the least intimate family life are training to be farmers.)

This greater definiteness of choice of occupation among those with the loosest family tie reflects itself in the youngsters' plans for the period immediately following graduation: Those boys most intimate with their families have a greater expectation of going on to college, while those least intimate with their families are more likely than the others to expect that they will go into farming or do some unusual thing. While more boys are planning to leave the community than to stay, a larger proportion of those least intimate with their families are planning to leave and this probably has something to do with their choice of miscellaneous plans for the period following graduation.

The pattern among girls is somewhat different: While the girls with least intimate family ties also are most likely to indicate that they have miscellaneous unusual plans for the postgraduation period, they differ from the boys in this category by including the largest proportion who are planning to go on to college. A greater majority of the girls than of the boys, and again the proportion is greatest among those with least intimate family ties, are definitely planning to leave the community when they become adults.

Plans for their private life are also most unusual for those with the least intimate family life. A larger proportion of them are planning to get married either at a very young age, at a relatively advanced age, or not at all. A larger proportion of the boys among them want either no children or a very large

## TABLE 5

## Expectations for Future Associated with Popularity in School

| Expectations | Very Popular Boys and Girls | Popular Boys | Average Boys | Popular Girls | Average Girls | Unpopular Boys and Girls |
|---|---|---|---|---|---|---|
| *For future chances in life* | | | | | | |
| Very good chance | 50.0 | 22.4 | 15.4 | 36.6 | 17.5 | 15.0 |
| Good chance | 22.2 | 57.2 | 49.6 | 43.9 | 41.0 | 25.0 |
| Average | 16.7 | 14.3 | 32.2 | 17.1 | 36.7 | 50.0 |
| Poor chance | 0.0 | 2.0 | 1.4 | 2.4 | 3.5 | 10.0 |
| Very poor chance | 11.1 | 0.0 | 0.0 | 0.0 | 0.4 | 0.0 |
| Don't know or no answer | 0.0 | 4.1 | 1.4 | 0.0 | 0.9 | 0.0 |
| *For age of marriage (in years)* | | | | | | |
| Under 20 | 16.7 | 0.0 | 1.0 | 5.8 | 6.9 | 5.0 |
| 20–21.9 | 50.0 | 16.3 | 11.5 | 37.0 | 37.1 | 20.0 |
| 22–24.9 | 0.0 | 46.9 | 31.2 | 38.1 | 37.1 | 25.0 |
| 25–27.9 | 5.6 | 20.4 | 26.0 | 8.0 | 7.9 | 10.0 |
| 28 and over | 11.1 | 2.0 | 6.2 | 2.9 | 3.1 | 10.0 |
| Don't want to marry | 0.0 | 4.1 | 6.7 | 1.6 | 1.7 | 15.0 |
| Don't know or no answer | 16.6 | 10.3 | 17.4 | 6.6 | 6.2 | 15.0 |
| *For number of children (wanted)* | | | | | | |
| None | 0.0 | 6.1 | 8.2 | 4.9 | 4.8 | 25.0 |
| One or two | 27.8 | 20.4 | 22.5 | 17.0 | 21.8 | 10.0 |
| Three to five | 33.3 | 51.0 | 39.9 | 63.5 | 53.4 | 30.0 |
| Six to eight | 5.6 | 6.1 | 5.8 | 4.8 | 10.9 | 5.0 |
| Nine or more | 22.2 | 2.0 | 7.7 | 2.4 | 2.6 | 15.0 |
| Don't know or no answer | 11.1 | 14.4 | 15.9 | 7.4 | 6.5 | 15.0 |
| *For staying in or leaving community* | | | | | | |
| Stay | 27.8 | 32.7 | 41.8 | 26.8 | 31.4 | 45.0 |
| Leave | 38.9 | 57.1 | 46.1 | 68.3 | 62.4 | 55.0 |
| Don't know | 33.3 | 8.2 | 10.6 | 4.9 | 4.4 | 0.0 |
| No answer | 0.0 | 2.0 | 1.5 | 0.0 | 1.8 | 0.0 |
| N | 18 | 49 | 208 | 41 | 229 | 20 |

PERCENTAGE GIVING INDICATED ANSWER AMONG:

number of children (the girls do not vary in this respect with the degree of intimacy of family life). The same tendency, to expect or plan on a relatively unusual adult life, was also found among those with least intimate family ties in the earlier study of University of Minnesota students. The evidence of the earlier study was that "responsible" behavior and "responsible" planning for adult life was most likely to be found among those with the most intimate family life, and the evidence from the present study—while not as definitive as the earlier one—suggests that this is also true among rural high school youth.

## FACTORS ASSOCIATED WITH PEER GROUP POPULARITY

We turn now to a closer analysis of another aspect of reference group behavior—popularity with schoolmates. We have already seen that popularity is somewhat associated with choosing school chums as the chief reference group. A much stronger correlation is noted in Table 5 between popularity and optimism regarding future life chances. Whether the estimation of personal popularity is based on the realities of the situation or not, apparently it and optimism reflect an important aspect of the youth's outlook on life. A curious finding here is that the proportion planning to stay in the community increases with progressively *lower* popularity. While this is partly a function of the concentration in the very popular group of those who say they do not know their future plans concerning staying in the community, it also seems to reflect important differences in general outlook on life.

Expectations for getting married at either a very young or a very late age do not seem to be correlated with estimation of popularity. But there is a significant minority among the unpopular who say they do not want to get married at all, which is not found among the other groups of youngsters. A similar pattern is revealed in response to the question concerning the number of children wanted. A fourth of the unpopular group do not want any children at all, which is a much higher percentage than that found in any other popularity group. Those wanting a very large number of children are concentrated in the two extreme groups in terms of popularity.

## REFERENCE GROUP VALUES
## AND EXPECTATIONS FOR THE FUTURE

Expectations for future adult life are linked to reference groups at least partly through the values which these reference groups hold. We sought to get at the relevant values of two major reference groups—parents and school chums—as well as personal aspirations for the future, by means of three projective-type questions:

1. Name three qualities or achievements you might have when you become an adult for which you think your parents would praise you.
2. Name three qualities or achievements you might have when you become an adult for which you think your school friends would praise you.
3. Name three qualities or achievements that you yourself would like to have as an adult.

Answers evoked by these directions are presented in Table 6, cross-tabulated by the reference groups of the boys and girls. The most general finding, which is supported by the percentages at several points in the table, is that where there is a discrepancy between what the parents and school friends would praise the subject for, those subjects whose reference group is their family tend to have personal aspirations reflecting the parents' values, while those whose reference group is their "school chums" tend to have personal aspirations reflecting the school friends' values. Other noteworthy conclusions that can be drawn from the table are:

1. The most frequently mentioned aspiration is an occupation. It is significantly more frequently mentioned by those whose reference group is "school chums" than by those whose reference group is "immediate family" or "organized groups." This differential is maintained when the occupation is farming. This orientation toward occupation on the part of those whose reference group is school chums—which seems to be encouraged both by their parents and by their school chums—helps to explain the previously mentioned finding that individuals in this category

## TABLE 6

### Reference Groups and Valued Qualities or Achievements
(percentages naming indicated qualities or achievements) °

| | Qualities or achievements praised BY PARENTS | | | | | | Qualities or achievements praised BY SCHOOL FRIENDS | | | | | | Qualities or achievements desired BY SELF | | | | | |
| | Among boys whose reference group is: | | | Among girls whose reference group is: | | | Among boys whose reference group is: | | | Among girls whose reference group is: | | | Among boys whose reference group is: | | | Among girls whose reference group is: | | |
| | School Chums | Family | Organized Groups | School Chums | Family | Organized Groups | School Chums | Family | Organized Groups | School Chums | Family | Organized Groups | School Chums | Family | Organized Groups | School Chums | Family | Organized Groups |
|---|---|---|---|---|---|---|---|---|---|---|---|---|---|---|---|---|---|---|
| 1. Get a job or specific occupation (excluding farming) | 68 | 28 | 45 | 100 | 57 | 69 | 73 | 21 | 25 | 85 | 48 | 49 | 97 | 20 | 38 | 84 | 45 | 42 |
| 2. Be a farmer | 39 | 17 | 18 | 5 | 0 | 0 | 36 | 13 | 16 | 0 | 1 | 0 | 35 | 16 | 19 | 0 | 0 | 0 |
| 3. Be successful: Generally | 39 | 29 | 27 | 10 | 20 | 17 | 9 | 26 | 13 | 20 | 19 | 35 | 0 | 25 | 0 | 20 | 18 | 12 |
|     In occupation | 48 | 50 | 33 | 19 | 38 | 23 | 55 | 43 | 32 | 15 | 29 | 28 | 62 | 57 | 44 | 15 | 31 | 42 |
|     In style of life | 10 | 15 | 3 | 5 | 5 | 6 | 0 | 17 | 0 | 10 | 4 | 0 | 9 | 24 | 0 | 10 | 9 | 12 |
| 4. Be a good family member | 0 | 7 | 3 | 38 | 17 | 6 | 0 | 0 | 3 | 20 | 9 | 21 | 0 | 2 | 6 | 20 | 12 | 30 |
| 5. Have a good family and home life | 19 | 21 | 18 | 19 | 19 | 29 | 18 | 15 | 10 | 25 | 19 | 21 | 9 | 35 | 28 | 25 | 33 | 60 |
| 6. Be socially adjusted and popular | 0 | 12 | 12 | 29 | 23 | 23 | 0 | 46 | 28 | 35 | 43 | 21 | 9 | 18 | 9 | 34 | 30 | 30 |
| 7. Have a nice appearance | 10 | 4 | 0 | 0 | 1 | 0 | 0 | 2 | 0 | 5 | 4 | 7 | 0 | 2 | 9 | 5 | 3 | 0 |
| 8. Have good character traits | 10 | 43 | 21 | 33 | 37 | 23 | 18 | 38 | 38 | 35 | 40 | 21 | 27 | 27 | 9 | 10 | 10 | 12 |
| 9. Be religious | 0 | 13 | 15 | 19 | 13 | 0 | 0 | 5 | 10 | 10 | 7 | 7 | 0 | 4 | 9 | 10 | 10 | 6 |
| 10. Be a good citizen and help others | 19 | 6 | 9 | 5 | 9 | 17 | 0 | 10 | 13 | 10 | 11 | 28 | 0 | 7 | 13 | 0 | 16 | 6 |
| 11. Have talent: Mental | 19 | 20 | 27 | 10 | 26 | 6 | 0 | 11 | 16 | 10 | 18 | 7 | 0 | 14 | 13 | 10 | 9 | 0 |
|     Physical | 10 | 9 | 15 | 10 | 11 | 23 | 9 | 15 | 16 | 15 | 13 | 21 | 18 | 11 | 13 | 15 | 9 | 24 |
| 12. Be happy and do what I like | 10 | 5 | 9 | 0 | 10 | 0 | 36 | 12 | 16 | 0 | 4 | 0 | 27 | 21 | 22 | 0 | 1 | 0 |
| 13. Miscellaneous and trivial | 10 | 1 | 0 | 0 | 10 | 0 | 0 | 1 | 0 | 5 | 2 | 0 | 0 | 1 | 0 | 8 | 12 | 24 |
| 14. Don't know | 18 | 20 | 45 | 3 | 14 | 58 | 37 | 25 | 45 | 5 | 29 | 34 | 7 | 16 | 37 | 30 | 300 | 19 |
| Total | 300 | 300 | 300 | 300 | 300 | 300 | 300 | 300 | 300 | 300 | 300 | 300 | 300 | 300 | 300 | 300 | 300 | 300 |
| N | 17 | 166 | 48 | 30 | 225 | 19 | 17 | 166 | 48 | 30 | 225 | 19 | 17 | 166 | 48 | 30 | 225 | 19 |

° Percentages add to 300 per cent as each subject was asked to give three responses to each question. Cases of "no answer" were excluded from the calculations.

are the ones most likely to be planning to go to work when they graduate from high school.

2. Material success is also very frequently mentioned as an aspiration. In most cases when success is the aim, occupation is specified. Boys are more likely than girls to mention occupational success as an aspiration for themselves and as a future achievement for which their parents and school friends would praise them.

3. Social adjustment and popularity are more frequently mentioned as personal aspirations and as achievements which school friends would praise than as achievements which parents would praise. In general girls think more of these traits than do boys.

4. Girls are also more likely than boys to think of being a good family member. They are especially likely to consider this a goal for themselves if their reference group is an organized group rather than their family or school chums. But when guessing what their parents would praise them for, girls are more likely to mention being a good family member when their reference group is their school chums.

5. Character traits and talents which are the goals of the ideal typical "inner-directed" personality are less frequently mentioned as aspirations and praised goals than are material success and occupations that we have already considered. This fact supports Riesman's hypothesis that other-directed characteristics are more highly valued than inner-directed ones (2). Notably, being religious and being a good citizen are infrequently mentioned. Among boys, those whose reference groups are organized groups are more likely to mention these latter goals than those whose reference groups are family or school chums.

6. Good character traits are generally as likely to be mentioned as personal aspirations as they are to be considered as something which parents and school friends would praise. This fact contradicts Riesman's hypothesis that the *trend* is away from evaluating good character highly, at least as perceived by the youngsters in our study.

7. Those whose reference groups are organized groups are consistently most likely to say they "don't know" what their personal aspirations are and what their parents and school friends

would praise them for. It is this category of our sample which is thus least oriented toward their future as adults.

8. In addition to Riesman's categories of "inner-directed" and "other-directed,"[1] one might distinguish another broad set of life-goals which is represented by our category 12, "Be happy and do what I like." We might label this the "gratification-directed" or hedonic personality. It approximates the ideal formulated by psychoanalytic theory. That it may be an increasingly frequent type of personality is suggested by the fact that it is mentioned more frequently as a personal aspiration and as a trait which school friends would praise than one which parents would praise. Further, those whose reference group is the immediate family (that is, those particularly oriented toward their parents) are less likely to refer to this trait than are those whose reference groups are school chums (for the boys) or organized groups (for the girls).

## SUMMARY

This study has examined just a few of the background characteristics, behaviors, and attitudes that might be hypothesized to be associated with the different membership reference groups held among rural high school youth. The statistically significant differences among youth with different reference groups were in regard to number of siblings, estimation of popularity among schoolmates, and plans for the period after graduation.

The most frequently mentioned reference group was the immediate family, and analysis was made of various characteristics associated with different degrees of reported intimacy of family life. Intimacy of family life was very highly correlated with fondness for father and mother, and was more characteristic of children who had either very few or very many siblings. Those very close to their families were also more likely than others to be popular with their schoolmates, uncertain about their future vocation, planning to leave the community when adult, get married at an average age and have a moderate num-

---

[1] Riesman has a third category of "tradition-directed" which we have not been able operationally to distinguish from "inner-directed" in this study.

ber of children. Planning to go to college showed different relationships by sex: Among boys, it was those who are the closest to their families who are planning for college, while among girls the opposite was true.

Popularity was associated with the desire to leave the community when adult and with optimism regarding future life chances. Those who did not want to get married or have children were concentrated among the unpopular.

Aspirations regarding personal qualities or achievements were found to be related to what were perceived to be the values of one's reference groups. Evidence was found supporting Riesman's hypothesis that qualities of the "other-directed personality" are more highly valued than are qualities of the "inner-directed personality." But there was no discrepancy in this regard between the youths' own values and what they perceived their parents' values to be. There was a tendency, however, for the youth to aspire to qualities of what might be called the "gratification-directed" or "hedonic" personality more than their parents were perceived to do so.

## REFERENCES

1. HYMAN, HERBERT, "The Psychology of Status," *Arch. Psychol.*, 1942, No. 269.
2. RIESMAN, DAVID, *The Lonely Crowd* (New Haven, Yale University Press, 1950).
3. ROSE, ARNOLD M., "Acceptance of Adult Roles and Separation from Family." Unpublished manuscript.

*Russell R. Dynes, Alfred C. Clarke,
and Simon Dinitz*

# OCCUPATIONAL ASPIRATION
# AND FAMILY EXPERIENCE *

*Whereas in the preceding research the author utilized
one concept, the reference group, in the light of which
he examined certain data concerning students, the research presented in this writing examines two—something
called "occupational aspiration" and something else called
"family experience." After each of these is* defined, *it
has to be* measured *and if the assumptions of science
are sound, and if the theory with which the authors
begin is correct, then some sort of* connection *ought to be
discovered between the two. In short, this study should
establish as fact something about which we had only
some sort of notion (hypothesis) beforehand. How did
this one work out?*

A recurring theme in the stratification literature emphasizes the
widespread acceptance of the "success" imperative in American
society. Upward social mobility is not only a possibility but
something to be actively sought. Although the rewards of mobility are consistently stressed, some individuals show a greater
desire to achieve these rewards, while others seem more "content" with their current status and expectations. What accounts
for this differential emphasis upon success? Why do some people
consider it more important to "get ahead" than others? Within

* Russell R. Dynes, Alfred C. Clarke, and Simon Dinitz, "Levels of
Occupational Aspiration: Some Aspects of Family Experience as a Variable," *American Sociological Review*, Vol. 21, No. 2 (April, 1956), pp. 212-
215. Reprinted by permission. (Italics by the editors)

a given socio-economic group, what social-psychological factors differentiate individuals with high aspirations from those who have lower aspirational levels?

Much of the psychoanalytic literature has suggested that unsatisfactory interpersonal relations in early childhood produce insecurity which is translated into neurotic striving for power, recognition and success. Adler and Horney, among others, have suggested that the quest for power is frequently used as a compensatory means of attaining reassurance against the anxieties produced by unhappy childhood experiences.[1] Some sociologists have also commented on the plausibility of these relationships. Ellis, for example, studying career women, found that those who had achieved upward social mobility showed a history of greater difficulty in their early interpersonal relations than did those who were non-mobile.[2] While the personality consequences of upward social mobility have been the major focus of previous research in this area,[3] there has been surprisingly little empirical attention directed toward understanding differential levels of aspiration. Does it follow, as much of the psychoanalytic literature asserts, that individuals with high aspirations are characterized by greater difficulty in their interpersonal relations within the family of orientation than those with lower aspirations?

## RESEARCH DESIGN

Investigation of this relationship required the selection of an appropriate measure of aspiration and some index of parent-child interaction. Although aspirations have been measured in varied ways, it was felt that an occupational referent represented one of the best single measures. The scale selected was developed by Reissman and was concerned with the willingness of individuals to forego certain satisfactions in order to achieve oc-

[1] See, for example, Karen Horney, *The Neurotic Personality of Our Time* (New York, Norton and Company, 1937), pp. 162-187.

[2] Evelyn Ellis, "Social Psychological Correlates of Upward Social Mobility Among Unmarried Career Women," *American Sociological Review,* 17 (October, 1952), pp. 558-563.

[3] See, for example, A. B. Hollingshead, R. Ellis and E. Kirby, "Social Mobility and Mental Illness," *American Sociological Review,* 19 (October, 1954), pp. 577-584.

cupational advancement.[4] In this scale, eleven considerations were specified that might prevent a person from advancing in rank and salary in his occupation.[5] Among these considerations were: leaving one's family for some time, endangering one's health, moving about the country, keeping quiet about political views, etc. Each consideration was evaluated in terms of three alternatives: (1) whether it might stop the individual from making a change; (2) whether it might be a serious consideration but would not stop him; (3) whether it would not matter at all. Only the first alternative was scored.[6] The logic behind the scoring was that persons who would permit these considerations to stop them from making a change were expressing lower levels of aspiration than those who would disregard these factors in order to attain higher occupational status.

Since this scale had previously been used simply to differentiate gross categories and had not been employed to measure individual differences, the sample was divided into "high" and "low" aspirers, similar to the division employed by Reissman. Operationally, respondents who received scores from zero to 19 were defined as "high" aspirers and those who scored 20 or more comprised the "low" aspirers.

A second instrument was constructed concerning affectional patterns in the family of orientation. Questions relating to the respondent's relations with their parents included: degree of attachment, amount of conflict, frequency of confiding in parents, feelings of rejection, parental favoritism, and fear of punishment from parents. Items were also included concerning sibling rivalry, childhood happiness, and coercion by parents through disapproval and unfavorable comparisons. It should be noted

[4] Leonard Reissman, "Level of Aspiration and Social Class," *American Sociological Review*, 18 (June, 1953), pp. 233-242.

[5] These considerations were ranked according to the frequency they were taken into account by the sample population in the original study and were weighted from 1 to 11. For example, a person who said that moving around the country would prevent him from making an occupational advancement received a score of 10. Conversely, if the item was not a consideration, it was scored zero. By summating the weighted responses to each of the eleven items it was possible to receive scores ranging from zero to 66.

[6] This method of scoring was slightly different from the method used by Reissman in the original study.

that all of these dimensions required the respondent's definition of his relationships. No claim is made that this definition was necessarily in close correspondence with the objective situation. *Even if the definitions were not objectively true to others, they were, of course, subjectively true to the respondent. The concern here was with the respondent's interpretation of the situation.*

The aspiration scale and index of parent-child interaction were employed in questionnaire form [7] and were administered to 350 university students enrolled in introductory and advanced sociology classes. Since the aspirational scale was phrased in terms of occupational advancement, the women in the sample expressed their aspiration in terms of advice they might give their husbands.[8] Using both objective indices of father's occupation and a self-rating on class position, the sample population showed only slight variations in socio-economic background. Over 55 per cent of the sample came from professional and managerial backgrounds. Only 8 per cent of the sample placed themselves in the upper class, and no one identified with the lower class, while 70 per cent identified with the upper-middle class and 22 per cent with the lower-middle.

## THE FINDINGS

Evidence obtained in this research essentially supports the relationship between unsatisfactory interpersonal relations in the family of orientation and high aspirational levels. The "high" aspirers stated that they had experienced feelings of rejection more frequently than did those in the "lower" group. As may be seen in Table 1, 42 per cent of the "high" aspirers indicated that they had experienced feelings of not being wanted by their fathers, while only 24 per cent of those in the "low" group had experienced similar feelings. When the data were classified according to the individuals' feelings of rejection by the mother, the percentages for the "high" and "low" groups were 34 and 20, respectively.

[7] All questionnaires were answered anonymously. Other dimensions, covered by the questionnaire but not included in this report, involved the relations between aspiration and religious ideology and the relation between aspiration and favorableness of attitude to marriage.

[8] There were 153 males and 197 females in the total sample.

## TABLE 1

### Feelings of Not Being Wanted by Parents in Relation to Level of Aspiration, in Percentages

| Feelings of Not Being Wanted by Parents | Level of Aspiration | |
| --- | --- | --- |
| | High | Low |
| Father | (N = 117) | (N = 223) |
| Some | 41.9 | 24.7 |
| None | 58.1 | 75.3 |
| Mother | (N = 122) | (N = 223) |
| Some | 34.4 | 20.2 |
| None | 65.6 | 79.8 |

Data concerning father, $\chi^2 = 10.7$; d.f. = 1; P < .002.
Data concerning mother, $\chi^2 = 8.43$; d.f. = 1; P < .01.

Similarly, the data regarding parental favoritism toward a son or daughter revealed significant differences in the same direction. Table 2 shows the result of this analysis. "High" aspirers defined their parents as showing more favoritism toward some child in the family than did the "low" aspirers. Furthermore, a significantly greater proportion of the "high" than the "low" aspirational groups indicated less attachment to their parents and had experienced a lesser degree of happiness during their childhood. (See Tables 3 and 4.) In addition, the "high" aspirers confided less frequently in their fathers (P < .05) and were more fearful of punishment from them (P < .05).

This pattern of difference was even more pronounced when the data were further classified according to sex, ethnic origin, or religion.[9] This finding would add some support to the observations which many have made that aspirational levels are closely associated with the person's position in the social structure. It should be noted, however, that the sample, on which this report is based, was relatively homogeneous in that it com-

[9] The details of these relationships will be discussed in a forthcoming report.

## TABLE 2

Favoritism Shown by Parents in Relation
to Level of Aspiration, in Percentages

| Favoritism Shown by Parents | Level of Aspiration | |
|---|---|---|
| | High | Low |
| Father | (N = 95) | (N = 188) |
| Yes | 45.3 | 30.9 |
| No | 54.7 | 69.1 |
| Mother | (N = 95) | (N = 188) |
| Yes | 41.1 | 25.0 |
| No | 58.9 | 75.0 |

Data concerning father, $\chi^2 = 5.56$; d.f. = 1; P < .02.

Data concerning mother, $\chi^2 = 7.46$; d.f. = 1; P < .01.

## TABLE 3

Degree of Parental Attachment in Relation
to Level of Aspiration, in Percentages

| Degree of Attachment to Parents | Level of Aspiration | |
|---|---|---|
| | High | Low |
| Father | (N = 110) | (N = 222) |
| Much | 33.6 | 50.9 |
| Little | 66.4 | 49.1 |
| Mother | (N = 123) | (N = 223) |
| Much | 52.8 | 66.8 |
| Little | 47.2 | 33.2 |

Data concerning father, $\chi^2 = 7.87$; d.f. = 1; P < .01.
Data concerning mother, $\chi^2 = 6.58$; d.f. = 1; P < .01.

## TABLE 4

## Happiness of Childhood in Relation to Level of Aspiration, in Percentages

| Happiness of Childhood | Level of Aspiration | |
|---|---|---|
| | High (N = 122) | Low (N = 224) |
| Happy | 72.9 | 81.1 |
| Average | 27.1 | 18.9 |

$\chi^2 = 4.04$; d.f. $= 1$; $P < .05$.

prised a predominately urban, middle-western, Protestant, middle-class, college population.

The "high" and "low" aspirers did not differ significantly in the degree of conflict with their siblings. Neither did they differ in the frequency with which they had confided in their mothers, nor in the amount of conflict with their fathers.

Since it is often assumed that aspiration is a by-product of the overt pressures of parental projection, it is interesting to note that there were no significant differences between the groups in their feelings that their parents compared them unfavorably with their siblings or peer group concerning accomplishments in school and athletics. In addition, the "high" and "low" aspirers did not differ in their estimations of the degree of disappointment their parents might have if their children did not live up to parental expectations. This negative evidence suggested that differences in aspiration are more closely related to subtle interpersonal factors than to overt parental pressures.

## SUMMARY

This study concerning the relationship between aspirational level and interpersonal experiences tends to support some of the current assumptions in the psychoanalytic literature. *Unsatisfactory interpersonal relationships in the family of orientation were significantly related to high aspirational levels and satis-factory relationships were related to lower aspirational levels.*

Since increasing attention is being given to the development of "happy" and socially well-adjusted persons by some of our institutions and social agencies, the question arises whether modifications will occur in the future to the success orientation of American society. It may well be that the increasing emphasis on personal happiness, rather than upon personal achievement, will serve to augment the growing quest for security.

## APPENDIX: ITEMS ON WHICH TABLES ARE BASED

### *Table* 1:

How frequently have you felt that you were not wanted by your *father?*
   (1) Very often   (2) Frequently   (3) Some   (4) Rarely   (5) Never.
How frequently have you felt that you were not wanted by your *mother?*
   (1) Very often   (2) Frequently   (3) Some   (4) Rarely   (5) Never.
In Table 1, response categories 1, 2, 3, and 4 were included in "Some," and category 5 was referred to as "None."

### *Table* 2:

During your childhood, who do you think was your father's favorite?
   (1) Older brother   (2) Younger brother   (3) Older sister   (4) Younger sister   (5) Am only child   (6) Yourself   (7) No favorite.
During your childhood, who do you think was your mother's favorite?
   (1) Older brother   (2) Younger brother   (3) Older sister   (4) Younger sister   (5) Am only child   (6) Yourself   (7) No favorite.
In Table 2, response categories 1, 2, 3, 4, and 6 were included in "Favoritism Shown by Parents—Yes" and category 7 was referred to as "Favoritism Shown by Parents—No." In some cases the respondents defined themselves as the favorite child. These cases were included since they were consistent with the purpose of the table, depicting a family "atmosphere" in which differential treatment of children was perceived. Cases involving only children were, of course, excluded.

## *Table* 3:

Amount of attachment between you and your *father?*
> (1) Extremely close   (2) Very close   (3) Considerable   (4) Somewhat   (5) A little   (6) None at all.

Amount of attachment between you and your *mother?*
> (1) Extremely close   (2) Very close   (3) Considerable   (4) Somewhat   (5) A little   (6) None at all.

In Table 3, response categories 1 and 2 were included in "Much" and categories 3, 4, 5, and 6 were referred to as "Little."

## *Table* 4:

How would you rate your childhood?
> (1) Very happy   (2) Happy   (3) Average   (4) Unhappy   (5) Very unhappy.

In Table 4, response categories 1 and 2 were included in "Happy" and categories 3, 4, and 5 were referred to as "Average."

*Part Four*

# THE STUDY OF SOCIETY

One of the omnipresent sociological "facts of life" is the human propensity for living, in some measure at least, by myth. Often in American society as elsewhere, this takes the form of "knowledge" that is fictional because it is based upon things as they *were* instead of as they *are*. Several of the selections in this section are, therefore, addressed to bringing us up to date—and sometimes sharply. Whyte in *Organization Man,* Riesman in *The Lonely Crowd,* and Mills in *The Power Elite* give many "that uncomfortable feeling" about the contemporary world. Insights such as these are instances of what Adolf Myerson has called "the great unlearning," through which all people sooner or later go—or ought to. What has to be unlearned is the oversimplified, idealized, past-oriented explanation of what the social world and social relationships "are." Unfortunately, but inescapably, most of us have "learned the facts" about society and human relations from those "teachers" often least competent to teach us these things *accurately*. First, the "authority figures" in our lives often did not themselves get matters straight in the first place. Secondly, for conscious or unconscious reasons, the young are often not given the whole truth, even as their elders themselves see and know it. Finally, there are the normal distortions of the "teacher's" own life experience—workings of perception, interpretations and memory, which so often warp the verities as they come out in the teaching-learning process. So what ought to be familiar often comes to one as new and strange—and sometimes threatening. But, one way or another, the truth will out.

Everything about society is not necessarily so startling, however. Some things are vaguely known, and further study simply confirms the original insight, and specifies more precisely something at first only suspected. The following readings dealing with urbanization, education, religion, stratification, the family, economics, and race are largely in this category. They constitute refinements and extensions, and in some instances critiques, of familiar ideas.

Here, as elsewhere, the sources from which we presumably could have drawn are abundant to the point of being overwhelming. We have tried to cull "a hundred pages worth" which can for one reason or another be recommended as points of reference, much as the soundings taken by a hydrographer in charting a body of water. Each sampling may contain considerable detail, but much is never fathomed at all.

First to touch upon theory about the nature of society itself, we draw upon Ralph Linton (page 226). Viewed in the most theoretical way, what can be said about the genesis and universal character of all societies, not just ours, not just this century, but human society universally?

The pioneer sociologist, Charles Horton Cooley, enunciated a proposition to which, so far as we know, all sociologists give fundamental assent. The individual and society, he said, are not separate; rather they are only aspects of one inseparable entity. That phenomenon is human life, which in one sense consists of the behavior of individuals, but in another equally obvious sense, concerns their collective nature. This is nicely illustrated in the selection from *The Organization Man* (page 229). The book focuses on men—a certain type of men who according to Whyte are now a predominant type in American society. But that being the case, the description of organization men is also a description of the society. The "ideology" of the Organization Man *is* the society which emerges simultaneously with the emergence of the organization man as a person-type. We have elected to open the discussion of society with this emphasis, in order that we might begin on a note of modernity. Whyte's thesis is challenging and constitutes an extremely fundamental understanding.

Modern American society is an urban society; less than 15 per cent of Americans make their living in agriculture and live in the open country. The rest are urban and of the urban ones over a majority live within normal commuting range of cities of 100,000 people or more. Two papers dealing with this phenomenon are presented, one of a somewhat more general and theoretical nature dealing with the reasons for the origins and growth of cities, and something concerning their nature (page 234). The second, an excerpt from *The Exploding Metropolis*, deals with the internal changes in what might be called the anatomy of the American city (page 242).

Yet every society, whether urban or not, has to be "run." In short, some kind of *power structure* has to exist so that collective decisions may be made concerning everything from garbage disposal to international relations. The immediate response to questions of social control is to conjure up an image of government—the constitutionally established agency for getting collective things done. And typically American is the reassuring conviction that being a "democracy" we can be reasonably sure that this is all done not only in the public interest but by public mandate. C. Wright Mills' *The Power Elite*, though by no means a completely uncontroversial statement of the matter, casts a long shadow of doubt across the terrace of complacency. From his well-known book we have taken an excerpt (page 248) in which he discusses how the "higher circles" are formed and how, in our innocence, we have allowed an extra-constitutional oligarchy to emerge and become solidified.

In the American ideology the key to solving all problems, collective or individual, is said to lie in education. While it is true that in recent years critics and critiques of education have been proliferated, there still remains the confident hope that a "free and democratic educational system, providing equal opportunity for everyone, is the great bulwark" which will insure the realization of our dreams. William F. Kenkel's digest of Warner, Havighurst, and Loeb's *Who Shall Be Educated?* (page 253) will raise some doubts not only about the democracy of the process, but also about the extent to which we can, in these times, afford to let slip down the drain so great a reservoir of talent as in fact we do.

If we hold to myths about education, so also do we about religion—at least in its organized forms. Liston Pope discusses the stratification of religious organizations in American society (page 271). In this paper he has summarized a number of "close studies of social stratification" as they are manifested in and through American religious organization. This is an excellent example of the ways in which one feature or aspect of a society—in this case stratification—influences another part. Particularly striking is the fact that an allegedly idealistic institution, namely religion, formally promulgating altruistic and democratic ideology, should itself become fashioned along non-democratic, that is, stratified lines.

Stratified or no, at least the majority of Americans are religious and becoming increasingly so. Of this there is abundant statistical evidence. More people today are members of organized churches than at any time in our history, and the proportion is going up. Precisely, however, what does this *mean* in the lives of the communicants? How "real" is it? (page 274). These statistical data raise some robust doubts.

Perhaps the "inexorable workings of stratification," as documented in *Who Shall be Educated* and "Religion and the Class Structure," not to mention *Organization Man* and *The Power Elite*, may not be as immutable as we sometimes think. While his thesis lacks statistical confirmation, an interesting assembly of facts and opinion is marshalled by Eric Larrabee (page 284) in "The Wreck of the Status System." This article is addressed to the proposition that there are forces at work in American society which countervail the gross stratification influences. At least it should be worth our while to consider this.

In all the standard sociological treatises, and just about everywhere else, one is reminded that American society is acquiring a characteristic called "complexity" and sometimes takes a special form called "bureaucracy." Instances of this are as common as flowers in spring. This would hardly seem to need any embellishment. Everything is said to be over-organized—too much to-getherness and belongingness; some call this the urban American disease. By implication, something which is not urban ought to be somewhat freer, namely rural life. Everett Rogers' description and interpretation of governmental agencies "serving" agriculture might come as something of a surprise to urban people and possibly also to rural ones, when the entire picture is assembled (page 288).

There is more than one way, however, to look at change. Social critics, including many sociologists, have tended to take the "ain't it awful" point of view: that is, they have been much more inclined to see dire conse-quences rather than any great white hopes wrapped up in the process of change. Just why this is so is not al-together clear, although it has been suggested in some published work that this is a function of their placement in the stratification system. In any event it must also be reported that some exceedingly objective studies of changing institutions appear in sociological literature, one of which is included on page 300: "Reshaping Core Institutions."

Another approach to change is comparative, that is, examination of the ways in which other societies struc-ture human relationships, presumably in an attempt to meliorate some of the structural tensions which we also have in our society. The Israeli Kibbutz discussed by

Kenkel (page 306) is an example of a society which has attempted by rational means to fashion a "better" way for meeting some urgencies in the sphere of men and women.

Sociologists, as everyone knows, also deal with race relations. There is at present an abundance of material dealing with the problems of desegregation of schools and other public facilities in certain parts of the United States. Sociologists have made numerous studies of such, and it is rather generally alleged that they were influential in the Supreme Court's decisions outlawing segregation. However that may be, most sociologists would claim that their chief contributions to the study of race relations lie not in the realm of public policy but rather in providing new knowledge and interpretations of the way in which the bi- and multi-racial system functions. In large measure this was the focus of Gunnar Myrdal's familiar and influential *An American Dilemma*. Among other theoretical contributions, Myrdal formulated the "Rank Order of Discrimination" hypothesis for whites and a corresponding "sensitivity to discrimination" hierarchy for Negroes. This was an hypothesis derived from various observations which Myrdal and his staff made, but it did not have a precise, empirical basis. On page 316 William S. M. Banks II presents one of the few, if not only, careful empirical researches designed to test the Myrdal hypothesis of Negro sensitivity. This is a careful work, presented as a sample of objective research in an emotion-laden subject as well as for the specific validations and refinements of Myrdal which it demonstrates.

Again and again it seems, sociologists and other students of society need to be reminded that the forces of social change emanate significantly, if not deterministically, from changes in technology. There seems to be a persistent reluctance to account sufficiently for the shaping of society by inventions in science and technology. We turn to William F. Ogburn again (page 332) for a brief reminder at the end of the collection of readings of the extent to which the contemporary world is shaped and reshaped by the inventions and the derivative influences which come from the ideas and gadgets which our inventive genius piles upon us in unending accumulation.

*Ralph Linton*

# SOCIETY *

*Theorists in sociology and anthropology have given considerable attention to what they variously call the "nature" of society, its origins, and its universal features. This is helpful to understand the other side of the coin when we look at the unique historical case manifested by some particular society which we are studying or in which we live. As we have pointed out in previous contexts, Ralph Linton's* The Study of Man *is a social science classic in which numerous broad theoretical concepts and explanations are to be found. His treatment of the universal characteristics of society, taken from a later book, is included here in an effort to give the student a general perspective while he examines numerous specific features of chiefly American society.*

Whatever the genesis of human societies may have been, all of them have certain features in common. The first and perhaps most important of these is that the society, rather than the individual, has become the significant unit in our species struggle for survival. Except by some unhappy accident, like that of Robinson Crusoe, all human beings live as members of organized groups and have their fate inextricably bound up with that of the group to which they belong. They cannot survive the hazards of infancy or satisfy their adult needs without the aid and cooperation of other individuals. Human life has passed long since from the stage of the individual workman to that of the assembly line in which each person makes his small, specific contribution to the finished product.

* From Ralph Linton, *The Cultural Background of Personality* (New York, Appleton-Century-Crofts, 1945), pp. 15-19. Used by permission.

226

A second characteristic of societies is that they normally persist far beyond the life span of any one individual. Each of us is brought, by the accident of birth, into an organization which is already a going concern. Although new societies may come into being under certain conditions, most people are born, live and die as members of old ones. Their problem as individuals is not to assist in the organization of a new society but to adjust themselves to a pattern of group living which has long since crystallized. It may seem hardly necessary to point this out, but one finds in many writings a confusion between the genesis of social forms and the genesis of social behavior in the individual. How such an institution as the family originated is a problem of quite a different sort from that of how the individual becomes a functional, fully integrated member of a family.

Third, societies are functional, operative units. In spite of the fact that they are made up of individuals, they work as wholes. The interests of each of their component members are subordinated to those of the entire group. Societies do not even hesitate to eliminate some of these members when this is to the advantage of the society as a whole. Men go to war and are killed in war that the society may be protected or enriched, and the criminal is destroyed or segregated because he is a disturbing factor. Less obvious but more continuous are the daily sacrifices of inclinations and desires which social living requires of those who participate in it. Such sacrifices are rewarded in many ways, perhaps most of all by the favorable responses of others. Nevertheless, to belong to a society is to sacrifice some measure of individual liberty, no matter how slight the restraints which the society consciously imposes. The so-called free societies are not really free. They are merely those societies which encourage their members to express their individuality along a few minor and socially acceptable lines. At the same time they condition their members to abide by innumerable rules and regulations, doing this so subtly and completely that these members are largely unconscious that the rules exist. If a society has done its work of shaping the individual properly, he is no more conscious of most of the restrictions it has imposed than he is of the restraints which his habitual clothing imposes on his movements.

Fourth, in every society the activities necessary to the survival of the whole are divided and apportioned to the various members. There is no society so simple that it does not distinguish at least between men's and women's work, while most of them also set aside certain persons as intermediaries between man and the supernatural and as leaders to organize and direct the group's activities along certain lines. Such a division represents the absolute minimum, and in most societies we find it carried far beyond that point, with an assignment of various crafts to specialists and the appointment of social functionaries. This formal division of activities serves to give the society structure, organization and cohesion. It transforms the group of individuals who constitute the society from a mere amorphous mass into an organism. With each step in the differentiation of functions the individuals who perform these functions become increasingly dependent upon the whole. The merchant cannot exist without customers or the priest without a congregation.

It is the presence of such a system of organization which makes it possible for the society to persist through time. The mere biological processes of reproduction suffice to perpetuate the group, but not the society. Societies are like those historic structures, say our own frigate *Constitution,* which are replaced bit by bit while preserving the original pattern in its entirety. The simile is not quite satisfactory, since the structures of societies also change through time in response to the needs imposed by changing conditions. However, such changes are, for the most part, gradual, and patterning persists in spite of them. Societies perpetuate themselves as distinct entities by training the individuals who are born into the group to occupy particular places within the society's structure. In order to survive they must have not merely members but specialists, people who are able to do certain things superlatively well while leaving other things to other people. Seen from the standpoint of the individual, the process of socialization is thus one of learning what he should do for other people and what he is entitled to expect from them.

*William H. Whyte, Jr.*

# THE IDEOLOGY
# OF ORGANIZATION MAN *

*The phrase "Organization Man" and at least some famil-*
*iarity with William Whyte Jr.'s book are quite general*
*among educated and informed people in the United*
*States today. His inimitable and somewhat frightening*
*portrait of the man who takes the "vows of corporation*
*life" and his wife who must know above all else "that*
*her husband belongs first to the corporation" can hardly*
*be taken very lightly even if it is, as some believe, some-*
*thing of an exaggeration. In the short reading which*
*follows, we have selected Whyte's discussion of the*
*ideology of the organization man, and how he has*
*emerged from the philosophical traditions of the Protes-*
*tant Ethic into a repudiation of it.*

This book is about the organization man. If the term is vague,
it is because I can think of no other way to describe the people
I am talking about. They are not the workers, nor are they the
white-collar people in the usual, clerk sense of the word. These
people only work for The Organization. The ones I am talking
about *belong* to it as well. They are the ones of our middle class
who have left home, spiritually as well as physically, to take
the vows of organization life, and it is they who are the mind
and soul of our great self-perpetuating institutions. Only a few
are top managers or ever will be. In a system that makes such

* From William H. Whyte, Jr., *The Organization Man* (New York,
Simon and Schuster, Inc., 1956), pp. 3-8, (Doubleday Anchor Edition).
Copyright © 1956 by William H. Whyte, Jr.; by permission of Simon and
Schuster, Inc.

hazy terminology as "junior executive" psychologically necessary, they are of the staff as much as the line, and most are destined to live poised in a middle area that still awaits a satisfactory euphemism. But they are the dominant members of our society nonetheless. They have not joined together into a recognizable elite—our country does not stand still long enough for that—but it is from their ranks that are coming most of the first and second echelons of our leadership, and it is their values which will set the American temper.

The corporation man is the most conspicuous example, but he is only one, for the collectivization so visible in the corporation has affected almost every field of work. Blood brother to the business trainee off to join Du Pont is the seminary student who will end up in the church hierarchy, the doctor headed for the corporate clinic, the physics Ph.D. in a government laboratory, the intellectual on the foundation-sponsored team project, the engineering graduate in the huge drafting room at Lockheed, the young apprentice in a Wall Street law factory.

They are all, as they so often put it, in the same boat. Listen to them talk to each other over the front lawns of their suburbia and you cannot help but be struck by how well they grasp the common denominators which bind them. Whatever the differences in their organization ties, it is the common problems of collective work that dominate their attentions, and when the Du Pont man talks to the research chemist or the chemist to the army man, it is these problems that are uppermost. The word *collective* most of them can't bring themselves to use— except to describe foreign countries or organizations they don't work for—but they are keenly aware of how much more deeply beholden they are to organization than were their elders. They are wry about it, to be sure; they talk of the "treadmill," the "rat race," of the inability to control one's direction. But they have no great sense of plight; between themselves and organization they believe they see an ultimate harmony and, more than most elders recognize, they are building an ideology that will vouchsafe this trust.

It is the growth of this ideology, and its practical effects, that is the thread I wish to follow in this book. America has paid much attention to the economic and political consequences of big organization—the concentration of power in large corporations, for example, the political power of the civil-service bureaucracies, the possible emergence of a managerial hierarchy that might dominate the rest of us. These are proper concerns, but no less important is the personal impact that organization life has had on the individuals within it. A collision has been taking place—indeed, hundreds of thousands of them, and in the aggregate they have been producing what I believe is a major shift in American ideology.

Officially, we are a people who hold to the Protestant Ethic. Because of the denominational implications of the term many would deny its relevance to them, but let them eulogize the American Dream, however, and they virtually define the Protestant Ethic. Whatever the embroidery, there is almost always the thought that pursuit of individual salvation through hard work, thrift, and competitive struggle is the heart of the American achievement. . . .

It is in America, however, that the contrast between the old ethic and current reality has been most apparent—and most poignant. Of all peoples it is we who have led in the public worship of individualism. One hundred years ago De Tocqueville was noting that though our special genius—and failing—lay in co-operative action, we talked more than others of personal independence and freedom. We kept on, and as late as the twenties, when big organization was long since a fact, affirmed the old faith as if nothing had really changed at all.

Today many still try, and it is the members of the kind of organization most responsible for the change, the corporation, who try the hardest. It is the corporation man whose institutional ads protest so much that Americans speak up in town meeting, that Americans are the best inventors because Americans don't care that other people scoff, that Americans are the best soldiers because they have so much initiative and native ingenuity, that the boy selling papers on the street corner is the prototype of our business society. Collectivism? He abhors it, and when he makes his ritualistic attack on Welfare Statism, it is in terms of a Protestant Ethic undefiled by change—the sacredness of property, the enervating effect of security, the virtues of thrift, of hard work and independence. Thanks be, he says, that there are some people left—e.g., businessmen—to defend the American Dream.

He is not being hypocritical, only compulsive. He honestly wants to believe he follows the tenets he extols, and if he extols them so frequently it is, perhaps, to shut out a nagging suspicion that he, too, the last defender of the faith, is no longer pure. Only by using the language of individualism to describe the collective can he stave off the thought that he himself is in a collective as pervading as any ever dreamed of by the reformers, the intellectuals, and the utopian visionaries he so regularly warns against.

The older generation may still convince themselves; the younger generation does not. When a young man says that to make a living these days you must do what somebody else wants you to do, he states it not only as a fact of life that must be accepted but as an inherently good proposition. If the American Dream deprecates this for him, it is the American Dream that is going to have to give, whatever its more elderly guardians may think. People grow restive with a mythology that is too distant from the way things actually are, and as more and more lives have been encompassed by the organization way of life, the pressures for an accompanying ideological shift have been mounting. The pressures of the group, the frustrations of individual creativity, the anonymity of achievement: are these defects to struggle against—or are they virtues in disguise? The organization man seeks a redefinition of his place on earth—a faith that will satisfy him that what he must endure has a deeper meaning than appears on the surface. He needs, in short, something that will do for him what the Protestant Ethic did once. And slowly, almost imperceptibly, a body of thought has been coalescing that does that.

I am going to call it a Social Ethic. With reason it could be called an organization ethic, or a bureaucratic ethic; more than anything else it rationalizes the organization's demands for fealty and gives those who offer it wholeheartedly a sense of dedication in doing so—*in extremis,* you might say, it converts what would seem in other times a bill of no rights into a restatement of individualism. . . .

Let me now define my terms. By social ethic I mean that

contemporary body of thought which makes morally legitimate the pressures of society against the individual. Its major propositions are three: a belief in the group as the source of creativity; a belief in "belongingness" as the ultimate need of the individual; and a belief in the application of science to achieve the belongingness.

In subsequent chapters I will explore these ideas more thoroughly, but for the moment I think the gist can be paraphrased thus: Man exists as a unit of society. Of himself, he is isolated, meaningless; only as he collaborates with others does he become worth while, for by sublimating himself in the group, he helps produce a whole that is greater than the sum of its parts. There should be, then, no conflict between man and society. What we think are conflicts are misunderstandings, breakdowns in communication. By applying the methods of science to human relations we can eliminate these obstacles to consensus and create an equilibrium in which society's needs and the needs of the individual are one and the same.

Essentially, it is a utopian faith. Superficially, it seems dedicated to the practical problems of organization life, and its proponents often use the word *hard* (versus *soft*) to describe their approach. But it is the long-range promise that animates its followers, for it relates techniques to the vision of a finite, achievable harmony. . . .

. . . In the Social Ethic I am describing, however, man's obligation is in the here and now; his duty is not so much to the community in a broad sense but to the actual, physical one about him, and the idea that in isolation from it—or active rebellion against it—he might eventually discharge the greater service is little considered. In practice, those who most eagerly subscribe to the Social Ethic worry very little over the long-range problems of society. It is not that they don't care but rather that they tend to assume that the ends of organization and morality coincide, and on such matters as social welfare they give their proxy to the organization.

# Chauncy D. Harris and Edward L. Ullman

# THE NATURE OF CITIES *

*A great deal has been written in an effort to explain the reasons for the growth of urban centers and their changing nature at different points in history. The reading which we include is particularly accurate in its handling of factual material and essentially typical of the way in which ecologists and urban sociologists see "the nature of cities."*

Cities are the focal points in the occupation and utilization of the earth by man. Both a product of and an influence on surrounding regions, they develop in definite patterns in response to economic and social needs.

Cities are also paradoxes. Their rapid growth and large size testify to their superiority as a technique for the exploitation of the earth, yet by their very success and consequent large size they often provide a poor local environment for man. The problem is to build the future city in such a manner that the advantages of urban concentration can be preserved for the benefit of man and the disadvantages minimized.

Each city is unique in detail but resembles others in function and pattern. What is learned about one helps in studying another. Location types and internal structure are repeated so often that broad and suggestive generalizations are valid, especially if limited to cities of similar size, function, and regional setting. This paper will be limited to a discussion of two basic aspects of the nature of cities—their support and their internal

* Chauncy D. Harris and Edward L. Ullman, "The Nature of Cities," *The Annals of the American Academy of Political and Social Science,* CCXLII (1945), 7-11, 64. Reprinted by permission.

structure. Such important topics as the rise and extent of urbanism, urban sites, culture of cities, social and economic characteristics of the urban population, and critical problems will receive only passing mention.

## THE SUPPORT OF CITIES

As one approaches a city and notices its tall buildings rising above the surrounding land and as one continues into the city and observes the crowds of people hurrying to and fro past stores, theaters, banks, and other establishments, one naturally is struck by the contrast with the rural countryside. What supports this phenomenon? What do the people of the city do for a living?

The support of a city depends on the services it performs not for itself but for a tributary area. Many activities serve merely the population of the city itself. Barbers, dry cleaners, shoe repairers, grocerymen, bakers, and movie operators serve others who are engaged in the principal activity of the city, which may be mining, manufacturing, trade, or some other activity.

The service by which the city earns its livelihood depends on the nature of the economy and of the hinterland. Cities are small or rare in areas either of primitive, self-sufficient economy or of meager resources. As Adam Smith stated, the land must produce a surplus in order to support cities. This does not mean that all cities must be surrounded by productive land, since strategic location with reference to cheap ocean highways may enable a city to support itself on the specialized surplus of distant lands. Nor does it mean that cities are parasites living off the land. Modern mechanization, transport, and a complex interdependent economy enable much of the economic activity of mankind to be centered in cities. Many of the people engaged even in food production are actually in cities in the manufacture of agricultural machinery.

The support of cities as suppliers of urban services for the earth can be summarized in three categories, each of which presents a factor of urban causation:

1. Cities as central places performing comprehensive services for a surrounding area. Such cities tend to be evenly spaced

throughout productive territory (Figure 1). For the moment this may be considered the "norm" subject to variation primarily in response to the ensuing factors.

2. Transport cities performing break-of-bulk and allied services along transport routes, supported by areas which may be remote in distance but close in connection because of the city's strategic location on transport channels. Such cities tend to be arranged in linear patterns along rail lines or at coasts (Figure 2).

3. Specialized function cities performing one service such as mining, manufacturing, or recreation for large areas, including the general tributary areas of hosts of other cities. Since the principal localizing factor is often a particular resource such as coal, water power, or a beach, such cities may occur singly or in cluster (Figure 3).

Most cities represent a combination of the three factors, the relative importance of each varying from city to city (Figure 4).

## CITIES AS CENTRAL PLACES

Cities as central places serve as trade and social centers for a tributary area. If the land base is homogeneous these centers are uniformly spaced, as in many parts of the agricultural Middle West (Figure 1). In areas of uneven resource distribution, the distribution of cities is uneven. The centers are of varying sizes, ranging from small hamlets closely spaced with one or two stores serving a local tributary area, through larger villages, towns, and cities more widely spaced and with more special services for larger tributary areas, up to the great metropolis such as New York or Chicago offering many specialized services for a large tributary area composed of a whole hierarchy of tributary areas of smaller places. Such a net of tributary areas and centers forms a pattern somewhat like a fish net spread over a beach, the network regular and symmetrical where the sand is smooth, but warped and distorted where the net is caught in rocks.

The central-place type of city or town is widespread throughout the world, particularly in nonindustrial regions. In the

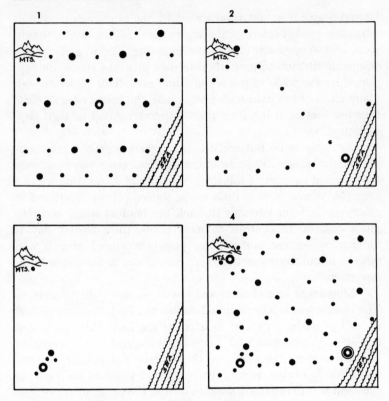

1. *Theoretical Distribution of Central Places*
   In a homogeneous land, settlements are evenly spaced: largest city in center surrounded by six medium-size centers which in turn are surrounded by six small centers. Tributary areas are hexagons, the closest geometrical shapes to circles which completely fill area with no unserved spaces.

2. *Transport Centers, Aligned along Railroads or at Coast*
   Large center is port; next largest is railroad junction and engine-changing point where mountain and plain meet. Small centers perform break of bulk principally between rail and roads.

3. *Specialized-Function Settlements*
   Large city is manufacturing and mining center surrounded by a cluster of smaller settlements located on a mineral deposit. Small centers on ocean and at edge of mountains are resorts.

4. *Theoretical Composite Grouping*
   Port becomes the metropolis and, although off center, serves as central place for whole area. Manufacturing-mining and junction centers are next largest. Railroad alignment of many towns evident. Railroad route in upper left of figure 2 has been diverted to pass through manufacturing and mining cluster. Distribution of settlements in upper right follows central-place arrangement.

United States it is best represented by the numerous retail and wholesale trade centers of the agricultural Middle West, Southwest, and West. Such cities have imposing shopping centers or wholesale districts in proportion to their size; the stores are supported by the trade of the surrounding area. This contrasts with many cities of the industrial East, where the centers are so close together that each has little trade support beyond its own population.

Not only trade but social and religious functions may support central places. In some instances these other functions may be the main support of the town. In parts of Latin America, for example, where there is little trade, settlements are scattered at relatively uniform intervals through the land as social and religious centers. In contrast to most cities, their busiest day is Sunday, when the surrounding populace attend church and engage in holiday recreation, thus giving rise to the name "Sunday town."

Most large central cities and towns are also political centers. The county seat is an example. London and Paris are the political as well as trade centers of their countries. In the United States, however, Washington and many state capitals are specialized political centers. In many of these cases the political capital was initially chosen as a centrally located point in the political area and was deliberately separated from the major urban center.

## Cities as Transport Foci and Break-of-Bulk points

All cities are dependent on transportation in order to utilize the surplus of the land for their support. This dependence on transportation destroys the symmetry of the central-place arrangement, inasmuch as cities develop at foci or breaks of transportation, and transport routes are distributed unevenly over the land because of relief or other limitations (Figure 2). City organizations recognize the importance of efficient transportation, as witness their constant concern with freight-rate regulation and with the construction of new highways, port facilities, airfields, etc.

Mere focusing of transport routes does not produce a city, but according to Cooley, if break-of-bulk occurs, the focus becomes a good place to process goods. Where the form of transport changes, as transferring from water to rail, break-of-bulk is inevitable. Ports originating merely to transship cargo tend to develop auxiliary services such as repackaging, storing, and sorting. An example of simple break-of-bulk and storage ports is Port Arthur-Fort William, the twin port and wheat-storage cities at the head of Lake Superior; surrounded by unproductive land, they have arisen at the break-of-bulk points on the cheapest route from the wheat-producing Prairie Provinces to the markets of the East. Some ports develop as entropôts, such as Hong Kong and Copenhagen, supported by transshipment of goods from small to large boats or vice versa. Servicing points or minor changes in transport tend to encourage growth of cities as establishment of division points for changing locomotives on American railroads.

Transport centers can be centrally located places or can serve as gateways between contrasting regions with contrasting needs. Kansas City, Omaha, and Minneapolis-St. Paul serve as gateways to the West as well as central places for productive agricultural regions, and are important wholesale centers. The ports of New Orleans, Mobile, Savannah, Charleston, Norfolk, and others served as traditional gateways to the Cotton Belt with its specialized production. Likewise, northern border metropolises such as Baltimore, Washington, Cincinnati, and Louisville served as gateways to the South, with St. Louis a gateway to the Southwest. In recent years the South has been developing its own central places, supplanting some of the monopoly once held by the border gateways. Atlanta, Memphis, and Dallas are examples of the new southern central places and transport foci.

Changes in transportation are reflected in the pattern of city distribution. Thus the development of railroads resulted in a railroad alignment of cities which still persists. The rapid growth of automobiles and widespread development of highways in recent decades, however, has changed the trend toward a more even distribution of towns. Studies in such diverse localities as New York and Louisiana have shown a shift of centers away from exclusive alignment along rail routes. Airways may reinforce this trend or stimulate still different patterns of distribution for the future city.

## CITIES AS CONCENTRATION POINTS
## FOR SPECIALIZED SERVICES

A specialized city or cluster of cities performing a specialized function for a large area may develop at a highly localized resource (Figure 3). The resort city of Miami, for example, developed in response to a favorable climate and beach. Scranton, Wilkes-Barre, and dozens of nearby towns are specialized coal-mining centers developed on anthracite coal deposits to serve a large segment of the northeastern United States. Pittsburgh and its suburbs and satellites from a nationally significant iron-and-steel manufacturing cluster favored by good location for the assembly of coal and iron ore and for the sale of steel to industries on the coal fields.

Equally important with physical resources in many cities are the advantages of mass production and ancillary services. Once started, a specialized city acts as a nucleus for similar or related activities, and functions tend to pyramid, whether the city is a seaside resort such as Miami or Atlantic City, or more important, a manufacturing center such as Pittsburgh or Detroit. Concentration of industry in a city means that there will be a concentration of satellite services and industries—supply houses, machine shops, expert consultants, other industries using local industrial by-products or waste, still other industries making specialized parts for other plants in the city, marketing channels, specialized transport facilities, skilled labor, and a host of other facilities; either directly or indirectly, these benefit industry and cause it to expand in size and numbers in a concentrated place or district. Local personnel with the know-how in a given industry also may decide to start a new plant producing similar or like products in the same city. Furthermore, the advantages of mass production itself often tend to concentrate production in a few large factories and cities. Examples of localization of specific manufacturing industries are clothing in New York City, furniture in Grand Rapids, automobiles in the Detroit area, pottery in Stoke-on-Trent in England, and even such a specialty as tennis rackets in Pawtucket, Rhode Island.

Such concentration continues until opposing forces of high

labor costs and congestion balance the concentrating forces. Labor costs may be lower in small towns and in industrially new districts; thus some factories are moving from the great metropolises to small towns; much of the cotton textile industry has moved from the old industrial areas of New England to the newer areas of the Carolinas in the South. The tremendous concentration of population and structures in large cities exacts a high cost in the form of congestion, high land costs, high taxes, and restrictive legislation.

Not all industries tend to concentrate in specialized industrial cities; many types of manufacturing partake more of central-place characteristics. These types are those that are tied to the market because the manufacturing process results in an increase in bulk or perishability. Bakeries, ice cream establishments, ice houses, breweries, soft-drink plants and various types of assembly-plants are examples. Even such industries, however, tend to be more developed in the manufacturing belt because the density of population and hence the market is greater there.

The greatest concentration of industrial cities in America is in the manufacturing belt of northeastern United States and contiguous Canada, north of the Ohio and east of the Mississippi. Some factors in this concentration are: large reserves of fuel and power (particularly coal), raw materials such as iron ore via the Great Lakes, cheap ocean transportation on the eastern seaboard, productive agriculture (particularly in the West), early settlement, later immigration concentrated in its cities, and an early start with consequent development of skilled labor, industrial know-how, transportation facilities, and prestige.

The interdependent nature of most of the industries acts as a powerful force to maintain this area as the primary home of industrial cities in the United States. Before the war, the typical industrial city outside the main manufacturing belt had only a single industry of the raw-material type, such as lumber mills, food canneries, or smelters (Longview, Washington; San Jose, California; Anaconda, Montana). Because of the need for producing huge quantities of ships and airplanes for a two-ocean war, however, many cities along the Gulf and Pacific coasts have grown rapidly during recent years as centers of industry.

## The Editors of Fortune Magazine

# THE EXPLODING METROPOLIS *

*Anyone who has lived over a half of a century in American society cannot help but be struck by the radical changes which have taken place in the internal structure of American cities. Architectural modifications like freeways with elaborate interchanges, sprawling suburbias, and slum clearance projects are but the outward manifestations of the volcano-like movements inside. Back of the outward manifestations of man are always psychological and sociological motivations and in the case of the rebuilding of cities, human purposes and intentions have a good deal to do with what finally emerges. The following excerpt from* The Exploding Metropolis *addresses itself to some of these current forces.*

More and more, it would seem, the city is becoming a place of extremes—a place for the very poor, or the very rich, or the slightly odd. Here and there, in pleasant tree-shaded neighborhoods, there are still islands of middle-class stability, but for young couples on the way up—most young couples, at any rate—those are neighborhoods of the past. They are often the last stand of an ethnic group, and the people in them are getting old. The once dominant white Protestant majority has long since dispersed, and among the Catholics and the Jews who have been the heart of the city's middle class, the younger people are leaving as fast as they are able.

When scarcely any but the well-to-do lived in suburbia, a

* The Editors of Fortune, *The Exploding Metropolis* (Copyright © 1957, 1958 by Time Inc.), pp. viii-xv (Doubleday Anchor Edition). Courtesy of *Fortune* Magazine.

home there was a desirable goal; now it is becoming a social imperative. By 1945 more Americans were home owners than renters; each year since, almost a million families have been joining the majority, and almost all of this increase has been taking place in the new subdivisions of suburbia. Between 1950 and 1955 the total number of people in the country's metropolitan areas increased by 12 million—going from 84,500,000 to 96,100,-000; within the city limits, however, the number increased only 2,400,000—from 49,500,000 to 51,900,000. In some cities the number actually declined.

Is this "urbanization"? The term is misleading. What is taking place is a sub-urbanization, and in this centrifugal movement the city has been losing some of its traditional strength as a unifying element of the region. While suburban neighborhood newspapers are showing marked increases, big metropolitan papers are barely holding their own. On the fringes of the city, people are no longer drawn inward toward the center, but outward to the new shopping centers. Los Angeles, which has sometimes been called 100 suburbs in search of a city, shows the pattern at its most extreme; there is hardly any center at all, and what center there is seems useful to most citizens chiefly as a way to get from one freeway to another.

Clearly, the norm of American aspiration is now in suburbia. The happy family of TV commercials, of magazine covers and ads, lives in suburbia; wherever there is an identifiable background it is the land of blue jeans and shopping centers, of bright new schools, of barbecue-pit participation, garden clubs, P.T.A., do-it-yourself, and green lawns. Here is the place to enjoy the new leisure, and as more people make more money and spend less time making it, the middle-class identification with suburbia will be made more compelling yet. The momentum would seem irresistible. It is not merely that hundreds of thousands have been moving to suburbia, here they are breeding a whole generation that will never have known the city at all.

Nor its values. Heterogeneity, concentration, specialization, tension, drive—the characteristics of the city have often been deprecated, but rarely have they been deprecated with such unwonted vigor. "I'm getting out of your skyscraper jungle," says the hero of the typical anti-success novel, and as he tells off the boss, inevitably he tells off the city as well. "To hell with your fur-lined trap, your chrome-plated merry-go-round," he says with pious indignation, and heads for the country and peace of mind.

Many of the people who are redesigning the city seem to have much the same frame of mind. Their heart is in suburbia—or, at least, suburbia as they would like it to be. As Jane Jacobs points out . . . in laying out the superblocks of the huge urban redevelopment projects, they banish that most wonderful of city features—the street—and they banish the singular, little enterprise, the special store, for which the city, far more than the country, has always been congenial. The results are not cities within cities, but anti-cities, and it is characteristic that they are sealed off from the surrounding neighborhoods as if they were set in cornfields miles away.

It is ironic that the "garden city" movement may turn out to have had its greatest impact on the central city. Ever since Ebenezer Howard first began arguing a half century ago for the self-contained garden town out in the country, the idea has exerted a great influence on planners—and much of it has been very much to the good. In America, notably in the work of Clarence Stein and his associates, it has produced such pleasant suburban villages as Radburn in New Jersey and Baldwin Hills in California. There have not been many of them, but they have had a considerable effect on the designs of the frankly commercial developments.

In its pure form the garden city is obviously not suited to the central city—its houses are two stories high, and there is a great amount of green space for gardens and playgrounds. But then, some twenty-five years after it was conceived, city rebuilders discovered Le Corbusier's "La Ville Radieuse"; in this plan towers concentrated such masses of people that there could be a high density of people per acre and lots of open space too. In its pure form it wasn't suited to the city either—it was far too stark and too patently collective. But it had a tremendous appeal to the ego of architects—instead of giving over green space to people to clutter up, it could be massed in great malls, and the architects' monoliths could be the better set off. By the late Thirties most public housing projects were being cast in this form. Today it is the standard design for every kind of big housing project, for rich or poor—the wrong design in the wrong place at the wrong time.

Even at its best the garden city is not a city, and were the design not so sanctified by utopianism some firsthand observation could have revealed this to planners long ago. It is not just the economics of green space; all the assumptions on which the design is based—from the uniformity of the apartments to the placement of the community stores—presuppose a suburban culture and a fairly homogeneous middle-class society. As visitors from the city can with justice remark, suburban developments may be all right to visit, but would you want to live there?

City planners (a surprising number of whom like to live in suburbs) have been beguiled by the garden city in another respect. To many planners, fortunately, the challenge of the city is meat and drink, but others, appalled at the chronic disorder of it, have turned their eyes outward and dreamed of starting afresh with new regional towns. These, the hope goes, would be more severed from the city than today's suburbia; clean and manageable, each would have an optimum balance of activities, would be nourished by its own industry and have an amateur culture of symphony orchestras, art schools, and little theatres, all its own.

This dream of glorified provincialism will never come to pass so tidily, but in its worst aspects it is uncomfortably close to the reality that the government is helping to shape, and the fact that it may be doing it unwittingly is scant comfort. The federal government harbors no coherent vision of regional towns, but like the state legislatures, which have always had little use for cities, it has been consistently favoring the country over the city in its highway and housing programs. The FHA shows partiality to the suburban home owner, and in its rules has created a "legislative architecture," ill adapted to city housing. In comparison to the money it spends on highways, moreover, the federal government has allocated little for urban renewal. Over the next three or four years $1.25 billion in capital funds may be spent for urban renewal—*if* there is no further holdup to the program—but for highways the U.S. has allocated some $33.5 billion. The effect, if not the deliberate design, will be the enlargement of suburbia.

And what kind of suburbia? The decline of urbanism is not going to be offset by a more attractive suburbia. As Francis Bello forecasts . . . , mass transit is going to be more and more supplanted by the automobile, and the result will be more scatteration—no nice clean regional towns, but a vast sprawl of sub-divisions, neither country nor city. It could be otherwise; as we maintain . . . , there are ways to channel the inevitable population growth into a pattern that saves some of the open space and amenity that people came out to enjoy. But this action requires that the rural and urban interests get together in common cause. At this writing, the anti-city bias of the rural counties remains one of the great stumbling blocks in the path of action that would help the rural counties as much as the cities.

There is no brief in this book for metropolitan super-government. It is obvious that there are many problems that are truly metropolitan—such as transportation, sewage, parks, and open space—and it is equally obvious that there must be much coordination between city and suburb and state. Such cooperation has been very slow in coming, and some people now believe that the only real solution is a metropolitan government that embraces the present suburbs and the city both. In theory, it would be administratively clean, and in its symmetry and orderliness it promises at one fell swoop to eliminate all the overlapping jurisdictions and political give-and-take that seems so messy to the orderly mind.

It is understandable that many businessmen are now off on a metropolitan super-government kick. It sounds so bold and dynamic—and so satisfyingly apolitical. One of the great cliches of civic luncheons these days is a series of resounding statements to the effect that our system of municipal government is obsolete, that the metropolitan area is an entity (at this point some shocking figures on the number of political sub-divisions in the particular metropolitan area), and that the thing to do is to set up an entirely new form of government. Recently one businessman was so carried away with the subject that he prophesied the dissolution of our 48 states and their replacement by 15 or 20 giant urban governments.

Actually, big-city government is surprisingly good these days. Many people may disagree with our choices in the list of outstanding administrations . . . , particularly those in cities awarded booby prizes, but there is no doubt that there has been a marked improvement in the caliber, not only of the mayors, but of the experts under them. This has not been a victory for "good government" in the usual sense—that is, a government in which policy and operations are removed from politics and put in the hands of hired experts and civil servants. The city-manager plan has worked well in many communities, but it is notable that in our big cities most progress has usually been made where the mayor has been a strong political figure as well.

In dealing with metropolitan problems he faces immense obstacles—and far too often he is surrounded by a ring of suburban animosities. But for better or worse these problems are going to have to be tackled through our existing political institutions, and those who believe the growing metropolis demands a new form of government tend to overlook that rather important institution, the state government. There are many obstacles to effective cooperation—Republican counties, for example, vs. Democratic cities, the over-representation of rural counties, and so on. But there is a real chance that in time the state and the cities and the counties will get together for more effective regional planning, and that there will be more metropolitan agencies to deal with problems that are truly metropolitan, like transportation or sewage. It is sheer escapism, however, for people to address their energies to a scheme that calls for counties and suburbs to help vote themselves out of existence.

*C. Wright Mills*

# THE POWER ELITE:
# THE HIGHER CIRCLES *

*C. Wright Mills is a forthright and vigorous critic not only of the condition of sociology but also of the condition of society. A long series of well-known books has come from his vigorous pen. His* White Collar *is probably without equal as a portrait and as an interpretation of the social forces which have brought about and caused differentiation within this mushrooming segment of American society. His* Sociological Imagination *is a sharp talking-to addressed to his colleagues who, he thinks, have missed some boats and followed some false Gods without realizing it. His* Images of Man *is a scholarly collection prefaced by some adroit understandings which any first rate sociologist can hardly ignore. When Mills writes something, it is likely to be controversial, but it is not something which can be ignored. It is so with the* Power Elite: *his graphic description and interpretations have given many an American pause to wonder about his own easy assumptions concerning democracy and all that the phrase implies. In the following section Mills explains how the "higher circles" of the "power elite" are formed and how they operate.*

The power elite is composed of men whose positions enable them to transcend the ordinary environments of ordinary men and women; they are in positions to make decisions having

* From C. Wright Mills, *The Power Elite* (New York, Oxford University Press, 1956). © 1956 by Oxford University Press, pp. 3-13 (Galaxy Edition). Reprinted by permission.

248

major consequences. Whether they do or do not make such decisions is less important than the fact that they do occupy such pivotal positions: their failure to act, their failure to make decisions, is itself an act that is often of greater consequence than the decisions they do make. For they are in command of the major hierarchies and organizations of modern society. They rule the big corporations. They run the machinery of the state and claim its prerogatives. They direct the military establishment. They occupy the strategic command posts of the social structure, in which are now centered the effective means of the power and the wealth and the celebrity which they enjoy.

The power elite are not solitary rulers. Advisers and consultants, spokesmen and opinion-makers are often the captains of their higher thought and decision. Immediately below the elite are the professional politicians of the middle levels of power, in the Congress and in the pressure groups, as well as among the new and old upper classes of town and city and region. Mingling with them, in curious ways which we shall explore, are those professional celebrities who live by being continually displayed but are never, so long as they remain celebrities, displayed enough. If such celebrities are not at the head of any dominating hierarchy, they do often have the power to distract the attention of the public or afford sensations to the masses, or, more directly, to gain the ear of those who do occupy positions of direct power. More or less unattached, as critics of morality and technicians of power, as spokesmen of God and creators of mass sensibility, such celebrities and consultants are part of the immediate scene in which the drama of the elite is enacted. But that drama itself is centered in the command posts of the major institutional hierarchies.

The truth about the nature and the power of the elite is not some secret which men of affairs know but will not tell. Such men hold quite various theories about their own roles in the sequence of event and decision. Often they are uncertain about their roles, and even more often they allow their fears and their hopes to affect their assessment of their own power. No matter how great their actual power, they tend to be less acutely aware of it than of the resistances of others to its use. Moreover, most American men of affairs have learned well the rhetoric of public relations, in some cases even to the point of using it when they are alone, and thus coming to believe it. The personal awareness of the actors is only one of the several sources one must examine in order to understand the higher circles. Yet many who believe that there is no elite, or at any rate none of any consequence, rest their argument upon what men of affairs believe about themselves, or at least assert in public.

There is, however, another view: those who feel, even if vaguely, that a compact and powerful elite of great importance does now prevail in America often base that feeling upon the historical trend of our time. They have felt, for example, the domination of the military event, and from this they infer that generals and admirals, as well as other men of decision influenced by them, must be enormously powerful. They hear that the Congress has again abdicated to a handful of men decisions clearly related to the issue of war or peace. They know that the bomb was dropped over Japan in the name of the United States of America, although they were at no time consulted about the matter. They feel that they live in a time of big decisions; they know that they are not making any. Accordingly, as they consider the present as history, they infer that at its center, making decisions or failing to make them, there must be an elite of power.

On the one hand, those who share this feeling about big historical events assume that there is an elite and that its power is great. On the other hand, those who listen carefully to the reports of men apparently involved in the great decisions often do not believe that there is an elite whose powers are of decisive consequence.

Both views must be taken into account, but neither is adequate. The way to understand the power of the American elite lies neither solely in recognizing the historic scale of events nor in accepting the personal awareness reported by men of apparent decision. Behind such men and behind the events of history, linking the two, are the major institutions of modern society. These hierarchies of state and corporation and army constitute the means of power; as such they are now of a consequence not before equaled in human history—and at their summits, there are now those command posts of modern society which offer us the sociological key to an understanding of the role of the higher circles in America.

Within American society, major national power now resides in the economic, the political, and the military domains. Other institutions seem off to the side of modern history, and, on occasion, duly subordinated to these. No family is as directly powerful in national affairs as any major corporation; no church is as directly powerful in the external biographies of young men in America today as the military establishment; no college is as powerful in the shaping of the momentous events as the National Security Council. Religious, educational, and family institutions are not autonomous centers of national power; on the contrary, these decentralized areas are increasingly shaped by the big three, in which developments of decisive and immediate consequence now occur. . . .

Within each of the big three, the typical institutional unit has become enlarged, has become administrative, and, in the power of its decisions, has become centralized. Behind these developments there is a fabulous technology, for as institutions, they have incorporated this technology and guide it, even as it shapes and paces their developments.

The economy—once a great scatter of small productive units in autonomous balance—has become dominated by two or three hundred giant corporations, administratively and politically interrelated, which together hold the keys to economic decisions.

The political order, once a decentralized set of several dozen states with a weak spinal cord, has become a centralized, executive establishment which has taken up into itself many powers previously scattered, and now enters into each and every cranny of the social structure.

The military order, once a slim establishment in a context of distrust fed by state militia, has become the largest and most expensive feature of government, and, although well versed in smiling public relations, now has all the grim and clumsy efficiency of a sprawling bureaucratic domain.

In each of these institutional areas, the means of power at the disposal of decision makers have increased enormously;

their central executive powers have been enhanced; within each of them modern administrative routines have been elaborated and tightened up. . . .

The people of the higher circles may also be conceived as members of a top social stratum, as a set of groups whose members know one another, see one another socially and at business, and so, in making decisions, take one another into account. The elite, according to this conception, feel themselves to be, and are felt by others to be, the inner circle of 'the upper social classes.' [1] They form a more or less compact social and psychological entity; they have become self-conscious members of a social class. People are either accepted into this class or they are not, and there is a qualitative split, rather than merely a numerical scale, separating them from those who are not elite. They are more or less aware of themselves as a social class and they behave toward one another differently from the way they do toward members of other classes. They accept one another, understand one another, marry one another, tend to work and to think if not together at least alike. . . .

The elite who occupy the command posts may be seen as the possessors of power and wealth and celebrity; they may be seen as members of the upper stratum of a capitalistic society. They may also be defined in terms of psychological and moral criteria, as certain kinds of selected individuals. So defined, the elite, quite simply, are people of superior character and energy.

[1] The conception of the elite as members of a top social stratum, is, of course, in line with the prevailing common-sense view of stratification. Technically, it is closer to 'status group' than to 'class,' and has been very well stated by Joseph A. Schumpeter, 'Social Classes in an Ethically Homogeneous Environment,' *Imperialism and Social Classes* (New York, Augustus M. Kelley, Inc., 1951), pp. 133 ff., especially pp. 137-47. Cf. also his *Capitalism, Socialism and Democracy,* 3rd ed. (New York, Harper, 1950), Part II. For the distinction between class and status groups, see *From Max Weber: Essays in Sociology,* trans. and ed. by Gerth and Mills (New York, Oxford University Press, 1946). For an analysis of Pareto's conception of the elite compared with Marx's conception of classes, as well as data on France, see Raymond Aron, 'Social Structure and Ruling Class,' *British Journal of Sociology,* vol. I, nos. 1 and 2 (1950).

*William F. Kenkel*

# "WHO SHALL BE EDUCATED?" *

*In 1944 W. Lloyd Warner and his associates, who were then making their famous investigations concerning class structure in the United States, published an important sociological work dealing with education. The title, Who Shall Be Educated?, is a question, and the book is in fact an answer to this and other questions. Who is being educated? How and why is it thus? William F. Kenkel's digest of the findings of this book was originally prepared for another purpose. It is presented here as a tight synopsis of the Warner study. The sociology of education does, indeed, include some startling facts!*

"The American public schools are, in the opinion of the people of the United States, basic and necessary parts of our democracy. We are convinced that they must, and we hope that they do, provide equal opportunity for every child. . . ." [1]

So runs the introduction of a book provocatively titled, *Who Shall Be Educated?* It questions how fully "those at the bottom" of our social-status hierarchy *can* compete, in our public schools, with those of higher status. *Who Shall Be Educated?* draws upon the results of various studies that describe how social status relates to whom and what is taught in our schools and who does the teaching. Chiefly, however, it is con-

* From John F. Cuber and William F. Kenkel, *Social Stratification in* 279. Used by permission. Title is that of W. Lloyd Warner, Robert J. Havighurst, and Martin B. Loeb, *Who Shall Be Educated?* (New York, Harper and Bros., 1944).

[1] W. Lloyd Warner, Robert J. Havighurst, and Martin B. Loeb, *Who Shall Be Educated?* (New York, Harper and Bros., 1944), p. xi.

cerned with the school systems in three towns: "Old City," a southern town of 13,000; "Hometown," a 6000 inhabitant town in the Midwest; and "Yankee City," a New England town with a population of about 17,000. . . .

## EQUALITY OF EDUCATIONAL OPPORTUNITY

If all children were able to continue their formal education as long as they were able to profit from it, and wished to pursue it, then we could say that educational opportunities are available to all. There is considerable evidence, however, that this ideal is seldom attained; a person's opportunity to remain in school seems to be closely linked simply with the socio-economic status of his parents.

Warner reports on a study of 910 Pennsylvania grade school children, all with I.Q.'s of 110 or above, and thus all "college material." The group was separated into those of "above average" and "below average" economic levels. It was evident that children of similar intellectual ability were not receiving a similar amount of education. Slightly over one fourth of the "superior" children of below-average socio-economic status did not even finish high school; approximately 60 per cent more finished high school but did not attend college. Not quite 13 per cent of these intellectually potential college students eventually attended college. About 57 per cent of the superior children of above-average socio-economic status, by contrast, attended college. Only a handful did not at least graduate from high school.

A study was made of a similar group of students in Milwaukee. From the standpoint of ability, the students were much the same; all had I.Q.'s of 117 or above. The yearly income of their parents, however, ranged from under $500 to $8000. Table 8 clearly indicates that the higher the yearly income of the parents, the more likely it was that the child attended college.

Other studies have also discovered this direct relationship between economic status and school attendance. If, however, the children of lower economic origins do not *want* to remain

## TABLE 8

### Relation of Parental Income to Full-time College Attendance of Superior Milwaukee High School Graduates *

| Parental Income | Per Cent In College Full-time |
|---|---|
| $8000- | 100.0 |
| 5000-7999 | 92.0 |
| 3000-4999 | 72.9 |
| 2000-2999 | 44.4 |
| 1500-1999 | 28.9 |
| 1000-1499 | 25.5 |
| 500- 999 | 26.8 |
| Under 500 | 20.4 |

* Adapted from W. Lloyd Warner, Robert J. Havighurst, and Martin B. Loeb, *Who Shall Be Educated?* (New York, Harper and Bros., 1944), p. 53. Used by permission.

in school to the same extent as do their wealthier intellectual peers, the statistics do not necessarily indicate a status-bias in our school system. Warner presents three types of evidence which would seem to indicate that economic factors bear heavily on the decision to remain in school. (1) One study discovered that many students give "lack of money" as their reason for leaving school.[2] (2) There was a large response to the National Youth Administration school program which offered financial aid to school students. It is difficult to estimate how many of the students would have dropped out of school were it not for this financial assistance. To be eligible for this aid, however, a child had to demonstrate he "needed" the funds to remain in school. (3) There is the fact that it *does* cost money to go to school, even to the so-called "free" schools in the United States. One study, for example, discovered that even ten years

[2] Howard M. Bell, *Youth Tell Their Story* (Washington, D.C., American Council on Education, 1938), pp. 64 ff.

ago, the "incidental" expenses connected with attending a public high school amounted to $125 a year.[3]

This type of evidence, though certainly significant, does not give us the full story. Many a lower-status child will probably say that he dropped out of grade or high school or failed to go to college because this is what he "wanted" to do. But let us investigate how the school system "works" in selecting students for higher education. Perhaps then we will better realize why it is that many lower-status children "want" to leave school.

## Separate School Curricula and Differential Social Status

### Elementary Schools

It may seem that social status would not affect the course of training in our elementary schools, since all students in the public schools usually receive the same formal training. We must remember, however, that the "best" families sometimes do not send their children to the public elementary schools. They register their sons, instead, at an "exclusive" military school and send their daughters to a "nice" girls' school where "music is emphasized" and where the "young ladies" can learn to ride and swim and cultivate the "right" friendships. Thus, children in our public elementary schools do not often even get to know their age-mates from socially prominent families. During Christmas vacation, perhaps, they may hear exciting tales of life in the different "cottages" or of strict but easily outwitted "headmasters," but all in all they learn little about how the highest 1 per cent live. In this manner, then, social status enters into elementary school education; at a very early age children are somewhat segregated according to the possessions and prestige of their parents.

But social status operates at this time of life in still other

[3] A committee of North Central Association of Colleges and Secondary Schools, *General Education in the American High School* (Chicago, Scott, Foresman and Co., 1942), pp. 17-20.

ways. A child in the higher grades in elementary school is well aware that in high school he can "elect" some courses or can choose from several different curricula. His parents, perhaps, have already instructed him concerning which courses he should choose and his teachers may have talked to him to assure that he will make a "wise" decision. Most children of lower status are not encouraged to talk about college-preparatory courses but are told of the "fine vocational courses" that they can take. Even while still in grade school, children of higher status begin to realize that high school, for them, is but a means of preparing themselves for college. Let us see, then, what happens when children of various statuses get to high school.

## High Schools

In Yankee City, a typical small New England town, the high school has four curricula. Two, the science and the Latin courses, prepare the students for college; the general and the commercial curricula are usually considered terminal.

The college-preparation curricula are said to be "better" than the terminal ones for these reasons:

1. Scholastic standards are higher in the Latin and scientific courses. A "D" is not considered a passing grade in these courses, whereas it is in the general and commercial ones.

2. The college-preparatory courses are taught better. The principal of Yankee City High School stated that the standard of teaching lowers as one goes from the college-preparatory curricula to the general and commercial ones. "It is like having two schools within one building." [4]

3. The college-preparatory courses are more difficult and comprehensive. The principal cited, as one example, the differences between the General Science Course III and the Chemistry course in the scientific curriculum. "The latter," he stated, "is more difficult and includes more material. . . ." [5]

4. The goals of the college-preparatory curricula are "higher." They prepare students for the occupations which di-

[4] Warner, op. cit., p. 62.
[5] Ibid.

rectly or indirectly can place them in a higher social position.

In view of these differences, one might suppose that the more able and ambitious students would choose the Latin and scientific courses. Social status, however, seems to affect the students' choice of curricula in the Yankee City and Hometown high schools. In general, the higher an adolescent's social status, the more likely he is to choose the Latin and scientific courses.

Thus, the status system is, in part, perpetuated. Children from families of higher status generally prepare themselves for higher statuses; many children of lower-status origin prepare themselves for a social position similar to that of their parents.

Table 9 indicates, however, that a sizable minority of lower-

## TABLE 9

### College Expectations and Social Position *

Proportion of High School Students Expecting to Go to College

| Class | Hometown Per Cent | Yankee City Per Cent |
|---|---|---|
| Upper upper | | |
| Lower upper | 100 | 100 |
| Upper middle | 80 | 88 |
| Lower middle | 22 | 45 |
| Upper lower | 9 | 28 |
| Lower lower | 0 | 26 |

* W. Lloyd Warner, Robert J. Havighurst, and Martin B. Loeb, *Who Shall Be Educated?* (New York, Harper and Bros., 1944), p. 66. Used by permission.

class children do enroll in the college-preparatory curricula. Some of these children will eventually graduate from college and will accomplish a substantial rise in status. But why do not more lower-status children prepare themselves for college? Several "reasons" are offered to explain this phenomenon.

1. *Lower-status children lack ability.* No objective studies support this theory. Intelligence differences between children of

different status are not sufficient to account for their differential preparation for college.[6]

2. *Lower-status children lack "ambition."* It is sometimes suggested that lower-status children lack the "will to get ahead" and that anyone with ability who "really wanted to" could manage a college education. Many high school students, however, have stated that they would like to go to college, but simply cannot afford it. Among those who state that they do not want a college education there are many, undoubtedly, who have accepted what they believe is the inevitable. Their knowledge of the cost of a college education and the experiences of their friends support this belief.

3. *Lower-status children lack encouragement.* It cannot be denied that some lower-status families encourage their children to pursue a course of study that will enable them to "get a job" after completion of high school. In many cases this is probably a quite "realistic" approach to the situation, because of the inability of the parents to pay for a college education. It is probably not as well known that teachers, too, dissuade students from preparing for college. Sometimes they "have a talk" with the student; other times they give failing grades to those who they think should not pursue the college-preparatory curricula. Warner implies that in Yankee City, status factors, and not necessarily achievement, enter into teachers' judgments of who "belongs" in the college-preparatory courses.

We have some evidence, then, that students' choice of curricula is in part dependent upon their social status rather than upon their ability to learn. There are some who do not like to admit that factors other than ability seem to determine who goes to college and especially that these "other factors" are closely tied up with our stratification system. Such people emphasize the fact that *some* lower-status children do, in fact, go to college. They point out, furthermore, that each year college scholarships are offered to able students and that a certain proportion of the scholarships always go unused. Later we will investigate factors in our schools, other than curricula differ-

[6] For conclusions regarding the relationship between ability and status and appropriate references see Stephen Abrahamson, "Our Status System and Scholastic Rewards," *Journal of Educational Sociology*, 25 (April, 1952), pp. 441-450.

ences, that are related to social status. Perhaps this will help answer these objections. Let us turn first to those schools that have but one curriculum for all students.

## SCHOOLS WITHOUT DIFFERENT CURRICULA

In some public high schools there is no differentiation of curricula; the same courses are available to all students. In general, there are three types of undifferentiated high schools: (1) the school whose enrollment is too small to permit different curricula; (2) the school whose population is similar in its status make-up; and (3) the school that is large enough to permit differentiation but chooses instead not to have hard divisions based on collegiate intentions.

*The small high school.* In Hometown, as in most small cities, the high school enrollment is too small to have a separate curriculum for the college-bound students. There are, of course, a certain number of "elective" courses, but students of all statuses are in the same "required" courses. It should be added, however, that in many such schools the curriculum is built around college-entrance requirements.

*The high school that serves a relatively homogeneous population.*[7] In homogeneous suburbs such as Lake Forest (Ill.), Grosse Pointe (Mich.) and Shaker Heights (Ohio) it is usually unnecessary to have different curricula. Most of the students are college-bound and the remainder seem to accept the curriculum that is built around the needs of the majority.

*The large, undifferentiated high school.* In some large cities the high schools contain no separate curricula despite the fact that their enrollments are large enough to make differentiation possible.[8] The distinguishing characteristic of the undifferentiated high school is the lack of the split between the college-preparatory group and the "others" and the differential prestige that is attached to the two groups. In such a situation children should have a greater chance to compete with one another and to demonstrate their ability.

Perhaps if we examine how social status affects still other

---

[7] Warner, *op. cit.*, p. 70.
[8] *Ibid.*, pp. 69-70.

aspects of the school situation we will understand why even in the undifferentiated high schools students who go to college do not come from the various status levels proportionately.

## STATUS AND THE "SECTION SYSTEM"

Some elementary schools have a section system by which the students in the same grade are separated into two, three, or more groups. In Old City, for example, each grade has three sections: A, B, and C. The sections meet in different classrooms and are taught by different teachers. In Old City the children are said to be divided into the sections on the basis of their ability. The junior-high-school principal explains that the "ability" of the students is estimated simply by teachers' judgments.[9, 10]

Accordingly, if ability is distributed more or less evenly among children of various statuses, we should expect to find the same proportion of children from each social level in each of the three sections. But this is not the case. The higher-status levels are represented in Section A up to twice as frequently as they are in the total sample, whereas there are over three times as many lower-status students in the sample as there are in the highest section. These facts lend themselves to two interpretations: (1) higher-status students in general have more ability than do those of lower status; or (2) students are placed in the section on the basis of factors other than ability alone. Perhaps the statement of two school officials will help us decide which is the more likely interpretation. When the junior-high-school principal was asked whether there were any status distinctions between the sections he responded: [11]

[9] *Ibid.*, p. 73.

[10] A recent study discovered that teachers in small schools can estimate a student's I.Q. with a fairly high degree of accuracy. Errors in estimates were made, to be sure, but the coefficient of correlation between teachers' rating of their students and their subsequent scores on an I.Q. test was discovered to be +0.72. (Robert E. Hubbard and William R. Flesher, "Intelligent Teachers and Intelligence Tests—Do They Agree?" *Educational Research Bulletin,* 32 (May 13, 1953), pp. 113-122. If we can generalize on the basis of this study, it would seem that teachers *can* estimate the ability of their students. The question in relation to this study concerns whether they estimate ability *alone* when assigning students to various sections.

[11] Warner, *op. cit.,* p. 74.

"There is to some extent. You generally find that children from the best families do the best work. That is not always true but usually it is so. The children from the lower class seem to be not as capable as the others. I think it is to some extent inheritance. . . ."

The principal's theory seems to support the first interpretation. A teacher in the junior high school had a somewhat different story when asked if there was "much class feeling in the school." She replied: [12]

"Oh, yes, there is a lot of that. We try not to have it as much as we can but of course we can't help it. . . . Sections are supposed to be made up just on the basis of records in school but it isn't and everybody knows it isn't. I know right in my own A section I have children who ought to be in B section, but they are little socialites and so they stay in A. . . ."

Studies dealing with the relationship between ability and social status would support this teacher's viewpoint that it is not always ability that places a student in the highest section.[13] Whatever the interpretation, however, the fact remains that higher-status students are overrepresented in the A section. By and large, students from a given status level are placed with one another, and thus learn to exclude those of quite different status.

## YANKEE CITY SCHOOLS

There are two kinds of groupings in the Yankee City elementary school system: (1) there are different schools for children from different sections of the city; and (2) the schools employ the section system for grouping the students in each grade.

Dorland School is situated in the south end of Yankee City. Over 80 per cent of the children in this school are either upper-lower or lower-lower class. Most higher-status children go to Ashton School, situated in one of the "better" neighborhoods. "In the case of those who live near the borderline of the school

[12] *Ibid.*

[13] For the relationship between academic achievement and social status see Stephen Abrahamson, *op. cit.*, p. 443, See also pp. 172-173.

districts the assignment of the students by the school authorities is based more on class status than ability." [14]

Social status is reflected in the physical facilities of the Yankee City schools as well as the make-up of the school populations. The Dorland School has the dubious distinction of being the only school in town without lighting in all of its classrooms. Its heating system has been called inadequate and even hazardous. In general, the school is dirty and run-down. The school authorities spend less money for this and other schools in the poorer areas than for other schools. With respect to this situation Warner concludes, "There can be no doubt that the powerful middle-class, by their influence on the schools, tend to contribute to the subordination of the lower classes by refusing equipment to schools which are predominately lower class." [15]

The Dorland School operates with a section system similar to that previously described. The children purportedly are placed in the sections according to their ability but the superintendent of schools commented that, "A section is for Hill Streeters, B for the middle group, and C for the Riverbrookers." [16] The school principal does not seem to like the implications of this remark and emphasizes that students are allowed more individual attention because of the section system.

But status differences among students in the three sections *are* evident. All of the upper-middle class (the highest class in the school) students are in A section, while 91 per cent of the students in C section are lower-lower class. Regardless of how we account for this, it is manifest that children tend to be segregated along lines of social status in some of our grade and high schools.

## COLLEGES AND THE STATUS SYSTEM

Most students are probably well aware that there are status differences among the many colleges and universities in this country. The "Ivy League" institutions and a few others largely

[14] Warner, *op. cit.*, p. 75.
[15] *Ibid.*, p. 76.
[16] *Ibid.*

attract the higher-status students. State universities and liberal-arts colleges draw mainly from the middle-status levels. College students of lower status are found disproportionately in our teachers' colleges and municipal junior colleges.

Equally as significant as the status differences among institutions of higher learning is the relationship between the curricula choices of college students and the economic status of their families. In a study cited by Warner, an interesting pattern is discovered when the college courses are ranked according to the median income of the families of students pursuing each. (The study was first published in 1940, so it is to be expected that the average incomes are lower than those that would be found today.) It seems safe to generalize from Table 10 that

## TABLE 10

### Parental Income and College Courses *

| Curriculum | Median Parental Income |
|---|---|
| Law | $2118 |
| Medicine and Dentistry | 2112 |
| Liberal Arts | 2068 |
| Journalism | 1907 |
| Engineering | 1884 |
| Teaching | 1570 |
| Commercial | 1543 |
| Nursing | 1368 |
| Industrial Trades | 1104 |

* W. Lloyd Warner, Robert J. Havighurst, and Martin B. Loeb, *Who Shall Be Educated?* (New York, Harper and Bros., 1944), p. 72. Used by permission.

status differences are often related to curriculum choices at the collegiate level.

Concerning social status and the school system Warner concludes: "The evidence from the Yankee City schools demonstrates that the school reinforces the class standards in the general community, from an early period in the child's life through high school and into college." [17]

[17] *Ibid.*, p. 80.

## Social Mobility Through Education

So far we have shown only one side of the picture, how the school system operates to fit students into social positions similar to their parents'. But there are always a number of "exceptional" cases. Some boys and girls of lower status are placed in the higher sections of elementary school, choose the college-preparatory course in high school, and eventually graduate from college.[18]

Education as a means of social mobility operates differently for different children, however. It depends, in part, on how far the mobile person rises and from where he starts. Warner cites some case histories of successful social mobility which illustrate how education fits into the picture. One is the story of Martha, a lower-status girl from one of the poorest residential areas of Hometown. "When Martha first appeared at school," we are told, "she was a shy, thin blonde child, looking like a fresh version of her pale, prematurely old mother." [19] She soon attracted the attention of her teachers, however, by her seriousness, her willingness and ability to learn, and her persistence in doing simple tasks for them during recess. Her teachers generally reciprocated with extra help in school work, and sometimes they gave her a book or two. As a result of her presumably pleasant experiences in grammar school, Martha had no misgivings about enrolling in high school.

Apparently Martha readily adjusted to high school and was very happy there. Despite the fact that her mother died and she was forced to keep the family going, she managed to remain in high school with the help of a scholarship arranged for by her teachers. Her school history was in marked contrast to her half-brothers and half-sisters who disliked school, were "kept back" at one time or another, and generally "grew to be unrecognizable among the other Boxtown children." [20] Finally, Martha graduated from high school and took a job as domestic in a "respectable" home.

From the Browns, Martha learned "refined ways" and "some

[18] *Ibid.*, pp. 81-82.
[19] *Ibid.*, pp. 88-89.
[20] *Ibid.*, p. 90.

of the niceties of living room conduct." For quite a time she was happy with them, then she announced one day that she was going to visit her mother's people in Indiana. The real story was this. She had become enamoured of a magazine salesman who professed both his love for her and his intentions of marriage. Martha's letter informing him she was going to bear his child had been returned with the conclusive stamp, "not known at this address." She bore the child in a maternity home in a nearby city and six months later returned to Hometown where she obtained a job through the assistance of her former employer, Mrs. Brown.

Another chapter in Martha's life began the night she met Dick Johnson, a run-of-the-mill lawyer, at a dance sponsored by a women's organization.[21] A few months later they were married.

And so the shy little girl from the tarpaper shack in Boxtown settled down in a neat white house in a "nice" neighborhood. Throughout her story many factors stand out as having contributed to her successful mobility. Martha had ambition; she was determined and calculating as well. She knew what she wanted and soon learned how to satisfy her wants. But we are concerned here with how education fits into the story of our socially mobile heroine.

From the time that Martha started school it was apparent that she was not like the rest of "those Boxtowners." Her clean clothes and person belied her lower status. Nor did she *act* like the typical "slum kids." She took an interest in school, helped her teachers, and so on. Her teachers, in turn, were willing to put forth some extra effort when they discovered that she was interested in "getting ahead." It was through their help that she managed to graduate from high school, a somewhat rare accomplishment for the "typical Boxtowner." Her first job was found by one of her teachers. Certainly education alone was not responsible for Martha's rise in status but it is almost equally as certain that it played an important part.

Most cases in which education contributes to a rise in status are not so spectacular as that cited. The more frequent cases are

21 *Ibid.*, pp. 94-95.

those of children who are able to raise their status only a little above that of their parents.

## Teachers and the Social-Status System

School policies and other features of the school system were shown to be influenced by social status. Teachers, too, fit into this pattern in ways that are not always understood. We would want to know, for example, what the position of teachers is in the status hierarchy of American towns and cities. From what point in the hierarchy did they come? Finally, and what may be even more important, how do status factors influence their role as teachers of American youths?

*The social status of teachers.* Most Americans, apparently, think that a public-school teacher has a "good" occupation. When jobs are ranked according to their prestige, the position of "public-school teacher" receives an "above average" rank. The job of teacher carries *more* prestige than such jobs as radio announcer, undertaker, and insurance agent, but it carries *less* prestige than such positions as physician, lawyer, and civil engineer.[22] In Warner's terminology, most teachers are "middle class." Table 11 shows how the public-school teachers are distributed in the status hierarchy in the three towns studied by Warner.

*The parents of teachers.* From Table 12 it is apparent that the parents of a generation of school teachers were largely farmers and businessmen. "It is safe to say," according to Warner, "that the businessmen are mostly owners of small businesses—grocers, druggists and the like." [23] It is significant that a sizable number of prospective teachers are recruited from the families of laborers. Apparently, the teaching profession attracts a large number of socially mobile individuals; in the study cited by Warner, probably over half of the students in the teachers' colleges will achieve a status higher than their parents.

[22] The relative prestige of these occupations is based on Cecil C. North and Paul K. Hatt, *Occupations Ranked According to Prestige* (unpublished manuscript). A partial reproduction of this scale appears in Logan Wilson and William L. Kolb, *Sociological Analysis* (New York, Harcourt, Brace and Co., 1949), p. 464.

[23] Warner, *op. cit.*, p. 101.

## TABLE 11

## Social-Class Distribution of Teachers *

|  | Hometown Per Cent | Yankee City Per Cent | Old City Per Cent |
|---|---|---|---|
| Upper-upper | 0 | 2 | 2.5 |
| Lower-upper | 0 | 1 | 2.5 |
| Upper-middle | 26 | 76 | 72.5 |
| Lower-middle | 72 | 21 | 20.0 |
| Upper-lower | 2 | 0 | 2.5 |
| Lower-lower | 0 | 0 | 0.0 |
|  | 100 | 100 | 100.0 |

* W. Lloyd Warner, Robert J. Havighurst, and Martin B. Loeb, *Who Shall Be Educated?* (New York, Harper and Bros., 1944), p. 101. Used by permission.

## TABLE 12

## Occupations of Parents of 1080 Women Students in Fifteen Teachers Colleges *

| Type of Occupation | Per Cent Engaged in Occupation |
|---|---|
| Professional | 8.1 |
| Manufacturing | 3.1 |
| Business (proprietary) | 42.1 |
| Farming | 45.2 |
| Public Service | 4.5 |
| Business (clerical) | 5.0 |
| Skilled Labor | 14.8 |
| Unskilled Labor | 4.0 |

* W. Lloyd Warner, Robert J. Havighurst, and Martin B. Loeb, *Who Shall Be Educated?* (New York, Harper and Bros., 1944), p. 102. Used by permission.

Thus, teachers are either born of middle-class families or have achieved this status by virtue of their occupation. Considering their status origins and eventual social positions it is not surprising that, as a group, they tend to take on and to emphasize the values of the great "middle class." [24] This affects their role as educators of American youth.

## The Boards of Education

In every community there is a group of citizens, usually elected, whose function it is to represent the general public in matters of educational policy. Several studies have shown that these boards of education are made up largely of business and professional men.[25] In terms of social status, the members of the school boards of Old City, Hometown, and Yankee City were somewhat higher than the teachers. A few board members were upper class, while none came from below the middle. It would appear, then, that the "middle-class bias" of the teachers would find approval and reinforcement through the boards of education.

## Democratic Values and Educational Facts

In the foregoing sections we have attempted to describe how the American school system is related to the social-status system. The school system simultaneously operates to perpetuate our existing social-status system and to provide for a certain amount of social mobility.[26] It is clear that children from lower social levels, many of whom have average or even above-average

[24] A recent study, for example, found that the vast majority of teachers in one community "identify" with a status level above skilled workers and, to a lesser extent, above white-collar workers. The teachers, moreover, were found to be "very conservative" in their views. See V. M. Sims, "The Social Class Affiliation of a Group of Public School Teachers," *School Review*, 59 (September, 1951), pp. 331-338.

[25] Warner, *op. cit.*, p. 118.

[26] The extent of social mobility is difficult to estimate and it is even less certain how much mobility can be traced even partially to education. As a result of a recent study Mulligan seems to conclude that the actual mobility through education is exceedingly less than the potential. See Raymond H. Mulligan, "Social Mobility and Higher Education," *Journal of Educational Sociology*, 25 (April, 1952), pp. 476-487.

ability, do not participate in our schools as frequently or for as long a time as do children of higher status. In view of the differential treatment that is afforded children of unequal status, this is not difficult to understand.

It should be made clear that Warner is not advocating a system of *identical* education for all children. Rather, he is stressing that it is in keeping with our democratic ideals that all children should have an opportunity to achieve as much education as they desire and from which they can profit. We have shown that this is not the case in America today. Warner also points out that America cannot afford the luxury of filling its top positions chiefly with the competent from among our higher-status citizens. "We must," he tells us, "use fully *all* our human resources if we are to have the necessary personnel to administer efficiently the work that society must have done." [27] With this in mind, Americans should be able to answer for themselves the provocative question, "Who Shall Be Educated?"

[27] *Ibid.*, p. 142. Italics not in original.

## Liston Pope

# RELIGION
# AND THE CLASS STRUCTURE *

*Liston Pope has published a number of important studies on the sociology of religion. One of the aspects he emphasizes is, we think, a very important one; that is, the influence of stratification upon religious organization. The brief reading included here is a summary of a number of his findings and the findings of others which he has integrated with his own.*

There have been a number of close studies of social stratification in particular American communities in the last twenty-five years, and they yield more precise information concerning religion and the class structure than can be deduced from public opinion polls. Their findings are too varied in detail (this is their great merit) to permit summary here, but generalizations based on them would include the following:

*Social Stratification.* 1. Every American community, from the most rural to the most urban, from Plainville through Middletown to Metropolis, has some pronounced pattern of social stratification, and religious institutions and practices are always very closely associated with this pattern. The number of classes, or layers, varies from community to community; Old City in the Deep South differs in important respects from Yankee City in New England; not all social hierarchies call their bottom class, as do the residents of Plainville, "people who live like the animals." However much details may differ, the stratification is found in all American communities, and religion is always one of its salient features.

* From Liston Pope, *The Annals of the American Academy of Political and Social Science* (March, 1948), pp. 84-91. Reprinted by permission.

271

2. Differentiation within Protestantism corresponds fairly closely to class divisions. Individual Protestant churches tend to be "class churches," with members drawn principally from one class group. Even where membership cuts across class lines, control of the church and its policies is generally in the hands of officials drawn from one class, usually the middle class.

Protestant denominations in their total outreach touch nearly all sections of the population. But each denomination tends also to be associated with a particular social status. Such denominations as the Congregational, Episcopal, and Presbyterian are generally associated in local communities with the middle and upper classes; the Methodist, Baptist, and Disciples of Christ denominations are more typically associated with the middle classes. The Lutheran denominations are harder to classify, because of their closer association with farmers, with particular ethnic backgrounds, and with skilled workers.

Though all of these major denominations have adherents from the lower classes, the religious expression of the latter has increasingly taken place in the last quarter-century through the new Pentecostal and holiness sects, which represent on the one hand a protest (couched in religious form) against social exclusion and on the other a compensatory method (also in religious form) for regaining status and for redefining class lines in religious terms. Some of these sect groups are already beginning to repeat the age-old transition toward establishment as respected churches, moving up the social scale (in terms of the class status of their adherents) as they do so. Christianity itself began among the poor, who accepted it less because they were poor than because they were marginal; most of its branches have long since permeated the higher classes of their societies and have relatively neglected the poor.

*Ethnic Division.* 3. Internal differentiation in the Catholic Church tends to follow ethnic lines more largely than economic lines. Ethnic divisions cut across the organization of Catholic parishes by geographical districts, though the latter have often themselves reflected the residential propinquity of immigrants from a particular country. Thus the local Catholic churches in a community may include a French Catholic church, a Polish Catholic church, an Irish Catholic church, and the like.

"Nationality churches" are found in Protestanism also, but they tend to be exceptional and to be associated more clearly with social (and often spatial) isolation than is the case in Catholicism. There is a great deal of evidence that nationality churches, whether Protestant or Catholic, are gradually losing their peculiar ethnic connections. As the number of foreign born has declined, sermons in English have been introduced to supplement—or to replace—the mother tongue.

The institution has found it very difficult to bridge effectively the cultural gap between its older and younger members. Of most importance, intermarriage is increasingly modifying ethnic divisions in urban centers, though some groups (especially the Jewish, Italian, and Polish) remain more endogamous than others; such intermarriage, however, "is not general and indiscriminate but is channeled by religious barriers; and groups with the same religions tend to intermarry." [1] Religious divisions may therefore become even more important indices of stratification in the future. Meanwhile, the nationality church continues to serve as a cohesive force, at least for its older members, and at the same time it helps to insulate them against disruptive and assimilative influences.

4. Differentiation within Judaism corresponds to a combination of ethnic and class pressures, with the latter probably stronger in the large. Higher-class and better-educated Jews tend to leave Orthodox synagogues and to join Conservative or Reform congregations, or to become secularized. Studies of this alignment are inadequate, but the general trend appears clear. This trend has not prevailed, incidentally, among the Jews of Great Britain.

*Church of the Middle Class.* 5. Religious organizations decline in influence at both extreme ends of the social scale, among the most privileged (though there is some contrary evidence) and among the most disadvantaged. In this very general sense, the churches are associated especially with the middle classes.

[1] Ruby Jo Reeves Kennedy, "Single or Triple Melting-Pot? Intermarriage Trends in New Haven, 1870-1940," *American Journal of Sociology,* Vol. 49, No. 4 (Jan. 1944), pp. 331-39.

## Glenn M. Vernon and Robert L. Stewart

# IS AMERICAN RELIGIOSITY REAL? *

*Religious behavior, like all behavior, has two faces, the public one which everybody sees and the private one which only a few people and the owner see—and sometimes the owner prefers not to look. In this reading, somebody does take a look and a factual one at that. Perhaps this will help us understand why a nation with the largest religious organization in its history seems to be particularly a-religious in the more total functioning of its people and institutions.*

That religion is very popular in America today is a common observation. We have now become "one nation under God." "The Ten Commandments" has been a huge box office success. Billy Graham has invaded "wicked" New York City and feels that his efforts have been rewarded. A prominent movie star tapes her evening prayers before she leaves for a night on the town, so that she can share them with her child. An author, an agnostic, pleads, via *Harper's* magazine, "Won't Somebody Tolerate Me?" And of course, church attendance and church membership are at an all-time high for Americans. Certainly in the United States today, religion and religious behavior are socially acceptable, and the public display of religious activity is commonplace.

Yet, there is another side of the picture. For example, even though the Bible continues to be a best seller, 53 per cent of a nationwide sample of our population, when asked to name the first four Gospels, could not even name one of them. And, when

* Glenn M. Vernon and Robert L. Stewart, "Is American Religiosity Real?", p. 14, vol. XIX, no. 1 (Jan.-Feb., 1959), reprinted with permission from *The Humanist,* Yellow Springs, Ohio.

thirty outstanding Americans were asked not long ago to rate the hundred most significant events in history, Christ's birth and crucifixion were listed in fourteenth place—in a tie with the discovery of the X ray and the Wright brothers' first plane flight.

Thus, questions have been raised in the minds of many of the students of society as to the meaning of this religious activity —questions as to whether the religiosity of our nation is changing, or whether some of our religious maneuvering has become as "tinkling brass and sounding cymbals."

A partial answer to this question was explored by the authors in a recent study of a group of students at Central Michigan College. In this study, evidence was secured which made it possible to make a limited comparison of two aspects of religious behavior which we will call, first, the outward or public manifestations, and second, the inner or private manifestations.

Our measure of the public or outward aspects of religiosity was secured from answers to questions asking the respondents to indicate specifically the degree of religiosity which they had. Questions such as "How important is religion in your day-to-day living?" and "How would you rate your feelings toward religion?" were included in this category. These answers were taken as an indication of the degree of religiosity which the individuals would like *others to believe* they had.

Our measures of the inward or private manifestations of religiosity were secured from a relatively new research instrument, the Twenty Statements Test (the TST) which asks the individual to provide twenty different answers to the question "Who am I?" These twenty statements then provide information about the individual's self-identification. Thus, it would seem safe to assume that individuals who have strong inner religiosity would include among these twenty identifying statements evidence of such religious orientation by making statements such as "I am a Catholic," "I like to go to church," "One of God's children," etc. Conversely, it would seem that individuals who had no strong religious identifications would not produce statements of a religious nature on the test. It hardly seems logical that an individual would voluntarily identify himself religiously in this unstructured situation without having corresponding inner religious convictions. The TST was, of course, administered before the questions dealing specifically with religion were asked.

A comparison of these two sets of answers thus provided our measure of how well the inner and outward aspects of religiosity match up.

Using either of these two measures we found that a large majority of the students evidenced religiosity. However, definite differences were noted. With reference to the outward manifestations, it was found that the students uniformly produced indications of high religiosity. These students evidently want others to think they are strongly religious. Answers concerning the inner self-identifications (from the TST), however, provided a somewhat different picture. It was clear that for the students studied, the outward aspects of religiosity definitely exceed the private aspects. For instance, 23 per cent more people said that religion was of moderate or great importance than identified themselves religiously on the TST. Eighty-nine per cent of the respondents were either moderately or strongly favorable toward religion publicly, while only 72 per cent identified themselves privately in these terms. Likewise, 78 per cent of the respondents who made *no* religious self-identification on the TST, indicated a high degree of religiosity on the question getting at the outward aspects of religiosity. Statistical tests indicated that the observed differences could not be accounted for by chance, and were thus statistically significant.

Thus, a major conclusion of our study was that using the measures which we did, there are outward aspects of religiosity which seem to have no inner counterpart. It should be emphasized, however, that this conclusion is true only in terms of the measures of religiosity which were used in this study. It should also be emphasized that since the students studied were not a representative sample of the rest of society, it would be inappropriate to come to any conclusions about society in general on the basis of the findings of this study alone.

The findings of this study as to the lack of correspondence between these two aspects of religiosity support the premise that in our society today it is expected that individuals will be religious, and that religion is defined as being good and desirable. Thus, in order to maintain one's standing it is important to indicate, when necessary, a favorable attitude toward religion, or at least no opposition to it. In other words, a favorable attitude toward religion might be one requisite of being a good American, while actually being religious is not. In our society, it may be sufficient to be for religion, without being religious.

## Smaller War Plants Corporation

# SMALL BUSINESS
# AND CIVIC WELFARE *

*Shortly after World War II there was considerable con-
cern in American society as a result of the continuing,
if not accelerating, trend toward large-scale corporate
organization in this country. "Small business," to which
a great deal of sentimental attachment has always existed
in this country, was feared to be going by the board.
It was, and still is. The federal government, through
such policies as taxation, loans, placement of government contracts, and in other ways, is in an effective position to accentuate or delay, or possibly even to reverse
the trend toward industrial concentration. The following
excerpt is taken from a study sponsored by a Senate
committee in an attempt to answer in a factual way
certain questions concerning the public impact of large
scale industry, especially in the one-industry towns and
cities. The results of the study proved hardly flattering
to the one-industry and big-industry cities. It is doubtful whether the differences revealed in this study between big business and small business cities are true
today to the same degree that they were at the time the
study was made, partly because as a result of this and
other investigations the management of big industry
has changed certain of its policies. Big labor, as well as
big business, made changes too. Nevertheless, not only
for its historical but also for its present implications,
this study is an important one.*

* Adapted from "Small Business and Civic Welfare," Document No.
135, 79th Congress, Second Session, U. S. Senate, *Report of the Smaller
War Plants Corporation To The Special Committee to Study Problems of
American Small Business* (Washington, D.C., U. S. Government Printing
Office, 1946), pp. 1-4.

A few gigantic corporations are now responsible for the bulk of America's entire industrial production and employment. . . .

How does this concentration of economic power affect the general welfare of our cities and their inhabitants? This is one aspect of the concentration problem which has received little attention despite its obvious importance. Does economic concentration tend to raise or depress the levels of civic welfare? . . .

This exploratory report is designed to shed light on the effects of economic concentration on civil welfare. It is based on a study of six American cities. They were selected in such a way as to provide contrasts in industrial organization and to make possible an evaluation of the effects of big and small business on city life. . . .

For purposes of this report a big-business city is defined as one in which (a) a few large firms employ all or most of the workers; (b) ownership of most of the industrial facilities lies outside the city; (c) business activity is concentrated in one or a very few industrial lines. Conversely, a small-business city is one in which (a) most of the workers are employed by a large number of small firms; (b) the bulk of the industrial facilities are locally owned; (c) business activity is diversified in several different industrial lines.

In accordance with these definitions three pairs of cities in the United States were selected for study in this report. The members of each pair were so selected that they had several basic factors in common—general geographical location, population size, percentage of foreign-born and Negroes in the population, etc. In the case of two of these pairs, however, the members differ sharply in one important respect. One of each pair is clearly a big-business city; the other is distinctly a small-business city. In the case of the third pair, there is also a differentiation with respect to big- and small-business industrial organization, but is not as sharp as in the case of the other two, and thus they constitute an intermediate check.

To these cities were applied standards of evaluation generally recognized by sociologists as suitable for the purpose. The figures used to measure the levels of civic life were obtained from official Government sources, from authoritative sociological studies, and from direct field investigation of the cities selected by a sociologist. Also obtained in the field by the sociologist was a considerable amount of information concerning non-quantitative factors in city life, such as the attitudes of civic leaders, the role in city life played by executives of the great absentee-owned industrial plants, and so forth.

Finally, it should be noted that the big-business cities studied here were chosen to represent the local manifestations of a national trend—the trend toward industrial concentration, absentee ownership, the dominance of giant corporations. Similarly, the small-business cities were selected to represent the typical community of small, locally owned, competitive enterprises.

At first glance, civic welfare may appear to be a highly difficult topic to measure or even to discuss objectively. Yet, there does exist a considerable amount of concrete, factual data bearing directly on the subject. Thus it was found that the chance that a baby would die within 1 year after birth was considerably greater in big than in small-business cities; in fact, the chance was almost twice as great in one big-business city than in the comparable small-business city. Public expenditures on libraries (per capita) were 10 times greater and on education (per student) were 20 per cent greater in one of the small-business cities studied than in the comparable big-business city; slums were more prevalent—in one case nearly 3 times more prevalent—in big than in small-business cities.

These facts are cited here merely to indicate the nature of the standards employed. The broad conclusions suggested by the study are that—

1. The small-business cities provided for their residents a considerably more balanced economic life than did big-business cities;
2. The general level of civic welfare was appreciably higher in the small-business cities;
3. These differences between city life in big- and small-business cities were in the cases studied due largely to differences in industrial organization—that is, specifically to the dominance of big business on the one hand and the prevalence of small business on the other.

The more "balanced" economic life provided in small-business cities was noted in several ways. First of all, industrial stability was much more pronounced. In small-business cities employment was more diversified; not only did a relatively large number of industrial firms operate in a number of different manufacturing lines, but a much greater proportion of workers were engaged in wholesale, retail, and other distributive pursuits. On the other hand, the entire pay roll of big-business cities was largely dominated by one or a few great industrial firms.

This economic dominance of a few big absentee-owned corporations in the big-business cities studied resulted in relative insecurity and instability. The mere decision of one corporation to move its local plant to some other area would be sufficient for economic collapse in a big-business city. Moreover, it has been contended by some economists that production and employment are typically less stable in monopolistic or quasi-monopolistic industries. In any event, it was found that in the big business cities studied, fluctuations in employment, wages, and even in the number of business enterprises were considerably greater, on the average, than in the small business cities.

Second, it was found that retail facilities were more satisfactory in small-business cities. They were more abundant, more efficiently managed, and offered greater variety. In the big-business cities, it was discovered, retailers hesitated to make substantial investments because of the business hazards incident to the economic instability referred to above. Thus, the residents of big-business cities often had to go elsewhere to buy.

Third, the gap between the incomes of the few very rich and those of the poor appeared to be greater in big-business cities, although available evidence on this point is not conclusive. In small-business cities it appeared that a larger proportion of the population earned medium or high incomes.

The final and most important test applied to big- and small-business cities was the measurement of the general level of civic welfare. The measure employed was that developed by an eminent social scientist. It gives weight to most of the important measurable factors which bear on the welfare of a city's residents, including, for example, numerous items relating to health, housing, sanitation, incomes, education, and recreation among others. A few of these factors—for example, infant mortality and slums—were cited above. The overall measure of civic welfare, summarizing all of these figures, showed that in each case the small-business city studied rated materially higher than did the comparable big-business city.

In the concluding chapter of this report certain tentative reasons are advanced for the generally higher level of civic welfare found in the small-business cities. It was found that in these cities, civic spirit was more pronounced, more widely shared, and more active. The economically independent middle class was more abundant in the small-business cities. For several reasons cited later, it was the independent middle class which usually took the lead in the voluntary management of civic enterprises. In the small-business cities they operated with the relatively widespread cooperation of labor groups.

In the big-business cities, on the other hand, the independent middle class was not only small but for the most part was not truly independent. In these cities the giant corporations were the real powers. Local executives of these corporations had little interest in civic enterprises as such, except insofar as such enterprises might impinge upon the profit opportunities of the corporation. The nominally independent middle class in these cities—directly or indirectly—was compelled to follow the dictates of the corporation executives. Whatever civic activities were undertaken by labor in these cities were instituted not in cooperation with other groups in the city but usually in conflict with them.

In short, in small-business cities the environment was favorable to the development and growth of civic spirit. The interests of the potential leaders of civic enterprise were generally mutual and locally rooted. In big-business cities, civic spirit was stunted or distorted. The potential leaders of civic enterprise were either powerless to act or were motivated by interests outside the city—particularly the home office of the giant corporation. These differences were reflected in the contrasting levels of general civic welfare found in big- and small-business cities. . . .

It is obviously impossible to state whether or not the conclusions derived in this report are applicable to all big-business and all small-business cities in the United States. An answer to this question would require a field study covering most of the cities in this country. Among big-business cities as well as among small-business cities, there must be many deviations from the patterns found in this survey. It is left for studies of the future to show just how important and how frequent these deviations are.

*Eric Larrabee*

# THE WRECK
# OF THE STATUS SYSTEM *

*Eric Larrabee is not a sociologist—or at least he lists no sociological degrees—he is a professional writer. But in his writing he displays an unusual familiarity with sociological materials. At the same time he often presents a fresh point of view which sociologists could well consider. In the late 1950's Mr. Larrabee published a series of articles in* Horizon *Magazine under the general rubric, "American Mores at Mid Century." "The Wreck of the Status System" is one in this series. It is a refutation of what he considers the sociologists' exaggeration of the extent to which stratification really dominates the behavior of the American people. After all, maybe we do need an antidote.*

Actually we are living not so much in a status system as in the wreckage of one, a storeroom full of broken monuments; for the process of exploiting status is self-destructive, and ruins each new idol that it raises. Once commerce gets its greasy fingers on a class distinction there is little enough left of it; and given the effort and incentive there is no honor, no eminence, no ornament that cannot be cheapened and coarsened and marketed to the millions. A hierarchy subject to merchandizing is no longer binding on the independent individual—and this is what saves us.

* From "The Wreck of the Status System," *Horizon*, "A Magazine of the Arts," Vol. II, No. 2 (Nov., 1959), pp. 22-23, 128. Copyright © 1959, 1960 by American Horizon, Inc. Included subsequently in Eric Larrabee, *The Self Conscious Society* (New York, Doubleday and Company, Inc., 1961). Used by permission.

The shell of the status system which we occupy can even now, admittedly, do damage to those unfortunates who go astray among its dingy, shattered statuary. But no one is required to. No one is compelled to engage in the bootless pursuit of symbols that have lost their meaning, or to keep up with Joneses who are merely seeking to keep up. The ordeal of competitive consumption is not mandatory, and there are many alternatives for those who can replace the search for pseudo-symbols with the search for something else—for competence, or merely for pleasure, or for some Grail of their own contriving. We are not condemned to take the worn-out system seriously; and its true victims are not the skeptics but the faithful, those who haven't yet seen the flaw within the marble, and still believe in the fallen gods.

The idea of social class is one of the most useful, and most risky, weapons in the armory of the social scientist. It has enormous plausibility. We all know that "class" exists, and we are continually confronted with evidences of it. Moreover, the more "scientific" of the life sciences, like biology, have passed this way before—and attained their present levels of reliability—by beginning with the Linnaean, or classifying, stage and dividing the raw material for study into families and species.

Once you have assumed that there is such a thing as "class," proofs of its existence follow with gratifying ease. Income levels distribute themselves across a workable scale; styles of living show welcome contrasts; and individuals turn out to judge one another's "place" with a satisfactory degree of unanimity. Obviously many people do not stay in place, and this leads to the equally plausible idea of "mobility," or moving from class to class—the unstable quality that presumably made the "high mobiles" in Ridgewood so vulnerable to stereo, soup, and carpets. On this theoretical skeleton can be hung a structure as complicated as the investigator desires, as adaptable to primitive tribes as to the status-graders of a modern industry. Like all self-confirming propositions, however, it is less useful than it looks.

For example, one of the modern sociologists who has leaned heavily on the idea of "class" is W. Lloyd Warner, whose Yankee City Series has handled a New England community on the hypothesis that it is composed of six classes: upper-upper, lower-upper, upper-middle, lower-middle, upper-lower, and lower-

lower. Warner uses what can be called the "subjective" rather than the "objective" meaning of the word "class"—that is, he is more concerned with the classes people think they belong to, or are assigned to by others, than he is with the class they would be placed in by income or by some other tangible factor. Warner argues, nonetheless, that his classes do in actuality exist, encompassing both meanings, and this has led some of his colleagues to complain. For instance, it has prompted C. Wright Mills (author of *White Collar* and *The Power Elite*) to insist that a good definition should be one-dimensional, so that you can make it hold still while other variables move; but Mills thinks that in Warner's hands the word "class" has become what he calls a "sponge word," so filled with various notions that you can never be sure which one you're dealing with. Mills would much prefer to define "class" in financial or similarly objective terms, and set aside the word "status" for the far less precise impressions that people have about each other, and themselves.

Yet even with this division of labor between the words, "status" is still a source of difficulty. The elements that make it up can be scored on an I.S.C., or Index of Status Characteristics, yet these will often differ from place to place, or even from time to time. One is hard put to demonstrate that status is *there,* inherent in the situation, and not brought along by the investigator in the baggage of his preconceptions. In such circumstances the test of an idea is not how sensible it seems, but how effective it is in solving problems that could not otherwise be posed. If "status" is simply a name for what we already know by other means, then its use will beg all the questions that we ought to be asking: what is it? how do we know? what creates it? what consequences follow? The sociologists themselves are in good part aware of this, and they handle their terminology—clumsy as it is—with a certain restraint. But in the process of converting to layman's language, many of the reservations and caveats get lost; and the results are subsequently served up to the public, with a spurious and unintended authority, as the pronouncements of social science.

"Status" has still another hold on the public imagination, derived from the parlor-game fascination that comes of putting people in pigeonholes; and this has been formidably strengthened by the recent emergence, during these postwar years, of a school of amateur and unofficial sociology, staffed mainly by journalists and dedicated to the proposition that one man's "insight" is as good as another's. Postwar prosperity brought with it an unprecedented opportunity for American self-consciousness to expand and exercise itself. When the late forties came we looked at one another with wild surmise and saw much that fell into patterns—like Madison Avenue, button-down shirts, grey flannel suits—and there were satisfactions to be had in naming the new categories, and guessing where one stood in them oneself. . . .

We are anxious now about status because it is problematical, which is another way of saying that the system no longer works. We are no longer bound by birth or bankroll to a fixed place in it, and there is the opportunity—though no requirement—for the individual to escape. In this disorderly turmoil it is difficult to discover who one is, but it is uniquely possible now to be free from the social self, that person other people think we are, and to be free also from envy—that most vicious of the sins inherent in a stratified society. Freedom is not necessarily a pleasure. Abundance may appear to be the palliative of our ills, but it is not. It calls in question the most fundamental principles; our own purpose, that of our people. There has never been anything like it before, and we are on our own.

*Everett M. Rogers*

# GOVERNMENT AGRICULTURAL AGENCIES: GROWING DEPENDENCE ON UNCLE SAM *

*Selections to document the complexity of American society are not hard to find. One does not have to read anything to know, for example, that living in an American city, at least for the people in the middle class, involves contact with a staggering array of intricately interrelated organizations. What may not be so clear, however, is that living in rural society, our stereotypes from another century notwithstanding, has become complex as well. If we select, as Everett M. Rogers does in the following, simply one aspect of the farmer's total life pattern, namely his relations with the federal government, and not even all of them, we see how this last bastion of individuality and isolation has been infiltrated by the efforts of the larger society to "render service."*

Government agricultural agencies are of increasing importance to farm people. Few farmers did not receive some form of government assistance within the past year. Before the Depression of the 1930's, there were few farmers who had ever received a government check. Some agencies had existed before 1930, the Agricultural Extension Service for example, but it was the Depression Period of the 1930's that rapidly multiplied the number of agencies. This increase in government agencies was not restricted to agriculture alone. In fact, almost every area of Amer-

* Everett M. Rogers, *Social Change in Rural Society* (New York, Appleton-Century-Crofts, 1960), pp. 285-295. Used by permission.

ican life now has at least one government agency to inform,
observe, or subsidize it. . . .

The following table lists the major government agricultural
agencies and their aims.

## Major Government Agricultural Agencies

| Initials | Name | Purpose |
|---|---|---|
| 1. USDA | United States Department of Agriculture | Coordinate and direct the activities of most government agricultural agencies. |
| 2. —— | Agricultural Experiment Stations | Perform agricultural research. |
| 3. —— | Agricultural Extension Service | Communicate information about new farm and home practices. |
| 4. VoAg | Vocational Agriculture (and Homemaking) | Train high school youth to enter farming (or homemaking). |
| 5. SCS | Soil Conservation Service | Provide technical assistance and secure the adoption of soil conservation practices. |
| 6. —— | Forest Service | Manage and conserve forest resources. |
| 7. ASC | Agricultural Stabilization and Conservation | (1) Restrict food surpluses, (2) maintain farm prices, and (3) pay farmers to adopt soil conserving practices. |
| 8. FHA | Farmers Home Administration | Provide loans and farm management to low-income farmers. |
| 9. FCA | Farm Credit Administration | Provide loans through local cooperatives (NFLA's and PCA's) for the purchase of farm supplies, equipment, land, and buildings. |

10. REA      Rural Electrification      Make loans to local co-opera-
               Administration            tives (REC's) who provide
                                         electric power or telephone
                                         service to rural people.

One indication of the importance of government in modern rural society is provided by a study completed in Henry County, Indiana, in 1951.[1] A total of 1,248 governmental officials and employees were located in this rural county at that time. Of these, 12 per cent of the total were federal employees; the remaining 88 per cent were mainly city, village, township, or county employees. There was a total of 327 different federal, state, and local government agencies in Henry County.

Government agencies are increasingly important in all phases of American life. They are especially important to the agricultural economy. For example, during the past 25 years over twenty-two billion dollars have been spent through government programs to help the American farmer; about half of this went to stabilize farm prices and incomes. In addition, twenty-two billion dollars were spent on other programs of indirect benefit to the farmer, such as the purchase of farm products for foreign assistance. In 1957, the U. S. government was holding more than seven billion dollars' worth of surplus farm products, mostly corn and wheat.

In 1958, one dollar out of every 14 budgeted by the federal government went to agriculture. With the sole exception of the national defense program, farm programs received the largest part of the federal budget. So, if Americans are interested in how their tax money is spent, they must be interested in government agricultural agencies. It is perhaps significant that almost every major farm magazine today has a Washington reporter and regularly carries news about changes in farm legislation and government agencies.

The author completed a study of the importance of governmental agricultural agencies in Miami County, Ohio, in 1959. A sample of 87 farmers were asked, "How many federal agri-

[1] Paul J. Jehlik and J. Edwin Losey, *Rural Social Organization in Henry County, Indiana,* Lafayette, Ind. Agr. Exp. Sta. Bull. 568, 1951, p. 421.

cultural agency employees do you think are employed in your county?" Twenty-nine of the respondents said they did not know; the remaining 58 farmers estimated there was an average of 89 employees in the county. One farmer said, "There must be a number equal to the number of farmers." Another responded, "I don't know, but there must be too many." The actual number of federal agricultural employees in the county was over 200 if part-time farmer employees are included.

## Why Do We Need Agricultural Agencies?

American farmers probably receive more help from the government than do many other segments of the business economy. Why are farm people given this special treatment? . . .

. . . There are at least four main reasons why the government has aided the farmer more than others:

1. The very nature of the farm economy is novel when compared to other areas of business. The excessive surpluses in agriculture cannot be controlled by individual farmers themselves. Four million farmers could not possibly enter into a voluntary agreement to limit agricultural production. Other parts of the economy, where there are a few large producers, can and do appropriately limit their supply to suit the existing demand. This is not possible for the farmer. So the government must intervene.

2. A second reason for public approval of government agricultural programs lies in the widespread fear of depression. The Depression of the 1930's was preceded by a drop in farm prices. Many Americans believe that a decline in farm prices and a surplus of agricultural products is an indication of a coming depression for the total economy. So the public feels that a government program to prevent surplus and boost farm price levels is good insurance against a general depression.

3. Another reason for the government's special treatment of farmers lies in the high value attached to the conservation of resources. Not to be concerned with the erosion of soil on millions of acres of farm land is not to be in vogue with current American thinking, whether one is urban or rural in his affections.

Everyone is "against sin and for soil conservation." This fact is well-known by legislators who have little trouble securing the passage of farm legislation if it is labeled as *conservation*. Of course, there *is* a real problem of conservation facing American agriculture. But it is socially acceptable to overstate the seriousness of this problem.

4. The fourth reason for special government aid to agriculture needs hardly to be mentioned again. This reason is the power of farm pressure groups in securing a type of legislation favorable for farm people.

## Changing Attitudes Toward Government Agencies

Farmers' attitudes toward government agencies are changing from resistance to passive acceptance. This is perhaps illustrated by the experience of one rural sociologist who was conducting a research interview with a farmer on his back porch. Several times during the hour-long interview, the farmer indicated his dislike for all agricultural agencies. He remarked, "There's too many people atryin' to tell me how to farm my place here." At the conclusion of the interview the rural sociologist thanked the farmer and started to leave. As he walked off, he heard the farmer yell in through the screen door to his wife, "Emma, have you been down to the mailbox yet? I don't know what we'll do if that government check don't come today."

Farmers' attitudes toward government agencies have become more favorable as they have (1) become more dependent on these agencies, and (2) gained more knowledge and understanding of them. A study of 1,500 New York farmers in 1952 found generally favorable attitudes toward most agricultural agencies.[2] One exception was the finding that farmers were about evenly split on their attitude toward price supports and acreage allotments.

Farmers have a generally favorable attitude toward government agencies in agriculture, with the exception of the acreage allotment program. There is evidence from another study that farmers' social values are somewhat opposed to attempts to con-

[2] Edward O. Moe, *New York Farmers' Opinions on Agricultural Programs*, Ithaca, Cornell Agr. Ext. Serv. Bull. 864, 1952.

trol farm surpluses.[3] In general, farm people eagerly accept means of increasing their production. In the farmers' thinking however, the *existence* of a surplus is a bad thing, but not the *production* of the surplus. In other words, the market is at fault, not the farmer. The idea of limiting farm production is contrary to the whole value pattern of farm life. Reduction of food production makes no real sense to most farmers. Farmers' opinions toward government agencies other than the price support program are generally favorable; these programs are more closely consistent with farmer values. For example, the soil conservation program encourages both production and soil conservation. And a New York study indicates that soil conservation practices of a production nature such as tiling were accepted more readily than such strictly conservation practices as contour farming and terracing.[4]

In 1957 a sample of corn-hog farmers in Iowa were asked their opinions of the Extension Service.[5] More positive than negative attitudes were expressed, but there were several farmers who reflected an unfavorable opinion of the Extension Service. The range of these statements is indicated by the following responses:

"Well, ah, I think they (farmers generally) feel as though they're (Extension Service) definitely helping and they're more than welcome, I feel, in the average farm home and on the farm. They (Extension workers) should be, they're qualified."

"The county agent probably knows what is best, but there are some hard feelings. Some say that he is just putting in his time."

"Well, I suppose we have to have those guys (Extension workers) to a certain extent. I know lots of farmers don't think too much . . . just a lot of added taxes."

[3] Horace Miner, *Culture and Agriculture: An Anthropological Study of a Corn Belt County* (Ann Arbor, University of Michigan Press, 1949), p. 87.

[4] Julian Prundeanu and Paul J. Zwerman, "An Evaluation of Some Economic Factors and Farmers' Attitudes That May Influence Acceptance of Soil Conservation Practices," *Journal of Farm Economics*, 40:903-914, 1958.

[5] Everett M. Rogers and George M. Beal, *Reference Group Influences in the Adoption of Agricultural Technology*, Ames, Iowa Agr. Exp. Sta. Mimeo Bull., 1958, p. 65. Used by permission.

In summary, farmers now have favorable attitudes toward most government agencies, with the exception of the farm price support program. This difference may partly be due to the farmers' basic values on increased production, which the surplus control program violates. There are some farmers who have unfavorable opinions of other government agency employees— such as Extension workers and agricultural scientists. The long-range trend has been for farmer attitudes toward government agencies to become more positive.

## Lack of Knowledge About Agencies

One reason that some farmers may have unfavorable attitudes toward government agricultural agencies is because they lack knowledge and understanding of them. Several government agencies have changed their names and initials since their origin. This adds considerably to farmer confusion. For example, the Agricultural Adjustment Administration (Triple A) became the Production and Marketing Administration (PMA) in 1945 and Agricultural Stabilization and Conservation (ASC) in 1953. Occasionally, one hears a farmer who yet refers to the ASC as the AAA.

A study of 1,500 New York farmers in 1952 disclosed that: [6]

1. Only 50 per cent of the farmers said they had heard of the Farmers Home Administration.
2. Four out of ten farmers in the 18 counties without a soil conservation district said they had a district. Two out of 10 farmers in counties with a district said there was no district or else did not know there was one.

Interviews with a state-wide sample of 104 Ohio farmers in 1957 disclosed the following: [7]

1. Only 32 per cent knew there was no direct connection between the Farm Bureau and the Extension Service.
2. Only 68 per cent knew there was a direct connection between 4-H Clubs and the Extension Service.

[6] Moe, *op. cit.*, p. 10.
[7] Everett M. Rogers and Harold R. Capener, *The County Extension Agent and His Constituents,* Columbus, Ohio Agr. Exp. Sta. Res. Bull. (in Press).

A sample of 600 Ohio farmers were asked about the relationship between the Farm Bureau and the Extension Service in 1957.[8] Only 70 per cent knew the correct answer, although most of the respondents were members of the Farm Bureau. Historically, there had been a connection between the Farm Bureau and the Extension Service, but the two organizations were officially separated in 1919 in Ohio.

## STRUCTURE OF GOVERNMENT AGENCIES

*A government agricultural agency is a public bureaucracy designed to provide services to rural people.* Most of these agencies originate outside of the county but operate within it. With few exceptions, agricultural agencies are organized under the United States Department of Agriculture. Each agency usually operates on state, district, and county levels. Most agencies have local offices in the county seat and their lowest level of organization is the county.

The goal or purpose of most agricultural agencies is to change human behavior. This change may entail communicating and securing the adoption of production-increasing practices. This is the goal of such agencies as the Extension Service or Vocational Agriculture and Homemaking. The goal of other agencies such as the SCS and ASC is to secure the adoption of such conservation practices as terracing, contouring, and building farm ponds and grassed waterways. Other agencies such as the ASC attempt to induce the farmer to restrict his farm production in order to decrease food surpluses. Still other government agencies provide financial loans through farmer cooperatives in order to help farmers purchase land, adopt new practices, or secure electric power. The common goal of most government agricultural agencies is to change people. The paid employees of these agencies are often called *change agents;* they attempt to secure the acceptance of changes by their *constituents,* the people in their assigned area of work. For example, as SCS worker—a change agent—employed by the Soil Conservation

[8] R. M. Dimit, *Factors Influencing the Organization, Function, and Membership of the Ohio Farm Bureau Federation,* Wooster, Ohio Agr. Exp. Sta. Mimeo Bull., 1958.

Service—a change agency—may attempt to secure the adoption of contouring by the farmers in his county—his constituents.

All of the government agricultural agencies included under the broad jurisdiction of the USDA are sometimes referred to by farm people as *the farm program*. Others use this term to include only agency endeavors, mainly of the ASC, to control farm surpluses and maintain farm prices. In this book, a distinction will be made between a *program* and an *agency*. A *program* is the activities or functions that an *agency* provides or sponsors.

## Types of Government Agencies

There are three main types of government agencies: (1) line action, (2) grant-in-aid, and (3) loan.

1. *Line action* agencies are those where a direct line of control and authority extends down from the federal level (USDA) through state and county levels to the farmer. The local change agents who deal with their farmer constituents are federal employees and their expenses are paid with federal funds. Most of the line action agencies are financed entirely by the federal government. Examples of line agencies are the ASC and SCS.

2. *Grant-in-aid* agencies are those where a grant of money is made by the federal government to the state or local level without a direct line of control and authority. The federal funds are often supplemented by state, county, or local financial support. The federal government may specify certain restrictions in the way the money may be spent by grant-in-aid agencies. There may even be federal employees who travel out from Washington, D. C. to inspect the agency and insure that federal restrictions are observed. Outside of these limits, however, the federal employees do not have authority over the state or local employees.

One example of a grant-in-aid type of agency is the Agricultural Extension Service. Federal funds are annually appropriated and distributed to the various state Extension Services. These funds are matched by state and often by county funds. Thus, the salaries and activities of the county agent are jointly sponsored by federal, state, and county governments. For this reason, the agency is often referred to as the "cooperative" Extension Service. The county agent is responsible to both the local people in his county and to the state Extension director. The state Extension administrator is not, however, subject to the authority of personnel in the Federal Extension Service, which is a part of the USDA. The Federal Extension Service mainly limits its activities to coordinating the state activities, supervising the distribution of funds, and carrying on certain other programs that could not be done more easily at the state level.

The state Agricultural Experiment Stations are also an example of a grant-in-aid agricultural agency. Funds are annually distributed through the Office of Experiment Stations—a part of the Agricultural Research Service in the USDA—to each of the state Experiment Stations. Other funds are secured at the state level and from other sources. The state Experiment Station director is the top authority in this agency structure. Funds, but not control, come from the federal level.

Vocational Agriculture and Homemaking is also a grant-in-aid type agency. Funds are granted from the U. S. Office of Education, Department of Health, Education, and Welfare, through state departments of education to local school districts where the federal funds are matched by local school district finances.

3. *Loan type* agencies are those in which a temporary grant of federal money at a relatively low interest rate is made to state or local organizations. In most cases these organizations receiving loans are farmer co-operatives. Examples of loan type agencies are the REA and FCA. The Farmers Home Administration provides loans to local farmers, but is a line action type agency in terms of its organization.

Let us examine the Rural Electrification Administration in greater detail as one example of a loan type agency. The Rural Electrification Act of 1935 provided for federal loans to any local organization which would provide electrification to rural people. These local organizations were not necessarily farmer co-operatives, but about 95 per cent of them were. Government loans were also received by municipal electric companies, partnerships, and corporations. The loans were at a low rate of interest—originally 2 per cent—and were repayable in 35 years. Many of these original loans have now been repaid. The local electrification co-op, often called a Rural Electrification Co-operative or REC, no longer has any connection with the federal government once its loan is repaid. While loans are in effect, the REA administrator in the USDA supervises the local co-op's financial standing and provides management advice.

In similar manner the federal government provides loans to local co-ops called Production Credit Associations who then loan this money to farmers for short-term purchases, or to National Farm Loan Associations who provide loans for farm mortgage and other long-term purposes.

The major government agricultural agencies are listed by type in the following chart. This chart also indicates the main pressure group supporting each of these agencies for federal appropriations.[9]

## Type and Support of Major Government Agricultural Agencies

| Agency | Type of Agency | Pressure Group Supporting Agency |
| --- | --- | --- |
| 1. Agricultural Experimental Stations | Grant-in-Aid | Association of Land-Grant Colleges and Universities; and American Farm Bureau Federation (AFBF) |
| 2. Agricultural Extension Service | Grant-in-Aid | American Farm Bureau Federation (AFBF); and Association of Land-Grant Colleges and Universities |
| 3. Soil Conservation Service | Line Action | National Association of Soil Conservation Districts (NASCD) |
| 4. Vocational Agriculture (and Homemaking) | Grant-in-Aid | Future Farmers of America (FFA); and Future Homemakers of America (FHA) [10] |
| 5. Forest Service | Line Action | American Forestry Association; and Izaak Walton League |
| 6. Agriculture Stabilization and Conservation | Line Action | No specific pressure group |

[9] The listing of pressure groups supporting each agency is partially taken from Charles M. Hardin, *The Politics of Agriculture* (Glencoe, Illinois, Free Press, 1952), p. 130.

[10] Very minor pressure group activities.

| | | |
|---|---|---|
| 7. Farmers Home Administration | Line Action | No specific pressure group |
| 8. Farm Credit Administration | Loan | National Farm Loan Associations (NFLA); and Production Credit Associations (PCA) |
| 9. Rural Electrification Administration | Loan | National Rural Electric Cooperative Association (NRECA) |

It can be seen that almost every governmental agricultural agency has at least one friendly pressure group that supports its claims in the annual contest for federal funds. Several of these pressure groups were originally formed as off-shoots of the government agency. An example is the National Association of Soil Conservation Districts, which is composed of farmers co-operating with Soil Conservation Service employees.

*Don Martindale*

# THE RESHAPING
# OF CORE INSTITUTIONS *

*It is something of a cliche that social institutions are ever changing; it is not so easy, however, to point out the how and why of their dynamics. The following description of contemporary American social structure, with particular emphasis upon the emerging of the present familial, religious, educational, and recreational institutions, constitutes a particularly lucid as well as objective description of the process.*

The core institutions of the nation are the state and the national economy. In accordance with the principle of consistency, all other institutions having features in conflict with the core are profoundly shaken and modified if not eliminated altogether. In accordance with the principle of completeness, no institution escapes reshaping. This may be illustrated by the family which was one of the core institutions of all original communities of mankind.

## CHANGES IN THE FAMILY

Originally the family consisted not simply of the conjugal pair but of all living generations centering in the same parent family. This group tended to be not only the consumption unit of society, but the productive unit as well. The family heads were, as family elders, also the authorities for the community as a whole. The family had powerful religious traditions, often the only

* Don Martindale, *American Social Structure* (New York, Appleton-Century-Crofts, 1960), pp. 500-505. Used by permission.

really important religion of the community. Complex economic, social, and political destinies of numerous people hung on the marriage arrangements of individuals. Under such circumstances, the decisions as to when and with whom men married were not left to individual initiative.

It is impossible to retain this kind of family relationship and still enjoy the advantages of contemporary life. The only near approach to this condition is in the most sealed-off rural and ethnic communities: El Cerrito, the Old Order Amish, or Chinatown. And even here the elders of the respective communities are well aware of the fact that once influences are permitted from the outside, the whole pattern is apt to disintegrate.

In America only those marriages are legitimate that are recognized by the government (whether arising from a civil or sacred ceremony), and only monogamous marriage is recognized. The government reserves the right to judge a common-law marriage, even if the rituals are not performed. The destruction of the claims of extended kin is illustrated by the lack of distinction between paternal and maternal relatives. Only the immediate conjugal family tends to count. The family has lost to an overwhelming degree all productive functions. Where the family is a productive unit, as often in the rural family, it tends to be organized on a business basis. Even arrangements between father and son on 4H club projects tend to take contractual form. Moreover, in the family as a whole even the preparation of food has in considerable measure been taken over by canneries, bakeries, frozen food processors, packing houses, creameries, and similar industries.

The reduction of the family to the conjugal unit and the destruction of most of its productive functions is correlated with an extraordinarily free choice of mates. Marriage arrangements in considerable measure cease to be a concern of anyone except the parties involved. One is able to marry in complete accord with conceptions of romantic love and is able to dissolve the marriage bond the moment love is gone. Under such circumstances both the marriage and divorce rates tend to mount, while with its decreasing ability to take care of dependent members, the family grows smaller in size (of course except for variations as in the World War II and postwar "baby boom") and less and less a haven for the old, the sick, the crippled, and the infirm.

As the institution most involved in the life of the young individual, the family, reduced in size and power and no longer a stable institution, loses the capacity to offer him the security he needs for healthy development. The juvenile delinquency rate tends to rise with the loss of power of the family. It is significant that in those subcommunity formations where the family remains relatively important, the juvenile delinquency rate is low and it does not matter whether they are urban, rural, or ethnic communities: El Cerrito, the Old Order Amish, Mineville, the Jewish ghetto, or the Chinese community. It is characteristic of modern man to deplore the fact that "the family isn't doing its job." The unconscious irony of the sentiment under the circumstances is often lost.

The changes in the family produce not only conditions that people deplore, but others they overwhelmingly approve. The family has become unusually democratic, with first the women, then the children, achieving emancipation. Women vote, hold public office, practice the professions, own and dispose of property, participate in paid work outside the family on a large scale, go to coeducational schools, participate in sports, patronize drinking places, have freedom of initiating courtship, and dress themselves when they choose in imitation of men's styles. The young are given a voice in family affairs, are reasoned with (and often win the argument) rather than being beaten, are given an allowance—at times entering into contracts with their parents, own their own cars, and enter the competition of a complex youth culture. The culture as a whole glorifies youth, strength, and competitive success.

## Changes in Religion

An adjustment to the requirements of the nation-state is also manifest in religion. The investiture struggles accompanying the rise of the secular powers in Europe dramatically illustrated the necessity for church and state to adjust to one another. The transfer of the papacy seat to southern France during the formative days of the French monarchy, the action of Henry VIII of

England in breaking from the Roman Catholic Church, and the backing of the Protestant movement by German princes were all historical aspects of the relation of church and state, indicating the need for them to interadjust.

There are two fundamental ways in which the relation between church and state may be stabilized, illustrated on the one hand by most European states and by the United States on the other: (1) by establishing an official church, and (2) by declining to designate any church as official. There were historical reasons for establishing religious tolerance as a formal principle and the strict separation of church and state in the United States. In colonial days the South was strongly Anglican; the North was populated by a number of intense dissenting sects which set up closed theocracies. The multiplication of dissenting groups and the schisms in the early theocratic period made it inevitable that any major collective action in the colonies would have to be nonsectarian. Moreover, the dissenting religions that became important in the United States had usually experienced only negative actions from government in England, as, for example, the Baptists and, to a lesser degree, the Methodists. Such groups had experienced government as an alien force; only a strict separation of church and state was acceptable to them. As a result, the principle of separation of church and state is observed in strict form. In the United States there are an extraordinarily large number of ecclesia, denominations, sects, and cults; a high degree of religious freedom; and extensive religious toleration. The formal principle of separation of church and state guarantees the plurality of religions as contrasted to the unity of the state.

Though the Protestant patterns that were dominant early in the United States had powerful Calvinistic elements, the doctrines of original sin, predestination, and election did not conform to American experience acquired rapidly with a continent being opened up and with nationalism and capitalism riding the waves. The tendency to emphasize the perfectibility of man and social progress has modified the earlier theological forms. An extensive secularization of religion has occurred with a fairly general abandonment of literal interpretations of the Scriptures and a displacement of religious experience in the direction of social service. The cleavage between fundamentalist and liberal beliefs tends to be manifest in all major groups.

Just as the family tends to be trimmed to its conjugal form, religion tends to move toward local autonomy. Moreover, the sect fragmentation has its corollary in evangelicalism. While an extensive commercialism is manifest in religious organizations, complete with advertising and formally organized fund-raising, moralistic attitudes once characteristic of the Sunday sermon have deeply penetrated political oratory. The best American political speeches tend to be sermons.

## EDUCATION

Though there are many private schools of both secular and religious type, the schools are primarily politically controlled. Thus a uniform education is in principle available to all groups. Though local and state governments are still primarily in control of the school system, there are beginnings of national control. The schools have represented the secularization of the optimistic confidence in individual perfectibility and social progress. The school system is supported by general taxation resting primarily on real property. This taxation is the source of conflict between large property-owning groups and other sections of the community and between religious groups, which wish to maintain their own school systems, and the rest of the community.

There is little doubt that the role of the federal government in education will continue to grow. Some pressure on the federal government for support of education has been present since the land grants for education contained in the Ordinance of 1785. The Morrill Act of 1862 provided for support of state agricultural and mechanical colleges. Federal support has been provided for the educational activities in connection with agricultural extension, the experiment stations, and the education of veterans. Some federal agencies have in-service training programs in connection with the colleges and universities. Federal expenditures on education run from $3,000,000,000 to $4,000,-000,000 a year.

The influence of the nation on education does not by any

means end with federal support. One of the objectives of education in the public schools is the inculcation of civic responsibility. Moreover, the federal government has provided an increasing number of positions, for which young Americans quite
consciously train themselves.

The way in which the federal government sets up the
requirements for its civil service positions determines not a little
the manner in which young Americans will tailor their college
careers. Whyte describes the "pipeline" from colleges into the
corporations. An even more important "pipeline" flows into the
federal government. The extent to which the federal government may take direct action affecting education has appeared
dramatically in conflict between the Governor of Arkansas and
the federal government over the integration of the schools of
Little Rock.

## RECREATION AND COMMUNICATIONS

The recreational life of the United States is drawn into national
patterns by the influences of the national economy and the state.
The agencies of mass communication—the newspaper, radio, television, and movies—are commercialized in the same manner as
other industries. They primarily carry out the standardization of
taste necessary for an economy resting on mass production. The
entertainment they produce is, in turn, a mass-produced product.
No local community can control them. The New England Watch
and Ward Society may ban a book for the proper Bostonians;
this may only advertise the book in the rest of the country.
Cleveland Amory reports that Richard F. Fuller, former head
of the venerable Old Corner Book Store and for 30 years President of the Board of Boston Booksellers, has been offered as
much as $1,000 cash by a publicity-minded New York publisher
to get a book banned. In the long run, only the federal government can control the mass communication agencies. Both in
form and in content mass communications move in a framework
provided by the national economy and the federal government.

*William F. Kenkel*

# THE FAMILY
# IN THE ISRAELI KIBBUTZ *

*From time to time accusations are made by friendly critics that sociologists' interpretations in the field of marriage, family life, and the sexual mores have been, despite our tirades about the dangers of ethnocentrism and our pretensions to objectivity, quite provincial. It seems to many that we have been too culture-bound, too inclined to rationalize today's, or more likely yesterday's, practices as the ones most clearly rooted in human nature and most likely to produce the greatest well-being. We think the critics are more than a little right. One way of answering questions about the universality of any social practice or answering objectively questions of function can be greatly facilitated by careful observation of other societies. This is what Kenkel has done with respect to the kibbutz. Some readers may be less interested than Kenkel apparently is in what the kibbutz should be labelled, but Kenkel handles his sources with professional care and writes with his characteristic cogency.*

In Hebrew, *kibbutz* means "a gathering" or "a company." Since 1921, kibbutz has come to mean a particular type of "gathering," that is, a collective settlement or village in what is now the state of Israel. There are at present over 227 separate kibbutzim and their total population numbers over 75,000. Sired by the ideologies of Zionism and socialism, kibbutzim have existed in spite

* From William F. Kenkel, *The Family in Perspective* (New York, Appleton-Century-Crofts, 1960), pp. 165-173. Used by permission.

of the stark realities of physical hardships, depleted and non-arable lands, warfare, and the scarcity of funds. But the kibbutz *has* lived. In the past four decades the kibbutz has passed from a dream to a fact. Kibbutzim, therefore, are no "wild schemes" or utopian visions. They are functioning and growing communal settlements, which have adopted some of the most unique social arrangements the world has recently witnessed. . . .

By some definitions of the concept, there is no marriage in the kibbutz. There is, however, a relationship between adult members of the two sexes that certainly resembles marriage. We could, of course, simply supply a definition of marriage that would include the kibbutz-type relationship and let the matter rest at that. But the existence or non-existence of marriage in society is not a matter to be solved by semantic quibbling and hair-splitting definitions. It deserves more serious attention. We can get closer to the root of the matter by investigating the regulation of sexual behavior in the kibbutz, ignoring for the time being the question of marriage.

All societies have established a relatively enduring social relationship between one or more men and one or more women within which relationship the principals are expected to find their chief source of sexual satisfaction. More than sexual privilege is associated with the relationship, of course, but the point is that everywhere the socially approved relationship we are describing does provide for the sexual gratification of the people involved in it. Society further prescribes who may enter into such a relationship, in terms of kinship and age, how many can enter into a single such relationship and the means by which the relationship can be terminated. Quite generally, too, there is a ceremony or ritual which marks the beginning of the relationship and following this the principals are assigned a new status in the society.

Sexual behavior outside of marriage is sometimes tolerated and sometimes disapproved, depending on the society and, within the society, on such factors as the age, marital status, and kinship relationship of the couple. Although there is considerable variation in the specific arrangements, all societies place some restrictions on the sexual behavior of their members and all recognize a relatively enduring sexual association of one or more men and one or more women. With these generalizations in mind, we will investigate the regulations of sexual behavior in the kibbutz.

The early kibbutz settlers were chiefly young people in their late teens and early twenties. Displeased with what they called the "false" sexual morality of the European cities from which they came, they set about to establish a rational sexual code.[1] A rebellion against the inequality of the sexes permeated the new code. Let us turn to the contemporary kibbutz and observe how this new code is implemented in the lives of the kibbutz members.

In many of the kibbutzim children are housed separately from their parents. Through high school there is no separation of the sexes in the dormitories, and up until high school the sexes use a common shower. Young children are discouraged from engaging in sexual play, however, and high school youths are discouraged from engaging in sexual relations and even from forming strong emotional attachments with one another. These things are frowned on because it is felt that such activities divert interests from the group and interfere with school and cultural activities.

A young person does not become a full-fledged member of the kibbutz until he has graduated from high school. From this time on, sexual affairs among the single are their own concern.[2] There are no taboos against sexual intercourse between these young people. In the private room of either the boy or the girl, or at some other convenient place, transitory sexual affairs take place as frequently as the couple desires. Young people at this stage of their lives have all privileges of other adults in the community and, as long as they are able to find a partner, can obtain whatever degree of sexual satisfaction they desire. One might speculate, then, that there would be no further changes in the sexual lives of the kibbutz members. But such is not the case.

Most commonly there is a "pairing off" among the young people.[3] A couple decides that they are "in love" and wish to

[1] Melford E. Spiro, *Kibbutz: Venture in Utopia* (Cambridge, Harvard University Press, 1956), p. 111.
[2] *Ibid.*, p. 113.
[3] *Ibid.*, pp. 113-116.

live together in a relatively permanent, relatively exclusive relationship. At this time they ask permission of the group for a double room. The term *marriage* is not used to describe this relationship, but once a man and woman have moved into a common room they are referred to as a "pair" or a "couple." The woman talks of her "companion" or her "young man," and the man uses comparable terms when referring to her. Sexual relations involving one of the pair and another party are definitely frowned upon, although not forbidden. The pair relationship can be terminated as easily as it was commenced. The couple simply makes it known to the kibbutz housing committee that they desire single rooms once again, and the pair relationship is then considered broken. Most pairs stay together, however. At one period it was estimated that the proportion of pair break-ups was a little less than the then current divorce rate in the United States.

One may well ask how this admittedly unusual arrangement between the sexes came into being. The answer is to be found in the kibbutz settlers' strong negative reaction to the traditional subordinate position of women and the corresponding dominant role of men. In the kibbutz, women, as well as men, are assigned a role in the productive economy. With the communal eating facilities and the common rearing of children there is no need for a woman to be "tied to the home." The equality of the sexes made possible in this manner was thought to be enhanced by the kibbutz-type "marriage." Selection of mates is purely a matter of the personal attraction of one for the other. There is no need for permission from the group, and the traditional Hebrew marriage ceremony has been eliminated. The woman, as an equal of the man, does not assume the man's name at the time of their "marriage," for this could be construed as a symbol of her inferior position. There are no legal ties between the couple as far as the kibbutz is concerned. Nor does a woman, or for that matter a man, benefit economically from the marriage. Each is entitled to his support solely because he is a member of the kibbutz. In a similar manner, a woman's importance and prestige in the group is derived solely from her own accomplishments. Whether he be a leader or a dullard, the man's reputation and prestige are in no way ascribed to his mate.

Equality of the sexes is reflected, finally, in the kibbutz provisions for terminating the "marriage" relationship. No woman need remain with a man she does not love simply because she would have difficulty maintaining herself otherwise, and no man need fear alimony and support payments which sometimes can prohibit remarriage. Just as the two join together because they are attracted to one another, so they are free to separate when they no longer like the arrangement.

The question that remains is whether this arrangement between the sexes can or should be called "marriage." Sociologically, of course, it makes little difference by what name the relationship is called in the kibbutz or whether the couple uses the conventional forms of address, husband and wife. What is important is whether or not the kibbutz pair relationship serves most of the same functions and has most of the usual attributes of what we commonly call marriage. Let us review the case.

In the kibbutz there is a relatively enduring sexual relationship between two persons of the opposite sex. There is a ceremony that marks the beginning of this relationship. It matters not, of course, whether a society requires the principals to a marriage to join their hands, exchange gifts, or dance around an oak tree in the nude. The point is that if a culture truly contains differentiated statuses for the married and the single there is usually a way to mark the transition from one to the other, a way of announcing to the group, so to speak, that a person has changed his status. In the kibbutz we have the request for a double room and the moving of beds into it, certainly a straightforward and self-evident way of proclaiming that a sexual relationship is being established.

There would seem to be in the kibbutz a discernible differentiation of status between the single and couples. Presumably the pair, after the bed-moving ceremony, consider themselves a social unit, and they are so considered by the rest of the group. The term used to describe the pair relationship is not used for lovers or those who are engaged in a transitory affair.[4]

What else, then, must we have before we can say that there is marriage in the kibbutz? The anthropologist, Murdock, found

[4] *Ibid.*, pp. 118-119.

in his studies of some 250 societies that marriage was characterized by a relatively enduring sexual relationship plus economic co-operation between the married members of the opposite sex. In all of the societies there was some kind of division of labor within the marriage, so that the married pair or group constituted an economic unit. Murdock concludes that ". . . marriage exists only when the economic and the sexual (activities) are united in one relationship, and this combination occurs only in marriage." [5] In the kibbutz, as we have seen, there is no economic co-operation between the parties to a marriage. The division of labor takes place within the larger group, the kibbutz itself. In short, marriage in the kibbutz seems to serve no economic function whatsoever.

Despite the fact that everywhere else marriage has been found to involve economic co-operation, we would venture to conclude that there *is* marriage in the kibbutzim. These pioneer settlements have an admittedly unique economic organization, one which happens to preclude a division of labor between mates. But there *is* a socially sanctioned sexual relationship, sufficiently enduring to make possible the procreation and birth of children. This would seem to constitute the essence of marriage, whatever other functions it usually serves.

It should be pointed out that what we have chosen to call "marriage" in the kibbutz does serve functions other than providing for the sexual satisfaction of the mates. These functions are difficult to define and describe, but one of them would seem to be the provision for a close and intimate type of companionship not otherwise available in the kibbutz.[6] Whether by nature or by nurture, members of the kibbutz seem to need this kind of intimacy or at least derive sufficient satisfaction from it to help motivate them to marry. In the kibbutz sexual intercourse can, of course, be obtained outside of marriage with apparently no group censure. But it would seem that the sexual association provided in marriage is sufficiently more satisfying and that the psychological security found in marriage is sufficiently reward-

[5] George P. Murdock, *Social Structure* (New York, The Macmillan Co., 1949), p. 8.

[6] Melford E. Spiro, "Is the Family Universal?," *American Anthropologist*, Vol. 56 (October, 1954), p. 842.

ing that, taken together, they create a powerful incentive to marry. Most adult members of the kibbutz *are* married, and there are other indications that most seem to think of the married state as the preferred way of life.

# Kingsley Davis

# THE DEMOGRAPHIC EQUATION *

*Almost every department of sociology has a course or two on population, a major part of which deals with the work of demographers. Likewise most textbooks in sociology devote attention to the subject. It is not always clear, however, what the language of the demographer means, or exactly what his logic consists of. Kingsley Davis is unusually clear and brief in his treatment of the demographic equation, and he should help to clarify what demography is all about.*

The science of population, sometimes called demography, represents a fundamental approach to the understanding of human society. Because of its statistical character, it has unfortunately acquired the reputation of being dismal and dry; but with modern data and modern techniques it can be fascinating.

The primary tasks of demography are (1) to ascertain the number of people in a given area, (2) to determine what change —what growth or decline—this number represents; (3) to explain the change, and (4) to estimate on this basis the future trend. In explaining a change in numbers the populationist begins with three variables: births, deaths, and migration. He subtracts the deaths from the births to get "natural increase" and he subtracts the emigrants from the immigrants to get "net migration" (either number may be negative). If $P_1$ is the population of a given area at an earlier time, and $P_2$ the population at a later time, then

$$P_2 = P_1 + (\text{Births} - \text{Deaths}) + \text{Net Migration}$$

* Kingsley Davis, *Human Society* (New York, The Macmillan Company, 1949), pp. 551-553. Used by permission.

In order to compare the population growth in different areas or in different times, the demographer finds it necessary to substitute ratios for absolute numbers. Thus he relates births to the population in various ways to get birth *rates,* and he does the same with deaths and with migrants. In this way he can state his variables in terms of processes (fertility, mortality, and migration) and he can talk about the *rate* of growth or decline in the population. If "r" is the rate of growth, then the following formula holds:

$$r = (F - M) + (I - E)$$

where "F" is fertility, "M" is mortality, "I" is immigration, and "E" is emigration. In other words, the rate of population growth is determined by the natural increase plus the net migration. If the area in question includes the whole world, migration drops out of the formula; for in that case only fertility and mortality need be considered. But if the area includes less than the whole world, then migration must always be taken into account.

It is clear that any factor influencing the number of people must operate through one or more of the variables mentioned. In no other way can a population be changed. For this reason we may call the four variables "the primary demographic processes." They represent the core of population analysis. The demographer consequently requires not merely census returns (enumeration of the population at one point in time) but also registration statistics (continuous recording of births, deaths, migration, etc.).

If the populationist stopped here, however, his work would have little to do with social science but would be merely a branch of biostatistics. What gives his subject interest to the social scientist, and social science interest to him, is in the first place the fact that fertility, mortality, and migration are all to a great extent socially determined and socially determining. They are the inner or formal variables in the demographic system, whereas the outer or ultimate variables are sociological and biological. Whenever the demographer pushes his inquiry to the point of asking why the demographic processes behave as they do, he enters the social field.

Population concerns social science in the second place because the demographer studies the number of people not only with reference to area but also with reference to their *character-istics.* He clings always to some definite area, but at the same time breaks down the total population within this area into groups or statistical classes, each having some definite, meas-urable attribute. Thus, for example, he may undertake to state the number of males and females in the population of the United States. He may go further and attempt to sub-classify each of these groups according to age—say in five-year age intervals.

There are, of course, innumerable characteristics. One might count the number of people with long noses, with brown shoes, or with pretty wives. The demographer must therefore employ some criterion of relevance in choosing the traits he wishes to count. Unconsciously he tends to adopt two criteria: (1) the importance of the traits in the social organization; (2) the im-portance of the traits for the purely demographic processes. Often, as one might suspect, both criteria lead to the selection of the *same* traits.

From a strictly demographic point of view *age* and *sex* are the primary characteristics. Not only are they important bases for the ascription of social status, but they are biologically re-lated to fertility and mortality, and indeed to migration as well. For this reason birth and death rates become most meaningful and are really strictly comparable only when the age and sex composition of the population is taken into account.

Most of the other significant traits selected for study by the populationist are not only socially important but are socially rather than biologically defined—e.g. marital status, literacy, citizenship, occupation, religion, income.

One should notice that the characteristics with which the populationist is concerned are in general those obtained in censuses. For instance, the United States census in 1940 [and 1950 and 1960] secured data on all the traits mentioned above except religion. In addition it obtained information on many other subjects, including migration (1935 to 1940), age at mar-riage of married women, and number of children born to mar-ried women. The census therefore yields information that is both socially and demographically important.

# *William S. M. Banks, II*

# THE RANK ORDER
# OF SENSITIVITY
# TO DISCRIMINATION *

*William S. M. Banks, II has made one of a number of factual tests of the more original and sometimes striking formulations found in the classic statement of race in* An American Dilemma *(1944). The following excerpt is from Dr. Bank's doctoral dissertation. In addition to telling us something about the question of discrimination, it may help the student to appreciate how theoretical formulations are ever subjected to reexamination in the light of new facts, new times, or simply the perennial doubts of investigators.*

## INTRODUCTION

This study is an attempt to test an hypothesis which Gunnar Myrdal termed "the Negro's rank order of discrimination." [1] In this epoch-making volume Myrdal stated that his observations led him to believe that whites in the United States insisted on the retention of discriminatory practices in a specific order according to type. He asserted that they insist most on retaining the barriers against Negro men having access to white women for sexual intercourse or marriage. Next in the order is their insistence on discriminations as far as courtesies and respect are concerned. Then follows their insistence on the retention of dis-

* Adapted from William S. M. Banks, II, Doctoral Dissertation (Ohio State University, 1949), pp. 1-2, 5-7, 9-10, 36-37, 94-99, 106-107. By permission of the author.

[1] Gunnar Myrdal, and others, *An American Dilemma* (New York, Harper and Brothers, 1944).

316

criminations in the accessibility of public services, facilities, and funds. Below these in rank are the insistence on the retention of political, legal and economic discriminations in that order. In other words whites insist most upon the retention of the discriminations in sex relations between Negroes and whites and least upon the retention of economic discriminations. This is what he called the "white man's rank order of discriminations."

Myrdal stated that "next in importance to the fact of the white man's rank order of discriminations is the fact that the *Negro's own rank order is just about parallel, but inverse, to that of the white man.*"

Thus the Negro's rank order would be:

1. Economic discrimination
2. Discriminations by law officials and agencies
3. Political discrimination
4. Discrimination in access to public services and facilities
5. Discrimination in the several etiquettes—courtesies and respects
6. Discrimination in sexual intercourse and inter-marriage

In other words the Negro resents, according to Myrdal's theory, and resists economic discriminations most and discriminations in sex relations and inter-marriage least. Was Myrdal correct?

## HYPOTHESES TO BE TESTED

In testing the Negro rank order of discriminations hypothesis, a number of related hypotheses are involved. These are advanced in order to give direction and order to the study being pursued. To this end the following hypotheses are advanced:

a. The ranking of the six general types of discrimination varies with the sexes of those doing the ranking.

b. The ranking of the six general types of discrimination varies with the age of those doing the ranking.

c. The ranking of the six general types of discrimination varies with the amounts of education of those doing the ranking.

d. The ranking of the six general types of discrimination varies with the place of birth and basic conditioning so far as Negro-white relations are concerned.

METHODOLOGY

## 1. *Locus of the Study*

Once the decision was made to test the "Negro rank order of discriminations" hypothesis, the problem of procedure became paramount. To test this hypothesis completely would involve a series of studies in various sections of the United States. This was out of the question for the present at least, because of the cost in time, money and personnel, among other reasons. But, the fact that a series of studies would be necessary to test the hypothesis suggested the feasibility of selecting a community and starting the series. If the test is to be completed, it must be started.

The selection of a locus for this study came next. It is generally agreed that Ohio is more or less representative of the midwest and in many respects of the whole country. Further, Columbus is generally representative of the entire state so far as race relations are concerned. There are reasons to believe that the attitudes and practices prevalent in Columbus will extend along a continuum which would include all patterns found elsewhere in the state. Concurrence on these observations was secured from several reputable scholars.

## 2. *Measuring Attitudes: Building a Scale*

This selection of a locus for the present study was a trivial task compared to that of deciding upon a reliable method of securing a meaningful ranking of the six types of discrimination by Negroes in Columbus. This latter task was made all the more difficult by the fact that no "pioneer" works were available to be used as guides. The writer has no knowledge of any previous attempt to make such a study. The question was: "What device could be used to secure this rank order of discriminations?"

It was felt that a paraphrased statement of the types of discrimination as suggested by Myrdal was too vague and general to permit an accurate and meaningful ranking. Therefore several weeks were spent interviewing Negroes at random. To some extent these interviews were kept within the scope of this study but no attempt was made to limit the interviewee's discussion of the related issues which he suggested. One standard question was put to each person: "What are the types of discrimination against Negroes by whites in the United States that you know about?" There were several more or less standard follow-up questions, once the interviewee had stated the types he knew about. "Which of these have you experienced?" "If you could get rid of these one at a time which would you get rid of first?" "Second?" etc.

After the first few interviews it became apparent that the matter of sexual intercourse and intermarriage was not being suggested as a type of discrimination. Therefore, the interviewer raised the question after the interviewee had run the length of his discussion. Generally, the response was to the effect that sex relations and intermarriage was no problem since "whites would not have it" or "only the lower class Negroes ever think about that." Several of the more sophisticated (sophisticated primarily in terms of advanced schooling and occupational prestige) Negroes stated that "although I don't want to do so, I still feel that I should have the right to anyone who wants me."

In order to ascertain the feasibility of trying to get people's attitudes through responses to the general statements given by Myrdal, the interviewer presented statements of the six general types of discrimination to a number of people and asked them to rank them. In practically every case it was necessary to give detailed explanations of each with examples. And when this was done, the interviewee was quite confused and the ranking suggested by him was quite often illogical and inconsistent with what he had said previously.

Following this step a number of situations involving the several types of discrimination were written down and presented to a number of people. They were asked to note the instances of discrimination in each situation and to indicate the order in which they would eliminate them. This device tended to yield a pattern approximating the Myrdal rank order for Negroes. At the same time the confusion noted in the other attempts at getting a ranking of the types of discrimination was eliminated. However, it was apparent that a scale which would yield valid and reliable data would have to be ten or more pages in length. Each situation would have to be written out in some detail and a maximum of three instances of discrimination could be included in each. Administering such a lengthy scale would undoubtedly encounter much resistance.

On a basis of these findings it was decided, nevertheless, that the scale to be used would be of the situational type. Thereupon 120 instances of discrimination against Negroes were listed. There were at least 15 instances of each of the six general types of discrimination. Each of these instances of discrimination was typed on a separate card. Then a group of "experts" were asked to sort these cards into seven stacks. Six stacks constituted the six general types of discrimination suggested by Myrdal. The seventh stack was labeled "Ambiguous or doubtful, overlapping, none of the six types." The experts included 15 members of the instructional staff of the Sociology Department of Ohio State University and two advanced graduate students.

The "instances of discrimination" were drawn from (a) the recorded observations of Negroes interviewed in Columbus, (b) those suggested by scholars in the area of race relations, and (c) those drawn from the literature relative to Negro-white relations. Each card was assigned a code number indicating which of the six general types of discrimination it was intended to represent. If a card was placed in any other category than the one it was intended to represent, this card was regarded as being "misplaced." Any card "misplaced" by three or more of the Judges was thrown out. A total of 24 instances were thus eliminated leaving 96 items for the scale to be constructed.

One of the major factors determining the effectiveness of a scale in securing the data it purports to secure is the wording of the "instructions." This is particularly true when individuals are obliged to rely primarily on these in filling out the scale. In this case, however, the administration of the scale was done wholly by the researcher. That is, he explained the instructions to each individual in person instead of sending them through the mail.

## The Scale

*The following is an abridged form of the scale Dr. Banks derived. Only 15 items of the 96 actually used are reproduced here for illustrative purposes. [Eds.]*

## Instructions

The United States prides itself on being the land of freedom, equality, fair play, and so on but many types of discrimination are practiced. Below are 96 instances of discrimination. Indicate for each whether you think it is *Very Serious, Moderately Serious, Not Serious,* or *Not a Case of Discrimination* by circling the appropriate number.

1—Very Serious (You are extremely resentful of such practices)
2—Moderately Serious (You mildly resent such practices)
3—Not Serious (You resent such practices very little if at all)
4—Not a case of discrimination

1 2 3 4    1. In certain towns no Negro can get a loan to expand his business.

1 2 3 4    2. Negroes in certain towns who "talk back" to white people are picked up and beaten by police officers.

1 2 3 4    3. In some counties only Negroes are actually required to meet the property requirements for voting.

1 2 3 4    4. In certain towns the institutions for juvenile delinquents do not accept Negroes.

1 2 3 4    5. In some communities Negroes must always address whites as "Mr." or "Miss" but whites never show this courtesy to Negroes.

1 2 3 4    6. In certain towns white men are known to have children by Negro women. Negro men are brutally beaten for speaking to the daughters of the white men for whom they worked.

1 2 3 4    7. Negroes discovered in the homes of their white "girl friends" may be lynched but nothing is done about white men who lived with their Negro "girl friends" in some states.

1 2 3 4    8. In some towns adult Negroes are addressed as "boy," "girl," "auntie," or "uncle."

1 2 3 4   9. In certain towns ticket agents refuse to sell Negroes pullman reservations.

1 2 3 4  10. The educational requirements for voting are enforced only against Negroes in some counties.

1 2 3 4  11. If arrested in some communities, no Negro can get out on bail.

1 2 3 4  12. The courts of certain communities never permit Negroes to serve as jurors.

1 2 3 4  13. In some states Negroes have to pass a difficult test in order to vote while whites only have to prove that they are residents.

1 2 3 4  14. In certain towns Negroes cannot use the public library.

1 2 3 4  15. Only Negro employees of some department stores are called by their first names.

## 3. *The Sample*

In brief, the sample used in this study, a total of 200, was randomly selected from the total universe—the 40,000 Negroes in Columbus, Ohio. A cross-section of the whole of the Negro population was interviewed, the sample being representative in terms of area of residence, age, sex, occupational and educational distributions. Each section of the city where significant numbers and types of Negroes lived was canvassed by the researcher.

[Note: We are omitting from this summary the technical discussions of sample determination, testing the validity and reliability of the scale, and other technical matters.

When the questionnaires had been administered to the 200 subjects, the results tabulated, and the hypotheses scrutinized in the light of the data gathered, certain conclusions were drawn. Eds.]

### Conclusions

The following conclusions based on the findings of this study and conceived within the broader framework of race relations theory are presented.

1. *The sensitivity of Negroes to different types of discrimination can be quantified.* Although this attempt at doing so is

somewhat limited it does present a basis for refining the devices and techniques to be used in such an undertaking. The writer is particularly aware of the need to devise means for getting more differentiating reactions to different types of discrimination.

2. On a basis of the findings of this study *there are no significant differences between the sensitivity of males and females to discrimination.* That is to say *sex is not a significant correlate of sensitivity to discrimination.* However, it is probable that by using a more refined scale some significant differences may be found, particularly with reference to certain types of discriminations.

3. *Age per se is not a significant correlate of sensitivity to discrimination.* Younger Northern Negroes are apparently less sensitive to discrimination than is generally believed. This is due primarily to the types of experience which these people have or have not had. In spite of the fact that the "35-44" age category evinced the highest sensitivity to discrimination, the writer is of the opinion that this was more a reflection of past contacts with the more flagrant instances of discrimination than a reflection of age differences. Approximately 57 per cent of this category were Southern born and had their first introduction to Negro-white relations in a Southern setting. Thirty per cent of the remaining ones had spent one or more years in the South.

4. *On the surface, occupation seems to be a significant correlate of sensitivity to discrimination.* The higher the occupational level, the lower the sensitivity to discrimination. Here again, however, other factors are of equal, if not of more, importance. It may well be that those persons in the professions enjoy a relatively high degree of economic security and therefore can circumvent or avoid those situations which involve flagrant discrimination. It has been suggested also that upper class Negroes attempt to dissociate themselves from the general Negro community.[2] There is an attempt on their part to identify themselves with the middle or upper class whites. If these observations are accurate, it would follow that the scores as recorded reflected a class bias rather than an occupational bias as

---

[2] Among the studies which indicated this is the American Council on Education series summarized by R. L. Sutherland in the volume, *Color, Class and Personality.*

such. Of course there is the counter argument that the two are closely related and cannot be considered separately.

One other observation tends to substantiate the belief that the observed differences are not merely functions of occupation. Over two-thirds of the professionals were Northern born and reared. This seems to be the more significant factor in accounting for the difference.

5. *Generally the greater the number of years schooling completed the less the sensitivity to discrimination.* The score variations of the different categories were not statistically significant as determined by the critical ratio but a pattern was reflected which seems to justify the above conclusion. It may well be that as one gets more and more schooling, he tends to find rationalizations for such treatments which were previously "unbearable." On the other hand, it may be that the more educated Negroes are more able to discriminate between the degrees of their sensitivity than the less educated.

6. The one variable which seems to be most directly correlated with sensitivity to discrimination is the place of one's early exposure to Negro-white relations. *Persons whose basic conditioning was acquired in the South or who spent several years in the South tend to be more sensitive to discrimination than those persons whose conditioning was acquired in the North.* This is due partly to the fact that the construct "discrimination" as a different meaning for Southern Negroes than it does for Northern Negroes. When the former think and talk of discrimination, their orientation is the background of personal experiences in which they had been "victims" of discriminatory practices. The antagonisms fostered by these experiences are reflected in their verbalization of their resentment of discrimination. It may well be that such verbalizations or recordings of their attitudes constitute an outlet for frustrations occasioned by these experiences.

On the other hand the Northern Negro tends to react to "discrimination" somewhat abstractly. For the most part his experiences have been devoid of the more flagrant types of discrimination. Consequently his sensitivity will reflect an intellectually oriented reaction to a phenomenon. Under such conditions it is not likely that a high degree of sensitivity will be evinced.

7. Finally, the *Myrdal Negro rank order of sensitivity to discrimination hypothesis is by and large an accurate portrayal of the sensitivity of Negroes in Columbus, Ohio to discrimination.* The obtained rank order differs from the Myrdal rank order but it correlates highly with it (.77).

*Brewton Berry*

# THE MYTH
# OF THE VANISHING INDIAN *

*Brewton Berry is a recognized authority in the field of*
*Race. His* Racial and Ethnic Relations *has won an im-*
*portant prize as an original contribution to the field.*
*In the article quoted here, Professor Berry brings us a*
*factual perspective on the American Indian which may*
*come as a surprise to some. As is true so often, this*
*article demonstrates that the easy common-sense ques-*
*tion may require a much more complicated answer and*
*one with more equivocation than the asker usually*
*realizes.*

. . . Modern scientists are finding, however, that the extinction
of primitives and underdeveloped peoples upon contact with
European civilization is not as universal and inevitable as we
had been led to believe. Consider the effects of such contact upon
China, India, Ceylon, Java, Egypt, Algeria, and the Philippines,
where population has grown at a frightening rate subsequent to
contact with the West. Even very simple societies, such as those
found on the islands of the Pacific, after some initial reverses,
soon were faced, not with extinction, but with problems of over-
population.

But what about the American Indian? Have not their numbers greatly declined since 1492?

Not if you consider Latin America. The population of
Mexico is estimated to have been 3,000,000 at the time of Cortez.
Today there are 6,000,000 Indians, and at least another 15,000,-

* From Brewton Berry, "The Myth of the Vanishing Indian," *Phylon*
(Spring, 1960), pp. 53-57. Used by permission.

000 in whom the element of Indian blood is very great. South America is thought to have been the home of some 9,000,000 Indians when the Europeans began to arrive. Today the Indian population exceeds 11,000,000, to say nothing of the millions of part-Indian mestizos.

Then what about the United States? Has not the Indian population here been dealt a shattering blow?

The statistics usually quoted would indeed so indicate. There were probably 800,000 Indians in what is now the United States at the time of discovery. By 1800 their numbers were down to 600,000. Smallpox, tuberculosis, massacres, and general dissipation took heavy tolls until the Indian population reached a low point of about 250,000 in 1850, and there it remained for some fifty years. Shortly after the turn of the century, however, it began to rise. The 1910 census reported 266,000 Indians, the 1940 census 334,000, and in 1950 there were 342,226. The Indian, on the basis of these figures, was indeed on his way to oblivion, but is currently staging a comeback, though he still has far to go to regain the numerical position he formerly held.

There are, however, two major reasons—and some minor ones—why these figures do not tell the whole story.

In the first place, there is no commonly accepted definition of an Indian. The Bureau of the Census instructs its enumerators to return as an Indian "full-blooded Indians, and persons of mixed white and Indian blood if they are enrolled on an Indian reservation or agency roll. . . . Also persons of mixed Indian blood if the proportion of Indian blood is one-fourth or more, or if they are regarded as Indians in the community."

The Bureau of Indian Affairs uses different criteria. It includes on its rolls only those persons entitled to the services of the Bureau, and these have changed from time to time with shifts in policy. Accordingly, these two federal agencies invariably find themselves at odds. For instance, the 1930 census reported 332,397 Indians, while the Bureau of Indian Affairs counted 350,541 in the same year. Finally, the Public Health Service, which also has a responsibility to the Indian population, uses still a different definition to fit its peculiar interests.

Obviously, then, the term "Indian" nowadays has very little relation to racial purity. Under the effects of different laws the same individual may be counted as Indian for some purposes and non-Indian for others. Officially classified as Indians are many persons whose ancestry is largely that of other races. Individuals with as little as one two-hundred and fifty-sixth part Indian blood have been included in allotments of tribal lands. At the same time there are many whose degree of Indian blood is considerable, but who are going, by preference or otherwise, as either white or Negro.

Several years ago Dr. J. Nixon Hadley, who has served in both the Bureau of Indian Affairs and in the Public Health Service, proposed that an individual, to be classified as an Indian in the United States, ought to satisfy at least three of the following conditions: (1) enrollment with an organized tribal group or on a reservation census roll; (2) general recognition as an Indian by the members of the local community; (3) ability to speak an Indian language; (4) retention of a considerable degree of Indian culture, such as knowledge of Indian arts and crafts, techniques of agriculture and hunting, participation in Indian ceremonies, etc.; (5) ownership of restricted property; (6) residence on an Indian reservation.

Dr. Hadley's proposal, whatever its merit, has not been adopted, and the fact remains that the definition of an Indian is quite vague, not only in the United States but in other American countries as well. Accordingly, population figures leave much to be desired. Even so, there is no evidence that the Indians are fewer in number than they were in 1492. This would be true (in Latin America, but not in the United States) even if we counted as Indians only the full-bloods. If, on the other hand, we followed the same practice with respect to the Indian that we do with the Negro (namely, "one drop of Negro blood makes one a Negro"), the number of Indians today would run into the tens of millions. But whatever the criteria, be they broad or narrow, it can safely be maintained that the Indian is by no means a vanishing race.

A second reason for doubting that the dire predictions of the red man's doom have, or ever will, come to pass is that there are, throughout the eastern United States, hundreds of communities of people who point—sometimes with pride, but not always—to their Indian ancestry, but who are counted as Indians neither by the Bureau of the Census, nor by the Bureau of Indian Affairs, nor by the Public Health Service. For that matter, their claim is received with some skepticism and amusement even by their white and Negro neighbors. Nevertheless, the tradition of Indian ancestry has persisted among them these many years, their racial features lend a measure of credibility to their claim, and they are not to be lightly dismissed as either impostors or dreamers.

These folk, whether or not they be Indians as they claim, are indeed America's outcastes. They, more than other class, might properly be called "forgotten men." They live their lives in a racial limbo—not quite white, not quite Negro, and not quite Indian. They are ignored, derided, rejected, tolerated.

Once in a great while they have their day. They step—or are pushed—into the limelight. This happened on January 18, 1958.

On that evening, near the town of Maxton, in Robeson County, North Carolina, there was waged the strangest battle in all the annals of Indian warfare.

A hundred members of the Ku Klux Klan had gathered for a rally. Its purpose, well advertised in advance, was simply to remind the thirty thousand Lumbee Indians living in that vicinity that they had better watch their step. It was feared that they might be "forgetting their place." One Indian woman, perish the thought, had been dating a white man! As if that were not enough, an Indian family had moved into a white residential neighborhood. The Knights, ever alert to such improprieties, had promptly burned crosses in the presence of the offenders. The situation, however, demanded sterner measures, and hence the rally.

At eight o'clock the Klansmen began to assemble, shotguns in hand. The Grand Wizard was present in full regalia. A huge banner emblazoned with the letters KKK was unfurled. A public address system was installed, and above the microphone there flickered a single electric light bulb. There were frequent flashes from the cameras of newsmen.

Across the road some five hundred Lumbees had gathered, also bearing arms. Except for their pungent jibes and raucous hoots, they were calm and orderly. The Klansmen ignored them.

At a given signal the Indians fanned out and crossed the highway, shouting war cries and firing into the air. The Klansmen dropped their guns and made for their cars, leaving all their paraphernalia behind. The Indians smashed the loud speaker, proudly grabbed the Klan banner, and bore aloft the rag-draped cross which the Klansmen, in their haste, had failed to set afire.

At this moment sixteen members of the highway patrol arrived on the scene, escorted the terrified Klansmen to safety, and proceeded to disarm the Indians, who offered them no resistance.

No one was seriously hurt, despite the thousands of rounds of ammunition that had been discharged. Four persons were slightly nicked by bullets, including one enterprising television cameraman. Only one arrest was made—a Klansman, who was charged with drunkenness.

The whole affair lasted barely thirty minutes.

The Indians then proceeded to stage their own rally. They marched triumphantly from the field of battle, bearing their spoils. They set fire to the cross, had their pictures taken with the Klan banner, and hanged the Grand Wizard in effigy. They had a roaring good time.

Next day the newspapers across the country headlined the rollicking incident. Reporters, newscasters, and columnists enjoyed a field day. "It seemed the Klan had just taken on too many Indians," said *Life*. "Look who's biting the dust! Palefaces!" wrote Inez Robb. "I am kind of proud of my Lumbee friends for busting up a Ku Klux Klan rally," began the syndicated column of Robert C. Ruark.

There is only one disturbing fact, however. The United States Census for 1950 reports no Indians living in Robeson County, North Carolina. How could they have missed these thirty thousand spirited braves, squaws, and papooses?

The Lumbees are but one of hundreds of similar groups of "quasi-Indians" (some would say "pseudo") to be found living in the eastern United States. They are not typical, however, for they are more numerous and more prosperous than the others.

Tennessee has its Melungeons, West Virginia its Guineas, Ohio its Carmel Indians, New York and New Jersey their Jackson Whites, Pennsylvania its Pools, Maryland its Wesorts, Delaware its Moors and Nanticokes, Virginia its Ramps and Issues, South Carolina its Brass Ankles, Alabama its Cajuns, and Louisiana its Sabines and Red Bones. Their numbers have been estimated at a hundred thousand.

Poor, isolated, and pathetic, these "racial orphans" eke out a precarious existence. Their Indian blood has been diluted with that of the white—and, in many instances, the Negro. They have forgotten their Indian tongue, cast off their Indian culture, and failed to remember their tribal identification. What is worse, they have in most cases lost even their pride in Indian ancestry.

But they have not vanished!

## William F. Ogburn

## TECHNOLOGICAL TRENDS
## AND NATIONAL POLICY *

*And always there are "things"—not only things which exist in the realm of nature like rivers and blizzards, but things that man makes. There is a cultural landscape as well as a geographic one and it changes far more rapidly and far more dramatically. William F. Ogburn, as we have pointed out, was a lifelong student of technology. His published works on the effects of invention are highly respected, and some of his phrases and theories are central to the thinking of most students of technology and social change. We end with this excerpt not with any intention to deny the significance of ideological sources in the shaping of social change, but rather to document the fact that the dynamics of technology must never be ignored as the prime shapers of human destiny in the twentieth century.*

An invention usually affects first the persons using it directly. If it be a producer's goods such as a farm tractor, it means at once the replacement of horses or mules, the purchasing of gasoline, and changes in various other farm practices. If it be a consumer's goods such as an air conditioning unit in a home, it affects the construction and use of the house, but of course the units must be fabricated and hence, for that purpose, factories must be created, marketing machinery set up, etc. All such re-

* From William F. Ogburn, *Technological Trends and National Policy,* Report of the Subcommittee on Technology to the National Resources Committee (Washington, U. S. Government Printing Office, 1937), pp. 9-10 (Italics by the editors).

sults are called the *primary influences* of the new technology.

These primary effects may flow out in different directions. Thus the X-ray is used for purposes of diagnosis in medicine and in dentistry. At the same time it is used in therapy as in the treatment of endocrine glands. It is also used in industry to detect minute flaws in the interior of steel castings or other solid objects. Indeed, manufacturers of the X-ray apparatus have noted some sixty different uses of the X-ray.

Similarly there are many different influences of radio. Some 150 were reported in the study of inventions in *Recent Social Trends*. Radio waves are used in guiding ships to port, as danger signals when a navigator is in distress, in flying airplanes, in program broadcasting, in point-to-point telephoning, in medicine, and in exterminating parasites.

These primary effects *are not all exerted at once.* Just as it sometimes requires 30 or 40 inventors working over a long number of years to evolve a complex major invention, and just as it may require hundreds of thousands of improvements spread out over time after the invention has been produced; so it requires a long time for the various uses of an invention to be determined. The phonograph was early used for recording dictation. Only later did it evolve into a musical instrument. Indeed, Edison, the inventor, did not think much of the possibility for the phonograph as a musical instrument, but thought it might have some use as a toy, and for recording the last words of dying persons. One does not yet know what may be the possible uses of the cathode ray.

Each of these primary effects may, in turn, produce *derivative effects.* Thus, as the tractor replaces animals on the farms there follows as a derivative influence less need for horse feed, which means that the land used for growing such feed is turned to other uses. This is a secondary effect. As land formerly used for stock feed yields other crops, the quantity is increased of other agricultural products, which tends to lower their prices. These lower prices are, in turn, mirrored in land values, perhaps in demands for tariff protection. Thus, these various derivative influences occasion effects secondary, tertiary, and so on. Each effect follows the other much like links in a chain, except that the succeeding derivative effects become smaller and smaller in influence. The effect of the tractor on lobbying for a higher tariff is very slight in comparison with other forces. A derivative effect in another direction is the stimulation the tractor brings to the cooperative movement in various ways but especially in the purchase of gasoline.

In general, the first primary effect of an invention is found in (a) the economic practices of production and (b) in the habits of the consumers using the finished product. The economic organization as a whole may be the secondary influence if the technologies concerned are important ones. Thus, the tractor has the influence of making farms larger because on the smaller farms a tractor will not pay. Time is required to purchase additional land and to consolidate farms. In other ways tractors influence the agricultural economic organization. They make the adjustment to a business depression more difficult than in the case of horses and mules, for in a depression it is easier to raise feed than to buy gasoline. The tractor also moves the farmer a bit closer toward specialized commercial farming as contrasted to subsistence farming. Very many of the great inventions following the so-called Industrial Revolution have been machines affecting industrial and economic life, namely, gasoline engines, motors, steamboats, chemical and metallurgical inventions. Very often, then, the first great social institution affected by these changes has been the economic organization.

Later derivative effects impinge on other social institutions, such as family, government, church. Thus, the great economic changes that followed the power inventions modified the organization of the family. Women went to work outside the home. Children were employed in factories. The home gradually lost its economic functions. The father ceased to be much of an employer or manager of household labor, at least in cities and towns. There followed a shift of authority from father and home to industry and State. In cities, homes became quite limited as to space. More time was spent outside by the members of the family. In general, then, these changes in industry reacted on the family life.

In a similar way inventions have impinged upon government. In some industries the nature of invention was to encourage monopolistic corporations dealing in services used by a large number of individuals or other corporations. Hence governments took on regulatory functions as in the case of the public utilities. Taxation measures shifted from general property, tariffs, and excises on consumption goods to taxes on personal and corporate incomes and on inheritances. In many other ways the government was forced to extend its functions, as in the case of interstate commerce. City governments, especially, had to assume many more activities than those exercised by counties, where wealth was produced largely on farms without the use of power machines.

Thus, the great inventions which first changed industry produced derivative effects on other social institutions, such as government and the family. Finally these, in turn, have produced still another derivative effect upon social views and political philosophies. The attitude toward the philosophy of laissez faire eventually undergoes change as more and more governmental services are demanded, despite professions of the old faith to the contrary. The philosophy regarding home changes too. It is not so clear under the new conditions of the machine age that woman's place is the home or that the authority of paternalism in the family is exercised as wisely as it was thought to be in the days of our forefathers. Also attitudes toward recreation and leisure time change, with city conditions and repetitive labor in factories. That these attitudes are so slow to change and are often near the last of the derivative effects of invention may appear surprising. It is true that these new attitudes always appear quite early with some few advanced individuals, leaders, and martyrs. The social philosophies of the mass of citizens do not change so early. Observation seems to indicate that the ideational philosophies hang on, become subjects of reverence, and are in general the last to change in any large way.

# EPILOGUE

And thus perhaps a picture, or better a mosaic, takes shape. But it is a changing one, one which the artist never allows the craftsman quite to finish. The configuration seen each day is imperceptibly changed for the next. If one could be absent for a week from the process, the change would be noticeable. In a year it would be striking. In a decade overwhelming. Meanwhile, everyone feels he "understands" the picture of which he is a part. But inevitably he understands it as it *was,* and not as it *is,* except perhaps for that small group who constantly focus on it. They may be attuned to each change, however subtle and however minute.

We would like to claim, by analogy, that the sociologist is this last mentioned man, and that the mosaic is the changing American society. But this, we feel, would be claiming too much. If there is anything to the analogy, it would simply be that the sociologist is the one who strives to see the changes in their incipient stages and to diffuse his information so that others too may know. But, of course, he, too, is part of the human menage and to a considerable, even if lesser, degree also relies upon the myths which are fashioned out of hopes and incomplete knowledge and too great a trust of the past. It is by no means clear that the sociologist is either the best interpreter of the current scene or the best prognosticator of what is to come. All that can be said is that he *ought* to be and that he *might* be.

And, even if the sociologist is best able to see the kind of world which is emerging, one of his most important findings will constitute for him a cruel irony: in our society no student of anything automatically possesses the power to control practical matters. The realities of power in our society, both now and in the foreseeable future, are such that overt decision and change by drift will probably stem from other sources. This is in itself inherently neither good nor bad, but it needs to be said, because there are those earnest and partly educated students of sociology who too naively and too hopefully expect more from sociologists and sociology than it is reasonable to expect. Possibly this may all change and in fact there is some reason to believe (or merely to hope) that the traditional "distrust of the expert" may, along with other ideological debris, be discarded. In any event, the tendency for each to be his own expert is a habit of mind better suited to our past than to our present realities.